THE COULOIR

by
Richard Manichello

Behler™
PUBLICATIONS

California

Behler Publications
California

The Couloir
A Behler Publications Book

Copyright © 2006 by Richard Manichello
Cover design by Sun Son – www.sunsondesigns.com

Library of Congress Cataloging-in-Publication Data is available
Control Number: 2005927107

FIRST EDITION

ISBN 1-933016-22-1
Published by Behler Publications, LLC
Lake Forest, California
www.behlerpublications.com

Manufactured in the United States of America

for
Margo

Acknowledgements

Melody Lawrence

Lisa Halle, Barbara Halle, Chenango Valley Writers'
Conference , Lawrence J. Hatterer Ph.D., The Arraoz
Family, The Cordova Family, Jean Marc DuBois, Jean Luc
Verdier, Pascal Charpontier, Philip Reviello, Nick
DeMarco, George Agalias, Bennet Windheim, M.Z.
Ribalow, Fred Pezzulli, John Bishop, William Styron,
Carlos Castaneda, Clarissa Pinkola Estes Ph.D., and all the
women who run with the Wolves, Robert Bly, Catherine
Townsend, Ginette Molina, Donna Mileti, John Heisse,
Franca Barchiesi, Barbara & Patrick Verdaguer, Tom
Woods, Peter M. Jeavons, ME Newmark & JK Perry, Andy
Selters, my brother, John, a teacher and scholar for life.

Kristan Ryan, Will Killhour
(special thanks)

Fanelli Café-New York, Farinet-Verbier, Eden Hotel-
Geneva, Mountain Air-Verbier, Auberge de la Diligence-
Crans Montana, Da Beppe Pizzaria-Crans Montana, The
New York Times, The Los Angeles Times

Janette Turner Hospital

In Memory
Dave Schultz and Gary Meyers

The descent beckons

        as the acsent beckoned

                Memory is a kind

of accomplishment

        a sort of renewal

                ~William Carlos Williams

cou·loir   (k$\overline{oo}$l-wär′)
noun. A deep mountainside gorge or gully,
especially in the Swiss Alps.

chapter One
NEW YORK

Down. Faster down. The line down, the skis nearly perpendicular, bending and carving an ellipse on the white edge of the world. It was beyond thinking, beyond skill. Only seconds to the safety of the col, to awaken from the nightmare. The crystal spray, high beside the poles, enfolding, plummeting in a frosted mist. Terrifying and erotic in the same instant. Undulating, riding, a sensual movement, pumping legs and arms. The sheer panic of solid earth, solid mountains falling away beneath my feet. The places. The slopes. No man belongs. The deep couloirs of vivid memory, the jagged turns, the steeps, gorges cut like scars in past descents. *Down. Steeper down.* Every fall, every drop deserved, the etched-on horror of the plunge, mine alone. There was no one else to blame for my survival.

Down the narrow dirt alleyway I ran, between our house and Sabatini's wooden garage, and into a field of ribbon grass, reed, and bearberry. We took countless photos in the field beside the river, every spring and every gray-brown November. I could scale the steep decline then, with abandon.

In jodhpurs and dark military jacket, my white shoes unscuffed, arms outstretched and pulling at the two adults on either side, I sailed down.

Blond, stocky and bowlegged, I looked like some English pug. Christ, I was ugly. I'd like to burn all those old photos. The large ethnic family insures interpretive remembrance of certain moments. Aunts and cousins embellish stories, decorate and disorder details, until poignant truth surrenders wholly to capriciousness.

"Eddie was so handsome." A lie.

"Eddie used to sit on my lap and laugh." I'd cry like hell.

"Remember the time—" the stories began, "when Eddie swam naked in the river?" I never swam naked in the river.

"*Look how far we've come.*" That I remember. I was clear about them. We'd run a short distance, stop and look back, and she'd say, "*Look how far we've come.*" I never remembered his voice.

They'd fly in, those thoughts, those scenes from other times. My mind a helicopter, hovering. I'd see everything down and away, an aerial view of parts. There was no choice in the matter the clear images just came. You'd attended the viewings and didn't make a fuss. They must mean something. An event re-opened. Perhaps there was something you missed. Pay attention. Who was that little man? The man before the journey? Was I ever really that small? Was I ever that happy? Where did it all go? And why so fast? Youth seeped in like molasses. It went out through a friggin' hole.

Body and spirit have made passages. Nothing can be taken back, really, and damn little resurrected. I'm hollow now and hardened like a steel drum. Regret rattles around inside like a loose stone. The inner man has clouded recollection, too. The membrane between memory and desire has grown too thin, or too fuzzy, to discern accurate detail from the avaricious urgings.

"*What you thought you came for*"

Yeah, yeah, I've heard.

Down a hill, I ran, weightless and free. A time when needs were small and uncomplicated. A routine repeated several times over, and in its repetition the seeds of memory. Patterns and rituals of transparent value find a moment and meaning in their re-discovery and re-play.

The mahogany office was a measure of distance, and meaning. Fabulous. Button-down, boardroom chic. Understated executive perks. The extrusion of manly achievement, a rendering after years of blood-sweat creative enterprise—an apropos New York benchmark—bestowed about the time I'd realized what an empty wish it was. Filled with career mementos and writing awards, old photographs, and a superfluity of comforts—putting cups and a humidor drawer, private john with shower stall, a wet bar—it made me yearn for less-weighty substance.

The accumulation, beyond the office, filled a Westside one-bedroom. There were U-Hauls-full of accumulation filling apartments left behind, the salvage of lovers, live-ins, a marriage and family. There were the contents of a locker at the athletic club, a car in a nameless garage on Tenth Avenue, a pair of skis at a friend's in Lake Placid, and two cases of '66 Latour in my brother's cellar—the detritus of a life lived on the run. A sizable wad of returned letters, lines professing revelation and insight reflectively, things that I could never quite accomplish veritably, occupied a small, crowded drawer behind the bar at Ethan's on West Eighty-second.

They were the parts of a man, the pieces I'd scattered about, the dots to which I drew un-connecting lines, monotonously. Afraid to be whole in one place, I'd parcel-out things, marking a perimeter, renting limited space in friendships, human interaction, and acquaintance.

The shadow of my time lengthened, heavy with heartache and reckless living, lies and betrayals, and scarred women. *That's what you do, isn't it?* Though the events themselves faded in intensity with time, the specter of their burden still grows long and dark in memory.

Kra-Bunch.

The office door flew open smashing against the paint-chipped and dented wall. And there she was. It was an entrance I'd learned to expect and grown to enjoy.

"Eddie, Jesus Christ, will you talk to Dexter? He's been busting my ass for the last half-hour. Will you talk to him? They don't pay me enough for this kind of shit."

In her feet—testy, intense—working the floor, fast and hard. Heels from hell, rail spikes on fuck-me shoes. Fishnet legs, and a biker's(excuse me, cyclist's) wide waddle, very open steps, lots of straddling air between the knees. Tight, red micro on the high side of perfect thighs. Blouse snug, eggshell crepe. Eggs, firm, self-supporting, the cleavage of champions. Face, stunning, dark, wild, a young Sophia Loren—from Brooklyn.

"You know, I don't know what's the matter with him."

"You seem a little, how shall I say, edgy? Hmm, Jude?"

"I mean, he's the chief, right? You're friends, right? Like he's got no balls, or somthing. I hate men without balls, you know what I mean?"

"Ouch. Yeah."

"Why can't he just pick up the phone and call you? What? He's, like, afraid of you or something? Instead, he busts my ass...go in and ask Eddie, just sneak in and get the name for me, go ahead, go in, ask Eddie."

"Ask me what?"

"Just like my husband, DeadDick, he's got, like, no courage, or somthing. No initiative. I have to do everything for him."

"I believe the character was Dead-Eye Dick."

"Yeah? Well, you don't sleep with him. My husband and Dexter, two pissy little weak guys, you know?"

"Your husband and Dexter are light-years apart, believe me. Ask me what, Jude?"

"Oh, yeah, about the book? It's so excite-innnggg. I'm so proud of you, Eddie. The whole office is buzzing, right? You're going to be famous, right? I'm-so-happy-this-is-great, Eddie, I swear." She'd pause and get a knit-the-eyebrows seriousness screwed into her face. "Is it scary, Eddie? I mean, like the thought of overwhelming success?"

"I'm scared shitless, kiddo."

"My mother gets like that when the whole family comes over for Sunday dinners, you know? Like, she knows her lasagna is good, and we know it's good, you know the immediates? And everybody always tells her how good it is, but she is scared. I'm talking scared-out-of-her-mind. O-my-god, every-single-time, not knowing how it's going to be received, you know, just anticipating."

"Yeah. I guess it's a little like...a lasagna."

"Anyways, feel better, Eddie. It's going to be good. You'll see." Her face brightened once again and she winked her assurance across the desk at me with a smile. If only I could've gone,to the bank on her confidence, I'd be as rich as a Sultan. "Now, Dexter wanted to know about the title. He says, is that the work-king title? Are you going to change it somehow before print-ting? Or, like, is that the title title?"

"Oh, he did, did he?"

"Yeah, that's because him and Brian, the little assistant shit, weren't paying attention during the meeting last Friday. Pisses me off. You know?"

I reached for the phone on my desk. Judy grinned, patently.

"Okay. Sit and relax. Watch this." I sidesaddled the edge of the desk and grabbed the tan demon's hand piece. Six lines blinking, six not, and Dexter's A-line was open. A touch of the keypad and a moment's wait. Judy's smile broadened.

"Brian? Eddie. Let me talk to Dexter for a sec, please." Judy mocked a limp wrist wave, pursing her lips. "Dexter. Goddamn it, what are you doing to my woman?" Judy raised her arms in triumph.

"Yesssss."

"Good day, Mate." The Outback twang. "I'm sorry, Ed. I didn't mean to break the little quiff's balls, you know, mate?" It was as though someone were twisting and strangling the phone cord with his words in it. "I just didn't want to bother you and all."

"We'll be hitting you with a sexual harassment thing, you know, so get ready."

"Right, right, Mate. Her ass or mine?" He growled then

belly laughed himself silly. "Listen, I know you're packing,
getting ready to shove-off and all that."

"All right, now get this, Dex, and get it straight,
'Heartache and Red Water' is *the* title. That's it. Four friggin'
words, Dex. No bullshit 'working title' or any of that stuff.
That's the title, *'Heartache and Red Water.'* Capital H, lower
case on the conjunction, capital R, capital W, *la fine*. Okay?"
Judy leaned in, smug and satisfied. "And no punctuation,
none of that, no commas or colons. You guys've got enough
assholes running around up on that floor, for Christ's sake."
Dexter laughed hysterically. I held the receiver out for Judy
to hear. She smiled and her face became a victory celebration.
Our team was beating up their team. She lived for it. Her
devotion and support of my every endeavor was vital to me.
We had a union of spirit, fully aware and reliant upon each
other's capabilities. It was an odd kind of love relationship, I
guess. A man could have such things with women—
unconventional love relationships. It was a lesson that had
taken me a lifetime to learn at a cost of unfathomable pain.

"Okay, Mate, you bloody bastard." The Perth
lobsterman's son came booming through the receiver again.
"Oh, Christ, Ed. You two are a scream. All right then, just the
facts. Got it."

"You'd better, you goddamn kangaroo. And leave Judy
alone while I'm away."

"Paris first, ay?"

"Yep. I'm going over for the Stirner diaries."

"Come on, Mate, you going to bring me something from
Paris, ay?"

"Yeah, French Ticklers. Make all your boyfriends gag."
Judy faked a gag and spun around on the chair, facing the
opposite wall, muffling laughter.

"Pervert. You're killing me," Dexter said, in final
submission. "Seriously, you know what I would like, Ed?
Really?"

"Say it and you got it, Dex—*une cravate, chemise sport...*"

"Two bottles of French champagne. Really. That's all. *Veuve Cliquot,* the gold label."

"Dex. This is America. We can get that stuff here now. You know? Since the friggin' Tea Party, I think. It's the modern world, Dex. It's amazing. Get with it."

"Yes, Ed, I know, but it's the sulfites. Nasty little American preservatives. French champagnes and wines don't have any, you see. Whenever I drink champagne here, I get all these horrid red blotches all over. It's awful."

"Red blotches?"

"Yes. All over. It's the sulfites. We're almost sure. If you don't believe me, I'll have my allergist call. You can ask her."

"Have your proctologist call, Dex. I think you're full of shit."

"I swear, Mate. It's true. Pretty please? Just two bottles."

"*Veuve,* huh?"

"The gold label."

"I got you."

"You're a bloody darling, you are. Thanks, Mate."

"Uhh, hmm."

"We been through a lot of shit together, Ed. I got to tell you, here and now, this book is the most thrilling goddamn thing. The whole bloody place is tingling. You're a star."

"Took me long enough."

"Come on, now. Don't be a poop. The wait was worth it, man. Nobody puts their balls on the footlights like you do, Ed. They're going to caress them this time, Mate. This one's going to tear through the list like a buzz saw, right to the top. That's where you belong. I couldn't be happier. It's a big one, Mate. I can feel it."

"Thanks, Dex."

"Have a great bloody trip. Get lots of rest. Dream about your next triumph. A play, maybe, huh? See you when you get back."

The phone snapped closed in my ear. Sunny Australia was gone with Brooklyn awaiting, and she was staring up at me with adoring eyes as if I were some Rock Star. I dropped the hand piece back onto the cradle, and opened my arms to receive my beaming assistant.

"Okay, Missy, what next?"

"Oh, Eddie, you're a love. Hugs, hugs, hugs." She sprung out of the chair in front of my desk, leaped onto me and we embraced with air-kisses cheek to cheek. "Huggie hugs. Okay, now one," She backed up, holding her memo pad in one hand, plucking a pencil from two dozen Orioles in the beer stein on my desk and then sat back down, perching on the chair this time like a barn swallow in a birch tree. Her red micro skirt was hiked to the 39th Parallel, the same latitude as her crotch. It wasn't awkward at all. So harmonious was her sensuality and demeanor, for Judy it amounted to an utterly benign fashion statement.

"Oh, one was Dexter," she giggled. "Okay, two, Gila called."

"Shit."

"What? We give her an itinerary?"

"No."

"Okay, three, the Old Man."

"Uh, I guess, yeah. Give him a schedule, the major points. Carl knows everything anyway. I think these little gremlins in airports all over the world have modems into Carl and they log-in the minute any of us steps off a plane."

"Four, Nick Agalias called. He'll be in on the twenty-eighth. Wants to do the Rangers-Penguins game, then "go Greek," whatever the hell that means. You guys into something strange, heh?"

"Dining, Missy."

"Right, right, Eddie. Five, I got you a car for Kennedy, four-thirty. See how I take care of my man?"

"What about my tickets?"

"Six. Tickets, right. New York-Paris-Toronto-New York. Evelyn called. She's working on the tickets. You know, the airlines really bust her chops. I mean, they're such shits. All goddamn day they do this to her. She'll send them up as soon as she gets them. That's it. Thanks for calling Dex. I'm out of here."

She was up and away in one swift move. The door left its port in the wall, as if it were trained to follow her out, and whammed shut with the same force that opened it. The office was still once more. The space, the void returned and the past began to fill the seams and crevasses of loneliness with old fears.

On the windowsill, a framed photo of a mountain sat dead center among stacks of manuscripts. Through the Levalor blinds, the deep stone canyons of Manhattan stretched beyond into a narrow infinity of islands, bridges, and harbor waters, gray and drab in the winter afternoon murkiness. The photograph was sharp and striking, blue, white, and grades of shining slate and granite. I held it in my hand, away from the office fluorescence and into the flat light from the window.

The black rock dome of the mountain thrusted into the sated cobalt blue of the sky, free of the heavy snows, pewtered, almost silver in the sharp rays of Swiss sunlight. A soft pink, the Alpenglow, tinted the uppermost snows and the bottommost sky where it shimmered along the mountain's broad shoulders. I touched the photograph, my fingers falling delicately on the glass pane gliding over the mountain's ashen ramparts.

"*Gelé,*" I whispered. One finger traced down along a white crag in the headwall, the thin, steep gorge coursing like a ribbon through the glistening solid mass, running the full length of the great mountain's southern face.

"*Gelé,*" I said again, aloud, and a memory pierced my heart, a memory both joyful and terrifying in the same instant.

"*Gelé.* Goddamn you," I remanded. *You have some part of me, some fraction. And I have all of you. Our souls are scarred, Gelé, marred together.*

More than ten years, you scarfaced mountain, you. Went by fast didn't it?

And look how far we've come.

chapter Two
P A R I S

"*Good Americans, when they die, go to Paris,*" the poet said, but I hedged my bets making the crossing three or four times a year. Imagine being there when "The Reaper" finally does call. How great would that be?

Arriving at De Gaulle, a welcome anonymity had already begun to settle in. I was feeling more and more the passenger within my own body. A certain detachment I'd sought was finally mine.

The *Rue de Seine* and *Rue Visconti* came together in a small five-cornered intersection made possible by the narrow alley, *Rue Jacques Callot*. The taxi deposited me on the wet cobblestone, as I'd asked, at the mouth of *Rue Visconti*. Alone in Paris at last, and cut off. I was trying to disappear, trying to escape the praise, escape the questions and smiles of those who praise and smile unconditionally. The fear of a new book succeeding was overwhelming me in a tidal wave of conflict and doubt usually reserved for total failure. To be triumphant, and yet to be deemed trivial behind your back. *Look at that lucky schmuck.* How would you know? Really, how could you tell? Half-hidden laughter was murderously double-edged. America loved a winner, venerated empty celebrity. Nothing was clear-cut, never will be. An author suffered the actor's lament—is it just applause, or is it love?

The daily diet of doubt. Why Paris? Why hide in Europe? Dig down, burrow the head and hearing, run from certain euphoria. Welcome disaster. *Yeah, I can deal with that.* The demand put upon success was to succeed again, and it had me plummeting into some trough wrought with old traps and sickness. In mid-winter Paris, I looked for punishment by way of a poisoned past. Success was some

too-good possibility. I was undeserving. The terror of
scrutiny, even the best kind, was descending, falling like dust
through a sunray, settling on the narrow, fragile sill of sanity.

I'd come here to retrieve six old and tattered diaries.
Handwritten in German, the books were unearthed in Berlin
during excavation and re-development around the old
Reichstag building, the seat of German governments since
1894 until the end of the Third Reich, when Hitler burned it
and Allied bombs buried it in rubble. The center of Berlin has
been under reconstruction and re-design, and a hive for
urban archaeologists, since 1992. The sketchy, but enticing,
first reports seemed to indicate the diaries belonged to a
Jewish theatre owner and producer who "entertained" high-
level Nazi officers and politicians, in non-theatrical ways.
Written sporadically all through the 1930's, certain passages
in the diaries, it had been intimated, could be historically
significant. The diaries end abruptly on a night during the
Pogroms in November 1938, one night before the fatal
kristallnacht.

The discovery, deep beneath the tunneled sub-terrain of
the third German empire, also raised questions about the
activities of the producer and the function of his theatre
during a time of Jewish expulsion and execution. These few
provocative inducements, and the authenticity of the hand-
scribbled journals of Yacov Stirner, were enough for the Old
Man, Carl Bested, and Atherton Books to plunk-down a
considerable sum of money to retain universal, literary, and
media rights for two years.

What Carl actually expected was for me to turn the story
contained in the diaries—within the two-year option of
course—into a blockbuster thriller with tortuous Nazis,
espionage, collaboration, sex, betrayal, subversion, murder
and suicide, war and persecution, Brecht and Weill, Dietrich
and Von Stroheim, all with a liberal dousing of the theatrical.

"Be inventive, Eddie, you know, make it exciting." I can
still hear goddamn Carl's missive.

Any one of hundreds of competent messengers could have collected the diaries, now in the possession of a Paris *négociateur*. Instead, I jumped at the chance to get out of New York.

"I'll do it, I'll go. I want to see the handwriting, the dirt and stains on the paper," I insisted.

Send a man to do a boy's job, I've always said. So, on that flimsy pretext, my time alone in Paris would help me cope with an on-coming curse. I finally felt a barrier here, the depth and breadth of the Atlantic. The gum bubble that was Paris put a sweet distance between all of that attendant pressure and my exaggerated fear of it.

At number 17 Rue Visconti stood the Hotel Balzac. It was unusually broad for this small street, and six windowed floors high to the copper Mansard roof. Black wrought-iron gates covered the two large glass front doors, and rococo ornamentation articulated all six floors of the stone façade. The stone was severely stained, of course, from 20th Century acid precipitants in the foul Paris atmosphere. To a city seemingly kissed by gods and artists, a plague of progress added its touch to classic architecture in long black streaks and pitted details. The Balzac's condition was worse since my last visit, but so was mine. I'd never stayed anyplace else in Paris.

Madame Desnoyers had been sent a fax memorandum from New York, I looked-up all the French in my *Larousse,* apprising her of my arrival and stay. She promptly faxed-back a confirmation. She didn't like computers, didn't trust them. The fax machine was a marvel, "*c'est incroyable, époustouflant,*" she'd said. It was as far as she'd go, technologically, in the 20th Century.

There, as always, behind the little Cambodian teak front desk-slash-bar, she waited as I entered. Rouge rubbed cheeks and thick, dark lipstick chronicled the burden of the hard years instead of concealing it. A life richly lived—post-war pleasures, by her accounts, taken liberally and often. She had the softness and story of use. A flowery print dress, much too short, snuggly wrapped her current *physique*—evidence that she was little concerned with seasonal style, yet much taken with the provocative. Jewelry glistened everywhere. A long, triple strand of niveous pearls fell between, around, and atop her huge breasts.

The fulsome Madame Camille Desnoyers suffered only anachronism in a world infatuated with youth and the ephemeral. Her efforts were honest, her natural beauty and refinement was but hidden, smothered really, beneath a veil of excesses and adornments.

"Monsieur Je'Nell-é, bonjour, bonjour..."

And that was about all the French I could handle at the moment, paddling like hell, mentally, I was trying to come up with some quick *mots*. She driveled on so fast I couldn't do anything but smile profusely and do some dribbling of my own.

"Oh, my, my, Madame Desnoyers, lovely, lovely, yes, *merci, merci, bon jour, bon soir, bon nuit, bon bon*." I French-i-fried my way through a few minutes of bullshit and niceties.

She embraced me warmly—cheek-to-cheek air-kisses—and I felt as though I'd suffocate in her dense perfume.

"Oui, Madame Desnoyers...le, le, top floor?" I rifled through the foggy French vocab section of the brain again. *"Eh...l'étage supérieur? Sommet, sommet?"*

"Au dessus? oui bien sûr. Certainement, monsieur Gen-elle." This went on for a few minutes more with me bowing a lot and smiling and bumping into her boobs until we agreed, and I understood, that I had the front room, top floor for at least three nights. Quite naturally, amid the lengthy greeting, a bottle of Calvados appeared from beneath the desk and Madame Desnoyers and I imbibed. We were hopeless Calvados lovers and the little groundbreaking nip together had become a kind of welcoming ritual. The brandy was

excellent and the earthy spirits sent a burning draft through my sternum like lightening through a pine tree. She welcomed me back with a few toasts, tried a bit of English, kept one hand always on my shoulder, and poured her effusive warmth over me like baptismal waters. Her pampering and endearment had made me feel pretty good, pretty much at home here over the past twenty-some years. I was lucky to be in her company just then and her charm was working a bit of magic. Europe had taught me to allow people to do their thing, not to stifle, and sometimes things would come up goddamn enchanting.

Madame Desnoyers backed me into the small, birdcage lift, talking all the while, touching my cheek gently like my Aunt Lil used to, and I *merci-ed* her to death as I floated up, up, and away through the Balzac's frescoed ceilings and out of sight.

The fresh flowers in my top-floor room were bursting with color, like a living, touchable Renoir arranged on a round bistro table in front of the windows. Nothing had changed. Nothing in the room had even moved since my last stay, perhaps since my first. A few dust-bunnies and cobwebs were rearranged, maybe, but the bistro table with its two bent-cane cafe chairs remained the quintessential French still life. The damn things were probably nailed to the floor.

The same Calvados, Coeur de Leon, and two bottles of mineral water and glasses were neatly arranged on a mirrored tray atop the dresser. The tray was a haunting reminder, holding the appealing ambiance of an apple brandy, but deeper it contained the many secrets of my time in this room, a small chronicle of light and dark passages, reminders of a journey that was, at times, blissfully radiant, and at times ripped with agony.

Three sets of floor-to-ceiling windows facing north toward the Seine framed and divided the luminous sky and the silhouetted rooftops with their clay chimneystacks.

This was the room that first July—end of junior
year—that first time on European soil, where Nicky Agalias
and I put a dozen of the finest French white wines—
Pulignys, Chassagnes, Pouilly-Fuissés, Chablis, and Loires –
in the little blue bathtub packed in ice and then roamed Paris
for the rest of the hot afternoon. We were going to taste and
savor and log every scintillating impression, wine by wine,
in a diary. We returned to find all the ice melted and twelve
wine labels floating randomly on the water above the bare
bottles. The wines were scintillating, however, even in their
anonymity. I think it was after bottle Number Six, a vintage
Six of what must have been a great year, that Nicky
proclaimed, "as I lay dying, a French wine should be the last
thing to touch my lips." I scribbled the would-be epitaph in
the diary, the first of many entries we would make under the
headings, Last Wishes and as-I-lay-dyings.

The afternoon was damp and bone chilling. Satisfied to
press my forehead to the cold pane of my sixth-floor
window, I held tight a glass of the aromatic Calvados and
entombed myself there. Misty white fog shrouded the top of
Invalides off in the distance, and Tour Eiffel couldn't be seen.
Tomorrow I'd venture out onto the avenues of poets and
sculptors, and into the museums and cafes, and sink
unceremoniously into the Parisian milieu. At the moment, I
was content with my cozy nest on the Left Bank.

My Paris visits, for so many years, were auspicious
searches for a single face among the millions, the resplendent
beauty of a woman who once enabled me to accept certain
truths and see the scars I'd left on the world, a woman who
suddenly ended all my descents. For such wisdom and
insight, I gave her up from the mountains of Switzerland,
gave her back to Paris. Everything's an exchange.
Everything. Paris was that hopeful stop in travels, a
sparkling city labyrinth of wishful possibility, of sifting
through phone directories, court records, seeking lawyers,
calling hospitals, walking every street and avenue, every

Quarter, *arrondissement*, and Paris suburb, looking, anticipating a chance meeting in a café or restaurant, a lead, some rumor or word about her, or an encounter with a friend. In time, the trips became desperate wanderlust, futile in the belief that two lost destinies simply could not rediscover their crossing.

The pale yellow lights in the windows along Rue Visconti were a broken patchwork of small squares, a lucent Mondrian of still, opaque curtains shutting-out one more winter's eve. City dwellers blamelessly composed the geometry of isolation. And my room at the Balzac was just one more window light among the many.

chapter Three
ELISSA

The Paris morning was brighter, drier, but still European-winter gray. The street life of this Quarter retreated for the cold season. The cafés were full, but the inhabitants pressed against the glass walls from the inside now, liquor and smoke hued, unsmiling, and as static as a Courbet. Gone indoors too, the street urchins, the booksellers and art hawkers, the curbside acts, and the ever-thinning numbers of prostitutes. Even the threadbare *marroniers* with their pans of hot, roasting chestnuts were scarce on the barren streets today. The flavor of Parisian sidewalk-café *joie* just wasn't the same in February. *L'entente de la vie* was hibernating like a big brown bear in a cave.

Young students seemed to brave the cold well, however. They crisscrossed the avenues briskly, in small groups, shuttling to and from the many art schools, the Collége, and the Sorbonne just a few blocks east. In the cold morning air, I turned up the collar on my long Navy bridge coat, stuffed my hands deep into the pockets, joined the sparse flock of students, and bucked the sharp breeze on an almost deserted Boulevard St. Germain.

The old train station on Quai d'Orsay had been converted in the mid 1980's into one of the city's showcase palaces of French painting. I could lose myself there for several hours amid the passionate and the pastoral. These were and have remained just French paintings and sketches, beautifully displayed. They were not the immortals we'd all seen in Art History books.

There was one top-floor gallery in Musee d'Orsay where I liked to end my visit. I'd plan a circuitous route through the other exhibition halls to arrive lastly in a brightly sky-lit room filled with *Degas*. So many of the works in his gallery were of women. The pastels of his later years seemed to connect with me, and I would sit and rest there for some time, feeling surrounded by a kindred spirit. His observance of the female in common situations, his emendation of her beauty, dignity, loneliness, grace, or innate desirability—catching a simple expressive movement of her will—touched a place of deep remorse within me. I'd sit, unable to accomplish some degree of self-forgiveness for my past, for my own twisted vision of female love and intimacy. I sat for hours in a room surrounded by one man's sight—by ballerinas and washwomen, actresses and *chanteuse*, young women *à coucher*—and envied Edgar Degas his delicate obsession.

The room was practically empty. Farthest away from the main galleries and crowds, it was quieter and smaller, with spotless hardwood floors, bleach-white partitions, and vaulted skylights. It smelled of fresh paint—the kind in gallon cans that went on walls—and one expansive area was being re-hung with a dozen-or-so large pieces. The work team appeared to be a group of young art students, late teens and early twenties, dressed in jeans and assorted work shirts and sweaters, and it was really quite fascinating to watch, like being backstage at a play watching some facet of theatrical magic de-mystified. The little army of students was well aware of my attention—I could hear the whispers and saw the quick side-glances.

One muscular, black-haired girl with a long braid trailing down her back had a commanding presence. As strong as any of the men, she lifted huge gilded frames easily. Her plaid hunting shirt, open and rolled and right out of an L.L. Bean catalog, draped her neck and shoulders and revealed, like theatre curtains, a mounded, sensuously curvaceous white tee shirt. The mounds moved and bobbed gently beneath the tee as she bent over and lifted. Faded blue jeans and sand-colored foothill boots packed a lower torso consisting of a sprinter's buttocks and a fashion model's legs.

And then, of course, there was her arch, that secluded cul-de-sac of erotic centricity, the wonderful isthmus, the architecture of my undoing—where less is not more, only more will do. Tight-fitting pants and high, vigorous gluteus muscles accentuated the truly exciting nature of the female sexual aesthetic. What it generated in men's imaginations, in a furnace of innermost needs, couldn't be measured, or faithfully predicted. It was a constant surprise to male muscles and fluids, maybe the only genuine surprise we ever experienced. Like many of the works in this museum, the young woman evoked impossible fantasies.

She was not Degas-like at all. She was the inversion of the A-frame Degas female, a stunning V-8 with squared, broad shoulders, the living, breathing ripeness of modern female youth. Robust and hormonally exceptional, she so suddenly made me aware. Just watching her was sensation enough, but then, what did men know of observation and control.

"Pardon, mademoiselle, eh, ma'm zelle?" I stuttered. She abruptly stopped cutting some picture wire and looked at me with wide, cautious eyes. The wire stretched between her two hands, the length of it just about enough for a man's neck. I smiled nervously at the readiness of her posture.

"Mademoiselle, j'regard tout, eh votre travail," I mumbled awkwardly and smiled again, hand gestured like a sort of "BoBo Sees Paris puppet." She froze solid, and watched me speak, as if I'd soon need an ambulance. *"Plus intéressante, mam'selle."* I went on. *"Fascinant, pour les* paintings...eh, the a *peinture, oui, les Degas, c'est magnifique. Oeuvre de génie, je pense. Excusez-moi, madame?"*

"Are you okay, mister?" She blurted-out, carefully.

"Huh? What? You speak English? *Eh, vous parlez...*"

"No, no, mister, please, don't do that anymore. Don't speak French. Please? You sound like an idiot."

"Well, excuse me, Mam." I recoiled, put-off and surprised. "Didn't know I was going to run into some smartass American kid hanging French pictures in the goddamn d'Orsay museum."

"Sorry," she said.

"No, not at all."

"No, really."

"No, you have a nice friggin' day, miss. Say, can you direct me to the men's shithouse, *s'il vous plait?*"

"Mister, come on, please? I'm sorry." She softened a bit.

"I suppose I can find it myself. Thanks." With that I started away, sweeping the wide, winged tail of my blue coat around in an arc, almost hitting her with it, taking long, heavy strides across the hardwood floor. And she gave chase.

"Mister? Come on, please? I'm sorry. I, I didn't mean to sound like a real jerk."

I stopped after about twenty yards, turned back around, and just stared at her. She stepped right up under my nose, practically, and looked at me with dark, serious eyes. She looked frightened just then, but her beauty and innocent fear belied a boldness and defiance—a completely unapologetic tyrant. The kid was a sphere-demolisher, a real ballbuster. She would break a man's heart into fragments like a cheap teacup, and he would simply smile and beg, "do it again, please?"

"Mister, please? Don't be so harsh. I said I was sorry."

"You're pretty cocky, aren't you?" I leveled at her. Her gaze went down to the floor, and suddenly I felt like I was scolding my own daughter. "I mean, I'm just sitting there, nice, you know? I'm admiring you working, the way you're handling things, you know? So, to be friendly, I try to say something, and I get shit. I get—was the French really that bad?" She looked up and suppressed childish glee, her eyes bursting with tears holding back riotous laughter. "The verbs weren't too goddamn bad, and then I get a mouthful from, from a goddamn American in Paris." She giggled again.

A broad smile opened up a lovely face, as if it were

suddenly brightened by Ferris wheel lights, and she glowed there in a carnival of smug satisfaction.

"So, you're not mad, mister?"

"Oh, no, I'm somewhat pissed, but I understand youth, you see. And stop calling me mister."

"Well, like, you're old enough to be my father."

"Yes, I am old enough to be your...Look. Enough about age, and no more mister, all right?" She laughed. "Name's Eddie. It's not fancy but it's easy. It works. Say it loud, I bark, say it soft and I'll pant, sometimes." She laughed again, sexier this time.

"You're cool." She smiled sheepishly.

"What do you mean?"

"I mean, sitting there. Like, we noticed you. You're kind of cool looking, kind of exotic."

"Exotic, eh? Yeah. Well, I'm old, older, but cool. Yes. Chuck Berry, the Beatles, Stones, Dylan, Springsteen, Annie Lenox, Ellington, Coltrane, Hootie and the Goldfish..."

"Blowfish. Hootie and the Blowfish."

"Blowfish, goldfish, what-the-hell. I forget sometimes. First thing that goes, you know? I'm old, remember?" She laughed aloud. Then, embarrassed, she peered over her shoulder at her mates. They were all looking at the two of us standing in the middle of the gallery floor. She made a face at them and they smiled and then she turned back to me.

"What school?" I asked.

"Beaux-Arts," she said. "It's my first year."

"Look, I don't want to keep you..."

"No, no, it's okay."

"Maybe we can have a coffee, someplace," I suggested. "You know, you could make this old American guy feel pretty good."

"Yeah, you know the way you were sitting there before, it was strange, like morose," she said. "You looked sad, a little, you know? Like, we thought maybe your mother died, or something."

"She did. She died."

"Ohhh, goddamn, I'm sorry." Crestfallen, she said, "Jesus, me and my big mouth again. I didn't mean it that way, honest."

I rolled my eyes upward, taking a pained gander at the huge skylight above.

"Mother died about twenty years ago." I sighed deeply. "And, fuck the psychiatrists, I loved her dearly and miss her. But I didn't think it still showed."

"Funny. Very funny," she said with a smirky half-smile.

"Seriously, I'd love to have a coffee, or a beer."

"Meet me at the Beaux-Arts in an hour," she said.

"The café?"

"Yeah, it's, like, right across from the school."

"Rue Bonaparte. I know it well."

"Great. I've got to run to the school from here, get something out of my locker, and I'll see you there. Thanks."

"For what? I didn't say I was buying." She laughed, a friendly and relaxed laugh.

"Right. Right. I'm buying. For the way I acted."

"Never happen. You're the starving artist, not me." *Now there's a joke, and how come I'm not laughing?*

"Well, I've got to get back over there." She shied, and did a sort of half-sashay in the direction of her schoolmates.

"Right. You got a name, Miss? I mean, for the café?"

"You could just yell, hey, Bitch...what I deserve."

"Then everyone will know we're Americans." She laughed again and each time she did she became more radiant. I was drawn-in more, too, with each reaction to my silly banter. I would have done it all day, made dumb jokes just to see her face light up that way. I would have stayed with her all day if I could have. It was comforting and easy. It was odd, and wonderful.

"Elissa Charogne. Newport, Rhode Island," she announced, like roll call.

"Nice. Two names. Now, go ahead, get back to your

crew. I'll see you at the café." I started backing away from her, the floor between us widened with light and shining lacquer.

"What about you? Eddie what?" She stepped after me, quickening deliberately. I backed away. She'd step in my steps, pacing after me.

"What is this? A Tango in Paris? Go on, get out of here."

"Eddie what? Come on, for the café." She kept after me, smiling and playful. I glanced around at the walls, quickly, trying to get away from her questions.

"Eddie...Eddie Degas." We stopped. "I'm a painter. From Pittsburgh. Porches. Parlors, parapets, pantries, kitchens, stuff like that." A veil of disappointment shadowed her beautiful face. She stared. Faux-mean knitted her brows.

"You're kidding me." Hands on hips, troubled. "You're a big bullshitter aren't you? You love to bullshit, I'll bet."

Hell, I wouldn't be a writer if I didn't love to bullshit. For the way she said it and the smile that followed, I suddenly wished I had a PhD. in it. The gods had disproportionately blessed beautiful women, I was sure. They could get away with anything—murder, lies, ruthlessness, betrayal, revenge, pantyhose—anything. There Elissa, Eve on the eve of womanhood, amidst Degas' immortalized, a beautiful, succulent masterpiece of female temperament and sensuality. Life and animal vibrancy, a tremor in a man's faultline, she had the temerity to shake the paintings off the wall. The "Last Wishes" list suddenly came back to me from that sultry July, and my sole entry of things pressed to my lips "as I lay dying" stood not ten feet away—the taste and touch of woman—the most exciting moment of living. It was the only thing I had ever wished for, in life or in death.

"You'll hear all about it at the café. Now go," I commanded.

She crossed her arms beneath those perfect soft mounds hidden in a white tee and watched me turn and march off.

The Restaurant des Beaux-Arts was a small café-bar, a hangout for some of the literary notables of the century — Oscar Wilde, Joyce, Hemingway, Miller — but its predominant trade has always been, and still is, the students and artisans who saturate the area each day, working in the nearby studios and classrooms. The lunch turnover was brisk and the atmosphere lively, the art world *cognoscenti* rubbed elbows with students and journeymen artists. Who knows who might be sitting beside you in any one of a thousand cafés? In the *arrondissement* that was midwife to half the world's fertile artistic emergence, every street corner held the possibility of eye-witnessing some gestation. Young Elissa Charogne of Newport, Rhode Island could be a future futurist, an incubating impressionist, or a dawdling Dadaist, her promise budding before my very eyes. Who knows?

She took long, deliberate strides across the sawdust floor, toward the small round table in the corner of the street-side bar. I'd been slowly nursing an espresso through the fifteen-minute wait. She unziped, unbuttoned, and unlatched several parts of a slate-and-green canvas waistcoat as she approached, then, like a runway model, had it off and neatly draped on the back of her chair in one seamless move.

"Pretty neat straightjacket there, Elissa."

"Moroccan Air Force pilot's jacket," she grinned, smartly.

"Surprised he didn't give you the plane to go with it."

"Surplus stuff. You can get it all over Paris. No big deal. I like confrontational fashion, like to stir-it-up once in a while."

"Your art's going to be confrontational then, I take it?"

"I suppose. Haven't given it a lot of thought yet. It's my first year. I mean, I guess I'll just know somehow."

Her skin had a blush from the cold air and her hair was a little tousled by the wind. Such a freshness and vitality about her in the first few minutes there, I hardly knew what to say. I was preoccupied with observation, roaming the intricacies of her face but never really able to take-in all there was. Some wonder in it seemed to renew every few minutes. She was probably very accustomed to this from men.

"You're going to eat something, young lady," I scolded her like a doting parent. "Please, eat whatever you want. And don't be bashful either. Lunch is on me."

"You're funny," she laughed. "You actually think I'm, like, starving over here?"

"No, but it's a hell of a good old cliché. Besides, it's the right thing to do. Honoring your parents. Suppose my kid were over here? I'd appreciate it if some American bought her a drink, or a sandwich. American's do that sort of thing, you know —intrude."

A cadaverous waiter appeared and stood directly over us. I made a kind of pleading hand formation at him for drinks. Elissa ordered a Campari-and-soda. I asked for a Ricard, with water, and another espresso. I then asked for the day's menu and the day's specials, in less-than-perfect French of course. Elissa stiffened at every French word I uttered. The waiter read-off the offerings du jour, and when I thought Elissa was about to burst open with laughter I turned the ordering over to her. She commanded the making of two special sandwiches—a luncheon deal with the Ecole—two salads, fresh fruit, cheese, and lots of extra bread. I dismissed the deadpan drone with a crude, bored hand wave.

"All right, that's it. That's the last bit of French from me," I blustered. "You handle all of it. I won't be humiliated anymore." Her laughter turned apologetic and soothing. "If I were your dad, I'd kick your ass, young lady."

She looked down at her hands and then away, scanning the room full of people, avoiding my eyes.

"If you were my dad, I wouldn't be here…maybe." She said it in tones much too sullen and serious, and all of the joy suddenly disappeared from that beatific face. I'd hit "white bone" as we used to say back home, a deep, hurtful pain close to the core.

One lousy choice of phrase, her mood shifted like a storm cloud, and suddenly I was terrified of losing her closeness.

"Say, I, I watched you when you came in. You didn't learn those long cowgirl strides in Rhode Island." She cocked her head slightly, and a half-smile creased her smooth cheeks.

"No. I didn't," she said with a sly pause, and then turned back at me. "How did you know that? You know a lot, don't you?"

"Yeah."

"Jesus. Modest too," she let out, under breath.

"I'm a writer. Writers know things. Have to."

"Well, Mister Know-it-all..."

"Drop the mister, I told you." She smiled, broadly. She was adorable and joyful again.

"When I left home, Know-it-all, I lived in Colorado for awhile then finally landed in San Francisco, where they caught up with me. Take short steps, people know you're from back East right away. You've got to walk Western. Anyway, you can put more distance between you and... things, a lot faster."

"Hmmm, is that how you do it? Got to remember that."

"We made a deal. I promised not to disappear again if they sent me to art school in Europe. Voila. Here I am in Paris. I'm happy. They're happy. I see them once or twice a year."

"Why Paris?"

"French is easy for me. Always was. Mom spoke it fluently, my Dad, sorta like you speak it. Charogne's a French name. Dad had some hot-shit ancestors you know. Both my parents were filthy-rich, actually, from filthy-rich Newport families, and I had a pretty pampered existence, I guess."

"How come filthy riches always look so luxuriant?"

"You-know-what-I-mean. I just had to cut loose. I couldn't stand Newport anymore. Christ, they had the guy they wanted me to marry picked out already. And then, everything was always a socially important, fucking thing, you know what I mean? Like a simple fucking tennis match, or..."

The full-color adjectives were spilling over onto the adjacent tables, and some of the lunch guests were glancing.

"Yes, Elissa, you're Newport accent went over smashingly in those circles too, I suppose? So. You headed for the wide open spaces."

"Yeah, my best friend and me."

"Thelma and Louise."

"Something like that. It was great. We had such a blast traveling."

"Left a trail of broken hearts across America, I imagine—you and your partner?"

"No, not really. Sometimes things are too important. I mean, like, the experience is too intense...know what I mean?"

I knew exactly. She had no need for some dumb ass, drooling male filling her head with false promise and insignificance just to get in her pants. I wondered what I sounded like just then?

"Yes, I know what you mean, Elissa. I was referring to the nature of young men, wanting to hold on to someone like you. Men love to throw themselves onto the rocks, in a manner of speaking, and we do it day after day for the scathing misery that beautiful women allow us to feel."

"Holy Christ. You're a Prince Valiant romantic aren't you? Right out of the Sunday comics." She said it with boasting self-satisfaction, stuffing it in my face.

"Well, burn-me-at-the-goddamn-stake, Marie. There are worse things in this world, my dear, much worse. Why, I'm just an old literary cowhand, searching for, and, ah...

discovering, actually rediscovering sort of, the, the, ah...
essence of Eros. The Essence of Eros, you see, yes.
Postmodernist, post-romantic view, of course, shifting
dominant, you know, retro, neo, pseudo, decon-O, E-cono,
regular, and high-test, naturally. And the, ah...metaphysical,
as it were, realm of...love."

"Impressive bullshit," she said, impressively.

"Important bullshit, too. Dark, lonely work, but
somebody's got to do it." We laughed together. "Sounded
good when the guy at Columbia said it." I fumbled with the
Lilliputian espresso spoon, banging the wafer-like saucer
beneath my cup. "I'm actually here on a...I'm here to pick
something up, for a guy back...I have a meeting
with...somebody."

Now, it was my turn to gaze away and look around the
room avoiding her eyes. This was the fan-hitting shit I never
expected to confront. The cycle doesn't help us at all. We
don't learn anything from it, men don't. The herd shifts, it
doesn't change. If I were a young buck, and had just met this
girl, I'd be the same stupid, pawing, fool-for-love dumb ass
with one stiff antler in the wind. It's not a lack of
commitment when we're young, it's a narrow agenda, and it
doesn't broaden much with age as long as we keep
pretending it's a bone, never admitting it's a muscle.

"What's going on now in the States?" She interrupted
my little rumination.

"Oh, reality TV."

"What's that?" She harked, with the shocked expression
and blasé contempt of the expatriate.

"It's just the same old television crap, I suppose, without
the laugh track." I couldn't define the indefinable on the
spot. "People can't tell the difference anymore between
drama and life so they label it now. These are actor-cops, see,
and these are real ones beating this black guy on the
ground." Now she looked at me kind of amazed. "And
here's the dummy you voted for, and here's the dummy-

actor in Washington running things. The subtitles help
people get their bearings on reality, they really do. Lots of
abs and buns, too." The look turned inquisitive and quirky.
"Abs and buns, fitness, aerobics? You know, all that vanity
appearance stuff," I continued. Her jaw hung. "The whole
exercise thing. Everybody's obsessed. Weightlifting.
Running. Stepping, spinning, Tae-Bo, Tai Chi, Tae Kwan Do,
tie everything up like a trussed chicken."

"You look pretty fit," she said with a kind of admiration
in her tone that flatters—an appraisal and a compliment in
one safe remark. I was impressed. "You were an athlete, I'm
sure. I can tell."

"Yes, I was. I stay in shape. But I refuse to be driven by
the perfect workout. A six-pack comes in cans for my
generation, you buy it in the store."

Lunch arrived and Elissa continued our conversation on
the same theme of "fitness" as it pertained to the male
physique.

We ate on the small round bar table with our elbows
banging against each other, picking the crusty crumbs from
the white table cloth regardless of whose sandwich they fell
from. She set the eating-talking pace, a fast one, and I
followed with all due gusto.

She ate like a horse—all of her food, half of my
sandwich, and my salad. She cut fleshy fruits and hard
cheese for me as she "discussed." I was amazed at her ability
to consume. Her definition was testimony to the efficiency of
the young body, placing varietal ingesteds in their rightful,
wonderful place.

Between bites and laughter, our lunch was as much an
interrogation about cultural goings-on in the States as it was
a repast. I provided much entertainment in my warped
assessments of the state-of-the-union, for her benefit of
course. Cynicism was applied liberally just to keep me on her
side. She laughed easily and often and somewhere between
the sandwiches, the chocolate mousse, fruit and cheese, and

the cappuccino torte a'la mode, she got whispery and sincere. The eyes went big, soft and watery, like a doe in dappled sunlight.

"I have a favor to ask," she said, eyelashes batting a thousand.

"Ask and it's yours. Hell, I've already paid for lunch. In New York that's real bonding. You've got me kid."

"Well, it's my drawing class."

"Need me to talk to your teacher?"

"No, see, tomorrow...well, you see we have these models. Live models. We sketch from live models."

"Yeah?"

"I was just wondering. I mean, could you? Would you? Would you sort of model for me?" Her voice went thin and little girlish.

"Sort of, live? Sort of, in your class?" I asked, straining at an annoying imitation of her shy inquiry.

"Well. Yeah," she said, with emphatic certainty. "Of course, live. Live. Sure." She looked at me like I was a dummy for asking. Then, the dummy plodded forward.

"Well. Just what are you sketching tomorrow, Miss Charogne?"

"What? What exactly?"

"Any particular body parts? Studies?" I said.

"Oh, no. No, no. No parts. I mean, yes...all parts. I mean, the whole body." She made broad gestures with her arms, nervous and apprehensive gestures. "I'm sorry. Shit. I shouldn't have asked you this. I'm just so damn impulsive sometimes."

"No, really. It's okay, Elissa. I'm flattered, I think?"

I smiled at her to try to ease the discomfort. "Of course, I hope you're working on Man-in-Decline?" I was looking for a laugh right about there, from either of us, trying to lighten the panic and concern, but Elissa remained deadly serious and very direct.

"What I need, Mr. Degas from Pittsburgh is your soul."

"Wow. Say, you're not *too* shy, are you? Pretty big request, girl. My soul, you need? Well. So do I, Miss Charogne. I need to find it and slap the son-of-a-bitch silly. Tell you what, find mine and I'll buy you dinner, sketch it, and we'll go on television together and make a lot of money."

"Please, Eddie? Listen."

I nodded. It was a shut up nod, a promissory nod of good-boyishness. She calmed, sighed and began again.

"I need the natural, available poise inherent in a state of being, a temporary state of being, of course, a state of inert emotion and, and, and...concentrated thought distilled in a single gesture."

"Impressive bullshit." I nodded again.

"Important bullshit, too. Yes."

"I'd better go back to my room and pose all night."

" 'Gesture is all and everything,' " she said, dreamily.

"Ahh...Brecht. 'The Will of Gesture.' Son-of-a-bitch, I like Brecht."

"Of course. A model may stand perfectly still and completely naked, and yet, reveal to the artist volumes of animated and lively stories embellished with layer upon layer of character and color and feeling, thought motion and sense memory."

"Excuse me? Did you say naked?"

"Well, yeah." She rummaged for words. "It's like...uh, they're like models, you know? I mean, if you don't want to?"

"I didn't say that."

"Really. If you're afraid?"

"Afraid of what?" My dander was up (whatever dander is, I could tell mine was up).

"You can wear your little underpants, or a jock..."

"Just. Just, just, just give me a second to...go over this. Just give me a freakin' second here to run this around." I was holding her at bay, non-committal. I was in control—like a fish with the hook half-swallowed trying to decide whether or not to meet-the-fisherman. "I'm going to pose for you in class? Standing there…what about boxer shorts?"

"No. No freakin' way. I'm not doing camouflage art."

"Black socks and boxer shorts with little red fire trucks."

"You wouldn't? You wouldn't dare." She was red and flustered. "Forget I asked. Please? Just forget it." She pouted and crossed her arms beneath those firm and luxurious breasts, hoisting them slightly in her huffing anger. It was to me like an offering, barter, contradicting the momentary tirade.

"I'm just kidding, Elissa. What time do you want me there?"

"Seriously? You'll do it?"

"Yes, I'll do it." Her sudden smile and gasp of delight relieved me even more than it did her. I'd be with her tomorrow, naked or clothed I'd be with her. I couldn't tease anymore and now I was stuck with a commitment. I glared down into my espresso, looking for some witch, or some fairy godmother to come forth through the black coffee and tell me I was completely nuts. "I can't believe I've gotten myself into this."

"Oh, Eddie, it'll be fun."

"Fun. The Senior Prom was fun. We've just met, for Christ's sake. What? I mean, how? What do I do up there…with…you know?"

"It's easy. You'll see. I can give you a book…"

"No, no." I shook my head like a horse.

"…or some pictures. But I really think a man of your… your…experience…a man of your…your…vast understanding and…your Knowledge. Yeah. Knowledge. Vast, that's it. That's what I mean. You have so much to draw upon. You're, like, a writer."

"So they…like…tell me."

"I think you can be very…you know…interesting…as a subject."

"You mean an object."

"Whatever."

I rubbed my chin between my fingers very vigorously. Then I ran my big, meaty hand through my hair to the back of my neck and grasped tightly at a strange whorl at the hairline. Elissa watched me, motionless. I squeezed at the back of my neck, rhythmically, several times and stared across the room. She stared at me, tapping a foot beneath the table.

"Do you mean, like I'm a guy throwing a discus, or a javelin or something, like some Roman guy, and I'm naked?"

"I hate sports," she said.

"Shit, Newport. Goddamn, this is..."

"Okay. Okay, okay, you can do something, sporty. But you have to make it interesting, Eddie. You know...inventive."

I stared down at the flat black espresso again and there wasn't a goddamn thing stirring in there except the distorted, shimmering picture of my fat nose and oval eyeball. I swigged it in one gulp. I practically threw the demitasse cup back in its little saucer, and grabbed my neck hard again, scratching my head, rubbing my forehead, going through more twitches than a third base coach. Elissa was silent, looking away, sipping her Evian.

"I can't believe this, I just can't believe my luck."

chapter Four
BEAUX -ARTS

At about seven-thirty the next morning I walked from the Balzac to the Quai Malaquais entrance to the Ecole des Beaux-Arts with all the trepidation of a six-year-old on his first day of school. My stomach was queasy, my bowels volcanic. A hazy half-light sparkled along the rim of the Seine—the sky was in the water— pink and blue pastel palates were carried on the flat center current. The river meandered on its journey west toward the Eiffel Tower, bending gently along the *quai*, threading the eyelets formed by the arching bridges and their reflections. On the opposite side, the buildings of the Louvre were sculpted in sharper sunlight and shadow, an unusual immensity, a look that history and time had heaped upon their monumental importance.

The air was filled with the acrid smells of Sicilian coffee and French tobacco, stale beer and brandy, expensive perfumes, the strong residues of wine and champagne—odors of sensuality overlaid with the fumes of burning diesel fuel in the bustling Paris rush hour. The frosted stone moorings along the Seine sent up an occasional plume of dank, rotting moss. Its greenness and bitter pungency pierces even in winter.

Milling around a small wooden door on Quai Malaquais, a group of men huddled against the morning chill. Round-shouldered blue-serge and frayed heavy sweaters mingled and interwove, soiled and cracked hands clutched cardboard containers, stealing the warmth of steaming coffee. Wide, flat cigarettes were pressed and wrinkled between nicotined fingers. The aromas of cognac and anise fused with the coffee and smoke and frosted

breath. A few of the men still wore white waiter's aprons that
fell straight out of their long, dark coats to the tops of scruffy
shoes and boots. Two men had grappling hooks hanging
from their wide leather belts. Raised and fleshy scar tissue
looked raw and red. Most of them were in tattered clothes,
faded woolens, and un-creased heavy trousers. Was it
possible? These, the forms behind high-priced works of art?
Dwarfish Punchinellos, hulking and scowling grotesques
with exaggerated limbs and appendages, warts and assorted
pustules—the sideshow muscular and the frail—their hard
features jutted forth into the Paris mist, and a wall of
contentious looking, deeply suspicious eyes peered at me,
puzzled. Was I some tourist, in the wrong spot for a bus
tour? Or did I belong? Did I have some augury to marvel? A
freakish birthmark the shape of Kansas, or Vermont,
perhaps, would score with this group, but the half-inch scar
just below my lower lip—a childhood memento from the
edge of a dining room chair—just wouldn't cut it here. This
was the Big Leagues of odd features.

After some guarded minutes of sipping coffee and
watching, an unlatching sound startled and redirected
everyone's attention. The Hunchback of Ecole des Beaux-
Arts, a small, bent man of undeterminable age, opened the
creaky little backstage door on Quai Malaquais and the
group rushed in to the hissing heat of the old school and just
then it was a toasty welcome.

The group became lively and talkative. They led, and I
trailed, through a maze of basement corridors, then up two
long flights of wide stairs to one of the main *ateliérs*. We
passed a huge classroom studio with windows stretching
floor to ceiling, twenty-five feet or more. Above the
windows, another long set of slanted, square transoms that
caught the first rays of sunlight.

Inside the room several people were busily working.
Men in blue overalls moved tables and desks, and students
arranged their workspaces. One bearded, distinguished-

looking man in a suit and tie strolled through the hurried activity, and amid all the commotion, I saw Elissa clearing a long oaken desk near the windows. This was our room, then, the room where the freak show of models, me included, would become the physical aesthetic in display of a good deal of dangling paraphernalia before the eager students of Ecole des Beaux-Arts. I watched Elissa setting-up her work area. At once, I wanted a look of reassurance from her, and I considered bolting back outside before she saw me.

She looked more radiant this morning, more reconciled to a classroom atmosphere. Her hair was pulled back again and braided, as it was the day before, but her dress was somewhat formal today, a short forest-green skirt over black tights and a smock-type thing draped around a white, collared blouse. She'd done a kind of Paris-Newport, urbane, arty, stylishness, and thrown-it-together quite well. Everything was a direct hit. Breeding seemed to facilitate an agility with style. Elissa had both in abundance.

The scrum, even more boisterous now, passed double-file through an ornately carved marble archway, graced from above by a gigantic gold-framed oil painting. A sinister, twisting male nude painted in the deeply shadowed style of Goya, or Delacroix, posed an ominous welcome. Another doorway, and into a room that was, by any definition the world over, a locker room. My discomfort and awkwardness suddenly dissipated, we'd reached familiar territory. A locker room was like the athlete's pied a terre. Men took to them like seals to a favorite rock. We appropriated in locker rooms. Hang one item of clothing, you'd established eminent domain, one fudged pair of under shorts, and it became forbidden territory. We were the bare-assed kids men longed to be in these rooms and all barriers and differences ceased to exist—the first fart reports, and you know you're among your species.

White robes, having a scratchy burlap texture, hung from rusted hooks that lined the wall space opposite banks of

the old school's dilapidated wooden lockers. Here we
marauded and grunted, undressing and rumbling, and
shouldered into actions that dissolved wordlessly into
another typically male specialty, imitation—the behavioral
modem of the hovel. This group, that only minutes before
resembled a local of the longshoreman's union, now looked
like an order of monks in prayer robes lining up for vespers.
Each man watched another for some Simian code or sound of
guidance. Unaccountably, it always happened, and we
moved out. And I was one of them, like it or not.

I was woefully unprepared for this nudity. What did I
bite-off here? I'd been involved in experimental theatre Off-
Off Broadway when I first landed in New York. Stage
nakedness then was commonplace. Hardly a play, especially
downtown, went up without a gratuitous scene of brief
nudity, or some provocative, full-frontal assault aimed at
audience squeamishness. Actors were trained for stage
nudity. Immersed in character, nakedness was just another
costume, but that state was the result of much conditioning.
Impulsively, I'd agreed to model for the student-apprentice
Elissa Charogne. *And what was I thinking?*

There were no theatrical characters for me to hide
behind, and try as I might to feign a costume of Hellenic
Olympism, or Greco-Roman statuary, I couldn't take myself
out of my body. I was there, fully, trembling and prickly
with chill. Elissa studied me intently, and I was *in the
moment*, as actor's say—and what a moment it was. I
perspired behind the knees and in my groin. Muscles
twitched. A deafness blocked me like a head-cold, then a
ringing siren screamed in my ears. The first few minutes
were total confusion. Body noise was at earthquake levels. I
could barely move. Itches arrived and disappeared. I didn't
dare go after them. Slightest movement was magnified.
Genitals shifted with all the subtlety of furniture pieces in a
small apartment. Beads of cool sweat on my scalp crept
slowly every few minutes and made their way down the

gorge of my spine. Sunlight through the transoms was medicinal and razor-sharp, falling on me like a prison searchlight. No shadows for a haven, no partial shade dimmed the vulnerability.

Elissa was a sublimely moving object in my periphery, downstage left and looking up. The wall, the windows, the faces were all a blur. I couldn't look directly at her for some time, and yet, I felt some sympathy, some tenderness and compassion coming my way, cutting through my fear. Elissa's eyes became a kind of strength. Their brown clarity, safety, and the appearance of solid earth down beneath me, gave collateral refuge.

The moments were Pinteresque—wordless deliberation, but a dialogue, nonetheless, of expressions, there to quell anxiety in the long pauses. She cloaked me in her look and I wanted desperately to see passion in her eyes and feel guiltless. So completely I had wanted to be stripped and find penance, away from that attendant praise in New York. To find reprove and lay bare the spirit, Elissa was my chance for a relevant atonement.

Artist and model in the final hour became a *Pietá*. In the end, it was not an exhibition—not in the way strippers taunted audiences with blatant nudity. I had invited a kind of harsh examination. I'd wanted an artist to unclothe me and peel away at layer after layer of false pride and aversion. Instead, Elissa cradled my vulnerability in warmth and understanding. My shame, my abasement, I'd have to accomplish on my own.

On my bed at the Balzac, I stared into the darkness, listening to the rain on the copper roof, replaying over and over my naked image turning and bending, sitting, standing through the three-and-a-half hours in the drawing studio. Ultimately, I became all of the things she wanted in that span—a stone Greek, a Roman marble, her bronze athlete, an alabaster Celt, perhaps her David, perhaps a Christ.

I'd been a good statue, I thought—conjured-up images in statuary remembered, ornaments along garden walls, heavy pedestals in public buildings, paperweights, and fountain deities. I prayed that a hard, pure rain might fall on me and wash away deep and pitted stains. No such luck. But Elissa had asked for my soul, a tall order for a statue. She made me realize how much like stone I really was. She gave no direction, not a word. I could hear, faintly, other students instructing their models with short commands and whispers. Elissa accepted, silently, whatever I gave. After a time, I was able to empty myself and feel exactly like some granite slab, Elissa's penetrating stare was the only touch to stir me.

I burned with fever lying on my bed, the memory of Elissa's eyes on me like a July afternoon. If only I could have it all back now, the summers, this room, those times, to feel reckless and free again, the way Elissa made me feel for a few flirtatious moments in a Paris museum. Some sickness of being beyond it, having done it, crippled me. Stranded here, alone and empty, I was left to race through the dungeon of memory again, all of it, with all the patterns. And for what?

A knock on the door. The darkness chilled and a fearful wish suddenly filled the room. *Open it. Open the door.* The wish, the danger, memory and desire would be standing there. *Open the door.*

In the frame, lambency startled. She stood silhouetted, haloed, against the golden-yellow light of the hall lamps, a grasp of deeply red-purple heather and heath in her right hand like a torch. We said nothing, then like a ship she sailed into my arms, parting me like still waters. Her hair was misted by the rain, her forehead, a smooth prow upon which to place my lips. Our shuffling feet scratched the wooden floor and our muffled sounds echoed along the empty hall. A rustle of damp overcoat and we suddenly erupted in each other's arms, humming, groaning, mouthing each other.

Places on her body, warm places between her shoulder and neck, chin and breastbone, I found, the fragrant places in her woman hollows, full of French soap aromas. A need to feel beneath clothes, a full emanation, the fuel and heat of my life. My act and all-consuming male identity, had always been this—female compliance, for the asking, for the taking. The basic deal. *What a simple blueprint, a man. How complex, a rib, anyway?*

Down on the bed she placed me like a stone statue in a museum crate. She had a presence of mind that my excitement overshadowed. *Women always do.* The handful of heather and heath burst into true radiance on the mirrored tray, my beacon from the past illuminated, and she moved through the room as if she'd lived here always. My room had suddenly become hers. Undressing in the darkness, her black figure skipped and chattered like a Muybridge negative against the blue windows. The outline thrilled me, each frame a dazzling arousal—a space of blue between her thighs, a hint of dark, thick hair, a breast swung under an outstretched arm as she bent down. Roundness, hardness, a dizzying anticipation of gifts, the animal rapture was coming, the ravishment approached communion.

Like a dance in darkness, we clawed and sucked and swallowed, entwining limbs like the bare branches of trees in winter. A soft curve of abdomen hovered over me like a low cloud, her warm spill seeped fresh into my mouth. *Again. A pattern begun again.*

In minutes, it wouldn't matter who she was, or where we were. She would fill it, the gaping hole of this sickness. I was easy. An archangel in a picture gallery anointed me with her smile and tender breasts and I was sucked into the Order again. That fast, the vows. I was easy for this god.

Her plaster athlete had come alive, stepped down from the garden wall and taken the sculptress in his arms. She slid along my body, breathing and licking. Then down she moved riding the taut camber of my belly, down between my legs with her warm face. Her hair dragged across my thighs.

A hand, firmed and warmed around me like a grasp of heath and heather, and then she took me in her mouth, gently.

Blood heat swelled, a pulsating syncopation and rhythmic stress in a most primal human music. *What's different about this day, Adam? Yesterday, it was all just fruit and innocent chitchat.* What was expected of us, anyway? We were in flight, Elissa Charogne and I, away from garden walls.

"Elissa? Look at me, Elissa." I raised on my elbows and peered down across the valley of my abdomen at her. She took me from her mouth, her eyes glistening in the blue darkness. A runaway's face stared up at me. In my Paris room, hidden from all that haunted us, we were found in each other. "Elissa. Be rough with me."

"What? What do you mean?" she whispered, her voice cracking.

"Please, listen to me, Elissa. Be rough. You must."

"Eddie, I don't understand," she cried softly.

"It's okay. Elissa, please? I need to feel the pain. Make me remember, please. Make me remember it. Make it hurt."

"But, Eddie..."

"Elissa. Yes, Elissa, please? Hurt me."

The innocence of a lamb's face turned suddenly grave and wolfen. Over me she hunched like a chimaera, and I lie back and wait. The room blackened and it began, searing, piercing a numb anurous rock of pain. My muscles constricted. A knot at the back of my brain tightened and I split the ceiling above and into the night blackness I flew until a whiteness finally burned-in behind my eyes. Whiteness. White pain that chilled like sunburn. Paris incinerated. The Mondrian patchwork of windows glowed white-hot and everything fell away. All searching ended. A white angel's wings fluttered, and the mirror's pale ghost cried out my final reparation. There was only whiteness and soundless pain, screams unvoiced in winter's moonlight.

~

Caresses then promises at dawn, the restorative morning as aftermath. Pawing coitus, tender embrace and time, the unhurried ointments that healed tremulous anxieties. Entering her was a meditation, the salutation pliable, slowed, and compressed. Sex was a steeplechase with my sweet Rhode Island roan, but her mount's been through the hedges. The dome of Napoleon's tomb, *Invalides*, glimpsed through the window as we sail over the jumps, rose into the morning sky. So young and strong, and I was at the center of her power, like a bow on the harp strings. She played me, extended the moments of ecstasy. We drenched each other in sticky love, her young-woman odors were unctuous and sweet. The sap and smell of sex and warm bedclothes was the amber abeyance that suspended all memory of events in this room—it confirmed my inveteracy.

She dressed in shadows tinted pink by daybreak. A naked puppet jumped and told bawdy jokes, making me laugh and take joy in her happiness—Rhode Island Red and her own *Crazy Cock* review. The vulgar became comical, propriety tossed aside for free expression. Burlesqueries abounded with raucous parodies of love and passion, sex, and our debauchery. She was funny. Giddy. She skipped across the floor, joyful and radiant, and leapt onto me as I hid under the covers.

She'd be late for class, but just then she was childlike and playfully unaffected. Exhilarated by our affair, she saw days ahead like this one, nights like the last. She was accustomed to the room, accustomed to my naked body as if she'd occupied both for extended periods. They were hers now, too, room and body. She and I had become, *we*. All of the functions our bodies could have, in this room, or in the bath, had been shared that morning. Lovers had no privacy, we perform sexual autopsy—at any time, anywhere. Territories claimed, organs and orifices suddenly free-trade zones, communal property vested in the anatomical joy of intimacy. We became a small country overnight with few laws—indomitable nudes, naked statesmen, answering to no one. Open, yet indestructibly sovereign. The secrets did the damage, only the secrets. *They always do.*

We were thrilled with each other. Our awakening had been gratified tenfold by varied and unbound sex. She was relaxed and confident, there was newness in the world, and she envisioned some days ahead. Hope was alive in her smile. I was good at this. In a night, belief seemed tangible. Inside her I'd set fields ablaze, a brush fire of dried heather and heath now consuming the room. I made promises for the afternoon and evening, for her days. I made lies. For every afternoon and evening, I had lies to suit the occasion. I was good at this, very good.

Eight-fifteen and young lover leaned over me one last time, licking and sucking at my mouth.

"Oh, Eddie(suck)goddamn it, I love this(lick). Why don't I just cut classes today(kiss, kiss, lick, suck)huh? We could stay in bed all day, Eddie?(suck, suck) Huh?"

"No, no, Rhode Island(kiss, suck). The world awaits a new artist. You are born everyday—Charogne Signs Work Today."

"You, Eddie, you're my work now," she took my head in both her hands, getting suddenly serious. "Let me work on you today."

"I'm finished, my love. I'm a finished piece." I sulked and she laughed. Then we laughed together, a sudden synchronization that linked us this morning to the beats of the previous night, one of those odd things that happened between two people after a first raging night of long, fulfilling lovemaking. She knocked me on the chin, kissed me again wrapping arms about my neck. Her trench coat was open, her legs spread like Willie Mays in a stance beside the bed. My hand fondled her inner thighs and crotch, making countless U-turns in that warm arch, along the silk-smooth panties, rubbing, running my fingers lightly beside ridges and stiffened hairs. She did Go-Go grinds and swooned, then pulled away from the bed, back out of the batter's box.

"You're an awful, awful man Eddie. Eddie. Why, you bastard, you never did tell me your surname. You son-of-a-bitch."

"Anonymous sex. It is pretty wonderful isn't it?" I put my hands behind my head, leaned back against a mountain of pillows and watched her fume. The face I first saw in the museum was back—the somebody's daughter, the someone's younger sister, a little tyrant, and the New England coed who made men drool.

"You bastard. I'm going to school, you deviant." She giggled like a drunkard. "Against my will, I am going to school. And when I come back, Mister Eddie Son-of-a-bitch, you'd better have a name, damn it. Like, a name that's listed, you know?" She wobbled and tried to control irrepressible glee, keeping a safe distance from the bedside. "Or. Or, I will call the ah...The French Sex Control Unit, or something, whatever."

"French Sex Control? Isn't that oxymoronic?"

"You wait, smart guy." She backed up to the door, teasing, waving goodbye, blowing me kisses across slender fingers. "You're after the 'Essence of Eros?' Is that it? I'm gonna ruin that venture, Sherlock." She grabbed her crotch like a Bourbon Street stripper. "Drink from this, porch painter." She burst with laughter at her own vamping, acting-out some organic freedom with her body, totally sensorial and invigorating. Some women craved unrestrained physicality and sexual abandon, and allowed it to rush forth freely like a Montana brook in spring. Watching Rhode Island Red strut the floor, it occurred to me that I'd made the unbinding of women purposeful in my life—to an extreme, to ruination—I'd sought it obsessively. Plagued with the recurrence of sexual illness, what did I need from Elissa Charogne, anyway? And how much? Illness like mine needed only a night nurse.

~

The afternoon train to Milan on weekdays was a short ten-car number. A double-Turbo engine was put on the front, the kind used for the bullet TGV, and on certain days with certain engineers at the throttle it was actually faster than the TGV. She hummed like the wind through the French countryside.

I opted for the red-cushioned comfort of Business Class. Sitting in the empty compartment I watched the slanted sunlight columns pour in and divide the cavernous train hall at Gare Lyon. Passengers and workers shuttled through the dark and light spaces like the flicker of old newsreels.

I was sick and depressed, and fleeing, running to avoid. The choices flickered, too, between dark and darker—the truth of last night and the lie of this morning. I came to Paris for distance, for self-deprecation, and anonymity. Instead, I found a way to plunder and maim. Exigencies flared, a young woman touched, and I was as lost as Atlantis.

Elissa Charogne's exuberance and compassion marked in my memory forever the Stirner trip to Paris—it overshadowed many others. We had woven together an experience, and into it I thread betrayal and disappointment. My only hope was that she sensed equal parts of my need and my odd expression of love.

The room at the Balzac had chronicled another visit, the mirrored tray absorbed another memory. Then, by train to Switzerland, I would chase the past to unravel ever-present distress. I remembered Madame Desnoyers' troubled concern at the front desk an hour before.

"Monsieur, I fear I will not see you again." Softly, she spoke with a quake and urgency in her voice I'd never heard before. Her English was concise, fluid, and very well spoken—something else I'd never heard before—and her eyes filled and sparkled when she forced brittle smiles. I hugged her tightly, and then held her shoulders in my hands.

"Madame Desnoyers, you must not think this. Of course, I will be back, trust that I will." I smiled, trying to elicit an acceptance of my promise. "Madame, rest assured, if you don't see me, or hear from me within six or eight months, I'll be dead and buried, no more, *c'est finis.* That is the only event that will keep me from coming back to the Balzac." I smiled broadly at her, the way people always do when they joke about death, but she gave me only her steady eyes. Her lips gathered tightly in a half-smile, and her silent accord chilled me to the bone.

"This girl, *monsieur J'nelle?*" She began again, changing her tone. "She is very young."

"Yes, madame, she is young, a very wonderful young girl. The young are so strong, Madame Desnoyers, *comme les boeufs, oui? non?* The young can withstand such difficulties, madame."

She'd seen me march into the Balzac with women throughout the years, young and old. It wasn't the girl that concerned her so.

"How can we be sure, monsieur? How can we be sure?" She kept after me.

"Because we are here, madame. We've survived to grow older, wiser, you and I." I kissed her cheek and quickly started for the glass front doors and Rue Visconti. She followed. I could sense she had something else to tell me and turned to her as I reached the doors. "I must go, madame. I will miss you. *Merci, madame.* Until next time."

"Monsieur J'nelle?" she said, stopping me with entreaty and regret in her voice. "You are my only American, *client...* *client?* uh, guest. Yes. Many, many years you are coming to the Balzac. And I am very happy to see you always. You know, I like you very much. You are very successful man, I think. Nice man. *E c'est tre, tre beau,* a very handsome man. Like the movie star in Hollywood. Women know. Many women, yes? *Ooouuulala, oui.*" Her eyes rolled and she laughed self-consciously. "I know, you see. You keep so very well, Monsieur J'nelle, so very nice looking, you don't seem to...*age*, like me." Her eyes squinted in deep concern and she brushed my cheek with the tips of her fingers.

"*Merci,* madame. You are very kind." A sudden disquiet spread through me, like a warmth that builds with shame.

"*Mais,* but..." She searched my eyes and hers were wet and filled with tears. "You seem to grow more sad, *monsieur.* All of these years, you seem to grow more sad."

Hurtling through the night in the south of France on a rocketing train, the blackness surrounded me, within and outside of the compartment. Past and present were moving at nightmarish speed, the decline unstoppable. The only stillness, my face reflected on the window glass and the prophecy of Madame Desnoyers' words ruefully etched in it.

Landscapes flew in and out of the eye sockets, roads and trees swirled about the nostrils, shadowy fields and empty barns were swallowed whole in the black caverns of my mouth and ears. Like misshapen creatures, amorphous lingerings that fly and dodge at the corners of dreams, the dark untidy figures were meant to haunt, meant to frighten.

Madame Camille Desnoyers' words echoed, the burning truth struck me through like a shaft of lightening ripping through a pine tree. *Lies are merely truths with bad intentions, Eddie.*

Yacov Stirner's leather-bound diaries, wrapped in sealant plastic, sat beside me in an open attaché. Maybe I had more in common with Stirner, than with Degas. The old betrayer, the Nazi collaborator and I made the swift transit together. His deeds silenced, dead in time and decayed in history, mine festered, corrupting each moment my life occupied.

The thunderous passage of this night soon gave way to sleep and dreams, and the plunge into memory. Deeper, I'd go. Back—five, seven, ten years, twelve, fifteen maybe. Who knew? Pick a year, it was all there—the covenant, and all the denial. The mistakes, the patterns that hurt, they were all there. Back I'd go, to the mountain, the high snows, back to the barren glacier, the desolation, and a vast wilderness of depression.

Soon the Simplon. A pitch-black entrance bored deep beneath the Alps. Sooner, the dreams—more ominous, yet an entrance from beneath just the same. I'd come this way before, across a Styx of my design, the river running faster, always deeper, indigo and wild. Down, always down it took me, into a lower world, a darker land. *The past is present. The lie is true.*

The journey was always a descent, a fall of some sort—the fundamental genesis. Without it, my understanding only represented understanding, and wondrous mystery then, was but a fallow symbol of the inexplicable.

chapter Five
V E R B I E R, 1985

The robin's egg was cracked, a lifeless substance oozes out. A cold killing air rushed in and something was dead, something unmoving and silent, revealing, but dead was lying there like February hoarfrost. A process was stifled, shut down without notice. Toxic fear compounding itself was leaching, contaminating streams of consciousness, streams feeding a river of thought. *Examine the condition. Re-examine it and wait.*

That was it. What else could I do? There were times when the best strategy was no strategy. Be patient. It's virtuous. How much damage could be done by being virtuous?

I liked the "oozing" bit. That was good. Morbid. Pungent, that view, that state of mind—finality, coldness, death, repulsion, putrefaction. I liked that.

The shadows of certain lies raced cross my path, a fraudulent rhetoric assailed my self-confidence—tell the first one, the rest are easy. *Guilt and Green Onions*, nineteen seventy-nine. I had something then.

An endless flow of minutiae leading nowhere filled the waking hours, the trite idea, greed, loathing, and the infectious patter of nonsense. The age of contagion. The virus, anxiety. Eighty-two, *High On Anxiety*, a real money maker. They ate it up in five languages, and Braille. Yuppie mental health. Turned it into a series of audio cassettes. They called it, Contentment and The Self in the I-Me Generation, or I'm Okay, *You're* The Prick.

I went on a streak, then something happened. A thing in New York, in court again. Then, Ann Arbor. Suddenly, the whole world was out to lunch, and I was on hold. Everybody was gone.

Shave your face, you won't look so bad.

It was a hundred-and-ten in the shade. Loneliness. Worse, an aloneness. Fever. Chill. Isolation, hibernation, an emotional hypothermia, apoplexy, mental lethargy, lassitude, irascibility, impatience with people, disdain for the most basic human inter-action, avoidance, and back to loneliness. I felt like shit.

Blocked.

Fuck blocked. I hated that goddamn word. Tonnage in the path, some friggin' lodestone jerked around in the brain like a meteor. Bullshit. I hated the blank page crap, too. A little time was all I needed, just a little time.

The telephone on the night table rang.

I rose to the surface like a harpooned whale. New York, I could tell by the ring. How the hell did they get the number?

It rang a second time. *Up Eddie, answer it.*

My Judy in thumbscrews. They had her kids hostage, probably. The unholy three—editor, publisher, agent. They sensed something. Potions, they brought. They tried to comfort me with a fake nonchalance.

"We were just thinking about you, mate. How're you doing?"

"Great. Couldn't be better, Dex." They were thinking about me? Who? The three of them? Or, was the "we" Katie, Larry, Brian, the new girl, the guys in production, travel, editorial, the grocer, the cleaners, my doorman, everyone west of the Azores? I hated this kind of intrusion.

"How the hell did you track me down?"

"February's centerfold for Brass Knuckles Quarterly sort of let it slip," Dexter said sheepishly.

"Better leave her alone."

"You lucky dog. How's the skiing? How're the women, mate?"

Dexter meant well, the big kangaroo. His voice linked

me again, bringing them all into my room. I knew they were
all there standing around my desk, no doubt. It was friendly.
What was wrong with that? Did I want this — the gesture, the
caring — or didn't I? I really didn't hate the intrusion. I hated
the decision.

"Don't bring back any famous Swiss diseases, Pecker."
Dexter kept busting me. "Hey, bring me one of them big cow
bells, will you, mate? I want to hang it on my door."

"Get lots of rest, Jocko, you're going to be riding a wave
of well-deserved success," Carl chimed-in. "This feeling is
natural, Eddie. Don't think about us."

"Right, Carl. Doing great. Just need a little rest."

Riding a wave? I'm friggin' body-surfing, face first.

Carlton Atherton Bested was owner and publisher of
New World Visions — New York and London — a haughty
collection of bi-monthly, biting fiction that I'd been writing
for, unimpaired and very happily, since seventy-nine. *New
World* was the literary glossy in Bested's publishing empire,
Atherton Books, a conglomerate slew of international
magazines, trade papers, art books and newsletters, all under
the Chimaera Paperbacks division, and *The Manichaean*, a
stiff-lipped, academic review, as thick as a Tokyo phone
book.

Visions was a literary duck blind, Carl Bested's private
skeet range for sniping at the clay pigeons of literary
pretention.

"You're our thoroughbred, Eddie. We need our number
one pony strong, now more than ever. You're going to be the
author of the decade, a Citation, for god's sake."

They shoot horses don't they, Carl? My wonderful boss
was an obese and unattractive man, but his size was a mere
wrapper for a tremendous intellect. He possessed enormous
generosity and warm-heartedness and could be quite
charming, in a sarcastic sort of way. He gathered coteries of
contrasting personalities around him, around us, his writers.
The sparks that flew from such blendings infatuated him

somehow. The more friction between types, the more he enjoyed it. He loved parties. He loved to mix the varied types in unusual ways and in imprudent situations, skimming off the boisterous dregs of heated arguments for himself, calling it adulation. Life was a grand gourmet stew of people and ideas, Carl was a ladle.

Author, he called me. The flavor of the month, more apropos, a burp beneath the phrase, "a novel by". Carl Bested adored me like a son. He prodded me with fatherly affection, something to which I was unaccustomed. A critic once slammed one of my semi-romantic novellas, "...it is a painful deliberation, he paints a chair with white-out forcing us to watch, and then, there are ten or fifteen pages of blood and passion, at times, sheer terror."

Carl teased me endlessly about that review. "A venomous sudden strike amidst the slithering-ly mundane," he chided his party guests with me on his arm. "A dramatic visualist," he would boast, "a slashing Lawrence, riding across the desert dryness and tedium of uneventful realism."

"I write fiction, Carl," my comeback, "none of which is fact, all of which is truth." And then everyone chuckled. Carl Bested paid me handsomely for such gentle parlance with his party guests, and for ten or fifteen pages of passion and terror.

"Eddie, darling, how are you? It's Gila, darling," The guardian agent sang into the speakerphone. British and puffy, a ditty, she was always having tea "and all that."

"Gila, darling. Feeling fine. Yes, everything's just 'darling' here, luv," I schmoozed.

"I'm so concerned about you. Don't try too hard to do anything, dear. Put your mind off of things, if you know what I mean. You'll come up and out into the beautiful blue, the beautiful blue and all that, Creation, dear, you know? Don't worry, these things happen."

There were days with Gila when I hadn't the slightest idea what in the hell she was talking about, but it always sounded soothing.

The conversation went on for some minutes more, laced with plaudits. Their wailing, sympathetic tone had the subtlety of Sicilian mourners. It concealed, haphazardly, a genuine panic. I was having a problem. I could stop writing at any moment for these people, a correspondence of marketable prose they had come to expect. The cycle? I don't think so.

A heady little novel—a novella with a novel's impudence—the result of four-and-a-half years, had brought me, surprisingly, to the foothills around literary Olympus.

It wasn't as if I were about to commit art. I put my balls on the footlights, and got a standing-O. End of story.

I spoke slowly, moving carefully through a minefield of praise, through comforting and courtesy, and made no apologies.

"Tomorrow, *domani*, later, soon, maybe."

Excuses came easily. I used them as much for myself as for them. They were satisfied and, for the moment, I was content with the hurried silence of the receiver.

Empty plastic containers surrounding the phone spilled and scattered, some fell to the floor. Halcion, Elavil, Ativan, Ludomil, Haldol—the heavy artillery. They'd kept me inside the railing. Judy had to steal from her father's pharmacy. Fucking Julio couldn't manage. Some connection.

"Eddie, man, I can get you cocaine, horse, chica negra, dust, poppers, the best hashish, nickle-bag, twenty dollar, some new shit coming down called Crack. Anything you want, man." Everything for the career junkie.

"Julio, this is no big deal. I need some pills, man, I'm getting sick, you know? What's the problem?"

"Man, what do I look like, Rite-Aid? Come on Eddie, man. That shit is tough to get, man."

It was an imperfect world. You got no help when real damage control was needed.

Something was rooted in deeper disturbances. An intimate aphasia, a soundless frenzy was on-coming, gravity pulling at me. A mercurial shift of moods and tempers straining at opposites drove the feeling of isolation further along the edge of a sort of madness. The travail of suffering through it, on your own, was somehow interpreted as an absolution and a penance all rolled into one. The reclusiveness disfigured. A razor to my face wouldn't accomplish anything. *To your wrist, Eddie. What about that?* I was angry. Days down, in and out of sleep. False insecurity harangued. I was stymied by something else, something completely new—paralyzing self-doubt. Of that, I was profoundly ashamed. I had never allowed myself such an antipodean indulgence.

The athlete, the fleet-footed halfback, All-Conference, All-State, All-American, stellar second baseman, four-letter wrestler, class beau, class president, big-man-on-campus, you name it, and I was all things to all friends and family. What would they think, seeing me like this?

A Spartan discipline had worked well, always. I was physically fit. Weakness offended me, sickness disappointed. The yellow-orange and red bars crossed the floor. I watched them on the carpet. Ten yellow, ten red. Day into night on a vagrant's schedule, the cold and the heat mixed. Paul brought plates of cheese, bread and coffee. He left them outside the door. I wouldn't let anyone in. I wasn't ready.

I thought I heard a titmouse scratching, running in the walls. He wouldn't come out to see me, not even for the cheese. *A mouse wouldn't look at me?*

Could I have done something? Was I not seeing a way out of the labyrinth?

A ski on fresh snow. A skate cuts blue morning ice. The images stung but said nothing. The frostbite was hot but not burning. The skin on the left hand withered and turned gray.

I watched a kind of death set in, I think. It began its long sleep next to my left hand. The crippling frost seemed to surround my every verdant impulse, every representation, every purpose, every emotion. Ideas lay there with a thin, frozen covering of complacency. Feeling had wrapped itself in lethargy. The cold face of immovability stared through the pane of intent.

Verbier, again. In times past I opened and closed the cafés, the clubs, and bars of this Swiss mountain resort in self-indulgent rituals that honored nothing more than excess. The excesses never hindered me, however. In fact, I was seeking similar patterns, similar rituals then—the smokey Café Borsalino, tables at Camargue and Au Mayen, cognac at Sacconaix, or the Aristo bar, a stupor of hashish, the icy rush of cocaine, limousine orgies, dizzying discotheques, the steep streets, the steeper ledges of snow and ice, some dream or obsession, some taste and touch of women, my brain and senses drowned in sex.

Some omen here helped me find a way to unlock. The ideas, the remedy triggered with such ease, before. Now what? What happened this time? One good book—like first sex all over again—and the extraordinary was ending in fear and inadequacy. Something else was in the way. I was drifting aimlessly between creativity and depression, desire and memory, awaiting the tides.

Snowy, white drugs blinded me when I wished to see elsewhere. They'd always been there to numb the memory, to blunt the fall when it came. The footprints of fallow deer disappeared between the curling drifts, the doe slipped away too fast. I chased sleep. Dreams recurred immutable and violent. A sane, logical grasp was lost. I searched the narrow path, trying to pick up the trail, some sign, a vision to catapult me through the stagnant, white delusions. Trapped on an ice floe, I jumped from piece to rapidly spinning piece, the spaces between widening with each leap. When would I fall? When, into the deep? When, the bottom?

The daily *La Suisse* slid under the door pushed by hands, by a friend, unseen. "Expedition Of Six Germans, Three Swiss Missing After Sudden Mountain Storm" the front-page banner glared in the narrow crack of hall light. I was stranded, too, in a sudden storm of personal loss. I had lost my son and daughter, my only real miracles—lost not to accident or disease, but to the catastrophe of bitter divorce and custody battles. Tradition and ritual brought people together in matrimony, civics took them apart. Father was a third class citizen—third after grandparents—merely a witness to a family. The seed had no right to the saplings.

My loss in the mockery of family court might as well have been a homicide, for some part of me it seemed surely had been murdered. The walls and floors of that old courthouse creaked of some unscrewed justice that morning. The warm, dark tones of Adirondack woods, their surfaces gleaming, belied a deeper-grained untruth. I lie still, in a darkened Verbier, hoping for some pure truth, a light overhead without shadow. Testimony, unlike vows, gave credence to the subversive nature of men and women in relationships. Intimacy was bartered in the time it took to draw-up legal documents. Man and wife tread mercilessly on privacy and promises. Why did men undress women with their eyes? To see if they were wearing listening devices, of course.

Others around me rejoiced that day. My heart raced toward a closed-circuit hell. I was unprepared.

My son looked strong and brilliant there in his tweed Sunday-suit and tie, emulating some man of distinction hidden in both of us—his emerging, mine suffocating on that day.

My daughter masked her crushing disappointment. A cherub face and smile, cheeks aglow like polished fruit, a manifestation of her indefatigable joy. Sophie was the unexpected gift, arriving only fifteen months after her brother. Many believe the unplanned ones were bestowed with special charms and graces. In fact, she had charmed almost everyone in the courthouse that day, even a stodgy old bailiff. Sophie lived up to the "unplanned" invention with an engaging personality, sophistication, and brilliance beyond childlike capacities. We guarded a secret pain together, she and I. We had shared a different common trial and survived. In many ways, this day was no match for what we had already been through together.

Sophie suffered with juvenile rheumatoid arthritis from the age of two. We had endured many hospital stays, tests, days and nights of pain and faded hope. Her little arms encircled my neck during our goodbye embrace and her silence seemed to consecrate a moment of profound and precocious understanding.

They say that small children sensed unhappiness and discord in a household, that an atmosphere of unrest between parents preyed negatively on sickness. I didn't know if that insight-of-innocence was true, but I never put on an act for Sophie's sake. I was honest about the deteriorating state of her parent's relationship, and I don't know how her body dealt with that unfair reality. Imperfection was abundant in adults, the myth of the ideal family was worthy of about a 30-second commercial. Adaptation was better than an alteration. Wasn't it? Truth, I'd idealized, would be curative in the long run. My wife thought otherwise.

"She gets worse, Eddie, she hurts for us, the way we are."

"What would you suggest, Newie? We walk around arm-in-arm, smile and laugh and kiss and look happy?"

"You could at least curtail your goddamn affairs for your daughter's sake."

"My daughter and I have a direct line of honesty and love. Stay off that line, Newell, just stay off. You and those goddamn doctors, stay off. And stop putting shit in her head about me."

"We do not discuss you, you and your whoring. God, I'll

spare a child that, that disgrace. I'd rather tell her you're out nights running drugs, or robbing banks, for god's sake. Oh, you are cruel, you bastard, you are cruel, Eddie."

She pleaded, she ranted, and sometimes even threw things, but she withheld tears through it all, through every railing fight. As if to spite me and not grant me the outside view of an emotional razing, she held back on tearful catharsis.

Canadian bred from English-French stock as stiff as they come. An only child with a surfeit of comforts and attention, she was as tough as nails. She expected a continuance of perfection, willed it to herself through an almost militant stoicism. She never wept over me. I admired that about her. My athletic nature respected the formidable toe-to-toe fighter she was. I admired her. I wish I could have loved her more.

"Must you tear me apart when I'm already in such pain? Can't you stop, Eddie? I'm not asking you to be loving again. Christ, I've given up that hope. Please? Just stop hurting me, the children, yourself."

A bloodless coup by "mummy's army" it was. And, as I had lost my father at an early age, so now a cycle seemed to be perpetuating itself. The thought alone of that prospect was punishment almost too great to bear. *Long shadows and early frost/the bud's lustre and bloom are lost.*

Some spark of joy in manhood died that day. My son saw it. I know he did. The look in his eyes reflected my failure. I would have that day forever. Its events would have an unending stage-life in my existence, active and vivid. *Pain is an event, suffering, a failure to metabolize.*

I drove to Ann Arbor, walked the campus there for seven straight hours. Waves of energetic, fresh-faced students engulfed me. The cold January air stung me hard, but failed to stall the mental replay of marital, familial collapse. Memories of some of the greatest days of my life, on the sprawling campus had lost their sheen. They were but the faded and distant images of yearbook photographs.

I was plunging into a trough of depression. I sensed it. Fast remedy was not coming to me. Escape seemed impossible. The imagined end game was unsatisfactory. I needed some place, some familiar landscape and people, somewhere to shed or exchange.

Sitting in empty Michigan Stadium that afternoon the place I wanted and needed came clear. The afternoon sun fell sharply across the snow covered, egg-shaped bowl and I saw the Alps of Switzerland rise up before me, all aglow in that same winter light. In the smooth, white drifts blanketing the rows of bleacher seats, I saw the deep cols and satiny contours of great, long stretches of snow, a seamlessness of sparkling white cover, endless and immeasurable in solace—an infinity of wonder.

I saw it all unfold.

I'd ski hard every day. Alone, I could set a punishing pace, testing myself on the most difficult ski trails I could find, Les Diablerets, piste Nationale, Plaine Morte, Neige Noire, Super-Diable, Saas Almagell, the steep cols of the Grand and Petit Combin, Dent Blanche, Taschhorn, Stockhorn, and Dufourspitz, skiing in places beyond my ability, off-*piste* – *ski d'sauvage* – the challenging and exhausting runs.

I'd skied them all before, but suddenly the agenda had changed dramatically. There was some business, some harsh reproof I needed to exact from these monsters. A finer fall line had to be traced much nearer the frozen edges of my fear. I knew them all, all the edges, all the spires. I knew the heart of Switzerland, the Valais, and the mammoth sentinels of the Pennine Alps. Their enormity and power could break me, the vastness of giants like those could devour all suffering, or kill me.

At sundown each day, I'd speed back to Verbier under a pink, Alpenglow ceiling of sky, hurriedly unpack my gear, bathe, re-dress, and race headlong into a night of mindless indulgence. Yes, I knew that well, too. I'd done it all before.

Verbier, in high or low ski seasons, was a hive of beautiful young women from everywhere on the continent. So plentiful and so exquisite were the women that their concentration in the village, during winter weeks, produced among most men a temporary madness. Time compressed, the meeting (or mating) place had been found, a frenetic pace developed and altered the normal search for ecstasy. Discretion and restraint gave way to obsessions and rapacious fulfillment. The proper mixture of high-energy activity and fun-seeking participants spawned a feverish drive to pursuits that weren't even remotely ordinary or normal. The impetuous hours spent in the nightclubs, cafés, and discos became feeding frenzies to satiate appetites gastronomic and libidinal.

Memory moved through narrow veins and knurls of dreams like the slow, steady drip of sap through maple trees. The sweetest syrup came from deepest recess. Year after year, the journey reinforced the path, bolstered the patterns, cut its silent gorge through sleeping recollection. I was awakening. Some viscous fluid of remembrance was moving. I was through the long dark tunnel, the passage was complete. A descent beckoned, the fall awaited. *Down, steeper down, Eddie.*

Verbier at last, and a morning mist was lifting.

Get up. Retrace. Begin again, from this room.

chapter Six
E A S T   E D E N

Ten days. Ten full days, alone. The Eden Est Auberge. The slatted French blinds strained and sliced the brief winter sunlight each afternoon as it moved slowly across the floor in yellow-orange, then sharp red bars. I couldn't watch them anymore. The room shook with the nighttime winds. The darkness enveloped, day and night. Sanctuary at the Eden Est, my small, musty skybox atop this tattered old three-story joint had served my needs well once more. Paul kept it chilly, like a meat locker, and dark, for me. Paul kept watch. He seemed to know what I needed—a desk, chair, a night table, an armoire—Swiss garage-sale shit. I could reach everything from the bed in this cell. An oil painting over the desk, its deep tones seemed to have an odd, exceptional quality for this place—lush, umber forest, shimmering Lake, and a moody Parzival glared out, one of those paintings with eyes that looked at you no matter where you stood in the room. Drove me nuts.

I was rammy. Ten was enough. Mornings were always bad, the afternoons worse. "A certain slant of light, winter afternoons," Emily wrote. Damn right, too. I'd made it there, now I had to do something. Even the mouse had gone, I hadn't heard him in days. I opened the blinds and the doors to the little balcony and let in the first full light since I arrived. The cold air moved into the room, too, another sorely-needed change. My room overlooked the commercial triangle, Place Centrale. The Eden and the Farinet, opposite Place Centrale, were relics by Verbier standards, sufficiently pre-War so that even I fit in the bathtub, a major concern. Miniaturization had made a strong impression on the Swiss. You got yourself a nice big tub, or in a few days you started to look like a Studebaker, from the back. The women always liked the big bathtubs, too.

The center of town was teeming with winter vacationers. Skiers coming down from the main slopes sped through the vehicle-free streets, the sound of their scraping skis a rhythmic relief from the commotion of automobile traffic. Crowds swelled during business hours, filling the narrow *ruelles*, rummaging, window-shopping, eating, making their way during Verbier's busiest time of the year. For most Europeans, especially the Swiss, it was winter carnival time, Fête d' Hivernal, a week of festivities capped-off by the World Cup Races the following weekend.

Events stateside had their way with me long enough. Days from the football stadium in Ann Arbor, it was time to start fighting back. I glanced over at the desk, at the stationary store of writing paraphernalia I'd brought with me. Could I deal? Soon, maybe.

Nothing in the room stirred but dust gliding in the sun-streaks. I took a pillow from the bed and threw it, hitting the Parzival, then bounding down on top of the writing pile knocking pencil packs and composition books onto the floor. A major breakthrough—that dust moved much faster. I paced over to the balcony opening.

There was a knock at the door, then fast, a voice in a phony French accent.

"Room service, monsieur?"

I smiled.

"Sorry, but I haven't ordered anything," I answered. "There must be some mistake. Can you get me the hotel manager, please?"

Another knock. Same voice.

"Hotel manager, monsieur?" I grabbed another pillow from the bed and slowly took the three short strides needed to cross the room, talking as I went.

"Your English is impeccable, monsieur manager. Where have you learned such perfect English?"

The voice then boomed through the door.

"Papa was a rolling stone, wherever he laid ma-ma was my home. Now open the fucking door, or I'm gonna bash it in."

I pulled the door open and the figure in the dimly lit hall stood surprised. I let the pillow fly, catching him square in the face. The red and black ski-suit and pillow rushed me with a bear-hug tackle and we went crashing onto the bed, wrestling.

"You son-of-a-bitch," he said.

"You bastard, get off me." I pushed hard and Linus Ellen Sinclair, the Third, plummeted to the floor. We were puffing hard and I threw the pillow at him again. "Liney, goddamn it, that wasn't a bad tackle."

"How much longer were you going to stay cooped-up in this hole?"

"Until you sent me some flowers. How come there weren't any flowers when I arrived?" I teased with haughty flippancy.

"I sent flowers. I did," he said, faking hurt sincerity beautifully. "They came back dead, because only an asshole can survive in a dump like this." I was smiling for the first time in weeks. Liney'd brought something into the room.

Linus was my best American friend on the Old World side of the Atlantic, and my groundwire to the social goings-on in Europe—the current scene. I never did anything there without checking-in with The Prince of Verbier first. Liney was Colonial-stock American, an expatriate playboy from Old Money. He was the heir, to an heir, to an heir of a Maine paper mill fortune in Portland and Bar Harbor— and that was only mother's side. Why Europe? A great-grandy got pissed-off at some U.S. Senator, and off they went with their money to live near Swiss banks, Paris museums, and Italian food.

Liney was content to just sit back and enjoy the fruits of legacy, and leave all the Sturm und Drang to his brothers and cousins. A trust provided him with an allowance fit for the sovereign of a small principality. He didn't need to work, he was never gainfully employed, not that I can recall. Liney did nothing, really. But he did it better than anyone I'd ever known.

Summers he sailed—the Med, the Pacific, the Caribbean, the Horn of This, the Cape of That. Winters, he skied—everywhere and anyplace snow fell. And his world never diminished in between.

He kept a chalet in Verbier dubbed, Chez Linéy. I never stayed there. He never offered—a courteous respect for the privacy I sought at the Eden—he sensed my needs somehow.

Leaning against the desk, sitting on the floor, he checked me over, searching for something.

"When I heard about you and Newie finalizing things, I figured one of you would show up here, sooner or later," he said, flatly. Bingo, to the point. How was this going to go down?

"A life of statistics, Liney, yards gained, most touchdowns, most points." He looked at me quizzically. "Now, I've become one, separated, waiting-for-divorce, single parent, absent father. I'm a baby-booming, consuming, percentile unit of analysis, a dot on the demographic survey. It's big stuff in the states, big stuff. All numbers, percentages, status, and the almighty American norm. Lifestyle shit. I hate that goddamn word." Not a bad start, I thought, a bunch of bullshit right off the top of my head.

"Excuse me? I think you skewed the sample a bit, old chum." He came back at me. "White collar, 30-something male, married, several extra-maritals. They had to make an extra curve for you, I think."

"Yeah, well. Erotic fantasies, they do get the best of us."

"Not like you, Eddie."

I walked away from him, looking out over the balcony.

"Remember Linus, women are like mosquito bites, if you don't touch them they go away. A lesson in pest control, my friend." I kept it light and self-deprecating. Funny thing, about pain, they say Christ got up after a few days down and showed his friends his scars. Was it a kind of theme with friends, or just with men?

"This from the man who tried to nail a Jehovah's Witness while your mother was at the supermarket?"

"Yeah, and I had to buy the goddamn bible, anyway. Come on, that was my bad time. The Wild Man was jumping around in my brain. I was impulsive. I was seventeen. Christ, your jockey shorts suddenly become like this slingshot when you're seventeen. Women are giants, and you want to take every one down with one shot. Shit, I was nuts when I was twelve."

"Tell me all about it, little David?"

"Listen, some kids collected stamps, or baseball cards. The first time I saw the dark between a girl's thighs, I knew what I wanted. And you can't lick baseball cards anyway."

"Man, they threw away the friggin' mold on you, I hope." He dogged me. His agenda was on the way. She was his friend. Was he going to let me have it for that now? "What in the hell were you trying to accomplish with Newie? What was that? You trying to rewrite the book on Open Marriage? Was that it? Miss Modernity, Mrs. Withit. Christ, Eddie."

He was a little pissed. Marriage was like a dogfight with me. I was a connubial kamikaze and Newell went down with the fleet. The previous relationship, long and obsessive, was defeating. When it ended I binged foolishly, looking for some semblance of new commitment. My search, my subsuming of Newell, was without soul or conscience.

The ravenous heart is easily deceived. The neon platitude flashed in my head. Nick Agalias always had one to fit the occasion. Aristippus Nicholas Agalias. I couldn't help but remember the huge figure of Nicky, in a natty black tux, looming over his warning like some ancient, implacable Sophist. Adonis to his campus harem, my compulsive college roommate, and best man at my wedding, he savored his self-appointed role as one of life's rudimentary impositions. A 235-pound linebacker could be a convincing imposition. Occasionally, he struck a very sober note of truth, as he did on the day of my wedding.

Liney introduced me to a green-eyed, Canadian schoolteacher in Verbier, and six weeks after we met, Newell Emerson Ingram and I married, a misdemeanor at the time that soon became a conjugal felony.

The conception of our children was incidental, and birth always debated—argued—for the first few months. Upon their arrivals into the world, Newell and I both claimed credit for inspired family planning. In fact, the children became my total focus, a purpose for my being and a window in my wall of deception and dishonesty. I walked all over the promise of marriage, destroyed any faith Newell had in the sacrament.

"I was just wondering when you were going to come out of the Eden, that's all," Liney said, still sitting on the floor "…not worried or anything."

"Just a little apprehensive, Liney." I sat on the edge of the bed, facing him. "It's like a screen door, you know, a failed marriage. You can close it, but it always seems open. Everything you've ever done and spoiled lies there, visible, the whole thing, just sitting out there a few feet away like last year's Christmas tree."

I searched his face for some indication of change. Would there be a new distance to our friendship? Some of Newell's friends had gravitated over the past few years. I wasn't quite sure how all of this side-taking worked. A bad marriage seemed to carry a stench, even good friends drifted steadily further from where they thought the odor originated.

"If she were sitting here, I'd tell her the same bloody thing I'm going to tell you right now," He looked directly at me through his bushy eyebrows. "Nothing has changed in the way I feel about either of you. I feel bad, it didn't work out. It's a car crash, everybody's shook up, injured, but nobody's dead."

"It's tough, you know? You just can't gauge how people are going to take it." I fished for some response.

"Well, this is the way it is. I'm glad you're here, you son-of-a-bitch. Hardly any Americans here anyway. I'm glad, honest. You'll get your mind clear, the Cup races are here, town's packed with all sorts of...things." He shimmied his head a little when he said "things." "It'll be good, don't worry."

"I wasn't worried about you, it's just..." My mind suddenly warped into garish flashback, seeing the stubborn old judge at Family Court pounding his mallet. "I got whacked in that courtroom, Liney. A father's just dead meat. No shit. Sixty-forty, we're beat before we go in."

"Bad, eh?"

"Bad? Christ. Justice isn't blind, she's blindfolded and getting raped...from behind, just more goddamn artifice, negotiation means you come out bleeding from the asshole."

"The kids? They get it? Everything?" His concern deepened.

"Yeah. I'm so friggin' depressed."

"Be careful what you take." A bullet-fast warning, with a hard look. I turned and surveyed the night table and the floor around it. The array of empty melancholia medicines, the caps and vials, gawked open like spent cartridges at a firing range, useless and hollow now. Enough shit to kill a Kentucky purebred, or at least get him kicked out of the Derby.

"I don't really know why I'm here, either," I said, not thinking and a little lost at that moment.

"You came here because we don't give a damn about status. You're the same Eddie with us. When we're here, we ski our asses off together. We party, we eat, we drink, we do some shit together." There was that little shimmy again. "And when we're gone, we're gone, no demands."

"I'm in this, this, it's like a paralysis, for Christ's sake. I'm fucking frozen, man. I don't feel anything. I can't write anything. I can't think."

"What? You and the Muse-es have a little spat?"

He made me smile again. I hung my head between my knees to erase the smile. This was good, I suppose. I was ready for a little rope-a-dope with Liney. He knew how to poke and prod and pull me along to a better place. He thought I didn't know when he did this, and I let him think it. I'd become a camera taking a picture of a camera taking a picture, or my peculiar dementia was analyzing the moments of our meeting like individual still frames instead of accepting simple friendly banter. I wasn't unhappy about it, but it was nerve-wracking. It was a symptom, the sharp imaging, like a high, overhead aerial view of the psychic terrain in conversation, nauseating in its detail. Suddenly, there was calibration and scrutiny and bothersome clarity where it shouldn't be.

"You're a pisser, Liney, you know that?" I half-laughed.

"No, come on, I'm serious," he said. "I'm trying to understand this thing about writers, really. People have this crazy idea of a little angel, or dwarf, or some goddamn little fruitfly, or something, you know…comes and talks to you?" He yanked my chain hard. I had to go with it. "I mean, you can have a disagreement," he reasoned, "with this thing. Right?"

"I guess you could call it that." I was lured in. Liney loved every minute. He was going to bust my balls and make me enjoy it.

"Just not talking to you, I suppose, huh?"

"Closed as a clam."

"Okay, okay, we're getting somewhere. Good. But I thought, you know, correct me if I'm wrong, don't you writers have different ways to trick them?"

"Not this witch."

"Witch? It's a she, then? I see, okay. And…she's not

some angelic fairy princess who sits by your mind's ear and whispers poetic, brilliant little gems?"

"No, not mine." I looked right at him. "I've got this trash-mouthed, gravel-throated, hairy motherfu..."

"Truth *and* beauty you want?" He exclaimed. "Nice. Wonderful. You writers, hell, you can't have both, Eddie. I mean, come on?"

"Yeah, it's a bitch isn't it? One lives at the surface and the other can't find it. I've got a monster, Linus. Listen... on a good day, on a great day. Let me put it this way, on your best day, you'd probably rather have Brünnhilde sit on your face."

"Sounds like the perfect woman for you, babe."

"Hey, she bad-asses all over, arrives late, leaves early, eats free, and leaves the place a mess." Suddenly, I had *him* by the short hairs. "The price of inspiration, my friend."

"And then what the hell do you do?"

"We have an arrangement, this harlot and I." I continued after him. "Something sort of like the Honshū wedding couple, you know, who are fitted with these hand-crafted belts when they take their vows? Each belt, you see, has this little brass bell attached to it. When the woman wishes to have sex, right? She rings her bell. The man, likewise, strikes his bell when an amorous impulse arises. They vow, however, that they will satisfy their physical desires only when the bells ring in unison."

Liney fell sideways, grabbed the pillow from the floor and winged it at me.

"You're an asshole," he screamed.

"It's just like sex," I boasted. "Not a lot of fun when somebody's bell's not ringing. You didn't know I could write Japanese, did you?"

"At least, you picked the perfect partner for something," he said, with great satisfaction.

"It's the luck-o-the-draw, Linus. We have no say. Some guys get a luscious Genie from a lamp, or an angel with little wings and big tits. Me? I get Redd Foxx's dominatrix."

"You sound just fine to me, Pecker," he said. "I hope they don't charge a helluva lot for those books you write. God help the poor bastards who read a load of your shit."

"No help from God, Liney. God's a writer, too."

"Oh, really, God writes, just like you, smart guy?"

"Oh, yeah, you don't know this?" I kept jerking his chain, and unexpectedly now I was having fun in the dungeon I'd made out of this room. "God writes trash, you know, pitiful short pieces, dime-novels, cryptic shit, dismal tales…just keeps cranking them out, you know? Then God gets published here on earth, yeah. The pathetic little stories are our lives."

"Hey, Eddie. You better stop chewing on that shit in those vials. I'm telling you, Famous, you need some cleaning-out. I've got to get you up the mountain, babe. I'm going to put your head in the fucking snow, make a frozen TV-dinner out of it." He looked at me with a half-demented leer and we both smiled and enjoyed a very knowing half-demented leer of long-standing with each other.

He rolled onto his back and stared up at the ceiling, thinking. He knew he had me where he wanted me, and I knew he was the cure, the only cure, wrapped in a protective seal of true friendship.

"Listen, speaking of heavenly objects, there's someone here, in Verbier, who knows you're here, and wants you to know she knows your here, and wants to know if you want to know…"

"Who the hell are you talking about?" I asked.

"Well, she's French, blond, she's from Paris. You met her before, here, in sev-en-ty-nine, eighty-one, two, I don't know."

"Great, that narrows it down." He rolled back onto his side and propped himself on one elbow. Long wait.

"Céline."

He almost whispered it, and the name fell. It descended,

and the sound of the name scattered in my head like first
snowflakes on a green hill. *Céline.* I heard it again, in her
voice. A silent snowfall was all that I could see, all that I
could remember, surrounding a luminous face. Liney knew
what he was doing to me just then. I gazed away, trying to
hold the image of her for a few more seconds. I could feel
Liney watching me, gauging my reaction, then he gingerly
dropped the rest of the apparition.

"Céline Decauville. Some years ago. Remember her?"

The full image pierced the entirety of memory, flesh, and
organs. It pierced, and burned like a draught of hot cider
swallowed too fast. Fever and agonizing pain spread
through my chest, it cut sharply through my groin. Blood
surged slightly faster through my arms and my heartbeats
hammered in my head—an intense movement of heat,
warmer with the thought and picture of her, hotter still with
an immediate need.

Sweetness arrived, a watery, pleasurable sensation in the
mouth, a viscous flow on the tongue, moving, then her
pungent nectar, sugary and sticky flooding my lips, a tasting
immersion. Impetuous. Irrational. Would there be enough of
her? And when?

Seeing Céline Decauville for the first time, I nearly
drowned in sensations, all of them impetuous and irrational.
The thought of this woman, in Verbier, ignited a firestorm of
disquieting compulsion, and a sexual addiction suddenly
awakened with a bellowing, hungry roar.

"Where?" I said, and it sounded like a threat, surprised
the hell out of me, too.

"Chalet Saléve. It's up behind mine, small one, up the
hill, way up. Remember where Stuart rented that time we
had the Christmas party?"

"Yeah, that was the Aspen." I kept remembering,
putting the visual puzzle together as he fed me the pieces.

"Right, a little further to the left than the Aspen, looking
up the hill. I don't know the street."

"Is there a number? You spoke to her, I take it?"

"Yes, for Christ's sake. Take it easy. I saw her a few days ago. But, she's not here now."

"What do you mean?" I turned back at him.

"Well, when you didn't come out of the Eden, she decided to go shopping, in Lausanne." Thoughts of her coming to me in the hotel sped through my mind, the dark den of the room glowing in her brightness. "She spoke to Jacky, I know. Jacky probably knows when she's coming back." I rose up from the bed. I needed to move, somewhere, anywhere.

"Christ. Calm down, will you? We'll see Jacky tonight," he yelled at me then glanced at his watch. "Now, come on, let's hit the Borsalino. Everybody's down. Time for *Ci-gîts* with 'The Gang.'"

"Yeah, yeah, okay." I was in a half-daze, staring out over the balcony railing, listening but not connecting. "Yeah, yeah, the Borsalino, 'The Gang,' yeah, that's good."

The mountains above town were bathed in the glow of the dying sun and for a moment I was alone with them, free of the confines and suddenly in their keeping. I shut everything else out, even Liney. I was here, in Verbier, where I wanted to be. New York, Ann Arbor, the courtroom, everything was behind.

Liney popped up from the floor in fluid motion. I heard him slowly approaching behind me. He sensed my remoteness, and gently put his arms around my shoulders, placing his forehead at the back of my head and neck, an intrusion so careful and kind.

"Hey, hey, easy man. Everything's going to be great. You'll see her. I promise you'll see her." Reassurance came over me, through my bones like sauna heat, in his soothing voice. "I'll have her arrested in Lausanne for shoplifting if I have to. No problem."

"Okay. Okay, okay, okay. Let's get out of here."

I broke his bearhug with my arms and jumped up on top

of the bed. "Get me the hell out of here." Pacing the bed like a cat at the zoo at feeding time, I kicked the rest of the empty plastic pharmacy bottles off the night table. Then, without touching the floor, I hopped from the bed to the top of the armoire. "Yes. Yes. 'The Gang'." Perched on the armoire, I talked down at Liney, my head just a foot from the ceiling, as I looked for the next place to leap. "Let's go to the Borsalino. I need a *Ci-gît*"

"That's it, break your neck, asshole."

"Get out of the way. We used to do this at school. The Wolverine Prowl. A wolverine never leaves prints on the ground. You can't track him down." The method of my escapes, explained.

"Eddie, Jez-zus Christ."

"No. Move. I want to kick the shit out of that writing junk."

"This just in, 'Man Found in Seedy Hotel After Fatal Leap'. " Liney jests. "You crazy fuck. I'm going up the hill to get the Red Head, I'll meet you at the Borsalino."

"The Red Head is here?" I asked, with dramatic gusto. "Great. Tales Of Hoffman. We're on."

"...and take a shower. You smell like an old whore."

"Unkind cut. An *old* whore?"

"I can't watch this," he said in fake disgust. "Borsalino. Half-an-hour. Stop by Deke's, see if your skis made it." Then, he opened the door and hesitated in the narrow opening. "And who in the hell is Redd Foxx?" *Exeunt*, slamming the door.

"Oh, you expat putz," I yelled into the ceiling, listening to his footsteps fade in the hallway. The desk awaited. The room was a mess, a sprawl of my occupancy. I could finally see the whole catastrophe from up here. It was visible now. The balcony doors were open, allowing light and fresh air in after days of hibernation. Linus Ellen Sinclair, the Third, had pulled me up from a lower, darker place. He opened a door, too, and the light and sweetness of a wonderful memory entered. *When can I have it?*

The pile that once occupied the desktop is scattered on the carpet in all directions. One of my composition notebooks lay open in a corner of the room, near the door. I jumped down from the armoire and picked it up. The unlined, scribbled pages indicated nothing but the disorder of mind and spirit I'd brought here. Some foreigner had marked my book, some Jonah ten-days trapped inside tried to signal and scratch at my ribs.

The cursive figures and formations wriggled unevenly across the paper, the crude, almost juvenile creations of an unsteady hand filled the page. Then near the bottom, two lines, clearly.

To this white part of flame
I run for burning

I closed the book and held it still in my hands. If I could only remember what in the hell I was running from.

Through the open balcony doors, I saw the top of Mont Gelé, Verbier's giant, a strawberry pink and slate black dome at this hour, rising high above the town. And from this dim corner, the room glowed magenta, too. All of the chaos in these confines, the dregs of my ten days, had a rosy hue.

I heard the mouse scurry in the wall again. *The Eden's not so easy to leave, is it my little friend?* Stay. I'll send for some cheese.

Parzival, above the desk, was shining in the Alpenglow. The rich dark tones and the old oil surface glowed an almost fire red in the light before dusk. Parzival peered at me. I was way over in the corner of the room, and his eyes were still staring at me. How did they do that?

chapter Seven
CAFÉ BORSALINO

I crossed Place Centrale to the Farinet. Chemin Colladon, a small, busy alley ran behind the hotel, and the high-tech, neon-lit window of Iron Mountain Sports glared brightest at dusk. It was very un-Swiss and not the only touch of Americana on this street. A faint, but distinct, stream of 60's Motown flowed from a small speaker situated above the door—Detroit, he took it wherever he went. Charles "Deke" Robinson stood in the doorway.

Deke left Ann Arbor in the middle of our senior year and fled to Canada vowing never to set foot on American soil again, and he never did. His skill as an entrepreneur made him rich in the drug trade during the soaring activity of the sixties and seventies. Deke could conduct a transaction anywhere in the world on short notice, and supply very wealthy people with the recreational drugs they so desired. His international clientele then were the Who's Who of Europe and Canada.

In the mid-seventies, he popped-up in Verbier flashing a Swiss passport, and soon after opened Iron Mountain Sports. People with large sums of money seemed to find places like Switzerland rather instinctively. Swiss discretion was, well, Swiss. Rousseau said, "the Swiss kept a secret so well that Switzerland was actually the largest country in Europe." Sunny sprawling Helvetia was the perfect ground for Deke, but he didn't hibernate, he invested in Switzerland's major industry.

Iron Mountain stocked everything imaginable for serious mountaineering and skiing—up-to-date equipment, seasonal sports gadgets, the latest European fashion wear, and state-of-the-art materials and innovations.

A tarnished California beach boy-salesman, Tre
Wunderlin, was Deke's U.S. supplier of techno-junk and
related accessories. Two years ago, Deke opened another
Iron Mountain Sports in Crans, on the opposite side of the
Valais, and brought Tre in as a full partner. Wunderlin had
been a major player on the supply-side network during the
"Wonder Years" of the drug trade. Complicity made for very
strong bonds. Deke and Tre remained as bonded and
profitable a team in legitimate world endeavors.

Deke spotted me walking down the alley toward the
store. Our smiles bridged the cobblestone alleyway.

"Hey, Famous, your skis have been sitting here for more
than a week," he yelled, and his thin voice echoed.

Deke and I embraced in an old Wolverine hug at the
doorway.

"The good-old PTT," I joked. "The mail may be late, the
skier may get lost, but his skis arrive promptly."

In his work apron, frayed denim shirt, shoulder-length
hair, and wire-rimmed glasses he was the picture of a
threadbare Sixties artisan, a Woodstock fossil symbolic of an
era of defiance, somber creativity, and worn-out idealism.

"Where you been, Famous?" He said, scolding me.

"Been hiding, Deke, you know how it is when the flow
gets going." We smiled the writer's lying smile.

Deke had written some very radical tracts at Michigan,
but he once revealed another passionate side of himself to me
in his poetry. Like so many others then, Deke abandoned the
poetry for the protest. He wore now the same tired smile
worn by a generation of wholly disillusioned people. I think
Iron Mountain Sports was his acquiescence to the capitalist
world he couldn't change, and it was a thriving business.

My own smile masked a kind of guilt that I always felt
around Deke. While he was putting everything on the line
for the dream of radical social change, I was part of the
Michigan athletic establishment, weaned on milk from the
ultimate, conformist teat, the team. I tried to be an activist-

athlete, got my name in The Michigan Daily and The Detroit Free Press for "benignly significant revolt against athletic gulag" next to a roll-call of campus rebels. But still I struggled to conceal an awkwardness in his presence, a tinge of self-reproach.

"You're looking good anyway, Famous. Writers are always stylish, handsome, the most charming liars on earth." He clopped me on the back of the neck with his big, dirty work mit. "You ever want to sit down and write our manifesto for the new order, you let me know."

"Sure, Vladimir," I chuckled. "This capitalist affliction of yours has put a damper on your grand manifesto days."

"Ahh, yes, the bright light of profit. How it doth shine." He laughed with Elizabethan charm. There was a savory glint now behind those wire-rims.

"I'm on my way over to the Borsalino. You coming?"

"Maybe later," he said. "Going to see 'The Gang,' eh? Well, everybody's here, Famous. This town's jumping, with Winter Festival and the Cup Races. You'll be swimming in women."

"What about the pharmaceutical situation?"

"Oh, I'd say that was peak also."

"Really?"

"Never seen anything like it, Eddie —the drugs, the money, the women. It's like a great tidal wave that just keeps circling the globe."

"Goes with a fast crowd like this, Deke."

"I don't use any more, Famous, but I know what's around, and, man, I'm telling you, anything you want, you can get—anything."

My mind drifted, momentarily, filling with thoughts of the anythings of times past, of the association of anything and Verbier. The word and the place together evoked fantasies of endless thrills and rituals connected with drugs, of Caligulan orgies, and of a recklessness of body and spirit that transformed all of us during those times into an alien culture.

"Well, you're all tuned and waxed, ready for the worst."

"And I'm looking for the worst," I kidded, halfheartedly.

"Ah. A business trip?" He smiled.

"That's right, I'm going up for the giants this time."

"A little self-flagellation, perhaps, up at dawn, pump those legs, work makes us free, the fit body houses the assiduous mind, that sort of thing? Always the athlete, eh?"

"No, just your same, basic coal-cracking show-off from Pennsylvania that's all. You know me." I jabbed him in the stomach and we both laughed. "I've got to go, Charles."

"See you later, Famous."

I continued on down the alley, but couldn't resist one glance back at Deke in the doorway. He was a reminder of that other era. Façades changed rapidly with each generation, but some people managed to keep the look of times and ideologies they embraced. Remnants of that time, expats like Deke, were scattered everywhere around Europe, but they seemed like artifacts now, curios housed in a museum of our own making, the Sixties. A new house of worship, hedonism, had risen. It stood prominent in the path of the Eighties, firm and implacable, very real, and pervasive.

Café Borsalino was a house of yet another hue. In style and content, it paid homage to the literary cafés of Paris, Rome, and Geneva. It had the scent of history and the somber, time-worn feel of a place that bore witness. The old station had heard the drinking songs of Gaul and Lombard wayfarers, and Celtic warriors once sharpened spears on stones that lay deep beneath in Borsalino's wine caves. The dark wood interior, saddled and stained by the larded hands of mountain hunters, gleamed like pewter in the cool, blue light bouncing in from the snow.

A certain crowd with a certain conviviality and sameness of thought defined the character of the Borsalino, and it changed in character, like all the great cafés, with the prevailing social whims of its inhabitants. It was like no other in all the Valais.

The café was filled to capacity. Aprés ski filled every niche, and hot liquid sustenance and friendly exchange fueled the favorite ritual of serious skiers—drinking, bullshitting, and trying to get laid.

Liney was at the bar with two blond ski bunnies—identical twins—and Eric Hoffman, a permanent winter guest at Chez Linéy.

"I think, therefore, I think I am…in the company of two beautiful thinking women." Eric teased the twins. They giggled on-cue. "There are two of you, I think?"

One of the super-skiers in our bunch—Liney and I named him Eric, The Red—he was a flying ace of the slopes with a bush of red hair. Eric was an intellectual, a bright, young would-be journalist from the Alsace educated at Dartmouth, Oxford, and the Sorbonne. He was a perennial student avoiding actual labor for as long as he could, but he often contemplated employment.

I grabbed Hoffman by the scruff of the collar, while Liney ushered the blond bunnies to some other site along the bar.

"Hey Eric, great to see you again, my friend."

"*Moi aussi, mon vieux.*" We embraced warmly. "Good to see you back in Verbier. The snow consistency is great, perfect granulation. Everything is just perfect," he said. Hoffman spoke like a Cornell physicist most times, everything exacting, as if there were reams of research behind every statement.

"Perfect? Perfect is an understatement." Liney wheeled back on Hoffman and me. Liney, however, was not inclined to exacting research. "Hot. Everything is hot, that's what it is. Lots of good things here. Verbier is hot, Eddie. Lots of parties, *ooouu la, la,* you know?" He wiggled. His enthusiasm was infectious, and Hoffman and I were hysterical watching him animate the juicy, layered meanings out of every phrase.

"He could be dangerous," Eric threw an aside to me.

"The Americans have landed," Liney yelled. "We'll take these Swiss for a few laps around the track. Women and children first, eh, forget the children, I take that back." He pinched my cheek. "The bastard looks great, doesn't he Eric?"

"Yeah. Keep him away from those luscious twins," Eric said.

Liney was wired, fully in his element, punching at my mid-section.

"We've got to go, come on, the table in the back. Now. Everybody's in the back."

Liney took me by the shoulders, and steered me like a sled, as we launched into the thick of a crowd that was three-deep at the bar alone. I waved at Eric as we were fast disappearing into a sea of colorful down parkas.

"Eric," I yelled back. "Send a *Ci-gît* over for me, will you?" He smiled and nodded an okay. I could see his bushy red hair moving.

A *Ci-gît* was a hot cider and Swiss brandy drink created here at the Borsalino. Literally, it meant "here lies" and many an unwary skier had fallen sleepily under its spell after just one or two drinks. There was some mysterious herbal additive also — we never asked — known only to a few tight-lipped bartenders in the cafés.

We were making our way back to a huge round table situated in a snug alcove off to one side of the main dining room. The Borsalino was completely taken over each day by the apres ski crowd, and this revelry was its lifeblood. Liney pressed-the-flesh as we waded through the parkas, tossing comments and greetings diplomatically side to side as we plowed through.

A mammoth fieldstone fireplace on the outside wall facing a log-hewn table roared and flickered with splits of fruitwood, its warm glow made everyone sitting there full-faced and blushed. The table was littered with mugs, and glasses, bottles and brightly-colored gloves and hats, and crowded with "The Gang," as we called ourselves, all puffed up in ski fashion *de rigueur*.

As Liney and I turned the corner into the alcove, a sea of red, gleaming cheeks transformed to smiles and crinkly-eyed laughter and surprise.

"Look what I just dragged in from New York," Liney announced and a spontaneous sigh and elation from "The Gang" overwhelmed me. For a single breathtaking moment, the love and affection that washed over me carried away the pain and heaviness I had borne for the past ten days. I was suddenly ensconced in the warm, protective circle of caring friends once more.

We were a core group, who sought out and enjoyed each other's company, winters and summers, in the mountains. One of those winters the group somehow coalesced, spontaneously, and christened Verbier our Holy Land, and made every bar, club, and café like some shrine, or reliquary. We all skied together, sometimes we just dined and drank, or danced and sang together. We did a fair amount of drugs together, too, but drugs were not the "glue of our cohesion," as Eric once pointed out. Being in Verbier together, seeing friendship grow and strengthen—that was "The Gang's" Magna Carta.

Friends came and went in "The Gang," they drifted out for marriages, careers, travels, and homes, changing societies and foreign countries, jobs, and just changing. And every now and then, someone drifted back in again, in Verbier.

Manolete Armendar and his little brother, Miguel, are the first to embrace me.

"Amigo. It's so good to see you here." Mano hugged me.

"*Con gusto,* Eddie," Miguel said, with a sparkling smile. "It wouldn't be the same without you. Now that you're here, all the crazy bastards are together."

These were the dark, very handsome, and wild-skiing

sons of a Madrid oil tycoon, but not the kind that came from trees and went on salads.

Manolo Armendar, head of Petrolera Armendar España, had created a crude oil empire, stretching from Venezuela to the Middle East. It was still a family business worth millions, to be inherited someday by Mano, Miguel, and their baby sister, Paloma, a little spitfire, a dark, snapping castanet, chattering, shoving her brothers aside to get to me.

"Eddie, Eddie, *cómo estás?*" She threw her arms around my neck and kissed me several times on both cheeks. "Oh, Eddie, you look-ed wonderful. We are missing you very much, *hay mucho, mucho.*" Her brothers laughed and rolled their eyes.

"We *missed* you, Paloma, not 'we are missing you.'" Mano corrected. "*Hay, los verbos,* she never gets them right."

Paloma was petit and so strikingly beautiful, her features radiated ten-fold through her bubbly personality. She had a face that neared the classical perfection of Spanish Renaissance portraiture. Resplendent and soft, Paloma was fine art in the flesh. She hung on my neck and I hugged her tightly.

"*Palomita, Palomita, mi amor,*" My Spanish was a bit better than my French. "I love you in my arms, but I delight in the memory of you, always." We laughed together and I stroked her black, wavy hair. "Because no one can take you from this big, hairy ape behind you, so I must be content with the memory."

The round, smiling, bearded face that came at me from behind Paloma was that of her husband. A mass of red and gold ski suit waddled toward us, reaching over Paloma to hug me, locking the three of us in an awkward, swaying embrace.

"*Amerikanisch,*" he yelled. "Is good to see you again, my friend." Helmut Schäfer—we called him Ham—was the cherubic, and perpetually smiling leviathan who made everything we did together a grand, unforgettable event, every meal a gourmet feast, every drink a tasting, and every day on the slopes an adventure in comic proportion. Ham was a character spiritually drawn from the loins of Sir John Falstaff, a plump fruit of gifted wit in all of the six languages he spoke, colorful, outgoing, full of anecdotes and pranks.

He wrote theatre reviews and art critique for Hamburg's largest circulation daily, published by Helmut's dad, and longer literary pieces for the monthly, *Rheinlande,* founded by Ham's grandfather.

"What's cooking these days, Ham?" I teased.

"Same stuff, Eddie. I am just coming back now from Stuttgart, where I saw a new opera by Philip Glass. Is very good, Eddie, very good. Such de-men-tion, such spectacle. Brilliant, I think. Do you know him?"

"Oh, yeah, both the dementia and, yeah, the dimension, 'Einstein On The Beach.' Big stuff. He's very big now in New York. The rest of the country doesn't get it, the Minimalism, you know? But...what do they know?"

"Tell me something?" Liney strolled in. "If this guy's the great minimalist, how come he's got two 'S's in his last name?"

Ham burst into a hearty belly-laugh, eyes twinkling, grin brimming wide, stretching his chin and beard like a big hairy coconut slice. He loved silly jokes and puns. Paloma laughed with him always, whether she understood or not. Love made some people radiate. I became a believer in the glow of Helmut and Paloma. I looked-on at happiness in a marriage like theirs and wondered about my failures, and Newell.

Ham, rest assured, carried Liney's little pun back to Hamburg and had another good laugh with his artsy-fartsy colleagues in the music and opera world.

Eric arrived at my side with my hot *Ci-gît* and placed it in my hand while my other hand and arm were being shaken vigorously by Stuart Hartman, and then by Ian Woods right beside him. They shook and shook, rattling my arm back and forth like a tennis racket. I tried to gyro my drink to keep it from spilling. These two Brits mirrored one another in almost everything, a Fric and Frac of jolly, fast repartee.

"Looking good, Yank. Very good to see you again." Stuart.

"Very good to see you, bloody good, Ed." Ian. It was like being in an echo chamber. "It's been quite some time, hasn't it? Yes, right. We'll do some blasted, ballsy skiing this week then, I suspect."

"Yes, ball-sy, Ed," Stuart chuckled.

"Yes, yes, ass-over-teacups, guys," I wedged in.

"How goes it in New York, Ed?" Fric.

"Yes, how goes it in the States, Ed?" Frac.

"Awful thing these days, about Iran-Iraq, isn't it?" Fric.

"Bloody awful situation, I should say. Barbaric." Frac.

Sticky time to begin discussing problems with the Moslem world, so I shook-down the greeting, quickly. There was an Iranian among us. I thought the world of her, and I simply couldn't tread that sensitive ground just then.

"Eddie, *mon cher*." Jacky touched my lips lightly with her soft, velvety cheeks. She wore a flashing two-point diamond in the nape of one nostril, and but for a heavy, half-drawn shade of eyelids, her eyes would flash to match the nestled gem.

She was just Jacky to us. No one tendered another name, no one ever asked for one. She was part French, it was said, the rest, stunning and dark, very reserved, and as mysterious as Persia itself. She co-owned Jacky's, a bar-disco that was one of our favorite nightspots.

There were many, very well-to-do Iranians in Switzerland. Most were sons and daughters sent here to boarding schools. The fortunes of their parents were heaped upon them, hidden in large bank accounts usually, in an effort to save what moneys could be siphoned-off and taken out of Iran before the fall of the Pahlavi Monarchy. The bank accounts grew faster than the children, and each day the possibility of never returning to Iran, for that group, grew as well. As a result, a young, very quiet sub-group of Swiss Persians had unceremoniously been given asylum. Their numbers were unknown, the size of their wealth, a secret, always.

Jacky was gentle and very generous. She worried about all of us like a mother hen, observing our excessive behavior, our excessive drug use, without being judgmental. She seemed more mature, but I suspect it was just an aloofness she maintained from the brash indulgence we Westerners gave vent-to in Verbier.

She watched over me with a fawning protectiveness. She had seen me in some unflattering conditions, moments of celebratory demise we called them. There was always a tinge of bittersweet regret behind her guard over me for something that might have been between us. I was aware of it over several visits.

"Jacky, *ma chérie*, how's business?" I touched her face, carefully.

"Fantastic, Eddie, really fantastic. The Cup races this week, the Fête, you know? We are packed every night."

"You look wonderful, Jacky, you really do."

"From some men that is a compliment. From you, it is defining, an appraisal to cherish."

"You think too much of me, Jacky." I pulled back, slightly, but Jacky was quick to grasp my hand and gently place a kiss inside the palm.

Suddenly destroying a wonderful moment, Jean Marc DuBois, owner of the Borsalino, immediately came up beside Jacky and grabbed my other hand. I was just about to ask her about Céline, and she slipped away from me like a candle through a dark cave, mysteriously, back into the crowd.

"*Le Eddie, mon vieux,*" DuBois bellowed, affectedly. "Tell me, is it you who is making Reagan again your president?"

Swiss, young, and gregarious, born and raised in the mountains near here, Jean Marc was surprisingly sophisticated and worldly. He was keen on Americana — a pain in the ass about it, really — loved to talk about anything that had to do with the States and considered himself an expert on politics. Basically, he loved to argue.

"This is the cowboy actor, no?" DuBois egged me on.

"Yeah, well, I really had nothing to do with that," I mumbled and scratched the back of my neck, not wanting to get into it.

"That's America, you know, John Mark?" Liney interjected, booming, ready to bust chops. "That's the beauty of the whole friggin' thing, you know? Anybody can become president, John Mark. Anybody in that goddamn country. Amazing. Anybody. I mean, that's what we always say, right, Famous?" Liney had a little spin on his emphasis now, a little zing.

"Liney?" I tried.

"I mean, it's a democracy, you know?" Liney revved up. "Weird shit, we are. Goddamn democracy. You guys know what that is, right? Ji-an Mark? Couple of piss-ants from Concord." More attitude was creeping into his speech now, considerably more volume.

"Liney?" Again, I tried.

"We even let women vote, right, Famous?" I figured that one would set DuBois off. Liney had his arm around my shoulder. I turned and talked right into his ear.

"You know what I'd like to put in your drink, Linus? My you-know-what. Don't start with this guy, please, come on?"

DuBois was not finished. He wanted to light-into Liney. He'd been saving something up and couldn't wait to get it out.

"The Americans, they put the car in the garage…" The Yank stuff was nigh, Europeans couldn't resist. "*Le poulet, uh,* how you say? *le* chicken in the pot, the steak on the table, and again the ham in the White House."

"Very cute, Jean Marc," I smiled, stifled an impulse to stick something in his drink. DuBois laughed excessively, and then like a contagion, everyone began laughing with him, or at him. The laughter around the table spread through the crowded alcove to include several smaller tables full of assorted groups of skiers.

Liney looked around, darting his head quickly, then put the smuggest look I'd ever seen on his puss and started singing the "Star Spangled Banner." It was vintage Liney, vintage Verbier. My only thought at the moment was, *here it goes*.

Liney marched stridently around the table, singing in a deep, serious register, affecting a teary altruism, at the least, befitting the opening game of the World Series. He seized the moment to get everyone's glass raised on-high to us, the only Americans in the place. Stuart Hartman and Ian Woods, to my surprise, suddenly joined in singing. They actually knew the words. Then Ham and Paloma and the others at our table started mouthing the words and humming along. Of course, Liney was conducting. Louder and louder they sang and it somehow sounded like a fair rendition of our National Anthem.

Then suddenly, from across the room, rousing, deep voices began like a chorus, rising-up, singing, "La Marseillaise."

"Holy shit," I whispered. "A war. We're starting a war, and we're going to wreck this goddamn place."

The French voices grew louder and stronger. One entire corner of the crowded café and a few more scattered tables joined in singing "La Marseillaise."

Then, voices from another part of the restaurant came bounding up, over-lapping.

"Deutschland, Deutschland uber alles..." The voices appeared deep and resonant and all of a sudden, Ham Schäfer had the most confused look on his face, and somewhere between the "rocket's red glare" and the "bombs," Helmut switched allegiance.

Liney was fueling the whole, riotous mess. Palomita giggled uncontrollably, and from the front, out towards the bar, the Swiss national anthem suddenly became faintly discernable, but growing very fast in intensity.

The singing was a deafening cacophony. It vibrated through the empty glasses that filled nearly every table. Skiers roamed as they sang. Groups faced-off at each other singing at ear-splitting levels, belly-to-belly, glass-to-glass, almost nose-to-nose. Liney pranced about the café like the master of ceremonies at a battle of the anthems pageant. He'd run out of "Star Spangled Banner" and was now onto the Notre Dame fight song. He was lifting his knees high, looking very much like a drum majorette marching around the room.

Before long, every national anthem turned into the Notre Dame fight song. None of the Europeans knew the words, but they all reveled in the melody and sang-out at exploding volume. Liney was doing high chorus-line kicks by now, his red ski boots flying up in the center of the room.

Two Frenchmen who, only moments before, had been singing "La Marseillaise" joined Liney on either side and the three began kicking in unison. As soon as they began kicking together, the Notre Dame fight song dissolved into the "Can-Can."

It was insane. People were dancing all over the place. The center of the Borsalino was a huge circle of Can-Can-ing, kicking, singing, skiers, Linus Sinclair, the Third, was at its center, waving his ski bandanna in circles above his head.

The madness was unstoppable, the laughter and singing tumultuous. The bartenders were out onto the main floor now, whipping their white aprons in front of them and kicking like true *Folie Bergere.*

This was Verbier in the best of times, spontaneous and completely nutty. This was the Verbier that had evolved from the repeated devotion to ritual, and these were the Europeans who made it memorable. They involved me in everything they did. Why? I never knew. They danced and flickerd in front of the fire, and their joy and revelry gave me the comfort I had sought.

I skied with all of them, with the best of them, many times. The *off-piste* skiing here was much more savage than in the States, and they indulged in it often. It took awhile, but I adapted to their expertise and daring. I skied everywhere they did, except in one place. There was only one place I would not ski, a wooded section just above Verbier called Jeavon's Run.

On a dare with some of "The Gang," I tried the fast skiing, through tight trees. But something happened. The trees and the late afternoon sun flickered and flashed, on the side, on the periphery of my vision. The spikes of flickering light came faster and faster. The shadows of the trees on the snow were like bars being pulled over me. It was maddening. Frantic. A spiking sensation. Intermittent bursts of light and dark, like the fast flutter of strobe lights in a dance club, caused pain at the back of my head, and I was suddenly gasping for breath. Everything chattered, stuttered, like a film loop lost in an old projector. I skied out of the trees and stopped. I shook uncontrollably and thought I was going to collapse.

Liney and Manolete skied over to see what was wrong, and I snapped at them like an angry dog. They were startled. I yelled, scolding the two of them in an illogical outburst. I beat the snow with my ski pole, screaming in a fit of anger, as everyone told it later. The spell subsided quickly and I suffered a bit of embarrassment, but within minutes felt as if nothing had ever happened. I haven't gone near Jeavon's Run since.

The smooth, round trees that supported the roof of the Borsalino were dark and friendly. People pranced around them as though they were Maypoles. And somewhere in the melee of wild dancing, the bartenders had taken the center of the huge circle with the two twin ski bunnies, enabling Liney to slip off to the side. He scooped up another half-full *Ci-gît* from the alcove table and headed straight for me. The restaurant was in a frenzy, even Jean Marc DuBois jumped and kicked like a disco queen. The floor trembled. The log pillars and beams, the old trees, shook.

"Some shit, eh?" Liney threw his arm over my shoulder and looked out over the moving, Can-Can-ing, kicking blur of swirling color like a man at a carnival who'd just set his carousel spinning wildly out of control. "Don't get much of this in New York, do you?" He yelled for me to hear over the ruckus.

"Only on New Year's Eve," I yelled back.

"I miss that sometimes," he said, and a glint of far-off fires registered in his gaze. Something distant and deep, a painful twinge of the expatriate came darkly over his face.

Liney stared at the revolving mass of people out on the floor, entranced. The Borsalino resonated. The singing shifted to softer songs, sung sweeter by tiring voices. The sound of "Edelweiss" drifted through the café, on very gentle voices, deep baritones, some lilting female mezzos, and the lyrical magic of German tenors. The Austrian lullaby hypnotized everyone.

"Christ, back to anthems again." I tried to pry Liney free, but some bigger voice from behind shook us both.

"You're a goddamn American romantic, Famous." I felt the firm grip of two large hands on top of my shoulders and that strong, deep voice could only belong to one man, Pierre Alain LaNoue. I turned around and faced a grinning Swiss giant, dark haired, tall, and framed like a bodybuilder. The best friend I had in this tiny country stood looking down at me, and we searched each other's eyes for a certain look, a look that came with the sudden confluence of a shared memory.

Years before, on one of my first trips to Verbier, Pierre Alain and I were caught in an avalanche. Skiing together, in a place we shouldn't have been, of course, we ended-up beneath a ridge that was being blown by the Swiss Avalanche Control. We heard the dynamite blast, the earth trembled, and we raced for our lives. We were buried, for nearly five hours, beneath fifty feet of snow, twisted and tossed beneath tons of loose, crystallizing snowpack, tangled together and dizzy. Lucky for us, someone saw us go under. Alive and frightened, we pounded-out a little compartment for ourselves, and waited like trapped coal miners, listening to the faint sounds of our rescue team above.

We told the story over and over, we shared it with friends and family, and it sounded more and more like an adventure with each telling. But for Pierre Alain and I, there was always the recollection of cold and darkness drawing life from our bodies, and of our miraculous escape from that death trap. That common memory of being together at a time so dire was ours alone.

"P.A., you son-of-a-gun, you look great." We gripped each other's shoulders tightly. "How is Marie and little Tarcis?"

"Very well, Eddie. Everyone is very well. The little guy is getting bigger everyday, bigger trouble."

"The Terrible Two's, we say in the States."

Pierre Alain was from Liddes, a small village in the Val d'Entremont, the valley next door to the Val de Bagnes. He married a hometown girl a year to the day after I married Newell. They lived full-time now in Verbier where they ran a crafts boutique. P.A. also played bouncer-and-doorman a couple of nights a week at Marshal's Club, Verbier's other hot nightclub-slash-disco.

On a few summer trips to the Valais, we'd made some spectacular hikes, together. Our friendship had grown steadily, steeled by the power and immanence of the mountains. "The mountain is a she-wolf, Eddie," P.A. once told me. "You and I are as Romulus and Remus to her." I couldn't share my feelings about the mountains with anyone but P.A. No one would believe the metaphysics of our mountain veneration anyway. It was ours.

"I saw Deke, and he told me you were here," P.A. said. "I'm on my way to the club, but I will see you later, no?"

"You will definitely be seeing us later, P.A.," Liney chided him. "You will be seeing us in our finer hours this evening, completely shit-faced, starving for affection, and you'd better goddamn have some beautiful ladies waiting for us."

P.A. laughed and grabbed Liney around the neck.

"Li-Noos, *ce vrai?* I am going to have an ugly witch waiting for you. *Ouuoo,la,la,* she will be so ugly."

"No, no, not for me. Eddie's been telling me about ugly bitches and witches. Now, get out of here." P.A. released Liney from the headlock and started off.

"*A tout*, Eddie. We can talk later, eh?" He rapped me on the back once more and winked.

"P.A.? You need any *bon bons?*" Liney asked.

"No, no. I am fine, thanks. *A tout alors.*" He waved and dodged through the crowd like a fullback, disappearing into the dim light and colors of the ski parkas.

"So, now you're happy, you've seen your little guardian angel here?" Liney said.

"Yes, I am. Little? Christ, I love the big oaf. Where are we going tonight, anyway? Where's dinner?"

"Cocktails at *chez moi* first," he winked.

"Christ, I almost forgot. What do I owe?"

"See what you want, first. Stash is fat. We've got plenty. You'll love it."

"When did P.A.?" I asked.

"He's cool. Just a little recreational stuff, I guess, nothing much," Liney said, casually. "Who knows what goes on in that gingerbread-house? Hanzel knocking Gretel's cookies off."

"Yeah, what do we know?"

"Tonight, we mix and match, we share, we rock'n'roll." Liney wiggled a little shake-and-bake dance. "It's all *così fan tutti*, you know what I mean?"

"Okay, Cuz, I get it, I get it. Where and when do we eat? I'm dying."

"Camargue, nine o'clock. Some wine, some raclette, plat Valaisanne, the whole nine meters." He pinched my cheek. "Glad your appetite's back, Famous. Lot's of good things here."

"*A tout, mon vieux*," I said as we hugged each other. I started off. "I'll come over about eight, eight-fifteen."

I dodged my way through the thinning, half-crowded café. Eric and Miguel Armendar were back at the bar, deep in conversation, and various couples had paired-off in dark coves and corners and nooks. Negotiations everywhere were fever-pitched for dinner engagements and nocturnal possibilities.

Outside it was pitch black. The crisp, new night air felt invigorating, and I needed to be alone just then for a few minutes, taking-in the past few hours with these friends and allowing for visions of the one missing, Céline. "The Gang" had lifted my spirits, but she came suffusively into the marrow of my bones. The power of woman, the invasive systemic authority of the female besieged my being.

The streets were crowded. The early shift of Verbier nightlife was just beginning. Skiers searched for warm havens, tourists searched for restaurants and bars, and as I strolled the Route des Creux, just then, a rescue sled came speeding down toward me, one skier, in harness at the point, and two more tethered behind. Someone injured and wrapped beneath the red blanket—the Swiss Cross blanket—was being taken off the mountain. The sled passed on the packed snow, and I was unnerved. A down-mountain rescue was a haunting vision, people standing, moving smoothly, swiftly, like a funeral in Venice. Fast and fluid, the rescue team turned into the Verbier hospital driveway and the bright lights of the emergency entrance.

I walked a bit farther, up the hill behind Verbier on the

Route des Creux, past a few more shops and restaurants to the edge of town. The mountainside rose steeply upward from this point and it sparkled with the thousands of lights from the chalets. I stared at the hill, squinting my eyes, making my own magical Christmas tree of the twinkling mountainside.

Somewhere, up on the hill, were the lights and rooms and hallways, the deep sleigh bed and thick, warm duvet inside of Chalet Saléve. I pictured Céline's room, seeing myself in the room with her, touching her. I imagined us moving, restlessly, over and around each other.

What of my reaction when Liney spoke her name, and the tremor of that memory through my body? What new discovery, a light out of long darkness, and something was stirred by the thought of her? The sky was velvet and stars flickered like diamonds. They seemed alive. What were we? What discoveries were left, what desires? Two bodies entwined, flickering like stars, searching for some belonging. Bodies in darkness, warm, loving, bodies in darkness—perhaps, that's all we are.

chapter Eight
La L Y O N

The "cocktail" hour at Liney's was much less eventful than the Mardi Gras of the Borsalino that afternoon. The rambling chit-chat that went hand-in-hand with the sharing of drugs was not terribly enlightening in these kinds of settings. One of the prevailing myths of the era was that great drugs automatically ignited the intellect, or caused quantum leaps in the creative spirit. I loved myth, put a lot of stock in it, but that one was mostly wishful hyperbole. The Wright Brothers got more lift than the affective suggestion of illusory flights and imaginative exploration brought on by drugs. Get-togethers like ours were much less prodigious and more like wine tastings.

The variety was impressive, testimony to the pervasiveness of goodies no matter how remote the venue. As was the custom with wines, where champagne often overshadowed even the finest, so, too, the champagne of drugs, cocaine, overshadowed nearly all other drugs of preference that year. It was our drug, La Cosa Nostra of our time. Cocaine was the white gold of the Eighties. It was everywhere, transcending economic, social, and cultural strata. It was the great white horse, messianic to our emerging, young and wealthy, Pop Culture.

A tacit acknowledgement of use was all that was necessary between friends and acquaintances. There were addicted users. I'd met some. We all liked the damn stuff too much, it was as simple as that. It was *the fashion,* the way booze-at-six first struck our parents.

Use was a private and very reserved affair. We never careened through the streets, or out of bars, dazed, loud and obvious. Not in Verbier. Long limousines cruised or parked, motors purring, all over the village nearly every night of the peak seasons. A fleet of low, catlike luxury salons roamed the streets of nearly every Valais resort. Their sleek, dark, concealing windows mirrored the peaceful streets of Swiss mountain life, while inside a mobile den was going full tilt, chocked with plenty of sex, drugs, and rock 'n' roll. As long as behavior remained civil and surreptitious, there were few problems with the Swiss authorities.

Dinner at Camargue was our usual feast-for-dozen-sedate-bacchanal, a surfeit of Valais specialities, all done over an open hearth. Plat Valaisan, raclette, chamois rotie, and Swiss wines seemed to blossom out of the wide wooden table. It was a country feast, typical of the Val de Bagnes. Our enthusiasm, depending on the ebb and flow of sobriety, exaggerated every tradition beyond recognition by anyone Swiss. Helmut created an irreverent, and ingenious, limerick for each of us. We roasted and toasted for hour upon hour of laughter, teasing, and storytelling. Each story, and dinner course, brought us closer together.

After dinner, we moved like a battalion on foot from Camargue, down the hill into the village, singing as we went, tossing snowballs at each other, and pitching them at the slinky black limo that shadowed us all the way to Jacky's Nightclub. A light snow fell and the lights of Verbier flickered softly as we approached. Jacky's was surrounded with more limos, the settlers were circling the wagons for the night.

My own aim from the moment I arrived was fairly narrow. I plowed through the wildness and insane thumping of the music to find the club's namesake, leaving "The Gang" at the door. Up a short flight of stairs behind the bar, I turned into a crowded but very organized office. Jacky sat solemnly at a large desk amid an array of extraordinary antiques, as if she were waiting for me, and my one objective suddenly stalled.

"My god, Jacky, these antiques." I rubbed my hand

across a small Colonial American desk. It felt warm to the touch. "You have some exquisite pieces here, I'm sure you're aware."

"I wish I could take the credit, Eddie. It's Henri, he's obsessed."

"Malouel?"

"Yes," she sighed softly. "I've never met a man with two passions and neither one of them is want of a woman."

Henri Malouel, Jacky's partner and roommate. A shadowy character, a freelance terrorist connected, some say, with the Red Brigades in Italy, Baeder Meinhof, and the Greens — you name the group, and Henri Malouel probably had them on his nefarious résumé. He was just another in Verbier's strange brew. Who, and what revolution, he was aiding at the moment was anybody's guess.

Malouel did logistics and documentation for terrorist activities—how to get five PLO from Istanbul or Beruit to Rome, or airline tickets, passports, ground vehicles, and lodgings for a small cell of operatives, or a car for a bombing squad in Brussels, or London, or Tel Aviv. He was an expert document forger and fence, and he had the odd physical make-up and facial features of someone who looked both Middle Eastern and European. A chameleon with command of several languages, he moved fluidly through countries and cultures on the fringes of international terrorism.

His other passion was antiques. When he was in Verbier he seemed every bit *beau monde,* wealthy, gregarious, a playboy-collector-skier *bon vivant.* He was, in fact, murderously charming. He was no one's friend, and yet, he was everyone's. Jacky and Henri Malouel were the village odd couple. She cared for him a lot, I was sure. He was an asexual man of mystery, of that I was equally certain.

"I'm learning about antiques, a little bit at a time," she said.

"Good choice, Jacky." Her stare changed, abruptly. As if seeing something from the inside, she spoke again, hypnotically, never taking her eyes off of the Colonial desk and my hand.

"My father was killed ten month ago." Flatly, blankly, she said it. "They hung him by his neck in Teheran, in the square." I stopped and looked at her. "They leave you to hang there, you know, in my country. When I was a little girl, I would hug him so tight around his neck. They will not allow my mother to leave. She probably wouldn't go, so…"

"Jacky, I'm sorry."

"I don't know yet, about antiques, Eddie, about the permanence of things." She stared at me now, as if to remark with her eyes about our impermanence, hers, mine, marriages, everything she could divine from my demeanor. She was seeing into me. "Henri, he try to teach me about some things that last, things with histories. He try. They are beautiful, aren't they?"

We were standing completely still. The antiques around us seemed to be whispering among themselves.

"There is someone here you need to see," she said. Bam. Direct. She affirmed my need. Jacky's mystery, again.

"Yes, there is," I answered in a trance. Weighty word, "need". Everyone was getting to know me too well.

"She is so beautiful, Eddie. French women, *incroyable, no?* She's in Lausanne. She come back Tuesday, in the afternoon."

"Did she say…?"

"Her younger brother, he ski for the, *equipe,* the team, the French team, you know?"

"No, I didn't know."

"Yes, he's the second level skier. She is in Chalet Saléve, of course. Chemin de Nifourchier. The name is on the plate, *au-dessus,* yes? She have a girl with her, a friend, Marie Terése. A very pretty girl from Paris. *Une minette,* know what I mean?" Jacky made a little kiss-kiss sound with her lips and I laughed. She smiled at me and her mood was different, more playful. What she'd said was very playful, very naughty, for Jacky.

A *'minette'* referred to a certain style, a manner of young French girls, a *terme d'affection*, typified by a swagger or affectation—a pair of tight, slender jeans creeping innocently, gently, around the vaginal area, accentuating a ripeness, a certain succulence equally appealing to men and women. *'Oooouuu la,la,'* Liney would say. It was difficult to explain.

"This one is *perfect*, Eddie, *vraiment*." We laughed together.

"Come on, Jacky, let's go back downstairs. I want to dance with the most enchanting woman in Verbier, before I have to give you back to your adoring patrons."

"So, I am an enchantress now, eh? Only until Céline come back, I think."

"Forever, Jacky. Your beauty is timeless." I took her around the waist and began to march her toward the stairs. She stopped us at the office doorway and took my face in both of her hands, looking straight into my eyes.

"Céline, she need you, too, Eddie."

There was that goddamn word again. Jacky's eyes glistened. Like a sandstorm, something came up fast from within her, some woman thing, a feeling, some message. She was an enchantress, stunning, Persian, dark and unfathomable in that moment. I drew her into me and held her firmly there. I was warm. I was as hard as a rock, and I wanted her to feel something of my desire against her body, something forbidden in her culture and denied her by an unresponsive man. She reached up, placing her arms around my neck tightly, and searched my eyes again, enjoying fully my heat and hardness. *Know what my body is exchanging for you now,* she was saying. I felt her vibrate against my hips. More than a messenger, she was there and then a surrogate in Céline's absence, passing some female passion to me, accepting the intent for Céline, savoring the embrace for Jacky.

~

Back down in the nightclub, the big Disco beat continued. The later hours quickened the pace of the ritual courting dances and patterns. It was a swarming phenomenon. Men in carnal anxiety—likened to the dance of honey bees, similar in body language, familiar steps and movements—they gave-off the same scents and secretions, spewed the same buzzing patter in the form of clichés, man-rap, and the spiel.

Looking out over the swirling mass — the young males hot and stomping, the females, their rumps round and inviting — I felt myself pulling away, just a bit, seeing it all through a whiskey glass, distancing myself from all that guy behavior.

Christ, men were dumb. *Men are dumb and women are crazy.* That was all Moses had on those fucking tablets. Forget ten commandments of anything, that's all there was. Read them backwards, or upside-down, sideways, that was it. The rest was bullshit.

"Want to dance?"

It was Eric Hoffman, goofed-up on something. So, for the next few minutes we got crazy, dancing together, mimicking and mocking the couples on the floor. Eric would throw his red hair back like a mare, and I'd gallop after him like the torrid steed. We swirled off the floor after some minutes of horsing around and watched the gala continue. Occasionally, Paloma or Jacky, or Liney, slithered by and tried to get us out onto the floor again. Eric and I shared our own oblique codes, quite capable of entertaining ourselves without ever trying too hard.

We observed three very handsome Italians swooping down on a number of beautiful young women. Even that game looked stale.

Some World Cup skiers from Germany, Sweden, Switzerland, and the entire Italian team were there. I asked

Eric about the Americans and he pointed over his shoulder, up the Valais.

"Crans-Montana," he yelled. "They're training, all week up at Crans. Tre Wunderlin saw some." I nodded, a broad comprehending nod, like Flicka, so he'd stop yelling.

Liney came over once again, dancing alone, and tried to entice us into a limo visit outside. We nodded a no to him. As he walked away, he pointed across the dance floor, about fifty or sixty feet, and looked back at Eric. Eric strained his neck to peer across and nodded back at Liney. Then Eric grabbed me in a kind of headlock to shut out some of the music.

"Remember Patric Verdaguer?" He said. I looked across. "*Quel différence, oui?*"

The person standing on the other side of the room did look very different. Verdaguer was a banker from Geneva. We'd known a different Patric, in different times, as a sort of Swiss yuppie, aggressive, polite and smart, a capable if unremarkable Genevois banker and businessman. What I saw now was, Giorgio Armani-meets-Wall Street, a nattily wicked executive.

"*Salop,*" Eric whispered in my ear.

A bastard, perhaps, but one who'd lived-up to the rumors of his incredible rise to wealth and power. Verdaguer was a money launderer, among other things, and not some rinky-dink mom-and-pop Laundromat. Patric was the big show. He worked through his central bank office in Geneva, and two branch offices in Sierre and Sion, two cities in the heart of the Valais.

Verdaguer had latched-onto Central and South American drug money early in the seventies, before anyone realized how enormous the scope of everything was. The sums of money he handled initially were staggering. The country of cheese and cuckoo clocks was the perfect Disneyland for Verdaguer's *foison*. And money begat money. Wealth, tremendous wealth, craved a currency market for its purchase and sale. The big players all came knocking at Verdaguer's door. They came out of the woodwork from everywhere—the good, the bad, the ugliest. Even the "goombah" money of worldwide organized crime was no match for the Colombian and Central American drug cartels.

"Banque Valais?" I asked Eric.

"*Oui*, he's like Fort Knox. The biggest in Europe."

Governments in the Third World still waited at his door, arms dealers wined and dined him to excess, and oil Sheiks kissed his brass-plated banking card all during their shopping sprees. There were crown jewels in some of his bank vaults, and expensive works of art were locked in apartments he kept in Geneva and Vevey and Zurich, the barter and the booty.

Banana Republics held huge accounts in reliable old BeyVey, stoked by their drug trade. The *presidentés* showered him with gifts of coffee, cigars, new investors, and, of course, bananas. Grungy-looking revolutionaries made deposits in one bank, and counter-revolutionaries took withdrawls from another. Some brought him rice, and some brought him beans – and the Carribean came to the Alps, borne on a lucrative tropical breeze.

Deke and Liney told me stories of the *clientéle* Verdaguer brought to Verbier on occasion, conspicuous and unsavory characters from places in Central and South America that even pack mules dreaded. They'd bring everything with them, too, even their women. Wedded to bodyguards, alone and armed heavily beneath their ski parkas they were suspicious or wary of everyone and everything. "Tainted wealth made lonely men of kings," my mama once said, "blood money, the richest man a recluse."

It was Verbier, just below the surface of things.

Next to Verdaguer near the dance floor, stood Fabian Thibaud, a Vaudois—Mister Limousine. Thibaud owned the limousine service that supplied nearly all of the cars that roamed the streets of the ski resorts. But his resort rentals were a pittance, merely pocket money. The real mean streets of the limo business were in Geneva, where, in the cause of world peace, the governments of the planet sent their emissaries to be pampered after the back-breaking labor of diplomacy. Three out of four times, the weariest heads-of-state leaned against the headrests of Fabian's fleet of jet-black stretches. From airports to offices, receptions to resorts, Fabian's cars chauffeured three-fourths of the world's representatives in the service of international relations. Arabs rented his cars, five at a time—just couldn't shake the caravan thing, I guess.

Thibaud owned Geneva. His rise to power, like that of Patric Verdaguer, had been meteoric also. City and Canton, he had a seventy-five percent share of the diplomatic carriage trade. And Verdaguer, it was rumored, had ninety percent of Thibaud.

The night was winding down, everything beginning to blend together in a haze. The loud music, the smoke, the drugs and drinks were having their effect. The group, our group, was a kind of blur of additions and subtractions, women from every culture in Europe breezed through teasing and dancing. Liney disappeared. Stuart Hartman and Ian Woods were blitzed, lost in a kind of candy-store stupor. Eric disappeared. Ham and Paloma swirled me out onto the dance floor and matched me with a beautiful brunette from Lyon. Manolete Armendar tried to sandwich her between us, shouting in song.

"Lyonnaise potatoes. *Sac de pommes d'terre, cette femme.*"

Finally, Lyon and I were pressed together so tightly by Mano, we stayed locked together until the music changed.

So, there I was, slow-dancing with a gorgeous brunette wearing slender black tights, a white turtle-neck, and a bright yellow and white ski sweater, and our hair was sticking to the sides of our faces like two sweaty teenagers at a high school dance. We kissed each other's clammy necks as we danced and soon the glandular green-light went on in both our bodies.

La Lyonnaise and I left Jacky's, refreshed by the cold air and light snowfall, as we frolicked drunkenly in the street on the short walk over to Marshal's Club. I had to see a man about a car—Pierre Alain. A long, black stretch sat directly in front of the club. It was no ordinary limo, no fleet rental. The license plate told me it was the 747 of limousines—low and dark, barreling *sotto voce* motor, little, dim opera lights on the sides, and the vain plate "Tric" of the Canton *Genéve*, it sat humming ominously.

We skipped up the three steps and into Marshal's entranceway. Lyon was under my arm and her affectionate play was continuous, her hands roamed underneath my jacket and sweater, rubbing and kneading my back and chest even as I spoke to Pierre Alain. P.A. smiled all the while, trying to get a better look at Lyon, jangling his car keys, trying to get her attention. Her face was buried somewhere under my sweater and she was kissing sensitive parts. I grabbed the keys from P.A.

"Where?" I shouted.

"Behind Ecurie, you know, across from the Eden, *a droit.*"

"*Alors, mon vieux, à demain.* In the gas-tank door, as always," I bellowed over the music's roar, rattling the car keys.

"*Toujours. Salut,* Eddie. You are very busy, I see," He laughed, and I stumbled back outside with Lyon tugging at me. P.A. had seen me in worse conditions, carried me on his shoulder on occasion. Ever ready he was, to rescue me from the jaws of Fate. Women were another matter.

Down the steps, and onto the road Lyon and I tumbled, my only thought being to get back to the Eden without any more stops. The night was fast getting colder on Verbier's hard-packed streets, and temperatures were rising in Lyon.

Suddenly, one of the rear doors of the gurgling, low limo

sitting in front of Marshal's swung open. Just the door opened, no one was visible. A spooky silhouette against the white snow, it hung there, open in the stillness like an arm outstretched. Even tipsy Lyon took notice. I wasn't squeamish, but it was a little freaky. We walked back to the open door and peeked inside. There was Fabian Thibaud sitting alone in one corner of the vast parlor of Patric Verdaguer's limousine.

Thibaud said nothing. He simply opened the palm of his hand and motioned to the sofa across from him, at the back of the limo. Lyon and I got in and sat down. The leather was sumptuous. It was warm inside and softly lit with more opera lights. Some type of elevator music played gently. I knew there were bars and tables and all sorts of gadgets in these limos, but they were nowhere in sight. Everything was sealed snugly behind stitched leather panels. Lyon and I sat quietly and stared across the wide carpeted space, waiting for Thibaud.

"The American, the *futbol* runner, no?" He said smartly.

"Halfback. It's different. Michigan." I was pissed-off already.

"Ahh yes, Mech-ee-gahn, *oui*. We met before, Eddie, some years ago, here in Verbier, I believe," he said.

"Yeah." I hated the way he said my name.

"Everyone in Verbier seem to like you, Eddie. Really, you have a certain way about you. People like you very much."

What the hell was this guy up to?

"I mean this," he pressed on. "I'm not trying to be, you know, critical or anything."

Lyon was holding my left arm with both her hands. Her head was nearly on my shoulder and I worried that maybe she was nodding-off with the sleepy monotone of Thibaud's voice. There was a long silence, then Thibaud reached into the right pocket of his herringbone sport jacket and took out a small, bulging plastic bag that looked yellowish in the glow of the opera lights. He then reached left to a row of switches on the back cushion of the front seat. Pressing one switch, a small counter top appeared out of the side panel next to Lyon, unfolding in front of her just off to the left. He tossed the bag, fully five feet across, and it landed squarely on the counter top with a soft plop. Lyon and I stared at it. It was white. The lights smacked it yellow, but it was white.

Thibaud pressed another button. The sound startled us. Two more side panels slid downward into the car's body revealing a well-stocked bar that sparkled with colorful bottles of brandies and wines and tinkly glassware. Another switch, and another panel slid open opposite the bottles. A tiny cloud of condensation rose from out of the opening into the light. Frosty bottles of champagne stood, gold-leafed and dripping, in the slender refrigerated compartment. Lyon and I sat like kids in a menagerie, watching all of the trap doors and walls slide, listening to the little motors that drove all of the gadgetry—buzz, bing, whizz. All of these machinations completed their sequence with a department store "bong." Lyon giggled and hugged my arm tighter, like a child watching a new set of trains on Christmas morning.

"Now, you don't have to stop at Sacconaix for your nightcap," Thibaud said, and a chill went through me. I hated shit like that. How would he know about my visits to some alleyway bar? Who the hell was watching me, and why?

The door opened, untouched, just as it did when we came out of Marshal's. Thibaud slipped outside like an eel. He was out on the snow before I could grab him. He was giving us Verdaguer's limo for the night. What the hell was this?

"Hey, Fabian." I stuck my face in the open doorway. "What is this? What's the ticket here?" I was flushed, I was up and sober suddenly, awake and in-his-face. The limo grumbled. The exhaust fumes climbed into the streetlight, in clouds, and some dark figure under a cap and visor held the door open for Thibaud. Fabian halted me with more of his reptilian charm.

"Patric like you, that's all. He like people who make an impression, like you, Eddie." Thibaud suddenly embroidered some animation onto his manner, quickly changing the plodding drone of his voice. He looked skyward, affectedly, as if drawing on some avian wisdom. "Please, you correct me if I make a mistake," he began, officiously. "The quarterback, he's the smart one, the leader, your captain, I think, yes? But, the halfback, *ce vrai*, ah, the halfback, the runner, he is the one who gets all the women. No?" He bent down, put his face in the open doorway and glanced at Lyon, then at me. "You have a good game, *Le Eddie*. They call you Famous. No?" Thibaud smiled and disappeared. I sat back. The door closed behind me, and Lyon and I rested for a minute just taking-in the sparkling array before us. The son-of-a-bitch even had Sinatra on the tape that was playing.

I didn't want to stay. Lyon didn't care, either way. She wanted to be amorous again and started snuggling, lifting my sweater, trying to undo my pants. She was tracking-down a one-eyed trouser snake, keeping the playfulness at an arousing level.

I tapped the black window behind the driver and he drove on, gliding slowly through the empty streets as Lyon and I began oral exams on the big leather seats and cushy pile carpet. If these guys knew so much about my patterns, the driver would know to take us back to the Eden.

He delivered us to the front door of the hotel. The snow pile glowed red under the flickering Cardinal Beer sign in the window of the small, front-room bar. We stepped out onto an empty Place Centrale and the limo lumbered away in that same low groan. Lyon and I watched it disappear down Rue de Verbier, and then went up to my room.

We never took a drink in the car. I pressed two switches to get rid of the bars, pressed another, and closed the fridge, hit another button, and put Sinatra out of his crooning misery soon after the car got moving.

I took the small white plastic bag though, put it in my jacket pocket. It would have been crushed anyway when the little counter top went back into the side panel. *Buzz, bing, whizz.*

I hated to waste.

chapter Nine
THE MIRROR

The painting over the desk had a strange sheen in the dim, pre-dawn light. I was mesmerized for a moment by the quiet of the room and the luminance of the painting, the distance, the rich greens and browns pulled me into the forest, the vaulting and imposing glades, and then there was the loneliness of his quest.

Lyonnaise was out like a mackerel, snoring chords. I kissed the sleeping brunette on the forehead, then on a bare shoulder. I pulled the duvet aside, exposing an exquisite French leg and hindquarter, and there was the shadow and curve and contour that excited like no other vision in the known world. *Cold shower.*

Six twenty-eight, and two thin hands of phosphor swept downward, slowly coming together, on the night table timepiece. The sun was on the terminator, and the edge of the sky was apricot. *Dämmerung, baby. I've got to go.*

The tiny town of Arolla sat at the very end of the Val d' Hérens. Arolla was a favorite spot and the highest station in the Valais, also one of the smallest Alpine villages. There was a small grocery store in the center of town that sold dark round bread the size of a softball and dried sausages that I craved.

Whenever I skied Arolla, I'd stuff two of each in my fanny-pack before I headed for the lifts. There, above Arolla, I'd find the peace and solace and some of the wonder I'd come to Switzerland to have. P.A. had introduced me to the mountains here near Arolla, on a few summer hikes, and the place affected me like no other. He sensed things about nature in an odd mountainman way, and so, too, the nature of the beast.

"This will be your spot, Eddie," he said. "This is good site for you. Every man has to find a place among mountains that makes him feel alone with his gods and demons." P.A. only looked a little like Mr. Clean with a full head of hair, there were times when he sounded like Descartes.

I skied the chutes descending the Pigne d' Arolla very hard, pressing the line, testing the outermost boundaries of my fear and skiing gumption. The skiing had to be shrewd and enterprising. A moment's distraction meant certain disaster. It was fast and terrifying along the jagged cliffs of the *Aiguilles Rouges*, the Red Needles. I was alone. Only the mountain spirits were near me in the needles.

Erase
begin again,
begin an instruction like the tenor
begins the great aria.
Placement. Placement. Ski, moment to moment
see how the notes follow
Trace, find serenity
the new line, white, then blue
down steeper down.
Remember — the knees, the feet, the hands, the heart.
Spring from memory, let the spirits guide.
Daring needs no witness. Submit.
Death, if it comes, will not brandish hubris.

I ran the steep cols all morning and as the noon-hour approached, I made my way onto the wide glaciers that surrounded the eleven-thousand-foot, Mont Collon. There, I put on my snowshoes, hiked a short distance, then put the skis back on for a long, thoughtful run along the glacial *névé*.

The sun was wonderfully warm. At the head of the Glacier de Cheilon, I parked myself in the soft snow, sitting against my skis, and ate my dark bread and sausages. *Be patient. You've had a brief morning meeting with the gods in the*

Needles. It was a process—patience. I sat and felt the sun. She'd come back soon, I told myself. She was in me already. *Be patient, Eddie.*

By mid-afternoon, I was on my way back to Verbier, via Sion. At four-thirty, I climbed the hill from Le Châble, P.A.'s little Fiat straining, winding steadily through and around the "S" turns in the steep ravines of the Val de Bagnes. The pink Alpenglow was descending slowly from the tops of the mountains and the lower valleys and foothills were already in blue shadow.

Finally, the first few lights and smoke streams of Verbier came into view and thoughts of the Eden, my room, my warm bed, and the thick white duvet filled every anxious minute of the climb. Verbier appeared. More lights. The chalets sparkled on the hill above the village. *Tomorrow. Tomorrow at this time, I'll be with her, I'll be with Céline.*

The after-dinner gathering spot was Marshal's Club—more loud music and the steady flow of gorgeous women—the feedlot of all the beautiful people. The wildness was wilder. The racers had begun training runs and the ski fans were all here, gassed-up and ready for World Cup craziness. And this night, Pierre Alain would be a part of whatever ensued for "The Gang." It would all continue this way, winding into higher gear for the Races on the weekend.

Marshal's mirrored walls seemed to double and triple the chaos. The moving bodies, the swirl of light, the loud music, and dizzying insanity created an energy unique among discotheques.

Members of the French ski team were present. I asked one of them about Céline's brother, Claude, only to find out he wasn't here in the Club with his group.

"Claude is a serious athlete," a robust teammate told me. "Ascetic and dedicated to an excellence in the sport," the young Frenchman insisted.

I smiled. I admired the remark. I was stoned, half drunk, standing, balancing skillfully on two feet, a drink in one hand, and speaking somewhat coherently at the same time, and this kid thought Claude Decauville was dedicated to excellence. I'd already imagined myself with Claude Decauville's sister, lustfully. I had imagined myself with sisters and daughters yet unborn, maidens and mothers, goddesses, dryads, naiads, and mountain nymphs.

In the swirling temptations of disco floors and singles bars, I saw only the women. There was nothing else to see. It was idolatry as satisfying as any drug, probably my most proficient indulgence. Excellence had nothing to do with dedication in my world order.

I looked at my own body in the disco wall mirrors. The dancing mass jumped and gyrated on the floor behind me. This was my sport now, a nightly blitzkreig, a stupor to anesthetize the pain and fear locked deep in my muscle.

Once upon a time, there was a halfback. He played without fear and laughed at pain. Where had he gone? The one that lived in me? The one like Claude Decauville with all that discipline and allegiance? The face and the eyes in the mirror told me, all too frankly. The eyes saw beneath the trim physique, deeply, an atrophy of spiritual muscle, a drawn and pallid will. The face was only a reminder of my youth, my calling card for collecting the female sustenance. Something had departed. Some vapor of the warrior was gone. How did my identical image hold me in such low regard? *Give a ghost a conscience, Famous.*

I raised my glass and toasted farewell. My reflected partner wouldn't bother me again, I'd make sure of it. I stayed away from that friggin' wall mirror for the rest of the night.

Our group enlarged considerably after a few hours to include new people, mostly young ladies, that Stuart, Ian, Eric and Liney had brought into it. Trips outside to the limo were considerably more frequent. I made several. Everybody was wound-up, to the tree line, as we used to say.

P.A. got out on the floor and had some fun dancing. He

was so uncoordinated, it became riotous. He danced like a walrus, like the Jolly Green Giant imitating a walrus. His wife, Marie, joined us at Marshall's for a while. I danced with Marie once or twice. She didn't do drugs, so I didn't understand a thing she said.

The three handsome, young Italians were there, their pose and their *motis* was unchanged. We created grazing land for the hungry herd like these discos and bars, the compromises the livestock made in them were entirely fitting.

Around midnight, I was dancing with a very thin, blond model from Paris. "Julliet" was the name she gave in a raspy, charcoal whisper. She had a stunningly carved face, a little severe, but very beautiful. She reminded me of the French rock singer, Sylvie Vartan, that I was wild about just then. Julliet moved elegantly, seductively, to the music.

On one brief visit to Liney's limo, we threw down a few grams of cocaine, together, and it was then, I discovered, that Julliet was actually a Jules, or a Jim, or a Bob. I really didn't give a damn at the point of discovery. She, he, was quite proud of it, wanted to show me everything. Call me old fashioned, but the evening suddenly became complicated. Prolong it no more.

"*Jamais, Julliet. Nnnnnnn'est pas possible,*" in my kindest, softest French. "Take the car, take the coke, take everything to your apartment, please, *s'il vous plait.*" *I'm out of here.*

I landed on the hardpack of Rue d'Rousseau behind Marshall's and began the long walk back up the hill to the Eden. An echo of humiliation rang loudly in my ears, it reverberated like thumping disco music. Halfway there, I started jogging and laughing, chuckling at first at my stupidity and then suddenly realizing it was worthy of a hearty laugh. I laughed even harder at the thought of "The Gang," knowing everything the whole time. I ran steadily faster, finally sprinting into Place Centrale. The rock music from the clubs was still faintly audible, resonating off the buildings. A few late-dates were scurrying along the sidewalks, ducking into hotels and alleyways, looking for warm beds and carnal treasure.

The little Swiss snow plows had piled and stacked the accumulation so many times in the open square, it looked like a fortress whose walls were ten feet high in some places. Children who played there during the day had made climbing notches in the fortress wall that faced the *Eden*. I climbed the footholds in three steps and threw myself up on top in soft, newfallen powder. I laid on my back, fully ten or twelve feet above the street, in the neon-red-and-snow-glow of the Eden's humming sign, looking up at the stars. The occasional limo slinked by down below. −

It started to snow, the first few flakes touched my face and melted. They ran down my cheeks like tears.

"What a piece of work is a man?" I recited. "What a piece of work am I."

The infrequent flakes began to cover me. A night full of revelry and surprises had ended. In a headlong sprint to satisfy the urge, I'd been aroused, unknowingly, by a man.

Aimless, hopeless, pleasure-seekers we'd all become, unable in our frenzy to tell the key from the ignition. The gods were having a rousing good laugh, I supposed, a thunderous good laugh, shaking heaven's walls and chipping the paint. The snowflakes fell faster now, bigger, falling in mirthful, somersaulting dance. The stars were falling from the black sky.

chapter Ten
CÉLINE

At dawn the next morning, I stepped from the doorway of the Eden to face a firing squad. They sat, smugly, silently, in a snow bank across from the hotel, waiting—Liney, Eric, P.A., Miguel and Manolete Armendar, Stuart and Ian. A few giggles escaped. I didn't say a word. The air was unbreathably thick with anticipation and no one in the group moved. Nothing in the entire town moved, not the slightest breeze.

They were waiting for Hermaphrodìtus to appear from the hotel, waiting to let me have it. The first light rays of morning pierced the ornate figurine of Minerva atop the Farinet across Place Centrale and one streak of sunlight, framed by the Roman's hilt and forearm, spanned the square, hitting me like a follow-spot in a burlesque show.

Liney started singing, a cappella, the old Mickey and Sylvia tune, "*Lu-uv, love is strange/too many people….,*" I broke stride suddenly and ran straight for Liney. But the Jolly Swiss Giant was in my path, and in a matter of seconds we were all rolling around in a huge snow bank in Place Centrale. I got the worst of it, but I did manage to snowwash P.A.'s face while the others sang on in barbershop quartet harmony.

We piled our gear and ourselves into two cars and headed for the ski station at Crans-Montana, a standard one-day jaunt across the Valais into the Bernese Alps. It was a way for us to get away from the huge crowds in Verbier and spend time together on the slopes instead of in the long lines, and our Gang skied the Montana station in typical fashion. We warmed-up on the long runs from the Plaine Morte

Glacier, ripped a few of the steep side cols coming off the Tubang, some of the off-limits rock and powder face cliffs, and the deep blue couloirs of sunny Mont Bonvin. It was one of our get-together ski days, a lot of fast, follow-the-leader nuttiness, aerials, and some extreme bombardiering.

Eric Hoffman and Pierre Alain never ceased to astound me with their total-abandon-style skiing. I knew their acumen well, but the terrain and jumps they navigated, at top speed, made us all shiver a bit.

My mind was hardly on the skiing. Preoccupied with Céline's return to Verbier that afternoon, I skied hard but not aggresively. We parked Pierre Alain's car at the foot of Piste Nationale, the long and famous World Cup downhill course, and at about one-thirty, just after a light lunch on the mountain at Lachaux, I bid farewell to "The Gang" and skied down.

I navigated the steep turns and aerial bumps as if I were skiing against the clock in the final run for Olympic Gold. The drive back to Verbier over the *autoroute* was no less a Giant Slalom of motorcar handling. I couldn't remember speeding across that highway with such Grand Prix precision and finesse, weaving and dodging everything through Sion to the Val de Bagnes. My body seemed to hum with a new music that afternoon, some song was returning.

I parked and went straight to the *Eden* to bathe and change. P.A.'s car keys—inside the gas-tank door, as always. My march up the hill to Chalet Saléve would be a one-way climb, I hoped.

By about four, four-thirty, I stood at the front door to number 14 Chemin de Nifourchier chilled and very apprehensive. It was like the saying, "seeing someone again for the first time." That same heavy, pressing pain shot through me, through the center of my chest and groin, when she opened the door as when Liney had first spoken her name that afternoon in the hotel. My memory worked in odd locales sometimes. I wondered how, or where anatomically, I'd remember the androgynous Julliet of the previous night.

There was a strange, long gap between our opening *"bonjours"* and the next few words in the minefield of dialogue. Her radiance filled a certain void, and yet, it created some momentary interruption in communication. Sad, wet, blue eyes glistened when she smiled. She entered me with that look, and the feeling I called pain suddenly became a warm viscous flow, gently dripping at seeing her at last. Excitement restored, anticipation renewed and my veins filled with new energy.

"You must be tired, Eddie," she blurted-out, breaking the spell. We were standing on the veranda of Chalet Saléve. We hadn't moved in the open doorway for some minutes.

"Yes, the walk up the hill was fast, eh, brisk," I said.

Then, again, the enormous silence. I stood enthralled anew by her long and undulating blond hair. Like a broad estuary streaked slightly by shifting black sands it all fell gently on the tops of her shoulders. Such dark skin she had, neck and hands — all that I saw—Moroccan brown, Basque brown, taut, and youthful. How would this umbered Gaul feel to my touch? Her soft lips pursed a gentle smile and my body burst with want.

"Céline," I shouted. "Do you remember when we first met?"

"Of course," very matter-of-factly, very French. "It was at the *ecole de ski*, the school for the children, no?"

"Yes, the little hill. It was snowing. I remember the snow on the hill—and your face." I swallowed hard. She'd preserved a memory, an attention most men shouldn't hear of.

"Such meetings are not forgotten," she said, so nicely. I felt more comfortable, a little more relaxed. We were on a roll with conversation. "You were with your boy, Michael, yes?"

"Yes." Such rhythm. The words flowed, like hard-boiled eggs were being gulped down between each one.

"I remember, I ask if you are married," she chided me. "And your answer to me, 'I'm flexible.' I don't forget such meetings, Monsieur Eddie."

I smiled, uneasily. I was flexible. I was compromising, desperate, agreeable, and lonely—all of it, everything contained in a sex addict's every waking hour. And I was available for passion, a pathetic infidel, for hire by the hour and willing—also included in the addict's repertoire. She had broken through something with her look that day years before, made me see, in retrospect, a behavior that was pathological.

"Things have changed in my life, Céline."

"I know. I knew they would." Like she had it fixed.

"Now, see, I don't get this. How do women do that? I mean, how do they know when a man's unhappy in a relationship?"

"We know everything."

"There were herds of single men here that February. I mean, why me? Was I giving-off some scent, some pheromone, or was it emblazoned across my forehead?"

"It was written on your heart," she said, dreamily French.

"Ah, *oui*, a cardiologist," I said, and she laughed. "Heart attacks caused by woman's penetrating insights, right?"

"Men are hilarious, you really are," she smiled and giggled as she appraised. "I saw an absence of love in your eyes, Eddie. Everything else was there, everything for me. But I wanted to know why. *Anormal, no?* How you say, *un* fluke?"

"No, no fluke, Céline. You see, men never rely on science. And we don't have intuition. We don't use it, I mean. Men look at the population of women, then some of us zero in on this seemingly unattainable sample, the tough-love set, see? Who are a) unhappy, and b) in relationships. The rest is right out of Las Vegas. Why don't you dump that guy?" She smiled again. "You understand Las Vegas, yes?"

"Casino, oui."

"Enchante, mademoiselle."

"I've waited two years to see something in your face, Eddie." Her words were sheer flattery, but I felt a little culpable for the way I'd behaved in that first meeting. We were getting clear of that now. "I wanted to know if such things can happen to people," she said, suddenly serious.

"And I wanted to be sure they could." The goddamn words fell right out of my mouth. How would I ever know when I meant it? Her face brightened and I saw a shimmering light in that impenetrable French stare, some ripple fluttered through her body and then resounded back in her eyes.

"Are you going to ask me in, Céline? Or, are we just going to stand out here and freeze in this pose?"

"I'm thinking," she said, coyly, looking for a reaction from me. I blushed like a schoolboy and she led me inside. The Alpenglow was just beginning to fall on the tops of the mountains.

Chalet Saléve inside was just as I had dreamed, the dark wood and high ceilings and a crackling fire ablaze within a large fieldstone hearth, warming the large living room. The spacious placement of the few furniture pieces gave the room an open, receptive ambiance. An immense, thick area rug of chocolate, pink and yellow swirl covered the expanse in front of the stone fireplace. The pink was the magenta of high peaks, the color of Alpenglow at dusk.

Everything was as I had wished it would be, except for the flowers. Fresh bouquets and arrangements were everywhere, big, bright, and fragrant, standing in tall vases — violet, blue, yellow, red — bursts of color gathered in wide wooden bowls, in pewter cups, and porcelain beer steins. And in the center of the rug against the deep chocolate swirl a handful of giant white lilies, moist in their own dewy mist, sparkled in the firelight. She had spent a fortune in Lausanne to have these flowers here, no doubt. I was speechless.

The room throbbed in the fire's glow. Only Céline's own beauty and grace matched the vibrancy of the flowers. Did I deserve this? Sharing moments, hours here with her? Something I wanted so, but was I bound by a lameness from my past? Events marked by extremes remain lucid somehow. A cogent reverie of love and the despair that attended its absence, to a man, becomes everything genuine, as if in the recall everything and everyone re-existed as before, true and tangible.

And a woman was always there. Men's ambitions and fantasies ran a circular path back to her, back to a female. From the beginning, we were aware of her, the girl in the second grade with little blond pigtails, at the spelling bee, when we got up on the two-wheeler, at our first dance, first party, on the first date, when we made the first touchdown, or scored the last run. A woman was always there. Why dream at all if not for her? Every woman's touch was always and never before, the same and, yet, forever new. I had no reference for the event of Céline in me. How lucky we were, given the chance time and again, how goddamn lucky we were to be near, to touch and hold miraculous creatures.

"Céline..." I began, nearly out of breath. We looked at each other for a long moment, charting the tension. I touched her face, lightly, letting my hand cup her cheek. My thumb wandered gently across her lips.

"Say nothing, Eddie. *Je sais.*"

"No, no, Céline. I want, Christ, I wish I could speak French now, damn it. Céline, it's just..." But French would be no help. I was tongue-tied and confused in my native language. I fumbled for things I couldn't voice.

Then, she stopped it all. She rose slowly and steadily like a dolphin breaching effortlessly from the waves, up into my arms, up to my face with hers, up her full, firm, body heavily against me, up, her mouth covered mine, up again her arms, up and over my shoulders, she took my neck, my head to hers. The firelight disappeared between us. We were like shadow art upon the walls, figures in a dance, like birds and fish and all the creatures of the earth when the message, the burning message in our brain, sent us clasping and clawing. Her body told me of consummation and rebirth, of ashen dissolution of fears, and a resurrection. And soon, my body understood and found its own expression. The language was new, again. We grasped, we nourished. We arose and swelled with animal ferocity, and never released from the very first embrace. Here was the renewal, the circular path, Céline was my return, my Isis, my Ouroboros, the snake consuming its own tail.

Like great white thunderheads rising steadily against a deep blue sky, we grew mountainous and billowing. And then down, our muscles brimming with sweat, backs shining and wet, we crushed together the white lilies. We glistened now as the flower petals did in the firelight. *Down steeper down* along sheer white walls. She spread beneath me the way fresh morning powder feathered open when I pressed down on the skis. Céline guided me down, and I rode, until the fire died.

The hunger was too great for sleep, an unraveling of our need, too urgent. To end the heartache... "That this too, too solid flesh would melt," he wrote.

That such a moment might disappear or be missed, we pushed sleep away. The snow played gently on the windows, the light tapping a constant syncopation with our breathing. And when we could postpone sleep no longer, we fell into short naps.

I watched her, caressing and kissing her when and where I desired. She, in turn, kept watch over me, cradling me in her arms, combing my hair with her fingers until I bid farewell to the conscious side. And always, the brilliant surprise of her mouth touching me, somewhere, took me from sleep and reverie, back to the supple perfection of her body.

Céline's body was toned and hard, an athletic body,

muscle elongated and sensuous, defined by training, and yet, sculpted and proportioned in raw female sensuality. When Céline's body moved it called mine to will. We seemed primitive together, fecund and Promethean as intimate performers.

On into the next day we continued, reversing an order in the world. The inexplicable became ordinary, the astonishing, usual. Somewhere in the middle of the night, we found a will to alter sexuality and consciousness, further tilting the world.

Through several grams of cocaine, like high priests, we waded, and sucked and licked at each other's fingers and lips as if the white drug were a powdered sugar. Disquieting aberrations developed into the commonplace. We were all things without restraint. The snow beat faster against the windows, rapping.

During some early morning hour, the comely *minnet,* Marie Terése passed through the house. We met in the hallway on one of my bathroom trips. My sagging nakedness didn't faze her, and we exchanged polite *"bonjour-bonsoirs"* then went our separate ways. Céline was hysterical when I told her of my hallway encounter with her Paris friend.

We never left Chalet Saléve. There was enough cheese and wine, and enough breads and fruits on hand to satisfy us. We slept intermittently, together, and occasionally catnapped separately, never more than a few feet apart. She read quietly while I nodded off, and I rummaged and paced, in the heat of another passion, while she slept.

Anything that appeared seemed to find a place, a category. I was looking for the line, the long curve upon which I traced effortlessly, rapidly, and moved through spaces unimagined. The mirage, the words and ideas that came without thought, shimmered up from the depths, continuous and connected, as if the great Milky Way had drawn closer overflowing and effulgent with stars, spewing a surfeit of constellations over a clear black heaven. From nothing it came.

I glanced at Céline's face as she slept and remembered how the motion, our movement, began from nothing and became some full and wondrous gesture, elongated, harmonious in phrase and mime, building in a kind of dance, vibrant with momentum and tone, color and music. The hours of complete immersion had dissolved ungainliness, pure body heat had melted buttery fears.

The second night occurred, and with it came the heavy snows beating on the windows. The snow accumulation now reached second level of the chalets in Verbier. We could literally step from the balcony of Saléve right onto a giant drift.

More snow. More cocaine. More recklessness and searching and the will, the weakness, to alter was ours again. To serve the addiction, we descended rampantly. A deep, black void between obsession and wondrous passion we claimed for our own.

In the array of drugs we'd compiled together, a thin, clear strip of cellophane lay randomly on a white hand-towel. The faint, reddish dots spaced evenly in a line along the cellophane strip caught my attention and sent a slight shiver of apprehension, mixed with titillation, up my spine. Liney's warning, "*watch what you take,*" echoed like a chorus in my drowsy head and I pushed aside the lysergic acid and chose an unrefined mescaline. The peyote composite turned out to be a bad choice. The experience was anything but good and there were hours of profuse sweating and sickness. We ended, in some morning hour, in the tub together swabbing each other down with wet towels.

Each night the equation was different. The desperate, piranha-like chase to devour was, however, much the same.

On the third day we decided to leave the chalet in the afternoon, shop for some food at the Migros, then take a long walk and see some of the practice runs for the Races.

By mid-afternoon we stood together at the bottom of the downhill run, hoping we'd get a glimpse of Céline's brother on his schuss across the finish line. We watched for an hour, but did not see Claude's run.

It was a gray winter day, the flat light took away all of the dramatic cut and contour of the beautifully manicured slopes. The bright banners and flags hung limp against a sky drained of color. Céline and I cared little about the day's tint. We were refreshed by the walk and happy to be out in the cold mountain air.

"How long has he been at it? Claude?" I asked.

"Not long, really. He tries very hard, he was the last one chosen for the World Cup team."

"It's a tremendous honor to be chosen, isn't it?"

"Not so tremendous any more." The words were cold, curt, and almost bitter. The journalist in me said, wherever there was an abrupt cut-off that was where you struck next.

"Liney told me that you were on the French swim team." My return went through her like a knife. She stiffened and gazed away, very far away, beyond place to some other time. "Céline, I'm sorry. Don't talk about it if you don't want to." I wanted desperately for her to share some secret with me. "It's just that I feel something in your body, there's something I want to touch in you, way down."

"Why?" She bristled and looked at me defensively. I searched for an answer and found myself falling back on honesty.

"Because, if I reach it, I think perhaps I'll find something of me." So much for journalism. "It's a selfish motive, Céline."

Her face changed, abruptly. She challenged me. There was a certain demeanor I had not seen before, calling me to an accounting.

"Can we be like this, Eddie?"

I knew this question was coming.

"I don't know, Céline. I don't know enough about myself to be sure. Every time I think I do, well, something changes. We're like this now, and something is happening. That's all I know."

"Yes, for me too, something wonderful," she said, happily.

"I am a frightened man, Céline. Not weak, but fearful. Like the mad dog that has just seen his image on the water. He suddenly realizes how vicious he has been all of his life just to be a mad dog, just to keep the reputation alive."

"I think I want to love the man you are, mad or frightened."

"Can you be one love in my life?" I asked. There was a confused look. Would she buy this Brooklyn Bridge? I watched her smile turn to frown. *Men are such dumb fools. Do some women know? Will they tell the others?*

"Can you help me to understand this? I'm not sure I understand," she said with trepidation in her inquiry.

"We don't forget, Céline. Men don't forget. It's a major flaw. Love piles into our hearts from the very first, like snowfall—fascinations, obsessions, addictions, infatuations... some woman does, I don't know...something, and we just never let them go. They mount, these women. It's an accumulation. Nothing and no one is insignificant. They all mean something. What we exchange adds up, never really melting away. It's all memory and sickness. Don't let me hurt you, Céline, stop me."

"Eddie." She stopped me, putting her fingers across my lips. She stared into my eyes with dangerous glee.

"I will give you everything and tell you anything," Her eyes implored and promised at the same time. "And maybe sometimes you'll wish I told you lies. But, you, you are dark, Eddie. The way we make love—there is something very dark. Two people don't make love the way we do and call it an affair. You have secrets. I will never probe there. I cannot. Some secrets...they must remain. Your secrets are your strength, Eddie."

"I'm not good with...words, Céline. Not these."

"You are beautiful with words. I have read some. You are powerful, Eddie, I believe this."

"I have but one power left, Céline. It's called truth and its going out-of-fashion fast, disappearing from the heart and soul of mankind."

"Truth cannot hurt us, *mon cher*."

"Once before I had...I was hurt terribly. I'm just a little more careful now. Aware of my fears, I guess. What's happening now is good, Céline, very good. Just let me be. Please, wait."

"I think I can wait for your words. I love the way I feel with you." She changed again, running her fingers through my hair, grasping it tightly. She owned me. "Now, what more did Linus tell you?" She jabbed me in the stomach, playfully, then hugged me and put her head on my chest.

"I swear, only that you were a swimmer for the French team...back in the thirties." She laughed, loudly. People around us looked, and she hid her face in my ski sweater again. The change to coquette was very brief, however. I held her closely but her body was already preparing an escape. She needed some distance just then, some of the space made available by the shared passion of our past two nights.

We walked away from the downhill finish area, her arm around my waist, as we headed for a cross-country ski trail that meandered through a stand of pine, and back toward Chalet Saléve.

"I wanted to be on Olympic team," she began, unsteadily. "To swim for France in Montreal. I was going to make it, I thought. But, the year before the Games, I came up against an East German—Kornelia, Kornelia Shöene—a beautiful girl, young, very muscular, very blond. I knew her. We smile at each other, like we are friends, you know?" Céline paused, as if seeing herself and the East German girl side-by-side on the starting blocks together. "We race three times against each other that year in European competitions and at Worlds in Bucharest. Three times she beat me...by hundredths,

hundredths, Eddie. The length of your hand, hundredths-of-seconds." She held her hand out in front of her, reaching for mine and staring at it, forcing some deep anger through it with her eyes. She clasped her fingers through mine, hard, and I felt her pain come into me.

"Three times, I came second, and we knew, all of us knew they were having the steroids, most of them. They knew that we knew, and everybody just laughed and smiled together." Her eyes were far away, and she softly sighed the girl's name again. "Kornelia, little Kornelia."

"You did go to Montreal, didn't you?" I tried to bring her back, squeezing her hand tightly, taking her in my arms.

"No. I didn't continue. I develop some injury and gave up my spot. So, you see, Eddie, my memory of being an athlete isn't like a memory at all. It's like a short, bad dream."

"Athletes are like actors, Céline. They never forget the plays, good or bad." The deep-harbored pain was releasing, I could feel her shiver.

"Neither am I a weak person, Eddie." She pushed away from me and started sputtering in French, fast and furiously. Most of it was expletive, surely, directed at the air and the ground. No standard dictionary in the known literate world contained what I was hearing.

"You okay?" I treaded softly toward her.

"Oui. Yes. *Merde alors.* I just get, *fou à lier,* you know? It hurt me so much, this thing. I have been unable to admit, to tell, how much it hurt, this thing."

The wild light in wolves' eyes fired like night tracers in her unruly gaze, and all my desire reflected brightly there. Her face was aglow, magnificent and alive, vibrant with a ferocious beauty. But I would never see Céline's face that way again.

That night, and I don't know why, I reached for the cellophane strip of candy-like dots—the LSD25. We'd embark, together, descending into an infinity uncharted. This was quite different, unpredictable and quite different every time.

I took two 200-microgram tabs and Céline followed, approximately forty-five minutes later, taking one. I also gave her two lines from Blake's *Auguries of Innocence* as an incantation, something to ease me through until I was fully shrouded in the drug's hypersensitive depths.

"You mustn't stray from this, Céline. Liney taught me this. We've helped each other before and this is very important."

"In English?" she asked. Her eyes pleaded with me.

"Yes. I think it's best. Slowly and calmly, repeat,

Hold Infinity in the palm of your hand/And Eternity in an hour.

Repeat it twice, just like that, and then say, Pass through the gate, Eddie. Gently, pass through the gate. Say nothing else, Céline, just that sequence for about ten or fifteen minutes.

I love the sound of your voice. It's the only music I'll need."

"Then, let me tell you now that I love you, Eddie. Take that dream with you and I will follow."

We held each other tightly for some minutes, until I surrendered to an uncommon relaxation in my limbs and senses. She kept my full weight between her arms and legs. Blake's words suited the otherworldly fire that both fueled and soothed a suppliant heart—a heart impoverished and anxious for the rumblings of creative disquiet.

So, I set off for the crease in the world cradled in Céline's firm embrace. Blake's gentle entreaty, borne on her trembling whispers began to filter through.

"Hold Infinity in the palm of your hand, and *Éternité* in an hour," she recited. "Pass through the gate, Eddie. Gently, pass through the gate."

Softly, the incantation resonated, and when she lay me down from her arms, I fell onto a bed of stars at the feet of my own patron saint, a smiling giant I knew to be Dionysus. Céline then became my blanket, a covering of tenderness and affection.

The acid ate through some human covering in the first clock-hours, and the basic human offerings, we plundered. We didn't know what we were seeking. Within ourselves, and in each other, a crossing of destinies was all we were aware of just then. We were on a tour through human impulse, the full spectrum.

Then I slid once again on deep purple hues and orange shafts the texture of stone. Céline's hair enveloped me and I coiled back down into her caresses. Her touch seemed eternal. And after the attending period, she too was fired in the kiln, granted a feral wisdom by the LSD — pure kindness, stunningly composed, beauty and compassion there beside me—I was permitted her.

An expanded or enlightened view of a very familiar cosmos was what I'd hoped for. The view from "a crow's eye" would expose weakness in a callous light, and that same light would illuminate any power or divinity. *A tricky place to be granted sight.*

The LSD came calling again, lifting me high above the dreamscape, one last time. Certain moments, certain intensities, touched upon violence. The trip was, in many respects, a flight, and who knew where we'd land? Some lab concoction transformed, and wherever I was going, whatever I had to see, Céline would be with me, harnessed to an unknown.

And she took me down once more, through the trees, through the flickering light of childhood fears and remembrances. Down, we went through those terrifying trees, the pulsing light, like fire from a furnace door, shining an orange light on my madness.

"No, not the stairs," I cried. "Not the banister."

The lights of the Christmas tree made magical colors on the wall opposite the stairs, through the pickets—shade and color, the bars of shadow and light. The long stairway stretched infinitely now, up from our living room, my mother stood at the bottom pleading.

"No, not the stairs, Eddie."

And in that little world revisited, there he tumbled, through the shadow and the color, through the light and dark shafts against the wall, a drunken acrobat fell on Christmas morning. Jack and I stood in our pajamas, by the tree, and watched his rolling, tumbling form strobe through the bars of our playful jail-on-the-stairs. And when he came to rest at my mother's feet, my father became my absence.

I saw it again in silence and I was the light. I was the incandescent filament, thin and ethereal, spraying tenuous particles through the white pickets over the pulsing stair—I covered my father. Then, down I plummeted through the flickering light and shadow, tumbling through the ratcheting lines, the lines covered me now in the horrid stripes that made my father like some falling zebra—brought down at my mother's feet by the bottled poachers of his own addiction. Céline was there, guiding me through the trees, through the light and dark. *How lucky we are. How goddamn lucky we are, sometimes.*

At some point in time, I ran naked from the balcony onto the snowdrift in front of Chalet Saléve, trying to extinguish some imaginary conflagration. Flailing in the snow like a hairy Yeti, I was engulfed by the LSD and was in danger. Céline, impervious to harm, rescued me from the snowy mound and brought me back inside, to our brown rug by the fire. There, the caked-on snow and my demons melted away. When shivering and memory subsided, I slept in her arms.

At dawn, I was on the empty streets of Verbier. Céline was fast asleep. The cold, fresh, morning air tingled against my skin and surrounded the sensations and thoughts I'd managed to salvage from the past ten hours. In the morning frost, I felt something quite new, a bit of optimism and belief.

Now, there was the forceful reality of a willful woman. She, too, was restored in restoring me. Whatever we had accomplished in the past three days and nights, only fear stood now in the way of what we truly wanted. The problem was not eliminating it, but transforming it. Elimination was easy, unkempt at times, like a bodily function – in transformation, worms became butterflies.

There was a grievousness and drama in my unconscious that I'd been too afraid to face for so many years, always backing down, taking refuge behind obsessions and addictions. When my father died some story died unfinished, some formation. The day was unwound by his absence. Orbits, and gravities, and movements, all found neutral in the moment just before my fall. I discovered a world within where I never knew he was, and suddenly, a continent was missing, a world lessened, a universe oddly out of balance. A comprehension of him was lost forever and I began a new clandestine search, misguided much of the time, for the meaning of his life—the man-father—in mine.

Rituals fell dormant, signs and symbols were suddenly mine alone to decipher. The squeeze-bunt, the infield-fly-rule immediately, fastidiously crystal clear, planets and constellations, the stick-shift, female anatomy, frogs and tadpoles, the moth and the flame, semen and ceremonies, all the shadows cast on men by men sliced sharp and prescient in the sudden, blinding whiteness of his death.

Suddenly, because of Céline, a celebration inside was taking place. Fireworks and Ferris Wheels lit the darkness in me, and I was ready to fly off a mountainside, a Monarch taking flight for Brazil. And Verbier was asleep. I felt like a bell ringer without a tower or a rope. I ran to the hotel and gathered my ski gear, then to the parking lot for P.A.'s little red Fiat—keys in the gas-tank door—he never failed. Swiss, go figure.

The frost underfoot crackled, the hollow morning drafts coaxed another memory and I stopped to think of the many instances when I'd walked these snowy little alleyways at odd times just to have a few hours away from Newell, to think on my shame, and review the ruinous life I'd led with her. Why did I drag others down with me? Why did I hurt them? Why Newie? She loved me, began a family with me. How many other lives were hurt?

As I drove down the mountain, through the "S" turns, I couldn't get the years with Newell out of my mind. And what of the life we'd built together? Was there no value in that effort? Our marriage was not made in hell, after all. I just took it there for regular visits.

chapter Eleven
THE ADAM CAGE

"Oh, you bastard. You bastard, you."

Words widened the distance between us one last time, they deepened the bitterness. The words echoed. The rage branded its mark in my memory. A clarification of humiliation, a wife's position defiled by flirtation, witchery, and seduction. The female's private rite with her male debased by what seemed like an army of her own gender. The adulterous husband, bewitched, seduced, serviced. A tempest of howling, *de profundis*, of wailing agony and anger, resonated through our apartment on Manhattan's Upper West Side.

It all sounded so Greek to me, so breast-beatingly sanctimonious. I could say that now, looking back over a trail of emotional debris. Given some distance from the pain I caused Newell, some distance from my own self-destructive past, it was easy to be glib about the hurt.

I'd heard it said in Parochial school, that Adam took a bite out of temptation and the serpents forever lost their legs, condemned to slither and slide as snakes for an eternity. At age ten, Sister Agnes Martin introduced me to a very real depression. The nuns at St. Anthony's were loath to indict, especially Adam, but there it was.

I remembered going to the reptile house at the Nayaug Park Zoo, faithfully on Saturdays, for months afterward just to sit and console the poor bastards. Silent, motionless for hours they'd lie, and I stared, watching their slivered, oval eyes for some twinge of persecution. Nothing came from their unmoving gaze. The limbless serpent (suborder Ophidia), its suffering continued — long after publication of the Bible I might add — wriggled along on scales, still without so much as a hint of appendages while we, in the lineage of Adam, embraced temptation with our two arms wide, and walked tall on three legs.

I still didn't get the joke.

Blessed or cursed with this basket of fruit between our two hind limbs — The Wild Bunch — the divining rod we waggled led us, usually, head and heart in-hand to the font of our masculinity, to the dark well of the historical male imbroglio. Sex was a sort of proving ground for Adams and a woman had the test track right between her legs—something like that. So, we slithered like snakes through the darkness, our trespass there, we imagined, our divine duty.

On Monday nights, it was Susan Littleton's apartment on East Eighty-Second. On the pretext of watching Monday Night Football with a friend, by seven-thirty my pre-game had already begun. If my team could cover the spread on Monday nights as well as Susan and I, the NFL would have been X-Rated.

Men often described women in bed as "banquets" or "feasts." In the spirit of that description, and those women, Susan Littleton was then a smorgasbord, a veritable buffet of sexual delight and innovation. Spontaneous and daring from our first encounter alone in an elevator, it was simply a matter of a few cups of coffee together, and a very short fuse was lit that ultimately reached a powder keg of romping, sexual dalliance.

Was it the sudden status of marriage that made me run for other playing fields? I don't know. Some men claimed that any binding situation was, in itself, the cause for their un-binding, extramarital sport. I can't speak for some men. In my case, status didn't matter.

Adventure was the heading for this affair. Anything and everything was on the table with Susan—including Susan—at least, for the length of the football season. Within a matter of a few weeks, however, it was time for league expansion. An appetite like Susan's could only grow. I didn't know it then, but so would mine. Her forte was variety, her hidden passion, geography.

Susan met me, albeit summoned me, just about anywhere on a moment's notice—empty offices, stairwells, airports, rented cars, movie theaters, and of course, the top of the Empire State Building. East Hampton beach houses, closed for the season, were choice meeting places. Susan's roommate was a real estate agent, kept keys to some of the most incredible mansions on Long Island. Susan and I desecrated most every stately room in those homes. High-flying, sexual intrigue with Susan Littleton was a decathlon of sorts. All I needed was the stamina and a map.

We tested our nerve nearly everywhere in the Greater New York metropolitan area, fulfilling benign sexual fantasies and creating a few new ones. Susan loved the danger. At times, she scared the hell out of me.

When my son was just an infant, I stayed home babysitting often while Newell shopped or went to some movie that I cared little about. Newie was a movie maven, much more so than I. She saw everything, with a friend, or more often alone. Perhaps it was a self-preserving respite from me she sought in those dark theaters. Maybe she knew everything all along. Women had a way of knowing such things, they just did. Sung like a Bacchae chorus, the ancient tune of men's actions in other nests echoed down through the aeons, but I paid little attention to Newie's private cathexis.

One evening, while little Michael slept, Susan Littleton appeared at my door delivering a pizza, dressed in a trenchcoat. In the box, a pizza with pepperoni and cheese, under the trench, Susan had no topping at all, not a stitch. A mixture of sex and fright was intoxicating, and habit-forming. Susan knew it all too well, she thrived on it. And I was as easy as pie.

Before long, the affair transformed. Lovemaking became an event, a contest, to arouse and tempt and court the danger, and at some point it lost all intimacy and fun. The pleasure we had derived from spontaneity and daring — and pleasure was the goal at first — became anti-climactic. The lust we craved was suddenly secondary to the logistics, or the convolutions, of something risky. The illicit, the adulterous trick, had become the primary inducement for the sybaritic cornucopia Susan and I fed from.

The patterns of the sexually addicted were remarkably simple. Actions were rooted in avarice and gratification, ours and the partner's we showered with so much attention. There seemed to be a great wide current of people with impaired souls, marred in a most infantile way searching for affection and approval. I tapped into this broad current, the swift, strong flow was a river of spawning pleasure for the skillful fisherman.

The ease of it all jolted me. Within minutes of meeting some woman, the contract, the promise of some future locking was signed and sealed. We knew each other like members of some secret lodge with some goofy sign or silly handshake. Some posture on a barstool, two sensuous, smooth knees weakly, gently falling apart, or a hand coming across the candlelit white tablecloth covering yours, or beneath the table the long manicured nails and strong fingers clamping your leg like a visegrip, moving firmly, determinedly, along your inner thigh up into your groin sending an unmistakable message, grasping, a hand of naked greed, gripping, fondling and turning the fresh earth of your need. In the benign frenzy, you push words into your looks, the covenant into your eyes, "Yes, when? Where? I'm just like you, tell me when."

I had entered into a circus troupe for infidels, and New York was the Big Top. And like the pachyderms in any big show who grasp for guidance at each other's tails to form an unbroken chain, I was agreeably connected, nose to tail, in an unbroken line of some wretched herd.

I'd visit a coffee shop on Seventh Avenue, New York's

Fashion District, in the morning, or stop-in to one of hundreds of side-street cocktail lounges at Happy Hour. I met many-an attractive buyer, or an up-and-coming young designer, that way and sealed a pact within an hour or two for some convenient fun. The Fashion District was an expedient well of talent I drew from often. They were a fun-oriented crowd that liked their action fast and uncomplicated. I was rapidly approaching warp-speed with my drug use and playing around, the ladies I met from Seventh Avenue seemed to live at that pace.

Men and women players alike avoided the women's movement condemnation of sexual exploitation. We were too mired in the addictive need to pay much attention to the changing body politic. We took the shortest path to sexual conquest, to our fix. We had to accomplish it, that was all—morality and any social context be damned.

The conquest was somehow interpreted as a rite of male existence, it was our task. We saw ourselves as that special, large-brained creature who spent much of his life on all-fours leaving five tracks in the sands of sexual history. So many women, so little time, the saying goes.

Woven through and around the logistics of screwball antics with someone like Susan Littleton, or bedhopping with the Fast'n' Fashionable, there was little time to waste for finding others—yes, others. There was no calculable saturation point, an obsession wanted only for opportunity. Agreement seen to, it was simply a matter of where and when. Less may be more to great architects, but more was simply, and necessarily, better for the hopelessly addicted.

An actress friend read me like an open script. She cautioned me one day,

"Good actors never lose themselves in their roles, Eddie," she said. "When they exit around a curtain or through a door, they think about their next costume change, their hair, their lines, or their next entrance."

Normal concerns, I thought. She told me I was "losing"

myself in the role, that I was "dangerous," and that someday soon I'd look in a mirror and see nothing, a real image, a soul, a value, anything truthful, would be invisible. Like the fool, I paid no attention to her. It was easier then just to avoid the actresses.

Most Wednesdays I met Ginette, a dancer-choreographer, for lunch at a favorite midtown *brasserie*. I tried to keep it friendly, confiding, Platonic, but it soon turned amorous and uncontrollably physical. Ginette introduced me to my codependent self. I remain indebted to her for that brief reflection.

"Let's make a deal, okay? I'll stop faking orgasm if you'll stop trying so goddamn hard to make me have it."

"But, Ginette?" I said. "I want to please you."

"Who died and appointed you Chief Fuck? Is that what you do with everybody? Is that what you see yourself as?"

"Well, yeah."

"I don't need to make love to an action hero, thank-you-very-much. You know, Eddie, everything was kind of nice. You're very tender, we were having some fun. I thought maybe I could go for a guy like you. But I haven't come across one yet."

"What are you talking about, Ginette? You know me."

"I don't know you...at all. And you don't know you. You're on the dark side of it, Eddie, the underside. You can't see it. You're going to screw me until I say uncle, aren't you? Or, until I say, I love you." She looked at me forlornly and I felt like a puppy who'd missed the newspaper, squatting before his master. "I don't know you at all, Eddie. I liked you better when we just had lunch. I kind of loved you then."

I lost more than a lunch and matinee partner that day, I lost a good friend. Ginette's sounds, her words, went through me. That should have been a sign that I was, in fact, becoming hollow. I thought about her sorrowfully, then looked for another friend to fill the emptiness. I had an opening on Wednesdays.

~

When Sophie was born, we realized we had to have a larger apartment. The initial search fell to me—weed out the "no-sees" and then bring Newie for a second look at the "go-sees." I went to a high profile real estate agency to save some time. They sent me out with an attractive, young, female agent named, Carmen.

On our third day of trekking Manhattan neighborhoods together, Carmen showed me a bright, two-bedroom up on West End—old, pre-War building, high ceilings, oak floors, river view, available in a month. It was empty. In a huge living room, with WBF (wood burning fireplace), and southern exposure, stood a six-foot stepladder and a painter's drop-cloth draped, haphazardly, over it. Surreal looking objects in the stark white room. Carmen leaning against a bleached wall looked like a wildly-sultry Caribbean watercolor.

"What do you think?" She asked, her dark, scabrous voice resonant in the hollow room. I stared at her for what seemed like minutes extended, stretched in the silence.

"The drop cloth is fine," I said. "The ladder...? Could be interesting. Difficult, but interesting."

I kissed her heavily, pinning her against the white wall. She returned the overture, enthusiastically. We attacked and gnawed at each other's mouths like animals who hadn't eaten for weeks. Rutting passion came into season with a fury that day for our species. Her body heat enveloped all professional restraint. A violent additive raced through our veins, hers as strong as mine.

"I knew you were trouble the minute you walked in the office," she said, panting, shimmying up my right leg with vice-like thighs. In seconds I managed her tight skirt up around her waist. My hand warmed and soaked between her legs.

"No trouble, chica, no trouble at all."

We tore at each other's clothes. She grabbed my hair tightly in both her hands after a few seconds and our sucking kisses stopped, the two of us breathing in each other's faces like salivating dogs. Her eyes were ablaze and intense.

"Men like you… in the heart, no trouble. In the pants? *Si. Apuro.* Much trouble."

"*Muchas gracias*, Carmen. This is a distinction I will remember always. Speaking of pants, chica…"

Her thin panties imploded in my fist, the elastic snapping easily and gathering in the force of my grasp, and they were gone in a flash. She lifted. Her eyes brightened.

"So, now, you're going to fuck me out of my commission, right?" she said.

The warm real estate that defined my being, I held in one hand. With the other, I fumbled to free the instrument with which I closed the deal—almost every time. *We are who we are.*

I took the apartment, bought it. Carmen got her commission, something that amounted to a little more than a month's mortgage payment. I got the key a week later, and for the next two weeks it remained empty, occupied only every afternoon from three to four-thirty by Carmen and me. I bought two more drop-cloths, and the ladder was interesting. Difficult, but interesting.

The Sixties extolled "free love" as counter-culturally virtuous. Behavior like mine was a hangover from that time, slightly modified, perhaps, and bereft of any virtue, freedom, or more apparently, love. Physically, I somehow managed to stay free of sexually transmitted diseases during it all — luck, pure luck interpreted, by me, as vindication, or some special dispensation.

I steered clear of dangerous encounters, no big boyfriends, no violent husbands. I took a long, cold look at my affliction after Ginette and Carmen — not long enough, not cold enough — and geared-down the pace of my pursuits.

A textbook term like "love addiction" was blatantly fraudulent. Romance addiction — another popular term in *nouvelle* psychotherapy—sounded apropos for high school juniors and seniors, but it clouded the actual driving purpose of men and women seeking a satisfaction that only came with a concomitance of flesh and sultry fulfillment. The heart was kept at-bay. A sex addict had a blind, driving need. All the frilly psychobabble in the current mainstream was a crutch. Nothing could unravel the mystery that I was hopelessly enthralled by a single, triumphant moment of sexual intimacy. It was my own narrow sacrosanctity, my manhood fulfilling a singular purpose.

I never denied the allure of love and romance, but candlelight dinners, bejeweled mementos, and walks in the park went out of fashion somewhere in the mid-70's. And the idea of the classic mistress simply didn't work on the tight budget of a struggling writer. Dark dens and secrecy—and the widespread acceptance of drugs—hid the rampant fraudulence of what men and women did together. The criteria had changed, morality and rules were out the window. It might have been love, could have been romance, but if I got home in less than fifteen minutes, for under ten dollars in cab fare, it was definitely perfect.

In the summer of '78, we took a house in Amagansett for July and August and we hired an *au pair* girl, a foreign exchange student from Belgium. Anja Severin was nineteen, slender and beautiful, blond, blue-eyed, drippingly sensual, and precocious. I immediately adopted her as my teenage daughter, welding that thought in my brain, emphasizing for myself the parent-adolescent distance and boundaries—a serious effort on my part to regulate my libido. In exchange for a brush-up course in French, I would tutor her in proper English usage. American slang, expletives, and bad habits were thrown-in as bonuses, a trade for the latest French insults and colloquial damnations. She was a good sport and the arrangement got-off to a pleasant start.

Anja was typically European, well-mannered, unabashedly affectionate, and she expressed a certain freedom and presence with her body that was very alluring and overtly sexual, yet innocent at the same time. Newie and I both noticed it, we thought it quite charming.

Anja and I explored eastern Long Island, did the grocery shopping together, and went to the beach daily with the children. Newell had taken a part-time job with a commercial film producer that summer. She was in New York three and sometimes four days a week. I made the train trek twice, reluctantly, every third week. Everything was going along swimmingly that July in the Hamptons. I felt quite comfortable, in paternal balance, handling my three charges while Newell toiled in the torrid city.

Anja met a strapping, young beach bum the first week she arrived — a sophomore from some Midwest university — kept their rendezvous a secret for several days, then brought him back to the house one evening where they "played" very physically out on the deck overlooking the ocean. Everything they did was physical. She 19, he 21, their hormones were at 212 Fahrenheit that summer. They were out of their minds for sex, I was sure, and I was completely unprepared for my response to her interest in the boy.

In the days that followed, Buckeye Bobby seemed ever-present. He met us at our little, yellow beach encampment, would pop out of the aisles at the supermarket, or the post office, or the snack bar at East Hampton Beach, put his arm around Anja, copping a feel here and there — a true-blooded American collegian. He was very out-going, very smiley, with white, straight teeth. Called me, "sir." His infatuation with Anja was intentionally overblown, I thought, he laid it on heavily just to piss me off. He exploited her European-ness, that bubbling, playful innocence and sensuality. She laughed incessantly at his insipid jokes and pratfalls. His antics dissipated some of his own rampant sexual energy, no doubt. I knew the feeling. She radiated in his fawning attention — a radiance that, suddenly, I couldn't avoid. Everything about her changed in some way.

(Correction) Everything about my perception of her

changed. Was I just being fatherly? Wasn't this the way fathers thought and behaved when their daughters took the flattery of other men? *Sure, that must be what it is.*

Bobby-beach-bum hovered over Anja. My patience grew thin. I wasn't sure why. Then one day it came to the surface, unaccountably.

"Monsieur Edwar,...?" she pleaded, in very coquettish, soft tones. "I have a feeling Monsieur Edwar does not like Bobby, my friend. I sense this when he is with me, correct?"

I never looked at her. We were preparing dinner, cutting and chopping an assortment of salad vegetables and fruits, spread all over the counter tops and in front of us on the butcher-block island in the center of the kitchen. Head down, I continued dicing and slicing, with enthusiasm.

"Somewhat correct," I said, my invented paternity shredding with every stroke.

"You don't like him, then?" She pressed me.

"No, I don't like him, Anja. I hate him."

The words came forth concisely with no apology attached, peeled clean, julienned by the sharp edges of my unexpurgated envy. The words surprised the hell out of me, the superlative of the remark. We stood silently, knives-in-hand, looking at each other across the green, garden array. All food preparation stopped, abruptly. Our thoughts stood naked for the first time, an open knowledge had stripped them of some protective leaf of ignorance, or propriety. A recognition of possibility flashed between us like heat lightening across a dark summer sky.

Some woman, unseen before, throbbed now within Anja. That laughing, innocent teenage protégé of mine stood pulsating with a rhythm, a beating of animal passion. She read my eyes, my body language, without fear or confusion. She knew, in an instant, that the issue of the boy was irrelevant. It was me, alone, lupine and making claim, alpha-marking the ground, the perimeter, with my scent. The unspeakable had been spoken, the original sin of jealousy exposed. A snake in a tree had taken Anja's attention away from me and I couldn't stand for it.

My barrier between father and lover came down and my all-consuming desire was now blatant. It hung like succulent fruit there in the heavy, humid air of July. Our garden, that kitchen, that afternoon became a field of early harvest. I took Anja's ripened offerings and left for stalks on the makeshift earth, my semen and my sweat.

We went on this way — for each other, by each other, of each other — the remainder of the summer. Anja became possessive and tireless, her youth and stamina exhausted me. She was like a nymph who had come to me from the green sea off Long Island. And like the dreamy sailor caught in her spell, I languished the long days in Amagansett bewitched by her charm and adoring compliance to my wishes. She dismissed the disappointed beach boy in a day and enslaved herself to me, literally. Or was it I who had become hers, a Humbert-Humbert obsessively drawn into the wellspring of this young girl's nascent and available sexuality?

It was the most active summer of my life. Newie was particularly "spunky" also, sexually speaking, her spirits buoyed by working in a creative endeavor again. Spiritually and physically, I was being siphoned-off by my wife and my *au pair* girl. At times, I felt like a doctor making rounds, when clearly I should have been the patient.

I had degenerated almost completely. Keeping-up a façade, running along a thin line of madness, seemed to take all the strength of a full-time job. Socially, I became suspicious of everyone. The slightest remark by friends about "that gorgeous *au pair* of yours" set me off like a cherry bomb. I felt like a highway billboard of guilt and paranoia. My writing output was next-to-nothing. What little there was, was trash, comic book, formulaic, and completely unimaginative—that, the writing, was the purpose of my summer off in the Hamptons. One passion suffered while another flourished. *Get a grip.*

Back-to-School spelled a kind of relief for me that September, as it never had in years before. Anja went off to Georgetown University in Washington. She wrote to us and sent the occasional snapshot. She would mention young men she'd met in her letters, but the photographs were always singular portraits, just Anja—a beautiful, smiling Anja—an angel amid the fall foliage along the Potomac. Each photo punctured me just a little, sending an oppressive pain of longing sharply through me. The photos brought back heavy thoughts of the sweltering, intemperate days and her supple, young body, its power over me, and of my captivated and corrupted soul impaled that July and August on a dagger unsheathed by my own will and uncontrollable addiction.

Later that fall, Nicky Agalias came to the city on business. Our reunions were usually the happiest occasions—dinners, Broadway plays, games at the Garden, nightclubs, whatever Nicky's imagination could dream-up on his flight in from Pittsburgh. New York was then a town for dreams and imagination.

On his first night in the city, we had dinner at Stavros, a favorite Greek restaurant of ours on the Lower East Side. Nick and I found the place together one Christmas break in our Junior year. By eleven that evening, we were piss-drunk. It was the kind of piss-drunk where certain perceptions, certain admissions, seemed to surface with a truth that was a hundred-proof.

"You just drag me here so you can dance with me," I said.

"Your ass is grass, that's bullshit," he stammered.

"Yeah, yeah, yeah you goddamn Greeks just want to dance around with other guys, I know."

"As a matter of fact, you're not a bad dancer for a Vowel...much as I hate to admit it, you bastard."

"Listen, if it wasn't for the Italians, the Greeks..."

"Oh, Jesus. Jesus no. Please, Eddie, not that Greeks and Italians shit again?"

"Okay, Homer, I'll save the next dance for you."

This went on for hours whenever Nicky and I got together at any of our numerous watering holes and downtown clubs. But at Stavros, our rituals took on added Mediterranean enthusiasm. Efthekios, the bartender, the waiters, busboys, and owners were all willing accomplices to our inglorious behavior. The Ouzo poured freely slowing our minds to a crawl, while the endless black, Greek coffee revved us out onto the dance floor all night long. It was just like being in a New York traffic jam, speed-up, slow down, zip-zap.

Nicky knew what I had been up to. He knew what I was doing to Newell, and the insane rabbit-run of my extramarital triple life. He had been silent all evening, never approached the subject. Nicky cared for us both. He was Michael's *compare*. At one point, sweaty and gased after dancing a fast *zebekiko*, we went into the men's room together and snapped down two full grams each. The traffic jam suddenly hit a blizzard, a white-out.

"Eddie, listen to me," he said, pinning me to the wall. "You're standing there, right in front of me. I mean, I see you standing there, you know? But, you're moving, Famous. You're moving, man, faster than I've ever seen you move."

"Nicky, who loves you, babe? Don't do this to me," I cajoled.

"No. No Shit, Eddie. Hey, this is Nick here, you know? This is Aristippus Nicholas Agalias you're talking to, goddamn it. I've seen you move, man. Eddie Genell off-tackle, Eddie Genell on a sweep, Eddie on a post-pattern. The last great, white halfback streaking down the sideline, moving like a fucking blur, man, afterburners going like a vapor trail." He gave me a little slap on the cheek. "But, it's like standing still, compared to how fast you're moving now, Famous." I thought he was going to really hit me, but he just leaned in, his forehead crashing into mine. "You've got to stop, Eddie. Get help. You've got to stop doing this."

Through the fog of the booze and drugs, the white tile and the white porcelain sinks and toilets seemed to grow out of the walls and floor, all smooth and shiny. They looked like snow drifts. It was Nicky and me all over again, like being back in Ann Arbor, stuck, standing there in the snowdrifts again. The icy wind of the cocaine was cutting through my sinuses now, searing my face and head like frostbite.

"Here we are in the dumper again, Nick. Back with the terlets and stinks. Jesus, you know how much tile we've seen in our lifetime? No, I mean, think of all the showers and locker rooms, and..."

"Eddie, come on."

"No, no shit. I mean, suppose they find that tile causes cancer in rats, or something? We're screwed, you know? We're fucked. Think about all the guys who went to the pros? Jesus."

Nicky had his arms around me now, from behind. He was holding me up like a rag doll under my arms, leaning against the mirrored wall, next to the blower-hand-dryer thing.

"Christ, Nicky, this place is white," I said. "You got any sunglasses?"

"Sure, Eddie. But first, you've got to take the blinders off."

"Heyyy, good one, Nick, very good. You remember when we used to talk about going to Vietnam, like if we got drafted and all that? And we'd be over there, you know, shoot-em-up and if one of us..."

"Shut-up, Famous. I don't want to talk about this." Nicky threw me aside and walked away, down along a line of sinks and mirrors.

"Naw, come on. Remember? If one of us got a leg blown off, or something, or, our nuts shot off? Remember what we promised? Do you remember what we said, Nick? What we promised?"

"Yes. Goddammit. Fuck you, Eddie."

"Nick? Just one, please? All it takes, Nick, Ari, Pussy? Right between the eyes, babe, right on top of this big, Roman schnozz here, Nick."

"Straighten up, Eddie. Straighten-the-fuck-up," he yelled.

"You promised." I pleaded like a child, a child on Lithium.

"We were kids, goddammit. Big. Kids."

"You promised, Nick."

"That was a war."

"This ain't?"

"Grow up, Eddie."

"Okay...like, when?"

"Between here and West 83rd Street, you son-of-a-bitch. Now."

"Jezz, that's...okay, okay." Nicky started walking toward the door. "Nick, Nick, you should of seen the *au pair* girl we had this summer, Belgian. You know, *au pair*, oh, peach, oh, melons?"

He walked out of the bathroom, back into the restaurant, never looking back at me. The door hung there for a moment, then began to close slowly on one of those pump things.

"Hey, Nick," I yelled. "We'll get a cab uptown."

The door closed with a soft thud and I stood still for a moment, alone in a plaintive echo.

There I was. Modern man. Post-War man, man-for-the-last-half-of-the-20th century. No Audie Murphy, Audie was gone, and not even necessary. Heroics, all gone. The enemies were all internal now. Where the hell was Knute Rockne, Bob Mitchum when you need them? Burt Lancaster? Gary Cooper? Victor Mature? Pat O'Brien? Where was the priest, or the coach, with that last bit of fire before sending the boys, the men, off to battle?

We hit a traffic jam on the cab ride uptown, zip-zap.

Nicky made me promise, I'd see someone, try to get some help, or, at least, talk with Newell and let the chips fall. She would help me, he said, she'd never abandon me. Of course, I promised him. Of course, I was wrecked that night and the promise was just another lie. I didn't go to see anyone. The "last great, white halfback?"

Are you kidding?

I stopped using, somewhat. I went home to Newell and the kids almost every night, stopped bar-hopping, stopped the lunches with women associates—the works. I quit freelancing, too. I met too many new opportunities that way.

A big publishing house offered me a staff position and I took it. For a while, I was getting miserably clean. Newie couldn't understand why I was home so much. She teased me about my new domesticity.

"Why did you marry me, Eddie?"

"I fell in love with you, Newell. We were in love. Marriage was love's status—once upon a time."

"But you belong, Eddie. You do belong, you know, somewhere else, somewhere out there in the dark."

"Don't make me out as some kind of vampire, Newie."

"I mean it in a most flattering way, Eddie, in a poetic way, really. I mean in the dark of the heavens, among stars and moons and goddesses. You're in a darkness between heaven and earth, darling, between my earthly love for you and that ethereal river of sex and playful, hallucinogenic sensuality. You would have been perfect in the mythological world."

"My very existence hurts you doesn't it, Newell? I'm not..."

"Hurt?" She exclaimed with exaggerated surprise. "What a strange word, Eddie...what a strange, odd, word. Much too simple and pedestrian for a writer of your ascending scholarship and ambition." She smiled to herself for being so accurate and discriminating with me. She chuckled softly like an infallible goddess in a Greek play.

"We've loved each other, darling, you said so yourself. Love, Eddie?...that is something so much more severe, so much more permanent than hurt...so much more destructive."

She stared directly at me, sweetly distant now, unreachable in her own exactitude. I fought the impulse to answer. The words would be pedestrian, as she'd said. Her laughter and jibes were bittersweet and close-to-the-bone, but still, I never opened-up, never came fully clean. Having me home nights was my big concession, my show of some reform. Newell would have to be satisfied with that. Deep-digging analysis was not part of my offering.

We went on this way—months, a year, a year and a bit, and then another year—with the kind of good, surface behavior I thought deserved some sort of medal for decency (more pedestrian nomenclature). There was no decency in my marriage, courtesy at a base level, but no decency. I thought the rules came from some universal governing body. I had committed war crimes and I was making reparation voluntarily, the record of my stalwart amends would be kept in Geneva, or The Hague, someplace weighty like that. I was flying, man, I was doing great. The sprinting halfback was in the open-field, nothing could stop me, but me. I went for weeks, sometimes a month or two, on good behavior, then rewarded myself with a little affair. A one-night-stand in another city, a flirtation, a shower of adoration and attention upon some receptive female just to test, just to see if I were still desirable, still pliable, still sure-footed and in control. I told myself I'd earned that type of digression. Venial sins, everybody had those. You just forgave yourself, a short act-of-contrition, you know, for spiritual upkeep, and you were right back to good sane behavior in no time. *Give him a bone.*

How did a self-curing addict reward himself?

With delusion.

I had an office at Chapman Publications, my first real position in publishing. I was writing travel. They gave me an editorial assistant, placed her at a desk right outside my door. Reward had arrived. Arrived? It was delivered to the damn doorstep.

Karin Scott was twenty-two, very bright, very stately and statuesque, a competent, cum laude-intelligent beauty. She was there with coffee, little sweet surprises, and brilliant new ideas for our stories every morning and we got along famously. We laughed and joked and, I dare say, our end of the floor was the most productive, Karin and I, the most laid-back and mirthful. We had an afternoon tea break together and talked about everything, mostly personal chatter, journalism, books, music, and such.

The tea break changed unexpectedly one day. Karin showed me a little tin-foiled gram-and-a-half of cocaine, waved it at me and waited for my approval. I gave it, and before long, it was tea and cocaine every afternoon, and I was giving her money to keep the supply steady, to keep her stores at a minimum gram-and-a-half to three grams per day.

We were ravenous together, and teatime became the highlight of our days. Within a few weeks, a very savage lust grew between us, too. It happened fast and just as fast we quenched each other's thirst for exceptional sexual contact. Behind the closed door of my office, the perversity of our behavior was spinning wildly out of control, our acts bordered on an aberrant lunacy. With our tongues saturated in cocaine, we would numb each other's organs in frost-bitten frenzy and delight—in every corner of my office, on every surface of furniture and floor, in every possible permutation of male and female inter-connectedness. We became so enamored of each other and so proficient at this type of sexuality, often times one of us would perform orally while the other conducted business on the phone.

The afternoons became precursors for the early evening hours. Karin left the office first and then, soon after, I'd taxi to her apartment and we continued right where we'd left-off in the office. *So much for venial digressions.*

The nature of our sexual fulfillments and experimentation

grew darker and darker, fueled by imaginations warped in a fast- growing array of drugs. The depravity that Karin and I were enmeshed-in became worrisome to both of us and a debilitating satyriasis eventually sent me searching for yet another woman.

Her name was Ilene Polokof, a psychiatrist, and I made my first frantic call to her while my cocaine-laden index finger was inserted, locked-to-the-knuckle, inside Karin Scott's rectum.

"Beam me up, Scotti."

"What?" Dr. Polokof whispered, incredulously.

"It was just a little joke of ours, nothing...."

"Go on, Mr. Genell. I'm listening...intently."

And I went-on for nineteen weeks, and Ilene — I dropped the "Doctor Polokof" at Week Three — listened and tape recorded, twice weekly, every sordid detail of my life that I could spew forth in fifty-five minute intervals. She was a haltingly beautiful woman with shining blond-frosted hair and soft blue eyes that always seemed on the verge of tears—empathetic—good for business I supposed. She spoke softly to me, but not often, from a comfortable this-was-my-daddy's armchair. I sat and talked sporadically, self-consciously at first, from a leather recliner. I liked her immediately, and she had my trust after the first few visits. Then, I wouldn't shut up. There was a long, leather couch in the room but I preferred to sit. So much of the story I told in those sessions took place at an Angle of Repose, I thought perhaps a new perspective would help. The air was fresh and filtered. The room was dark with only a floor lamp, at a low setting, beside Ilene. The lamp lit her most flatteringly. She was trim, very shapely and athletic looking with smooth, toned skin and sensuous musculature, and expressive, strong hands.

Shadowy action photos of lacrosse play hung by the bookcases. Dimly lit diplomas from Trinity College and the University of Pennsylvania hung behind her desk along with other citatiae that I couldn't see well enough to read. She didn't smoke cigarettes, and discouraged any intrusive habits like gum chewing, candy lozenges, or any pacifier to distract from the business at-hand. She offered me a fruit drink each week before we began, and each week I declined. Music, however, was conducive for some patients. I could have had music if I wished, but I declined again. Why score the misery? "Auntie Mame" was a great musical. Fuck the overture, and let's get on with the show, I figured.

Weeks Two & Three, I filled four tapes with Newell. Newie before, Newell after we wed.

Week Four, My son. My father.

Week Five, My daughter. My struggle with the sickness gods.

Week Six, The Doe. A woman named, Donna. Rough session. Deep, hurtful memory. Blind storage. Ilene dropped the Mr. Genell, for the less formal, yet professional, "Edward."

Week Seven, The college years. Patterns begin. "Women, women everywhere." A passionate cheerleader. Broken promises. Drugs. The "Edward" was dropped for the familiar, "Eddie."

Week Eight, First session, Ilene wore tight-fitting blue jeans, drank fruit juice, brightened the floor lamp beside her by one setting. Second session that week, I didn't remember.

Week Nine, First session, She wore a skirt for the first time, sat atop the desk from minute twenty-three to minute forty-one swinging a handsome leg back-and-forth as she listened, just kicking it out from the desk. I made mental note of the leg, a muscular calf, and petit, adorable feet. I was ill, I wasn't dead.

Second session, we talked about sexual perception, parents to parenthood—I was like a guest on a Talk Show.

Weeks Ten & Eleven, The Affairs. A compendium of stories that appeared to sketch rather accurately my life's work, more or less. The free-associative Decameron was a rambling account of how an intelligent, well-educated male had subordinated ambition, inspiration, initiative, a work ethic, trust, truth, value, morality, nearly everything worthwhile in life, all for the touch and repetitive adoration of women—a supplicant at the carnal altar—and for making that kind of intimacy, time and time again, an end in itself.

Week Twelve, we swapped stories of first love. It was a remarkable turning point, I thought. But then again, I wasn't the psychotherapist. The atmosphere changed, of that I was sure. I made her laugh, often. A beautiful laugh. I caught her by surprise with the story of the snakes at the Nayaug Park Zoo, and a tiny trickle of fruit juice shot through one of her nostrils when she broke-up with laughter. The kind of thing you couldn't forget when it happened to an unfathomable blond beauty like Ilene Polokof.

The transcriptions of those sessions edited most of Ilene's laughter, they left out all of the tears.

ISPOLOKOF, File, Genell-MC,Tape#23 [EG VOICE] (tape start up) "Luckily, the guilt doesn't last very long. Before you know it, you're in your prime, thirteen, weeks away from fourteen. There's hair growin' all over you, your voice is going nuts, and all you think about, awake and asleep, are legs and asses and breasts. Everywhere you look women are arousing you, the specter of female sexuality looms perpetually in your disturbed consciousness…billboards, mannequins, underwear ads, movies, magazines, tight sweaters and budding bosoms, your brother's girlfriends, your cousins, your aunts, almost every older woman, even National Geographic. My brother Jack and his buddies would have parties in our basement and I'd sit on the stairs and watch the girls dance. His girlfriends—17, 18-years-old, bubbling over with sex—they teased me sometimes, playfully taunting in some suggestive way. Little did they know, I could have licked them all like candied apples, right there on the cellar floor.

The suffering builds, you know, Doc? It builds fast when you're thirteen and you think you're going to strangle if something doesn't happen for you soon.

Television hit me hard. Nature shows were out. There was an immediate and natural urgency in my own body now that needed attention. Suddenly, I was flicking through the dial just to find the women...the teenage women, the older women, it didn't matter, Bandstand, Dobie Gillis, The Mickey Mouse Club, Loretta Young, Miss Kitty in her lacey corsets, Donna Reed, Lawrence Welk. No joke. I watched the youngest Lennon Sister sprout breasts right on TV. [Polokof inaudible] I didn't give a damn. Television was an undecipherable scientific phenomenon—still don't understand it—the women on it were miraculous visions.

It was the shape of things that I was after, Doc, the landscape of the female body, the true curvature of the earth. I hungered to see it day and night. I didn't give a shit about David or Ozzie or Harriet. I just wanted to see who Ricky was bringing home. Ricky was the one getting it. A year earlier, I thought "The Jackie Gleason Show" was funny, now I just tuned-in to see The June Taylor Dancers, all those legs, and busts, those incredibly smooth thighs all in a row, rows of beautiful women kicking those long legs and smiling at me."

[POLOKOF VOICE] "Everyone has obsessions at that stage of adolescence, Eddie. [giggle] I remember, I was, I can't [inaudible]—the year in the Sixties, it was when the Beatles first came here, remember? We were crazy, girls were, after that first tour they made. I bought life-size posters, black and white, I think, of Paul and Ringo—never forget it. And I'd pasted them onto the wall and the door of my room...Paul was on the back of the door. And every morning, on my way out to go to school, I'd kiss Paul right on the lips, several times. I was crazy. We were all crazy, obsessed, for God's sake. I mean [inaudible]...kissing that picture of Paul McCartney every morning." [giggles]

[PAUSE IN TAPE] [LAUGHTER SND.OVERLAP].

[EG VOICE] "Jesus. That's really...that's interesting, you know? I had this picture, this poster, life size, on the back of my door. My brother Frank gave it to me...of Rita Hayworth. Unbelievable. Beautiful, you know? What a goddess. [inaudible] She was a woman you could dream about, I mean dream. And anyway, every morning, on my way out...to school, I'd kiss this poster of Rita Hayworth, you know? Once on each breast. [PAUSE IN TAPE].

And then, anyway there were the girls at my school, St. Anthony's, my female classmates. Little potential Rita's.[laughter] Same sex, hard to believe. They were warthogs, most, some looked like frogs. We called them everything under the sun and, up until then, we had avoided them. Suddenly, a few appeared to me like rare amphibians emerging from the waters, coming ashore, incandescent and lovely to watch in the new light of womanhood. They were exciting. Something was happening to them. Their new contours made wonderful shadows and curves and elevations in the light. Their clothing bulged now in different places...made me stare, made me want to touch. Unnoticed and ignored for so long as bothersome toads, there came little women. It was a divine revelation. On the surface it seemed as though some June Taylor Dancer was locked underneath, pushing, struggling, stretching the blue and green scotch plaid uniforms, trying to burst free.

It was time, Ilene. My body was telling me, it was time. By some quirk of nature, my ears were able to hear the secret croaking of slender, wet frogs. Perhaps they too had some urgent need. It was time for me to find my Frog Princess."

"You mean, Frog Prince. You ninny," she said. "You're confused, Eddie. It's the Frog Prince."

"No, Maryann," I said. "I'm not confused. I mean, my Frog Princess."

We were sitting on the stone wall of the bridge on Orchard Street, the bridge over Gunpowder Creek. I had walked there with Maryann Grabowski after school. Maryann was my classmate at St. Anthony's, but she and her family belonged to St. Nicholas, the Russian Orthodox church, the "Onion Church" we used to call it. She had long auburn hair, blue eyes, and very lively, fresh skin that seemed to glow all the time like it had just been washed with Ivory soap. She was athletic, and she played the piano. When she played the piano, she'd pull her skirt up on her thighs. She smiled easily, and wasn't pimply or anything, so I figured maybe she had a better handle on the puberty thing. We liked each other enormously. I felt I could talk straight with Maryann, come right out with things. She seemed more mature. She was already fourteen.

"I know what I'm talking about, Maryann," I said. "Honest. My brother, Frank, he's in the Navy, you know? He told me that for so many years girls are just like frogs, frogs with pigtails, just noisy frogs with pigtails. They're just around. You don't pay any attention to them, just avoid them like a head cold."

Maryann was listening, intently. What a great woman, I thought. This was really our first serious talk together. She was swinging her leg back and forth, just kicking it out from the stone wall while she listened, and a beautiful leg it was, too. A little thick in the calf, but I liked that.

"Then, something happens," I said. "...and I'm telling you this from deep in my heart. You don't look like a frog to me anymore, Maryann."

"Jesus-god, thanks Eddie. I'm blushing, man."

"I didn't mean that," I said.

"Have I told you lately, you don't look like a bulldog anymore, you big shit."

"That's what you thought I looked like, Grabs? Nice, a bulldog, a friggin' bulldog?"

"Maybe not me, but some of the girls did."

"You didn't seem to mind at the last three parties, Grabs. We've been makin-out pretty good, like 20-minutes at

Conroy's party, no Post Office, no games, just making out like mad. And what about Linda Thomas's swim party last summer? I was feelin-you-up pretty good under the water."

"Okay, Okay, I get the message."

"I am trying to tell you something, Grabs. This is serious stuff. I mean it." We looked out over the creek. Neither of us spoke for a long time. I was acting, I remember, trying to seem hurt and serious. I wanted her to be interested in the subject, curious. "Everything's changing, Maryann, but fast, like really fast. My body. Your body. I look at you now, Grabs, and it's different. Something is happening. You've got to feel it too, you must. I think it has something to do with all this hair growing."

"You got hair too? Jesus-god."

"Yeah, you?"

"Yeah. I mean like, lots," she said.

"I know you got your period," I said.

"How do you know that?" she screamed. "Goddamn you, Eddie."

"Grabs, Jesus. You're sitting there one day with your legs apart and I could see these little red stains—I'm not blind, for crying out loud."

"Nice, Eddie. You son-of-a-bitch. You're looking up my dress all the time, huh?"

"You bet I am."

"Goddamn you. My sister was right. She said, watch out with that Eddie Genell, he's like a too-horny guy. She says she can see it in your eyes."

"Your sister Annette is a very intelligent, very perceptive woman," I told her. "And, she's built like a brick shit-house."

"I'll knock you off this friggin' bridge, Genell. You're hot for my sister Annette, is that it? I'll kill you."

"Would you believe, Lassie?" I yelled. "Grabs, do you get what I'm going through? It's a female thing right now and I'm reacting to something...which brings me back to my original point, Maryann, *the* male and *the* female animal."

I had stopped her tirade, kept her close to the main topic. The argument was suddenly getting very erotic. This, I could do. I could see that my words were having some effect. Her protestations were not like stone walls, they were more like a labyrinth of curving, gentle hedge rows begging me follow the path, follow the lush, green entreaty, turn this way, then that way, speak more about it, about our sexuality, say the things that excite and titillate, talk about us bursting at the seams, but follow, Eddie, follow until you reach the reward.

"I don't care how stunning your sister is, Grabs. She's almost eighteen, she's a dream, she's like some pin-up. It's you, you and me I'm talking about, Maryann. I think I'm in love with you. I mean it."

In that second, I saw something in her face, a softness that drifted through her body and then came back into her eyes, something I read as want and female vulnerability. It mirrored my own desires, the constant screaming want of my own throbbing innocence. It was real, it was pure, this time.

Those words had caused a momentary disarmament, a melting signal of capitulation and submission in Maryann Grabowski's face that was like my first shot of a strong drug. It was easy, too. That feeling, that look that I had caused became like a Holy Grail. I would seek it, with woman after woman. More and more I would want it. Now, it just felt wonderful to elicit such a response, such warmth, as Maryann's.

"Jesus-god, Eddie. You are scaring the shit out of me."

Maryann just stared down into Gunpowder Creek. There we were, living in this grimy little town in the Pennsylvania coal and steel belt, where waterways were blackened by backwashing mines throwing up their slag and waste, and I remember at that moment that shitty little creek seemed like the babbling brooks of smitten English poets. I saw nothing but beauty and light that day. Wind pushed through the trees around us and our feet hung together off the Orchard Street bridge, high over the rushing, dirty creek water. It was one of the great moments in life. We stared down together for a long time. I put my hand over hers and held it tightly. She had a fearful look on her face just then and I wanted her more than ever. I felt an enormous responsibility suddenly mounting, too. It was growing inside me fast, like the breakers paying-out tons of shiny, wet anthracite at the end of a long conveyor belt, minute by minute, the mountains of new coal rising and spreading — my own impetuosity filling a void as deep and empty as an abandoned mine. I had reached out for a young girl's hand, but what I suddenly held was the possibility of a woman's love. Everything was different.

"What, what do you mean, Eddie...when you say, you love me?" She asked, softly. And I still don't have an answer.

Maryann Grabowski and I went together for almost two years, and then we went to different senior high schools. If I stuffed two thousand books of the greatest romantic poetry and prose in history, a couple of foreign films, and a couple of letters to-the-Playboy-editor into my recollection of those two years, it could not adequately describe my love for her. We were initiates for each other. We brought each other into an idyllic and exciting world of passion and desire so great it overshadowed all other growth of that period. I saw her nearly every day and expressed my adoration and an undying devotion to her, in some way, on every one of those days. At times, I ignored family and friends to be with her, to dote on her. Men do get idiotic and a bit goofy when they're in love. She seemed like my reason to live, a reason to get up in the morning and go to school. My attendance record was perfect during those years.

We were in two school plays together. We hid in basements and rec rooms, locker rooms and the church auditorium, the old bell tower, even empty confessionals, to rehearse made-up love scenes and explore each other's bodies. We went to the movies often. While the huge gray figures on the screen kissed and petted, so did we. We took walks and had picnics in the wooded mountains above the strip mines and swam naked with each other in the clean streams near the high farms. Every kiss, every touch was the most exciting moment of living. It was an obsession of sorts, the need to be near her and touch her, the filling of my conscious and unconscious life with her vision and mystery, the belief that sensuality like ours was as close as we'd ever get to perfection. We found out more about our bodies—their wonderful powers and frightening needs—in those two years than in the whole of our existence before. If that wasn't love, then I don't know yet what is.

Maryann was the goddess. She became my religion, my introduction to a sacred feminine, the portal through which all life and learning came into the world. If there was something holy to be experienced, then she was the experience, the sensory reality, and at the expense of sounding corny, a first blessed taste of a divine infinite, the *Yin* to my *Yang,* the completion of the cosmic androgyne.

Ilene Polokof listened to it all, she chuckled occasionally, sniffled a few times, and she stared at me now, tearfully.

"Ilene, you must help me," I pleaded. "I've found expression for my obsessions since I was thirteen....easy. I've never found reasons. I've debased not only the women I've misused, but the women I've truly cared for, too."

"Eddie, you tried...?.." [inaudible][TAPE RUNOUT].

That session lasted one hour and thirty-six minutes. Ilene and I had coffee and scones together afterward at a little cafe on Madison Avenue. She told me of the boy who first made an attempt at sex with her. It was hilarious. We were in that cafe for fifty-two minutes more, laughing.

Week Fourteen, I related an event that was extremely traumatizing. I had refused an opportunity for quick, hassle-free lovemaking with a woman in my playwriting group. I shook uncontrollably all during the session. Ilene placed me gently on the couch and covered me with a woolen afghan. She sat on the floor beside me, her hand on my shoulder, and we did a gestalt sprint to the session's end.

Week Sixteen, I told Ilene that the only light remaining in my existence was in our morning sessions, that I lived only for them. I told her, I couldn't think of anything but being in her office, in the therapy room, with her. Temptation surrounded me every day, I pleaded, "I think only of being here with you." Tears filled my eyes, involuntarily, they welled-up with my words, and I saw something in Ilene's face, a softness that rippled through her body and then came back into her eyes.

There was an 18-minute gap in the last tape of Week Sixteen. No conversation was discernable during that time frame, only the incongruous sounds of a few caresses and movement, kisses, the sound of our skin against the leather couch, the rustle of clothing, soft and barely audible, disconnected talking — a word here and there — the sounds of Ilene Polokof and I making love. Eighteen minutes. Then, whispered goodbyes. The tape recorder got it all.

Weeks Seventeen, Eighteen & Nineteen, We talked during those sessions, but the tape recorder was never turned on. The leather couch was a pull-out. Who knew?

We carried on, randomly, for three more weeks in her apartment, not the office. Then it ended, amicably—twenty-two weeks, five thousand bucks, and tenderness off-the-clock.

The whole mess crossed my desk one day, a less-than comprehensive case study of a codependent 31-year-old male with infidelity patterns, passive-aggressive tendency in inter-relationships, addictive predisposition, and proclivity to exhibitionism(nice), neatly typed and edited into a sixteen-page article, _The Adam Cage_ for _Mental Health Today_ magazine, a Chapman Publication, byline by one, I.S. Polokof, Phd.

The story editor, then, at MHT was an old friend, Karin

Scott. She sent me a pre-pub copy—and the typed
transcripts—inter-office with an I-Luv-New-York apple stick-
on note attached,

> *Imagine, E.G.? All this and not a word*
> *about pull-out sofas. Tsk, tsk...What am I*
> *to do about journalistic integrity?*
>   *love, Scotti*

I sent it back upstairs, inter-office, with a note,

> *Let's have "tea"*
> *—and talk about it.*
>   *baci, Captain Kirk*

I had no sage insights about "the talking cure." It could
be called "the listening cure" as well, for what we really
heard was most probably what initiated change. But not for
me. A heart as deaf and dumb as mine hungered for some
new language, some new sign. I talked and I listened. And
then I saw the form of a woman in the dim lamplight of Ilene
Polokof's office, I saw a shimmer of female passion race
through her body, then back into her eyes.
We are who we are.

Marriages don't just fail, someone causes them to fail.
That's what my fortune cookie would read if these last five
years were a Chinese dinner full of lies and deceit. I accepted
all the blame. I had to divorce Newell Emerson Ingram. That
was inevitable. I'd slip out of the marriage through the back
door. My life was a shambles but I had caused this
intelligent, Canadian beauty more suffering than I'd ever
dreamed I was capable of causing. It was time I stopped
dragging her down into the muck with me.

You're supposed to feel great after all of that purging. I
didn't. Everything changed and nothing changed. I was
more distraught than ever about a man's function. Was this a
weakness, or really a strength? Is this who men and women

really are? Woman. Doctor. Man. Patient. Was my ethic any worse than hers?

Standing on the subway station platform at 42nd Street, I thought of throwing myself in front of the next speeding A Train, the 8th Avenue Express, but I had just bought a ten-pack of tokens. I amused myself with such thoughts, they were still in the humorous realm. Soon enough the comedy would turn black, and patterns would return. A new darkness enveloped me. Everything in the name of action and creativity and change betrayed me in a quietus.

Separation papers, lawyer talk, divorce proceedings—all of it began calmly. We emptied the apartment on West End Avenue. I occupied its absurd vacuity for another year-and-a-half. Newell and the children went to Ottawa for an extended visit with her family. She never returned to New York. I went home to Pennsylvania for a weekend visit. Family could be, sometimes, a salve on deep wounds.

Uncle Lou took me aside after a big Sunday dinner in my grandmother's kitchen.

"Men fall in love with the same woman, over and over," he said. "Different models, different years, but the same basic design. Ford, Chevy, and Chrysler—that's all there is, kid."

My Uncle Chick had a more organic view.

"Love is a rush of shit to the brain," he said.

We drank homemade wine for hours and talked about the women we'd known and loved. I listened. They exaggerated and advised. I wanted to write them a check for five thousand dollars, but neither one would take it. Then we all passed-out in the backyard on the spotted old lawn chairs under the mulberry trees.

I crossed the bridge on Orchard Street the next afternoon. Gunpowder Creek rushing beneath was as clean as a Scottish brook since the mines had closed. The years had also healed the strip-mined mountainsides back behind our old house. Blue-green trees covered everything, now. The incline beside Sabatini's wooden garage didn't seem so steep anymore, and the field by the river was waist-deep in wild grasses and weeds.

I spoke to Father Makarov, the pastor at St. Nicholas's Russian Church. He told me Maryann Grabowski married a chemistry teacher she'd met in Graduate School at Penn State. She had two kids and lived in Montclair, New Jersey. I called Maryann. The conversation was brief. She had heard that I was going through a divorce and offered sympathy. I said I'd called because I needed to tell her something. I needed to tell her that when we were fourteen and fifteen, I loved her. I loved her more than life itself, and that everything I'd said then was true.

"It was real, it was pure. That truth will exist forever, Maryann…" I told her, "…frozen in time."

I thanked her for loving me, and said goodbye.

Inside the empty shell I'd become, down beneath street level, I was all twisted like a bunch of subway tunnels, twisted and turned and tangled around myself, wrapped like snakes around a tree. Some ghost that looked like me, was caged down there in the cavernous maze, wandering through a vast, empty unknown.

A distant son of Adam was lost and searching, far, far from the delightful garden, filled with the fruits of manhood, and yet still hungry, desperate, and famished for the true sustenance of his desire.

chapter Twelve
THE GODS IN THEIR EYES

We get no points for simply remembering. The deeds finished, the outcomes warranted, even if unpredictable. What was there to be done about past events with current knowledge? No sight was better than insight when you're too late for revision.

I'd ski my ass off that day, stay alone, and search for the interior landscape. I'd let the mountain spirits surround me, and try to hold onto the promise of Céline. I tried.

I skied the late morning hours above the small town of St. Luc in the Val d'Anniviers. Lunch was not a major concern. All of the drugs Céline and I took during the night had obliterated my appetite almost completely. In my pocket I carried a few strips of *viande sécheé*, the lean, dried meat of wild mountain chamois, an indigenous specialty that resembled American beef jerky. I ate most of them on my lift ride to the top.

The colored brochures in the tourist office on Fifth Avenue never seemed to capture the feeling of the Valais. They couldn't come close to this "immensity of earth and sky." Filled with it again, I hung there in the chairlift like a dewdrop.

It was nearly twelve-thirty when I saw the last of the valley below, the last glimpse of towns, roads, or mountain *cabanes* on the lower foothills. I caked-on the Piz Buin cream in a blazing brightness just before I crossed over onto the back tundra of the 10,000-foot Bella Tola, then made my way onto a high snow plain and skied southward, toward the peak of Le Tounot.

The snow sweltered a bit in the sun, mirage waves rose and liquefied the horizon. This was winter's equivalent of a shimmering African desert. I was far above the tree line. The rolling snowfield changed with each crossing of smooth depressions or small cols into more desolate landscapes of rock, drift snow, and fracture ice, and then back to glaring snowfield. Ahead of me and miles in the distance, the broad flanks of Weisshorn and the towering granite chutes of Dent Blanche dwarfed everything else before them. Farther south and to the left, the Matterhorn was just a nipple on the skyline.

Suddenly, the sharp report of a few scattered abdominal pangs registered and I slowed my pace slightly. I tried to ignore them, but the pains deepened quickly and brought me to an abrupt halt on a flat terrace of windswept powder. I took deep breaths and did some callisthenic bends and short squats over my skis. I leaned back in my boots using my poles like parallel bars to support my weight and tried to relieve the pain. The cramps continued and grew, hitting me sharply on all sides of my abdomen like body shots from a seasoned welterweight. I grabbed handfuls of snow, rubbing it in my face, breathing deeper all the time, stretching and twisting at my waist, trying to unknot the spasms. Then, lightheadedness started to complicate matters. The trauma worsened rapidly.

I snapped out of my bindings and walked vigorously in circles for some minutes, jogging and walking, lifting my knees into my chest. Lying prone, I tried rocking on my belly, and then lying on my back I tried short, alternating sit-ups and leg extensions. I couldn't stem the waves of pain.

The stomach spasms were buckling me, bending me in half in fits, and my dizziness was suddenly being zapped by flashbacks, fast flickering pictures of the previous night, fiery shocks of image and light flashing onto some back-screen of vision. I knew then that the source of my pain and sudden reverberation was the lysergic acid Céline and I had eaten only hours before. The overwhelming desire for the pleasure mixture of drugs and sex clouded every restraint or warning about the risks involved. Clouded too, the unknowns lying dormant in the psyches of the users.

The "auras" coming to me then may have sprung from some deep-seeded and unresolved pre-disposition, or some hidden genetic misalignment stamped-out generations ago by a mad ancestor. Who knew? We were all the descendants of warriors, murderers, and gladiators anyway, I reasoned—history's parentage of clowns and cutthroats, geniuses and morons, beggars and kings. Perhaps the drugs only served to liberate and unbind sublime desires forged centuries ago. What a frightful choice of time and place to take a quick spin through the psychogenetic family tree.

My heart was beating very fast and I was sweating profusely, the cold sweat of panic and hyper-metabolism. The residue of LSD, some psychedelic foam, was rolling through me again like a riptide, cutting a turbulent path through my body.

Flashing pictures of Céline, swathed in torn sheets, tied and writhing furiously, continued to whack at my brain in short, vivid bursts. Some ungodly exhibition of twisted passion was being revealed to me in re-play.

I dove into a drift, burying my head deep in the cold, rubbing the snow and sweat around my neck, soaking my hair. In between the auras, I flailed and groped, searching the horizon for some reference point, and there was nothing but sky and snow mingled together, no definable light source, no protrusion, no change, just a white, milky hue.

Everything had flattened, all terrain and its perceptible contrast. The real earth had become surreal, it heaved like a billowing bed sheet. The landscape scattered in fractals, twisting and bending in odd shapes, splitting in a geometric kaleidoscope like broken mirror glass. It was a universe suddenly gone haywire, toying with my logic. All that was left was either up or down, the mere sensation of ascent or descent.

I scrambled back to my skis, stumbling and rolling twice in the snow like an enraged animal when Céline visited me again, her crying face pleading with me between her twisted arms, her arms wrapped in frayed strips of white sheet, my teeth scraping against the handsome, hard muscle of her back and buttocks.

My eyes teared and I was wringing with sweat as I pushed-off slowly, gliding, moving almost imperceptibly on a frozen, and calving glacial ice shelf. Like a child's first steps, I skied the skier's first anxious slides, letting the fall line draw me into the vertical path, in gravity's tow completely, I let it pull me down into a nondescript, white emptiness.

The blank tundra was flatter still, a white screen where only quick flashes of Céline appeared from time to time as I skated gently, half-consciously down then up, over the endless *névé*. Mounds after contours met with only more endless white mound after contour, barren and monotonous. There was no end and no beginning, no there and no here. Drifting aimlessly, I circled in my own path most probably, hoping to come upon a remote mountain *cabane*.

I knew these mountains. I'd studied the maps, but with this sickness and pain, all of that knowledge was suddenly irretrievable among the mental rubble of this disturbance.

The spasms propeled my body into alternating sweat and chill and rapid heart palpitation. I was delirious and shivering. My yellow and black jumpsuit was soaked and getting colder against my skin. Time was immeasurable, distance distorted and inestimable. The horizon seemed to be continually swallowed by a voracious fissure of infinite depth and capacity. The sun's movement played havoc with my uncertain passage, my shadow on the snow jumped all around me, or I around it. I was on a fool's treadmill, always moving, never arriving, and going nowhere.

I talked incessantly, the otherworldly nonsense of a disembodied voice. This feeling of loss had locked itself in somehow, sometime before. My thoughts drifted. I talked and talked. My mind loosened, like a door swinging open on a hinge, and these present shadows gave way to random-accessed sensations and images.

Hypothermia was beginning and in my confusion I did all the wrong things. I ate handfuls of snow, sucked at the cold water, trying to quench an unfathomable dryness and thirst. Hot now with a false fever, I rubbed my neck and head in the icy crystals clinging to the palm of my wet glove. I threw off my hat at some point—couldn't remember where it flew—and whenever Céline appeared I covered my eyes in the new fallen powder gathered from the surface of the granular base, hoping to somehow freeze-out her weeping image.

I walked. I moved like a cross-country skier, sliding and pushing my skis through the thin cover, never lifting my feet. My boots and skis felt steadily heavier and heavier, the snow sucked at my feet like mud. The sickness was beginning to subside under the steady, slow tracking of my arms and legs at the skis and poles, but this constant movement and trauma had made me extremely tired.

In the final stages of hypothermia, a strong desire to sleep overrides all better judgments. I knew well, the dangers. I was better versed than the average skier on the perils of the elements in winter, and yet, I succumbed to the seductive impulse and I laid down to rest.

As I reclined on my side gazing across the wide stretch of snow, I envisioned a long, white, mountain beach lulling me into a comforting slumber. The coldness that enveloped every part of me then glowed of sunny warmth. Windblown snow hurried off the tops of drifts like sand sifting off the edges of dunes. Sweat ran across my face, across my lips—a last lick of bitter salts, and the sweet smell of suntan cream. But for the sound of cold mountain wind, instead of waves crashing, it could have been a day at East Hampton Beach.

My eyes closed one last time. Color bursts and spirals,

flashed and coiled on the backside of the darkness like Dali and Miro scribbling behind my eyes. The heavy curtain that fell soon cut-off all sight, and out of a deeper blackness a theatre of absurd images and voices suddenly came forth. I told myself repeatedly—some voice did—that I was just lying down to rest for a few minutes, that I'd awaken soon and ski away refreshed and reoriented. A few more fading pictures of Céline, serene and soft this time, appeared and then in succession—an image of my mother standing at the base of our stairs, my son throwing a new white baseball, and a doe-eyed woman running her hand across my forehead, pushing my hair aside. Memories came, like smoke from distant fires rising in thick gray strands, then disappeared into the timelessness of delirum. A face. The eyes of the doe. Darkness. Then, a sound.

"Eddie?" A female voice called. *A blue light.*

"Eddie?"

"Céline?" My voice called.

"Eddie, don't worry." Stronger now, the voice pleaded.

"Mom?"

"Eddie, don't worry, we'll send it to Warner's."

"Donna?" Donna's voice. "Donna?"

"Eddie, we'll send it to Warner's, we'll send it around. We're not turning-tail and heading for the hills are we?"

"It's not commercial, Donna. Go ahead, say it. It's not rank, it's not the imbecilic blockbuster comedy that'll make a couple of Hollywood mini-minds overnight geniuses."

"Eddie, I didn't say..."

"It's not the lame-brained sitcom, or the drooling tit-parade with a string of brothel jokes. It is none of those great cinematic achievements that this pisshole-on-the-San Andreas is so enviably famous for. Say it...won't hurt my feelings."

Please don't say it.

"Careful, Babe, it's a long fall from that high-horse you're on."

"I can't write that shit, Donna. Some guys can. There are thousands of them all over this town. God love the bastards."

"They know how to play the game, Eddie. They play ball first, then they do whatever the hell they want. You've got to be in the league to play the game, Famous."

"This place is nothing but games, Dee, games and tricks. That's what everybody does here, turn tricks. Nobody reads anything, nobody comprehends. They decipher codes, Honey. If this doesn't happen on page twenty, or this on page thirty, or there has to be a screwing scene before page fifty, oh yeah, got to have a screwing scene."

"You're getting vile, Eddie."

"One guy reads every sixteenth page. No shit. This son-of-a-bitch lands like a helicopter every sixteen pages...that's about seven pages out of a hundred-and-twenty-page screenplay. And he knows, mind you, this genius knows if it's a hit."

"Please, you're getting all worked-up."

"Can you imagine if this asshole had been handed Casablanca, or the African Queen, or Chinatown, or Spartacus?"

"Eddie, stop it, please."

"They're all decoders, Donna. Sons-of-bitches talk like brain-damaged marmots. Hey, not bad, brain-damaged marmots, got to remember that one. Pour yourself another scotch, Eduardo...why-thank-you, yes, don't mind if I do."

"You're getting wrecked, dammit."

Donna watched me head for the scotch on the bar. That crushed expression on her face meant that everything was backfiring. The hurt was supposed to be mine, my little tantrum. I hated hurting her.

"They drive the most vulgar cars through a choking atmosphere," I was rolling. "Surround themselves with the most conspicuous, hideous accessories, including people."

"They do give great parties, though."

Check-friggin-mate. Beautiful, Donna. She knew how to

play me, how to fan my fire, and how I loved to burn long and languorously in fights, ranting ad infinitum about everything until I just wore myself down. She dared me to continue with her deftly placed counterpunches. What a prizefighter she'd have made. Behind that crooked little smile of hers, she was beginning a standing eight-count, mine.

"Oh, Christ," I blathered. "Do you really get your jollies on the star bullshit?" Her smile broadened. She knew she had me, she radiated smugness. I was entertaining her. She really loved me, too. *I think.* I wanted every fight to be the best fight of our lives. "You like this kissy-face shit, don't you? Cord Saunders spilling his drink on your bosom, all that ass grabbing?"

"I like, Eddie? I thought *we* came here to do something." She pressed down on the *we.* "I thought *we* wanted this— this, shit. You wanted a shot at Hollywood, you wanted to try a screenplay. I wanted it too, Eddie. I wanted it with you."

"Ahhhh, whip me, beat me with your magnanimity."

"You're a bastard, you know that? Bleeding hearts don't get Jack-shit around me, Babe. I listen to you rag and bitch at that typewriter, watch you throw pages onto the floor, yelling and screaming...goddamn this, and friggin' that...and I think to myself, here is a happy man. Oh, the creative agony, the pain, the joy, the heartbreak of inspiration — the Muse arrives, and she departs. This man, I tell myself, is fulfilled."

"Say, now that's great stuff, Donna," I warbled. And it was. She was so goddamn beautiful right now, I wanted to jump on her and lose myself in the only truly inspired act I'd ever performed. Couldn't she see how much I wanted her? Couldn't we have fallen into each other's arms just then?

"I pour the scotch," Her patience was fast disappearing from her voice. She was rolling now. "I listen to the dialogue, pour some more. We talk about the scene, the characters, the development, the plot. I correct your spelling, your grammar, your punctuation. I re-type, I Xerox, punch holes, type letters, I lick stamps and envelopes. Lick? My friggin' tongue can go Express Mail from here to East of Eden, for Christ's sake. What the hell, Eddie, I'm part of it, aren't I?"

I was too slow and stuporous to answer, drunk and wobbling around the living room. Part of it? She was the whole thing. I only wanted it to impress her, something big to prove...something. What? What did I want to prove, anyway? *Men are such damn fools, especially when we're young.*

Donna scooped the car keys off the bar, clicked her heels across the foyer, and slammed the front door behind her. Her exits were great theatre. But the night was not mine for stellar performances, not even if she'd gone straight to the bedroom.

I absorbed the silence for a moment, and then befriended another bottle of scotch. I coaxed it out onto the rear deck of the house with me, overlooking the shimmering Pacific.

An hour passed and I finally seduced the last half of the bottle down to the beach.

Malibu. Our first big move together — out of New York, out of the cramped studio on East 47th street, we'd broken new ground. Donna was producing segments, from L.A., for the network's Morning Show. Donna Martin was her on-air name, Donna Morelli, the name of the brilliant Wellesley brunette at the center of my world. She was an excellent correspondent, far better than the show's two happy-talk hosts. Her pieces were a weekly staple of topical people and current issues, solidly reported.

Malibu was a chance for me, at Donna's expense, to shop my work around Hollywood. Some early short fictions and a one-act I'd written were an *entré* to a Los Angeles agent. The agent promised "traffic lanes" to some of the studio decision brokers and a possible tie-in to a gold-card director. He'd made good on another promise already—getting me in to a pitch meeting for one of my treatments. It was his way of letting me see my own blood spilled in the executive suite. It was effective.

Donna decided to sit back and watch my adversarial enthusiasm, assured it would play itself out, knowing all the while it could undo the best writers with the best intentions. Slowly, our ambitions, the dreams we'd dreamt together, and our two years of unmarried bliss, were beginning to suffer.

I sat there in the warm sand of Malibu under the stars, left to reel-in all the insults and stupid remarks and re-play them through a haze of acute inebriation. I started to refill the emptiness that always followed our quarrels. So elusive, the beast called happiness, and so obvious the loneliness that attended her every departure.

Love seemed to hide itself in a dense forest after we argued, camouflaged at times, while faults and weaknesses flaunted their apparition. The difficulty was in the vigilance, the watch over what we both cherished in one another — how to keep that from getting lost in the trees.

Suddenly, things became clouded in drink and disappointment. Success was a seesaw for two, but failure needed to be dealt with alone. So I thought, so I'd convinced myself. We were a Broadway hit together, we were happy, and life was in-balance. Our second act was a little bumpy, anxiety escalated, and the addictions were always waiting in the wings. *And isn't that where I was headed without delay?* This time it was booze and self-loathing. *What did the future hold?* A pattern was beginning—love and equilibrium kept me sane, fears of success or failure, or loss, and like a house of cards, I destroyed any semblance of balance, and love.

Donna was analytical. She had the clarity of vision that my passion and impatience blurred. She nurtured our areas of individual growth. Considering the area I needed, it was an act of supreme sacrifice.

"You can dream all you want, for as long as you wish," she gently teased with loving certainty. "We're just right, you and I, I know we are. You can be a vendor of clouds, Eddie. And I? I'll be the collector of stones."

The following day, we helicoptered down to Ensenada on the Baja Peninsula, where we met with the macho, and rapidly fading movie star, Cliff Garvin, and his small entourage. It was Donna's assignment and we traveled with camera crew and assistants, and enough equipment and film, to capture Garvin, at leisure, fishing on the high seas in his seventy-five-foot luxury yacht, *Stiletto*. A knife-in-the-water, sleek and streamlined, *Stiletto* suggested speed and windy adventure just sitting in its slip. The boat was named after one of Garvin's hit movies, *The Silver Stiletto*. The ship was rigged for sport fishing with two fighting chairs on an elevated poop deck in the stern. Garvin, of course, had his own customized chair. Its gaudiness made it the most striking, and conspicuous, feature since the last voyages of Leif Eriksson.

In one of his period epics, Garvin played a Viking warrior, or some Norse King, and he got to keep the ornate throne the production had built for his war ship. It was the kind of back lot collectible the movie society fawned over the way archaeologists cringed over fossils. But Garvin's leisure and collectibles were not the stories that brought us to his floating R.V.—neither was his autumnal career.

Garvin had been co-habitating with the sexy European film star, Jan Braun, for slightly more than eight years. Braun made the classic period-adventure pictures— Roman Wars, Greek epics, Biblical sagas, Faustian-dark cinematic tone poems—lavishly produced, with huge casts of musclemen in loin cloth and scantily-clad females. It was Epic Melodrama with breathy love scenes cut about ten feet short of an X-rating. It was soft porn for the history buff.

Jan Braun was a stunning centerfold for these types of B-minus eight-reelers. The dialogue in these films was written on a matchbook, but the action, the epic scale, the hot, sweaty bodies and the marquee value of a voluptuous — also hot and sweaty—heroine were enough to sustain the genre, at least during Braun's prime, roughly eight years.

With a sudden drop in the prime, Garvin asked Braun to move out. She, in turn, brought suit against Garvin seeking an enormous property settlement and a monthly allowance commensurate with his earnings during their eight-year live-in arrangement— alimony from a man who was not her husband. California suddenly had a landmark case on its hands. Common-law did not apply in the Golden State, and no contract had ever been drawn-up between Garvin and Braun. Companionship, it seemed, should have some equitable value, or should it? The courts were stymied, but the litigants were pushing to try it. It might have been an open and shut matter, with an amenable settlement, but for the suggestion of alimony and Hollywood's peculiar brand of co-habitation. So, the routine split of two consenting adults, two of Tinseltown's rich and A-list famous, became a national issue, and the newest portmanteau, "palimony" rang through the land.

Donna had managed an exclusive with Garvin while the rest of the talk shows were doing full hour programs with Jan Braun and other women spurned, as she was, by live-ins, fiancés, and long-term boyfriends. Listening to the arguments on these shows, any woman who had spent so much as a weekend with a man was entitled to some settlement. One brainy L.A. lawyer even drew up a one-night-stand agreement, with a compensatory clause for bad sex.

Braun was the perfect talk-show guest, she was doll-like and possessed a kind of Bambi-ish innocence — sympathetic and appealing to the afternoon audience — and then she turned her good looks into something sensuous and jiggly for primetime. She clearly knew how to handle herself in front of cameras and was getting tremendous mileage out of the publicity.

Garvin was much older than Braun. He came across

poorly in the print media—looked lecherous in photos—like a sneering flesh merchant who had somehow enslaved this innocent young beauty. His macho screen persona didn't help him either.

Donna had seized the opportunity to give Garvin a fairer hearing, on a reputable show, and allow a different audience to hear the other side of the story. Garvin appreciated her even-handedness during an effluence of women's rights clamoring that skewed the public, sympathetically, toward Braun's appeal.

Donna's only proviso was that the story not be a photo-op for Garvin, no shots of weeding the garden, or doing the laundry.

So, on the clear blue sea off of Baja California, we were rightly in macho-movie-star Cliff Garvin's element, preparing to do battle with the ferocious yellowtail and the savage Bonita.

The show was already buzzing with anticipation. The producers decided to give the story episodic treatment. It would appear in four installments the week before Braun's and Garvin's lawyers gave opening statements in Los Angeles—coincidentally, November Sweeps Weeks in Ratings Land.

It was a coup, the kind of scoop reporters lived for, and shows, like the Morning Show, lived-on with. In the news business it was a grand slam in the bottom of the ninth, winning the World Series.

Donna was suddenly walking on the waters of TV News. Anything she wanted, she could have, helicopters, two crews, extra lighting, deluxe accommodations, an associate producer, two production assistants — anything. She asked her executive producer if I could go along on the Garvin Fishing Shoot.

Billed, presumably by Donna's boss, as "a writer," I was a sub-species in the Hollywood hierarchy just below the vertebrates. I was there to observe, lend support, and stay out of the way. As a mere earthworm I was non-threatening enough to the Star species to be a guest on the shoot.

I conceded testosterone levels to Garvin and two of his adventure-flick pals, and let them gush all over Donna. In that way, I figured, the day would pass uneventfully, which was just what I needed. In the battle for levels, alcohol was winning the day among fluids in my body.

I finally ran aground the previous night on the living room floor surrounded by the ghost ships of Galleon-sized Cutty Sark and Johnny Walker bottles, their empty mouths gaping, aimed at me like an armada's canons. The day could only improve, first a helicopter, now a boat. I felt like a Swiss Army Knife. Some parts were extremely sharp, and others, dull and useless.

Coming aboard I accepted Garvin's welcome soulfully. It was Donna's party, I'd behave and resist the temptation to be caustic. I'd try. Donna had heard enough wily sarcasm for one 24-hour period. Asked if I liked sport fishing, I replied, "No, I'm into clubbing baby seals." Temptation got the best of me at the worst times. Donna shot me a fierce look on that one, and I quickly launched into a serious discussion about suntan lotion, always a popular topic in Southern California.

Watching magnificent creatures yanked into the air by men with cables, rods, and huge steel hooks, was not my idea of stimulating entertainment, and I found my way to the opposite end of *Stiletto* with my composition notebooks, pads and pencils — and my tanning cream — and spread myself over a perfectly padded sunning niche in the bow. From the V-shaped, vinyl sofas the hubbub of activity at the rear became just a distant murmur.

Max, a crusty Old Salt, and another Garvin movie crony, steered us beyond Ensenada's busy Bahia and we set-off for the serene coastline south of the *Punta Banda*. In among some wide-reaching bays and coves, the waters were flatter and there the Garvin interview would be shot while we drifted on lazy currents.

Alternating strands of white beach and rocky cliffs rolled
past in the distance. Trolling and drifting through these
pastel waters we encountered groups of small artisanal
fishing boats. From the prows of these boats, the shiny, dark
bodies of young Mexican boys were perched like statuary.
Sometimes the boys waved, flashing their white teeth in
exuberant smiles, and then they'd dive into the clear water.
Their frog-like strokes propelled them down and out of sight
for several minutes. Then they would break the water's
surface once again, raising high the small yellowtails and
covacha impaled on their reed-like spears.

The interview got underway, finally, with Garvin
looking rather stately and star-like in his Viking fishing
throne. Donna came forward during a break and sat beside
me. We stared silently at each other for a long moment—our
standard method for expiating common pain—the pain we
always caused each other in arguments. Her face was proof
that the creative force was not concerned so much with
perfection. Donna was, rather, evidence of a divine
imagination, an intellect infused with artful ecstasy. Donna
was umber-hued, like the deep earthen brownness of rich,
freshly-turned Apennine hillsides. Brown-eyed, dark-
pigmented lips that never needed artificial embellishments,
she was moist to my kiss even in desert dryness. Her dark
chestnut nipples, unusually big and striking, rose from
fulsome breasts. Rivet-like they stood through shirts and
lingerie of any weave. She was the square-shouldered
daughter of a Boston seafarer. In heels, she was as tall as I,
and her long and muscular legs harnessed a sprinter's
power. A fathomless dark well of passion, she quenched the
thirst of my need. The chief between my thighs ran a
warpath after her touch, needing no urging, no provocation.
Her sultry, silent stare, the soft look of the doe—knowing
and penetrating—bore through my shame, always.

She broke the silence, admonishing me for the "seal"
remark. Then, doubling-back on admonition, she admitted it

was a funny line—the joke was tactless, but it was good tactless. I wanted her to touch me. The thought barely occurred and she ran her hand over my forehead, fixing my hair in the sea breeze.

So beautiful, yet so dangerous, navigating the deep waters of our relationship. Some giant formless truth swam beneath, coursing between us, moving silently through the light and dark of a consuming passion.

She headed aft to continue the interview, the long shadow of her figure lingered there on the deck before me. When she turned back to me, her face glowed in the soft light coming up from the water.

"This afternoon we're going out to deeper seas, really far out. Are you sure you don't want to fish?"

"Naw, skip me," I said. "I'm working on a scene about some guys hugging trees up in the Northwest." She smiled, a broad and beautiful smile.

"I love you, you idiot." She laughed. "I'd love to see you get sea sick today…serve you right. Johnny Walker goes to sea. Was it Johnny at the helm last night, sailor? Hmmm?" She made me laugh. The laughter hurt my head, but in her looks the aftermath of the previous night was missing. It disappeared when she touched me.

"Going to come and watch me fish later? We're going to do some B-roll of Garvin and me in the fighting chairs." She egged me on.

"That's what we need, my love, fighting chairs." She looked stunning now against the pale sky as she sauntered back to the interview set, peering over her shoulder with a seductive glance.

During the next roll of the interview, I wandered below unnoticed to find the restroom. The facility called a "john" on land is dubbed the "head" at sea, two words that accurately defined cause and effect of all of my present discomfort.

The quarters below decks were a vast complex of suites and compartments, surprisingly spacious. It was posh, like an expensive motel. But Garvin's touches, or perhaps Jan Braun's, were as ostentatious as the Norwegian fishing chair. A sprawling cocktail lounge was the central feature, heavily stocked with every liquor imaginable. The mere sight of fourteen different brands of scotch, side by side, made me shudder.

I encountered two young Mexican boys who had run of the kitchen and all other amenities below. I tried to be cordial, but the two boys were preoccupied and seemed a little out of sorts, bothered by something. I offered the few Spanish words of congeniality I had command-of, and the boys mumbled something back about "no whales today," "*ballenas, ningun.*"

If the Mexican boys were bothered by an uncommon absence, I wondered what the sea might contain instead. Nature's exchange, I ruminated—something always replaces something else.

The interview finished. The crew and assistants reloaded the cameras for their cover shots and hand-held cutaways, and *Stiletto* turned and headed west for deeper waters. The land mass diminished to a thin solid line behind us, and then finally disappeared altogether. The Garvin muscle pals were baiting the hooks for Donna and Cliff, and from the bridge, the captain was keeping the rear appraised of sub-marine activity by reading from a sonar device called a Fish Finder. It was a gadget that reported where, and at what depth, schools of fish were situated. With equipment like the Fish Finder aboard, it wasn't long before man and woman and fish were squaring-off on sport fishing's field of combat.

Fish were flying-up from the water and hitting the deck of *Stiletto* in great numbers. The laughter and excitement coming from the stern indicated that the humans were dominating play. Donna was having a ball. Every strike on her line was accompanied with infectious laughter that produced ever more flattery from the men.

The film crew was getting great shots, from every

conceivable angle, except the fish's. Only a few big fish were kept and stored in a customized cooler in the ship's hold. Dozens of others were tossed back, presumably returned to their classmates in the schools just for being good sports — for taking a hook on the jaw and hitting the deck without too much complaint.

It was a fun afternoon for non-aquatics, all in all, until Garvin took a strike on his line that sent a small tremor the entire length and breadth of *Stiletto*. The heavy line slapped the fiberglass railing three times, knocking loudly. Some creature on Garvin's line signaled a readiness to fight. Everyone on the boat noticed, even I felt a slight roll of the lumbering yacht. The line cracked and whizzed, screeching like a tape recorder in super-fast rewind. The huge fiberglass pole coming out of the Viking throne bowed like a branch in a hurricane, twisting and buckling, making hollow, gnarling sounds under the strain.

The jubilant staging area for sport aboard *Stiletto* was suddenly stilled and silent, all attention riveted on the bending, whirring rod. Garvin and his two pals dashed to the chair. Max came out of the steering house, onto the portico overlooking the rear deck. The two timid Mexican boys were peering aft from the top of the steps that lead down into the galley, I could barely see the tops of their heads. Garvin was strapping himself into the Viking chair while the musclemen scurried to tie everything else in, everything unnecessary to what was happening between that chair and whatever had hold of the speeding line.

Donna and her crew were incidental now to the three men manning Garvin's chair, they'd become peripheral and took up stations away from the area of the fighting deck. Something had changed. An air of seriousness, that was not present all afternoon, suddenly seemed pandemic on the afterdeck.

The line whizzed from the reel, hundreds of feet paid out. The men stood patiently around the chair, watching the line disappear into the heaving sea. Silently, they listened for a hesitation in the sound, a break in the huge fish's stride. Then, a slackening came, the buzzing line stopped, and Garvin lurched backward, his two arms outstretched grasping the pole, he pulled with all his energy. One muscleman was behind the throne chair, his arms locked around Garvin's chest, pulling the actor back and down into the seat. The other aided the bent pole with one gloved hand, pushing it up, straightening it, then alternately touching the line and pole as if listening with his fingertips for the creature's angered message to his foes.

This then, was the game—the strength of three men against an unimaginable single force and fury from beneath. As much as I hated this sport, I was captivated. The teamwork, the wordless communication and nuance, motion and change, strength and momentum, the interplay of elements, and the beauty of these three men straining against the arc of the fishing pole—it was something to admire. Writhing in unison, they became a part of the rod and the line, pulling and releasing, searching for their opponent's weakness. Their backs bent in an ancient rhythm against the sea, and they summoned images of a timeless struggle.

They spoke not a word, the team. The sinew of their shining arms, their bowing heads, tousled hair and wringing brows, however, spoke volumes of the battle's progress. The great and wondrous beast beneath worked in silence, too. From hundreds of feet below, unseen, he ran his field, he pulled to match his own back against the men.

During the course of the next twenty-six minutes, Garvin looked, at times, like a man in the throes of convulsive fits, spasmodically thrusting and recoiling when the creature called him to the fight. The musclemen too, began to tire. The men mopped each other's sweat, they took the pole in turns, reeling-in furiously and letting-out, sparring with the fantastic fish. The powerful creature sapped their strength, minute by minute.

The vigilance they kept was focused on one moment in the long fight, the moment when the great beast would break the surface of the water, trying to unleash himself from the line, leaping wildly through the air in search of his freedom. Symbolically, it was the first tally — when creatures of the sea left their element for ours — the first register of advantage.

Thirty-two minutes passed. The line was still angled sharply down. The stubborn fish gave no sign of coming up. Instead, he swam belligerent patterns, fiercely erratic and zigzagging. He snapped the line again, three more times, cracking it like a whip against the hull.

The men, in whispers, talked now of his size and weight, of time and tenacity, of his kind — sailfish and blue marlin — sea giants who would stay the fight. I watched them guard the chair and line, and in that moment a rumbling sensation came from deep within. Traces of my hangover were gone completely, it had nothing to do with booze. A sane and sobering tremor of something quite different vibrated through my body, and suddenly, I felt that I knew what swam beneath us at the other end of the line. I grabbed the railing, my blood pulsated through my arms and chest as if the angry creature had just swum through it. Enraged and terrified, the great beast that I envisioned, I knew would not surrender to any sportsman's rules. Only in the grasp of death would he break the blue surface in bloody submission, only destroyed would he lie on *Stiletto's* deck and concede defeat.

I trembled at the thought of a great shark swimming, panicked, frenetic, pulling and gnawing at the unrelenting line, the line lacerating and cinching, the hook tearing at his flesh. Pictures came to me, suddenly, Sunday sports page pictures of great white sharks, tiger sharks, hammerheads, threshers, makos, dun-colored, gray, blue and sand, black slender missiles, sleek and beautiful, hung in infamy, their perfection inverted, defiled on some marina gallows by gaudy vigilantes, smiling all there in stupid hats — the photo record of the catch—pictures of the sea's majesty reduced.

I wished for the power just then, the breath and stamina to dive and swim, fast and far to his deep dominion, cut him free, and watch him fly through the green darkness.

I stood on the white deck now and my heart pounded for that beast. As the line came up nearer and nearer to the horizon, I watched for his signal. Surprisingly, no one ever guessed shark, not the three men who'd felt the pull of many great fighting fish, not the captain who sailed these waters countless times with sportsmen, nor Donna and her crew, the innocents afloat.

Finally, at fifty-one minutes, about thirty yards off the starboard side, the great shark rose to the top. He lifted his head a few feet out of the water just once, his gaping jaw cut and spewing blood, and then rolled onto his back and bared his white underside to the afternoon sky.

Unconsciously, I moved toward the stern, watching the scene unfold before me. The sea undulated gently and the body of the shark rolled with it as the men dragged him across the water toward the jet-ski winch at the back of the boat. In the small swells the shark's full length and mass were revealed. He was not a great white, but his horseshoe-curved jaw stretched at least three feet across. From nose to tail, he was just under eleven feet. It was his barrel-chested girth that was so terrifying, so impressive, a muscular bulge of breast and flukes that reverberated with his frightening power.

The three men and the captain busily prepared the afterdeck for the shark's arrival on board. Donna remained quietly by her chair. The two Mexican boys had left their safe haven on the stairs and situated themselves by the larboard railing on the fighting deck, watching. The film crew captured the scene from above on the captain's portico, and I stood amidships, able to see the men and the shark, overlooking the ritual that ended nearly every big catch.

There was no jubilation yet. The men worked like altar

boys at high mass, quietly and fast. The captain put one pistol shot through the shark's head, and then the grinding winch dragged the limp beast onto the fighting deck, tail first. Tangled and trussed in the fishing line that tethered him to the fight, his clefts were cut and vented, probably in the final gasp that brought him up, they were crisscrossed in still more line. His full mass finally fell onto the deck with a boom that rocked *Stiletto*. It listed starboard from his weight. Gallons of reddened water from his open mouth flooded the deck, swirling around the chrome pedestals of the fighting chairs, moving like a tide, curling back, touching everyone's feet. The bloodied water rushed and swirled back to the shark, surrounding him. *Stiletto* leveled once again and it was done.

The men whooped and yelled banshee cries. They laughed and screamed, embracing one another. The Mexican boys relaxed and smiled at each other, flashing white, exuberant smiles, and Donna looked up at me. Anxiety spoiled her beauty in the glance. She sighed uneasily, a half-smile telling me of some mixed feeling, of vulnerability, of how her heart was hurting just then, as mine was. I was wishing to hold her in my arms, at that moment, and she seemed oddly distant and unreachable.

The film crew hurried down the stairs to the fighting deck, getting hand-held close-ups of the men and the great shark lying at their feet. They took cutaways of Donna and the Mexican boys, shots to describe all of the celebrative relief. The magnificent creature lay leaning against the side of the boat, the eddies of his own bloodied seawater swirled around him.

A series of photographs were taken, in every permutation of people and fallen shark possible, enough to fill a dozen scrapbooks. The Mexican boys were comical, timid and fearful of the dead animal even as it lay there motionless.

When the photo session was finished, the captain took a

short piece of rope from his pocket and fashioned a bowline in a few fast movements of his hands. He placed the loop over the shark's snout and lower jaw and tightened the slipknot, sealing the rows of ratcheted teeth safely inside.

Garvin then opened a small hatch in the starboard railing and took out a large knife. The knife looked to be about a foot in length, but as Garvin turned it flashed brilliantly in the sunlight, and I saw that it was no ordinary fishing knife. It was a silver stiletto, ornately handcrafted by Mexican artisans expressly for the insert shots of Garvin's hit movie.

In one swift and skillful motion Garvin placed the knife against the white throat of the shark just behind the rope cinch that held his jaw closed, and ran the blade the length of the shark's soft and bloated underbelly. A thin red line raced after the knife's sharp blade, like blood chasing after a surgeon's scalpel. The red incision widened slowly and then burst open, and another flood, a deep vermilion wave washed across the shining deck. The gash grew larger. More and more it spread as the shark's bulging gullet pushed forward, pushing something through the opening. Then in one more spasm the shark's stomach sac, like a swollen embryoid, forced through the opening onto the deck.

Donna screamed and everyone jumped back fitfully. All were now looking down at the huge egg-shaped organ shining in the afternoon light. I was paralyzed. My eyes shoved forward, painfully straining, staring at the horror on the deck.

There, pressed against the clear, unbroken membrane of the shark's stomach was a small hand, the small left hand and forearm of a boy, all bleached and ghostly. The five fingers of the hand opened out and gently touched the clear tissue, as if reaching or waving from within the shark's innards. As serene and still as the birth sac suspending the unborn life, the glazed and veined transparency held the child's arm and hand in calm repose. It was the only body-part visible, but it seemed connected to the whole, the intent of the boy's reach captured and stilled in an instant completely intact with his thoughts and his bodily motion. There was peace in his gesture there, a tranquility apropos of a long and restful journey. *This little Jonah had met his whale.* Death had accompanied him back to a beginning place, filling his ears again with liquid, stopping the sounds of any fury, of any trauma.

I watched Donna's distressed breathing, as she quivered tearfully alone in the radiant sun. The silent lobe on the deck once beat a similar, distressed cycle. Life suspended in life. Here we were isolated and alone, all suspended in a journey, in a cycle, alternately swallowed whole and thrust up, breaching for some meaning, searching for an understanding of the fearful—all caught-up in our own "phenomena." *What of this heartache? Why, the pain Donna and I cause each other? Why?* The organs of my own body swelled suddenly, erupting, trying to escape me, pushing everything inside, out through my throat.

I ran, back toward the bow, my eyes bulging, hurting. My head filled with blood. I jumped and fell to my knees on the vinyl sofas, throwing my arms around the steel spar that projected out over the water. The sea turned bile green beneath me and some rotten bloodwater stench filled my nostrils. The wind rushed over me, like black smoke, as the yacht started moving.

I clung to the bowsprit, waiting for the great lump of my sickness to come up. It never did. The pushing, hurting clot of sorrow and revulsion stuck there, pushing against my heart.

The sound of the wind increased as the boat redoubled its speed. A silence from the wind just then would heal, but that was when I heard the laughter. The faintest echo of deriding mirth was drifting forward, seeping through the wind, a guttural, steady, chuckling ridicule—barroom laughter, locker room scorn, open contempt. Like hunter's gathered around the kill clanging whisky glasses, they drafted pride, taking manly measurement of their deed, tearing at the fresh meat of inferiority. The raucous bellowing laughter of hunters lording over the hunted grew louder.

I sucked deeply at the salt air, still clinging to the spar. Where was Donna? Why hadn't she come forward? I pressed my head down against the fiberglass deck, hoping the drone of *Stiletto's* engines would drown-out the sounds of the men. And then I heard her sound, Donna's sound. Her laughter mingled in and she was laughing with them. Her sound cut through the rest. It came through the spar, through the wind, and a crack in the world was opening, a fissure, thin and secret and unstoppable, suddenly dividing the universe between us. Her little laugh, a giddy, haunting betrayal, spontaneous and perhaps innocent, entered me like a harpoon. Our severance widened with each passing second.

Stiletto's numbing engines came loud, through my skull. I looked down and watched the bow's blade furrow the dark green water, opening a deep cut across the surface, folding back the ocean's smooth skin, exposing a painful whiteness on the sea.

The memory of love dies slowly in some men's hearts. It rushes back in moments of stillness, swirling around us like reddened water. A persistent tidal bore overwhelms and we suffer deeply when love fails. We're unrepentant as hell, and some things we simply cannot forget. Hurtful flaws, both.

I sought eternal love with Donna, and found it. Only the terms were different. Everything's an exchange—something always replaced something else. *Where is the darkness? The silence?*

~

A rasping, breathy sound began deep in the blackness of the suspension. Then, a tactile sensation, scraping against my face, a flat scratchy pad rubbed rhythmically along my cheek and hairline. The scratching pad and breath were hot, lapping at the dried salt of perspiration on my temples and forehead.

I opened one eye, just a slit, and the lapping stopped abruptly. We stared at each other, breathlessly still for a long moment, his unblinking glassy, black eye fixed squarely on mine. His head cocked, quizzically, with every twitch of my face or eyes. The huge head and conical curved horns of a buck chamois were just inches from my face. The sleek and beautiful mountain ram looked down at me like a sad dog, his eyes limpid now like two pieces of wet coal, disappointed that his newfound lick had just become animate. A single disbelieving thought flashed through my mind—was this it? Had I crossed over? Was this the Great Perhaps? And God is a chamois? Not bad. What a surprise for the racist-feminist argument. In my savior's deepening gaze, however, I saw something benevolent and powerful, something so regrettably unattainable.

Envy his beauty, this was real. I had not crossed over. I moved slightly and he jumped back, startled. He planted his stocky front legs spreading them wide. His head lowered, as if readying for a charge, the rounded horns flashed in the light.

I reached, and he jumped again.

Suddenly, a shot rang-out. The chamois turned his head toward the blast. His four legs bent low. He glanced back at me and then, with a forceful thrust he sprung like some winged griffin and became airborne—I'd never seen a leap that high. I rolled over on my stomach and another shot whizzed through the silence, the bullet thud hit the snow like a wet wad of paper. I saw the chamois dash away behind me, cutting a zigzagging path through the chunk toward the edge of rock cairn where two light brown fawns were waiting. He stopped short, about fifty feet away, when another bullet chinked the rock next to one of the frightened fawns. The shot echoed across the broad mountainside, deep into distant ravines. The big brown ram froze still. He cocked his head back in the direction of the shot, and then cocked it back again and stared at me.

You've dodged three, big fella. You'd better get moving. The next shot'll have you, big guy. You'll be a goddamn trophy.

The buck and his fawns stood staring at me across the bright expanse of snow. The gods in their eyes spoke then of an innocence and need in the living world. The tenderness in their looks imparted some compassion for my own frailty, for the impermanence, and my helplessness. In their shiny black eyes, the momentary impasse held a message of common and tenuous truth — of shared sorrow in our short passage on this earth. *Why have I been allowed to survive?*

I reached and grabbed a ski pole lying next to me, and with failing strength I lifted the pole and slapped it hard against the snow, spraying the crusty granular pack high in the air. Ice crystals flew in an arc skyward twinkling like a shower of white diamonds. The chamois and his fawns bolted out of sight.

I rolled onto my back and stared at the sky as the sounds of two voices, speaking in German, came nearer and nearer.

What followed immediately was pretty much an insensate blur of sounds and movement, lifting and walking, riding and sliding in a sled, accompanied by the murmurs of my two *Swiss-Alemagne* rescuers. I'd collapsed, it turned out, a short distance from a mid-mountain cabin, and too short of any downward trails to safety.

On the journey back to the cabin, I continued to fade in and out of my sickness and disorientation. Certain moments were clear and cogent, like the fire in the cabin and its warmth, the yellow flames, big and hypnotic, while other events seemed half-imagined. The voices of the two Swiss hunters were a distant din, a mumbling background ambiance for the light and color streaks of half-remembered, dreamlike actualities. The night ensued.

Asterix and Obelix — never got their real names — were

Swiss-German. Their spotty French was adequate, but not expert. They were not certified Alpine Guides, *bergfuhrer*. They wore no official patches, and they possessed no special equipment. These guys were throwbacks, I was sure, from an era long since past in the Valais, Helvetian mountain men, as purely Swiss as a yodel. Their crude appearance spoke of a life close to nature, hewn on the mountainsides of the Val d'Anniviers. Finding a man in the snow, any man, required mountain men of good, Calvinist piety to restore him, help him regain strength enough to face the mountain once again. This seemed to be their sole unprepossessing body of law. And to that commandment of their giving, they went about speaking in muted mumbles mostly, tending to my recovery. I sipped hot liquids, I recalled. By Bunyonesque hands and forearms, I was undressed then placed gently in a straw bed.

The sunrise brought a clear-headed awakening. The hunters were almost wordless as they prepared hot *muesli* and a powdered chocolate drink. I tried talking to them, but they were serious and somber, rather curt. Their replies were limited to about two or three universal grunts and hand signals. I wondered if I'd said some vulgar thing, or made some insulting remark in one of their languages during the night to make them pissed-off at me? I drank and ate as they placed each edible in front of me, the *muesli*, some hard bread, a piece of dried fruit, and the hot, muddy chocolate. They watched me curiously.

When I finished, they cleaned the earthen bowls and wooden utensils I'd used, doused the fire, and waited just outside the door as I dressed in my dry warmers, socks, leotards, and ski outfit. I was a bit freaked. It was as if all of my clothes had been sent out for an overnight clean and pressing.

I emerged from the cabin into a fantastically bright, blue morning. The Val d'Anniviers was just below and plainly visible once more. I could see St. Luc, and the small village of Grimentz on the opposite side. Looking left, I saw clearly, all the way down to the valley's end where thick gray strands of chimney smoke rose steadily, straight from the town of *Zinal*.

Harpo and Groucho were positioned like statues, hunting rifles in hand. Their snowshoes were laced to their gaiters and feet with strips of brown, furry hide—the unlucky chamois become a shoestring ornament. My skis and poles were propped—clean and shining—against the outside wall of the log hut next to the door. Everything I said during this time drifted, unabsorbed and unrecognized out onto a nothingness of cold morning air. It was like talking nonsense just to see the clouds of my breath. I talked continuously, creating a dialogue with myself while Wilbur and Orville remained cold-shouldered and unresponsive.

They watched me stonelike as I fumbled with my skis. I snapped in, put my hands through the pole straps, and made another feeble attempt at spoken gratitude, in a tongue I thought resembled German rather closely. I elicited nothing verbal. Instead, each man, in turn, stepped forward and grabbed me brusquely about the shoulders and hugged me, bear-like, squeezing the air out of me and rapping me on the back once or twice. Then each stepped back in place like a soldier on guard duty.

Rocky and Bullwinkle then pointed to a meager opening in the thick evergreen forest that surrounded the cabin, and I took this to mean, "so long, Bud, there's your way back." The directive was reinforced in what I recognized clearly as French,

"*Saint Luc, ici,*" one said, as the other nodded. Stoic, economical, but poignant parting words—Swiss ebullience.

I pushed-off and cruised toward the hole in the dense forest with the same spirit of ceremony, never looking back, but giving thanks, nevertheless, in my own silent kyrie for the kindness shown me by the hunters and the hunted.

St. Luc and the mountains above it were unchanged by my visit. Even the tracks of my skis would soon be gone, covered by the night snows and winds. My rescuers and I never exchanged names or phone numbers, doubtful they'll remember me when next they ate from wooden bowls, or hunted the deer and chamois of the Val d'Anniviers. So much of the day and night was, and remained, a mystery.

I drove back to Verbier that morning in a condition akin to a light hangover. For the next twenty hours, I rested alone at the Eden, taking hot baths and sleeping for a few hours at a stretch. The way to death was relatively easy up in the high snows, much easier and much closer at hand than anyone could ever imagine. In a matter of hours, I was shown one simple and straightforward way—a peaceful cold sleep, unencumbered, folded for an eternity in nature's frozen arms. But the event of my salvation, the interrupted sleep, proved puzzling, mystical, even Felliniesque. In the time of a bullet's flight, I'd seen the fate of all endangered species. And in the eyes of brown mountain rams, reminded of a thin and fragile mortality.

The images that came to me before my blackout—the dreams, the voices—I jotted down everything in one of my notebooks. I only guessed at the meaning, or the selection of those particular pictures, at that moment, in that sequence. Maybe there were other scenes in the dream-sleep moments. Maybe. They'd slipped from memory. What remained was supposed to.

Near the end in darkness I thought final, the hurtful and the joyous, a boy and a woman, heartache, red water, and loss. I wrote down everything I could remember, no more, and closed the notebook.

I wouldn't eat viande séchée for quite some time, I vowed—a small homage to the still-eyed chamois with the raspy tongue. It was the least I could do.

chapter Thirteen
F R A N C A

From the hotel, I tried calling Céline several times. In a
somewhat stronger condition, I climbed the hill again. There
was never an answer to my phone calls, and no one was at
the chalet. I assumed she was on the mountain somewhere,
watching her brother Claude. The Special Slalom was in first
run. The Downhill event had finished. I'd missed the Giant
Slalom and the Downhill, missed two days completely to the
strange events in the Val d'Anniviers.

The day was brilliant. The crowds were huge and
enthusiastic at the finish area, and the snow conditions were
perfect for one of the premier Alpine events. It was a Swiss
day, Alpine skiing, the World Cup in the heart of the Alps,
sunshine, and pageantry. Thousands of spectators lined the
snowfence the complete length of the Slalom run. Unlike the
Downhill or the GS, the Special Slalom could be seen from
start house to finish line. From the wide braking area at the
finish, the skiers looked like falling leaves, wafting side to
side, as they navigated the blue and red gates. The crowd
chanted with each skier, a sound that matched the rhythm of
slalom skiing—joop, joop, joop—and the hillside resounded.
Swiss cowbells rang louder and louder as the skiers neared
the finish.

Wineskin bladders deflated everywhere, and the
drinker's boistrousness inflated in direct proportion. College
football had its tailgaters, and for the Swiss, a Saturday
afternoon of La Coupe du Monde was the sports fan's
Elysium.

"The Gang" was here in full force. I hadn't seen them for
almost all of four days. Of course, they occupied a prime
position in the grand finish stadium, to see and be seen.

"He is risen." Deke Robinson was the first.

"Was he lost in the Jura?" Eric asked the group.

"No, in the Saléve," came the reply from P.A., and everyone had a hearty laugh. Paloma Armendar had a huge smile for me.

"Eddie, you look wonderful —if you know what I mean?" The suspense was killing her.

"Palomita, I feel wonderful. Things are going beautifully." Her face lit up and I needn't say more about my reunion with Céline.

"What happened to you, man?" Pierre Alain asked, pulling me aside. "The car was gone for two days. I was about to send out a search party."

"Search party? Me?" I joked with P.A., all the time replaying in my mind the miraculous rescue by the *Schweizer menschen* in the Val d'Anniviers. "Someday, over six or seven cognacs, I'm going to tell you a story, P.A."

"Something happened, I can tell. Eddie? You in trouble?"

"No P.A., no trouble. Actually, something good, really good. I think I'm in-tight with the gods these days, at least, the ones in Switzerland with nice eyes."

"Who was she?" He smirked.

"It's a little hard to tell. Do me a favor, though, stay away from the viande sécheé for awhile, will you? The stuff's bad for you, man, clogs the arteries, lots of triglycerides, fatty acids, shit like that, you know?" P.A. screwed-up his face, stepped back and looked at me guardedly.

Just then, amid all of the cheering, a woman emerged from the crowd directly below our position. She captured my attention, and nearly everyone else's interest at the same time, at least, every other male in "The Gang." Her manner of dress was not ostentatious, but her casual air, her posture and gait, and a classic European elegance were conspicuously attractive.

"Okay, I'll ask." I turned to "The Gang." "Who is she?"

"I don't know, but I've seen her in the shop once or twice," Deke replied, set in his own trance. "She buys only the best."

"Who cares?" Manolete was hypnotized. "She obviously doesn't come to the clubs. If she did, she'd cause a riot."

"She's Italian," Liney spoke with ringing authority. "Franca Marchese—from Florence, I think. They have houses everywhere, very important family in Italy," he said. And whenever Liney said *important* it usually meant something other than wealth, some incalculable value given to blood line. Liney just knew that sort of thing, he related intrinsically to a sense of breeding. "It's only her second time in Verbier. They used to frequent Zermatt, St. Moritz, Gstaad—"

"They?" I asked.

"The three wild Italians—at the clubs?" Eric quizzed.

"Oh, yeah." I suddenly connected. "Manny, Moe, and Giacomo, the Siamese Pep Boys, joined at the ego." I remembered the three swooping down on the females in Jacky's and Marshal's.

"The big guy's her brother, Lorenzo. Italian equestrian team," Eric said.

"Listen," I said, riveting on her hypnotically. "Any female from the country that gave the world extra virgin olive oil and Sophia Loren, is worthy of serious consideration."

"I think Liney means she's got titles and shit, Famous," Deke wisecracked.

"She's an aristocrat," Liney defended. "Anyone can see that Deke, almost anyone. The title is Contessa, if you're interested, and that beauty down there in the black ski suit is endowed with an abundance of class *and* money."

"All right, alright, boys. Uncle Eddie's got to do the leg work. All of this talk. Talk, talk, talk. 'Gentlemen'…" I boasted. "'Start your engines.' The hormones, the old bones, the estrogen, the collagen…'what a day for a daydream.' "

"Christ, Famous," Deke whined. "Some things don't change, do they?"

"Yeah, I know." The words floated out of my mouth, automatically, with a captive's resignation. *We are who we are. Caged into it.* "Gents, I'll have a full report filed in no-time."

And with a nod to "The Gang," I jumped into the crowd, weaving my way down to the statuesque Italian beauty standing alone. She stood alone but there must have been ten thousand eyes upon her. I felt them as I got closer to her, and the glares of my friends behind me, smiling and shaking their heads. But, I'd never met a Contessa before.

"Bad day for the Italians," I blurted it out, right behind her, looking off, up the hill at the skier coming down. She turned and looked at me and I had to fight the impulse to look back. That face was beaming and without even a glimpse of it, I felt a power in her beauty. Her dark eyes burned into me. *Maybe she doesn't do English?*

"*Buon giorno, signorina,*" I tried.

Céline was light and softness over dark. This woman was pure blackness, shining blackness, an animal beauty, equine and savage. The gods bestowed beauty like Franca Marchese's to punish men for their lies and digressions, as if to say, "*See, virtue can have rewards, here is grace, beauty, and mystery. It is here, next to you. Be nice.*"

She was coy, and she was ignoring me.

"Italians prefer boxing and baseball," I said, still not looking at her. I tried again. "Joe DiMaggio, Rizzuto, Marciano, Benvenuti, Rocky Balboa...," Her face suddenly lit-up with a broad smile, challenging me. I saw, out of the corner of my eye, a sly sense of humor intensifying.

"Well, I know everybody call you, Famous, *Famoso*," she said, in savvy retaliation, and in English as thick as Bolognese sauce. "You are American, and you stay in the Eden East."

"You're batting a thousand," I replied, looking at her.

"Someone who stay in that place is either an eccentric millionaire, a hotel inspector, or a masochist."

"You just dropped down to three-hundred." I laughed, and saw that she was a player. "That's quite a bit of casual information you've come by. Funny, I didn't know a simple thing like checking in to a hotel could become a character study, signorina Marchese, or is it, Contessa? *Firenze?* yes?"

"*Fiesole*—near enough." She stiffened. "And how do you know my name?" That fine Tuscan profile came up closer to my face to interrogate me.

"Wait, signorina, we go in order. You're first."

"Well, let's see..." She was cool and smart. "I had you followed by my private investigator. He follow to the Eden, then, he pay the concierge a big stack of Swiss Francs."

"Hold it, hold it, no, no, no, Franca. May I call you Franca, Contessa? Thanks. I've always thought you Italians watch too much T.V. Now, look, Beauty, you had a good plot line, but it was flat, hack, you know? Predictable. First of all, the concierge at the Eden wouldn't tell his mother who I am—not if she nailed one foot to the floor and made him run around in circles." She smiled, grandly. "But, try this, Franca, see, your private eye, he follows me to the Eden, hears screams coming from the third-floor front room."

"Aaaahhh. Aaaahhh," she screamed, acting the role. She was game. *What a face.* I can't concentrate, the eyes, carved cheeks, mouth and skin shining, it's too much.

"He goes in and gets the key off of the board," I continued. "Which is easy, because Paul hangs them right there, where anybody can grab one or two. He gets into my room, Franca, and can't find a plane ticket, passport, wallet, anything useful. He starts going through my clothes. Figures, a monogram, maybe. This guy's a vain Yank, he thinks...got to be something with initials, a belt buckle, a shirt. He sees that all the labels on my clothes have been cut out, picked out, unstitched. Ah, ha. C.I.A., he thinks, naturally. Because nine-out-of-ten Europeans believe that seven-out-of-eight

Americans are C.I.A. anyway. Then, he sees the hotel
stationary. There, a big 'E' at the top of the page."

Franca laughed out loud, and there was a childlike glee
in her expression, like a little kid listening to a mystery comic
book story.

"Such a story, signore Famous. It's an opera."

"This guy you hired is no Rhodes Scholar, Contessa. He
tears the stationary sheet off and brings it back to you.'

"...and, I throw the swine out."

"Obviously. You're livid. Now, the private eye goes back
to the Eden to stand beneath my third-floor window,
listening."

"Ah, yes, the screams, the screams?" She said, very
involved in the plot.

"No. The plaintive cries of ecstasy."

"Oh? *Ecco?*"

"Yes, the plaintive cries of ecstasy. Always change it,
never, never cover the same ground, the echoes, you know?
Advance the, uh, the what-cha-ma-call-it, raise the, uh, you
see, you build the..."

"Tension?"

"No."

"*Esspectation?*"

"No."

"*Intrigo? Quale?*"

"No, no. *Vieni qui, bella.*" Her beautiful face came up
very close to mine again. "The, ah...smut."

"As-*mota?*" The brows go up, heavenly.

"Smut."

"Smm-utt? *Che cosa, smutt?*" She said, bewildered.

"The Smut Plot. The underlying, perverse, prurient,
lacivious, lustful, immoral intention of the primary text. All
American bestsellers have it, or they don't sell."

"Oh, I see," She wondered with grave concern.

"Yes, and soon television will learn the value of *il plota
smutta*, for without dirt, where will we find virtue?"

"My, you're very insightful, mister, uh?"

"Eddie, Eddie...but you can call me Famous. It's O.K."

Just then, the race announcer on the loudspeaker drowned-out our conversation. He was screaming excitedly about a skier who was on the hill at that moment. I turned to listen, and it was Claude Decauville having the run of his life. I couldn't see the blue and white-clad young Frenchman managing the gates from where Franca and I were standing. The crowd pressed in toward the finish area, squeezing the two of us out of the line of sight. Claude's split-time was a half second faster than the current leader, a remarkable feat for a first year World Cup skier starting in thirty-eighth position. Quickly, I scanned the crowd, looking for Céline, but couldn't find her.

"What is going on?" Franca asked, tugging at my arm.

"A young Frenchman. The brother of a friend."

Céline? A friend? Did I really say that? Like a reflex the lie just kicked out in front of me. I lifted and strained to see over the heads of the foreground crowd, trying to see Claude's finish. The announcer was blabbing a-mile-a-minute. Then Claude came into view about a hundred meters from the finish, and the bells, whistles, and screaming were deafening.

The crowd waited. The announcer kept repeating, "bap-a-da-bap-a-da-bap, Decauville, bap-a-da-bap-a-da-bap, Decauville..." And then, the announcer stopped, hurriedly. The crowd sighed in unison, deflating like a bad spare tire. Claude Decauville had missed a gate and crashed into the orange snow fence about four seconds from the finish.

My heart sank. Visions of Claude, then of Céline flashed through my head.

"What's happened?" Franca brought me back.

"Missed a gate. Not a good day for the French either," I joked, trying to distract myself and Franca.

"Let's do something else, Eddie *Famoso*, I'm bored with the skiing," she pouted. "I've had enough for today."

"Yeah, me too," I said, still thinking of Céline.

"I know," She said brightly. "Let's go back to my chalet and make mad, passionate love all afternoon." A straight-faced zinger tossed-out to the air. She was wild looking, devilish.

"Good, that's good—shock, surprise, good opener."

"It's much too early for champagne, anyway. *No?*" Spoken with the perfect combination of flippancy and insouciance.

"Excellent," I commended her. "Boredom, condescension, tedium, preoccupation. You've got tremendous potential, Contessa. You're getting the hang of this. In reference to your offer, could we try interval lovemaking—thirty and thirty, you know?"

"Ahhh, espresso, *eh?*" The black eyebrows went flying.

"No. No, *signorina,*" I blushed.

"*Presto?*"

"No. *Primo, Contessa.* We must first get to know each other. I like to sip and savor, you know what I mean?"

She burst out with a hearty, gravel-ly laugh. Striking, her face was, alive and striking, fully expressive, open, beatific. "Your beauty inspires beauty. Do you know that, Franca? Of course you know, what the hell am I saying? Men cannot fathom beauty as deep as yours—not with our minds."

She paused and accepted the flattery graciously with her eyes, the long black lashes mesmerizing me. She'd heard it all before, knew what to do, and how to play a man like a mandolin. Could a man be original for her? Novelty, maybe. Original? No.

"Well then, tea by the fire," she said. "And we'll begin at the beginning." I looked at her sideways, puzzled. "*Carissimo,* the screams, the screams, remember? Aaaahhh. Aaaahhh."

We started off toward town, making our way through the heavy crowd. People seemed to part in front of us like the Red Sea before the Israelites. It was a strange phenomenon, celebrity, extraordinary beauty, wealth. In societies that venerated the three, as we do, those possessing any combination had an unquestioned power. As we walked, I felt again the eyes upon us, lots of them. Whispers went with the looks, "Who are they? Who is she?" Franca put her arm in mine, and the moment was complete. Sometimes one gesture by a woman, and a man rejoices in being just a man.

"So, come on Eddie, what happens to my private detective?"

"Well, under the window the second time, after the first stupid mistake with the stationary, he hears a woman's cry, 'Oh, God. Oh. Dear God.' Now, he thinks he's got a name, or the woman's writing a letter." Franca roared with laughter again, almost pulling me down in the snow. "Aren't they silly?" The people must have been whispering.

Chalet Arosa was one of the monsters of the mountain. A three storied, six-bedroom Swiss style mansion, beautifully maintained. It had a spectacular view of Verbier and the lower foothills leading up from the floor of the Val de Bagnes. It was just west of Liney's chalet, on Chemin des Luys, and the pattern of the morning and evening mist, as it floated up and down the cols of the dark valley, could be seen best from this area of the mountainside. Sky and earth and mist of heavens were in magical confluence from this spot. It was prime real estate in Verbier, winter or summer.

The bottom floor of the chalet was an open carport, occupied entirely by three shining automobiles—a red Lamborghini, a track-modified, black BMW coupe, and a white, futuristic Japanese prototype, Formula-C Mitsubishi. The Axis Powers equally represented in a single garage.

"Let me guess," I prodded her. "You're the Mitsubishi."

"No. The BMW," she said, casually. I raised an eyebrow. "I like black," she quipped. "It's so easy to dress for. Besides, I like to get where I'm going fast." She gave me a sly glance and put her arm through mine again, forcefully.

Just then, the door to the chalet sprung open and three young, dark men bound down the front stairs. They were, in fact, the same extremely good-looking three I'd seen in the clubs. A man didn't usually make that sort of observation, but I must admit, they were strikingly handsome men. They say, men can't recognize beauty in other men—some hormonal thing. They can. Men simply won't admit it—some other hormonal thing.

"Ah, yes." Franca watched them approach with a mild intolerance. "The boys. My brother and his two friends—the Lamborghini and the Mitsubishi, respectively."

"*Franca. Che fai?*" Lorenzo Marchese, the big guy, leaned over and kissed his sister on the cheek, affectedly. Franca received the Italianate gesture coolly.

"Lorenzo, I'd like you to meet," She hesitated and some mischievous glow suddenly came across her face. "My American friend, Eddie God."

"*Dio? Ma che?*" Lorenzo screwed a grimace into his face.

Franca and I looked at each other and burst into laughter. Lorenzo and his two friends were too puzzled to laugh. Before they could recover, I thrust my hand forward at Lorenzo Marchese. Our eyes met first. Lorenzo Marchese and I locked eyes and then hands, and something happened in that moment, some chemical, visceral activity began in our inards. In mine, I was certain.

In the hierarchy of male wolves, two Super-Alpha males could never face each other, thusly. All the genetic, prehistoric codes clicking just behind their eyes, would forbid it. How thoroughly blood curdling, and how exciting, the primitive struggle must have been. Here we stood, all locked in social baggage, the amenities, holding hands that once executed our will like the claws of our natural cousins.

He never took his eyes from mine. His head was firm, cocked straight and flowing with black curls of hair. I pictured him atop his medal-winning steed, the team captain, pompous and so self-assured, Lee on Traveller,

Alexander on Bucephalus—beauty, strength, and confidence. What did I look like to him? Roy on Trigger?

"So, God is an American?" He said. Wit, too. His two friends laughed at his little pun.

I'd turned over the beautiful petal of a flower in Franca and I was seeing some pitted underside, some danger.

"You knew all along." I tried to match his levity, tried to be cordial, open to some other feeling, but it wasn't working.

"These are my two friends," he said, graciously. "Giancarlo Bruni and Alberto Cannegia." The two stepped forward and shook my hand firmly. Franca, meanwhile, was getting a great kick out of watching the sparks between the four of us.

Franca and I spent the rest of the afternoon together. And at six, there was champagne. There was cocaine. Plenty of both. My mind went bubbly and white, too, and the hours passed.

Ferried around in a limo that evening that simply appeared when she wished it, we dined elegantly at *Au Fer à Cheval*, danced to conventional music at Auberge de la Diligence, and sipped cognacs around midnight at Sacconaix. I'd never taken a woman in there before. Philipe, the frail barkeep, looked at me kind of cross-eyed. Franca and I were wonderfully silly, half drunk, and very playful. I consent to almost anything in that state, and at some point I agreed to go skiing with her the following day.

The slinky limo drove to the side door of the Eden. Franca wanted to come up to my room and look for labels in my clothing, but we laughed instead and made-up more "smut plots." We managed to get each other very excited there in the back seat and on the floor of the limo. Franca was moist. The word "regret" blinked on-and-off in my brain like a neon beer sign, the condition of having a woman like Franca Marchese in my arms, and four or five bottles of champagne—plus cognac, drugs, and assorteds—rattling around in my head. I bid her farewell there in the backseat. I dared not turn regret into stupidity.

"*A domani, Edouardo, domani di prima mattina. Provocante. Animali,*" she yelled to me, throwing me kisses like a Homecoming Queen from the backseat, through the rear window, as the limo sailed-off.

In the dark lobby of the Eden, one little nightlight behind the front desk burned constantly for late returnees, like me. The illumination there was enough to reflect off of a small piece of notepaper, a white-on-white lily and green stem drawn on its front. The note was tacked to the keyboard underneath my key.

> *'Eddie, mon cher*
> *…was at the top of le Slalom today.*
> *Missed you, horribly. Claude, very depressed,*
> *wants to quit. Call me.*
> *I love you, Céline*

Damn-it. If I called now, I'd lie. I'd lie about Franca, I'd lie about tomorrow. I looked out of the front window, to the hill of chalets. Franca's limo was still climbing the Route des Creux, and somewhere up there in the maze of sparkling lights, Céline was looking, waiting for me to call. The hill full of chalets and lights pulsated and I felt that at any moment all the chalets would begin to slide in a great avalanche, tumbling down into Place Centrale, all converging, piling together at the Eden three stories deep.

chapter Fourteen
ZERMATT

Six-thirty, sharp. I was standing outside on the little balcony when Franca's black BMW rumbled down the hill and stopped in front of the Eden down below. She parked as though she had Diplomatic plates, right in the middle of Rue d'Verbier, and gazed up at me through the windscreen with an enchanting, seductive smile, looking as fresh as a flower. I felt like death warmed-over. Champagne, cocaine, and cognac — the C Vitamins — an embalming mixture for the Jet Set.

Into the front seat I slid, eyes completely covered by glacier glasses. She rubbed my temples, giggling all the while. Her smirk filled the air with gleeful satisfaction. She kissed me softly, many times, all over my face, then strapped me into a seat belt and a shoulder harness. I was a hung-over ragdoll. She was cradling-me-in so that I'd nap while she drove to wherever we were going. How nice. No chance.

I didn't think anyone could ever drive the hairpin "S" turns down the mountain the way Franca did that morning.

"A nap? Jesus Christ, Franca. Out of the question," I yelled. "What a waste, to be asleep when the end comes. The last great adventure embarked upon and the best part of the journey missed." Franca laughed all the way down the hill. "Just what I wanted my dearest, a day on the black-macadam slopes with Emerson Fittipaldi."

"Tell me you'll stay with me tonight," she yelled back. "Or I'll drive faster." She chuckled again, pressing the accelerator.

"Slow down, *Speditiva*. Or we'll be together forever — never mind tonight."

Just then, a thought of Céline flashed through my mind.

A turn here, a turn there, over the edge and no need to worry about anything. To die, and take the lies with me. Fitting, for a life that lies had essentially undermined.

"*Amore mio*, think of it," she said sporting a devilish grin. "You won't have to worry about your hotel bill."

"Damn. You'll pick up my laundry, yes, Contessa?"

"*Laoun-dree?*" She said, with affected benign horror. "*Ma che?* What is this, *laoun-dree?* I never heard this word."

"Drive, you little aristocrat." She laughed again as she downshifted, with emphasis. Every time she giggled her face glowed like a child's. Men would die in a fiery crash, gladly, with this woman. The BMW screeched and whirred, around and around, down and down we caromed. Franca was loving every minute of my fright. Men are never at-ease when women are behind the wheel. If they say they are, they're lying—a sexist thing, very sexist.

"Where are we going, anyway?" I asked. "You haven't told me. And me, I never bothered to ask. I'm under your spell, Franca. You control me now. You know that don't you?"

"Of course, my love. We are on our way to Sion."

"Sion? What are we going to do there, sauna? swim?"

"Agh. What kind of girl do you take me for? *Bestia*. But, it's not a bad idea."

"Okay, surprise me," I said.

"I wish I could," she replied, and I saw a little sadness in her face for the first time. The wheels behind that Florentine brow were turning, I sensed it. I felt myself give-over to her in that second, erasing all thoughts of Céline, of everything. I was with her now, with Franca.

I touched her thigh and squeezed gently. She glanced over at me with a gleaming smile. Something in her eyes imprisoned me, wrapped me in a cage, a thorny bramble of her dark passion. She placed her hand atop mine, firmly, and then moved my hand between her legs into a warmth and softness, holding my hand there against the tepid pulsation of her hardness.

The BMW got the best of whatever Franca was feeling at that moment. I sat back, unmoving in her heat, and gritted my teeth. The drive down the hill was nothing compared to the race across the autoroute. The city of Sion appeared in seconds.

She drove, expertly really, right to a small airfield on the edge of the city. A shiny yellow and white helicopter sat waiting for us, a rakish, gray-haired pilot stood by its door. Franca drove through the metal gate giving access to the main terminal buildings, past a few service vehicles, and onto the tarmac airstrip, unannounced, practically up to the door of the chopper. We stepped out of the BMW, and magically a white-jacketed waiter appeared from the small office of Aereo Pennina adjacent to the main set of terminal buildings. He carried a tray with two cups of *caffé* and a small white plate with sugar lumps sitting on it, intercepting us halfway between the car and the helicopter. What choreography. What orchestration. We sipped as the waiter stood waiting.

Out of the corners of my eyes, I caught quick glimpses of two or three attendants scurrying, ferrying our skis and poles from the BMW into the chopper. Then, the gray-haired pilot came forward to greet us. The nearer he got, the more he looked like William Holden (an older Holden) in *The Bridges at Toko Ri.*

"Vittorio, *giorno.*" Franca held out her hand, her arm automatically rising like a crane, straight out. Vittorio kissed her hand as if they'd done this routine a thousand times.

"*Buon giorno, signorina,*" Vittorio replied, reverently.

"My American friend, Eddie. Eddie, Vittorio." Franca finessed the rapid introduction after the hand kiss.

"Vittorio, a pleasure, *Piacere, molto.*" My Italian stuck to the roof of my mouth, boiling off with the scalding espresso.

"Well, shall we get going?" Franca said with her usual nonchalance and stunning flippancy.

"I have the transit visas, round up the usual cowards," I joked in my best Claude Rains.

"*Cattivo, basta.*" She squeezed my arm tightly and then smiled that mischievous smile again. The pilot and the waiter were dumbstruck, watching her dreamy-eyed and grinning all the while. She clinked her cup back down on the tray. I clinked in-kind. Then, Franca marched me to the helicopter as if I were a wounded soldier.

The waiter disappeared as magically as he had appeared, attendants flew off in several directions until they were unseen, and I crawled, reluctantly, into the hold of the chopper.

It was a modified gunship, Sikorsky H-3, secondhand Vietnam vintage probably, spruced-up for the ferrying of several skiers—or a Swiss army patrol—to their favorite glacial drop spots. It was actually huge inside, skis were standing straight, strapped against the side wall. I clung to the sidewall, too, groping for my bearing. Bill Holden slid into the cockpit, tied a white silk scarf around his neck, and cranked-up the old war machine.

I hated these goddamn things. The engine roared. I buckled-in and suddenly remembered all the helicopter rides I'd ever taken in my life, realizing that each one followed a night of spiritual or corporeal debauchery, or alcoholic misuse. Sure that my complexion was a pale green by now, I took a few deep breaths through my nose, loudly.

"*Amore mio,* are you alright?" Franca asked.

"Me? Fine. I love the smell of chopper fuel in the morning." I sniffed harder. "Listen, Franca," I yelled over the engine's building revs. "We don't have to do this if you don't want to. How about some over-the-edge tobogganing, or something?"

She laughed again, those beautiful white teeth were moist and flashing. If I felt the way she looked, I could have flown the Valais naked and without a helicopter, doing aerial acrobatics all the way. Then, she leaned over and kissed me on the lips, twice.

"What about a snowball fight?" I tried. Something in my question must have been Vittorio's cue. The yellow Sikorsky ripped into the sky, due-vertical, as though dodging enemy rocket fire. My stomach followed minutes later.

Aloft, over the great Pennine Alps, and I felt better the minute we leveled-off, but I continued to let-on that I was suffering. It was useful playacting, and entertainment for The Contessa Marchese.

Most people swooned over aerial views. For some unknown reason, I didn't. Suddenly, the greatness and majesty of the mountains was reduced. The spires and peaks flattened as we gained altitude and before long, we were looking at just another map. Man again, assuming a god's view of the world.

Franca held my arm tightly. She wanted to keep me beside her, clinging to a new, best friend. Now, only the little, dark Italian girl remained. The Contessa was gone. She was full of wonder and excitement, a *bambina* by my side. Little Franca hugged my arm. She would not let go easily.

I was her plaything for the day. They do sometimes fall in love with their subjects, I mused. Could I handle that? Live in a stone palace in Italy, accept all that privilege? Men did think this way — could I schmooz with other royalty, have an asshole for a brother-in-law? But then, I thought, who doesn't have a brother-in-law who's an asshole?

I'd be a player, but I wouldn't kid myself. Franca wanted an adventure, not Count Edward, "The Yank."

We changed into our ski boots midway into the flight across the Canton. Naturally, I asked the dumb question "What about our shoes and socks?" And there, you see, was the division, the telling separation. One simply did not ask a question like that when one was "to the manor born." Of course, our shoes and socks would be taken care of. There

were people in the service of people like Franca Marchese to
see to such things.

By the time we were booted and zipped-in, the grand
Mattertal Valley was beneath us, the Visp River sparkling in
the center of it like a strip of molten lead — half-frozen, half
flowing. At the end of the valley, standing like a church spire
in the sunlight was the Matterhorn, Le Cervin. Vittorio
turned and headed straight up the valley, decending steadily
as we flew southward into the sun, toward Zermatt. The
landscape rose slowly up from the map, bringing the
magnificent contours and outcroppings, the cols and snowy
ravines into near normal perspective once again. The valley's
small towns of St. Niklaus and Täsch passed beneath us.
Cows and people, skaters and children running, children
sledding could be seen again—life, on a human scale,
rediscovered.

"*Gornergrat?*" I yelled.

"Yes," Franca screamed back, over the engine's grind.

Franca got up, as if she'd worked this run many times,
and slid the large side door open. Just outside the opening,
two rather unique projections pointed outward and down at
about a sixty-degree angle — strangest things I'd ever seen.
They extended out and over the struts, and looked like two
wooden, stretched-out toilet seats. This was heli-dropping
Alpine style?

Boots on, we moved to the open door and watched our
journey, Franca holding me ever tighter to her. The
helicopter was a brilliantly made machine, and I realized that
as we moved around the compartment. It was rock steady,
and the cabin wind turbulence was insignificant. We put on
gloves, goggles, hoods and scarves, looking like two
beekeepers in search of a hive. Vittorio would signal us to sit
in the elongated toilet seats when the time came, I guessed.
We waited and watched the earth draw-up beneath us.

Zermatt passed below. Vittorio turned east, and the
broad shoulders of Sunnegga and Riffelalp, folded in

morning shadow, led our way up along the Findelen Glacier.
Franca squeezed my arm again, a thrilling light beamed in
her eyes. The Sikorsky beat the thin air as we climbed. The
Gorner Glacier was to our right, but hidden behind the front
massifs of the Hohtälli and the Rote Nase. On our left, we
sailed past the Unterrothorn and the smooth white face of the
Oberrothorn. Vittorio was taking us up and over the back
side of the Stockhorn, practically in the shadow of 15-
thousand-foot Monte Rosa.

In minutes, a white, seamless stretch at the head of the
Gorner Glacier came into view, and Franca guided the way.
Placing our skis on either side of the toilet seats, we snapped
in. The seats, as it turned out, were not what I'd envisioned.
We'd stand in them, not sit, like racers at the starting gate of
the Giant Slalom, two side-by-side holding blocks for an
aerial descent, wonderfully smooth wooden tracks waxed to
a brilliant patina.

Vittorio leaned back — gray hair, dark glasses, white silk
scarf — and gave us a nod. Vittorio had a career, Franca told
me, doing aerials for Fellini, Pasolini, Di Sica, and Bertolucci
in the heyday of modern Italian cinema. She skimmed-over
the part about the aerials for Mussolini, in Il Duce's Big
Produzione. Only certain references made it onto the résumé
in Europe. The past was a place, for some, where odd jobs
were better forgotten.

"He'll make one pass to show us where," she yelled. We
were standing at the top of the wooden slides, in the
doorway.

"It'll be the shortest ski jump, or the longest fall, I'll ever
make, Contessa."

Monte Rosa looked near enough to touch. We made a
pass over a wide and gently-sloping snowfield. Vittorio
brought the Sikorsky down to about twenty or thirty feet and
slowed our air speed. Again, I was amazed at the solid glide
of the heavy aircraft. Vittorio waved a gloved hand, and

began to circle up near the huge Monte Rosa again in preparation for our flyby drop on the next pass.

Franca stepped up and into the wooden slide, holding onto the overhead lifeline hanging in the open doorway. I followed her lead, grabbing the line and hoisting up. We flexed our knees a few times. Then she grabbed my face in one hand, leaned over and kissed me once, squeezing my cheeks.

"*Bestia.* See you in paradise." She pointed down below as we approached the drop area. "We must yell something together when we jump, Eddie. It's our custom." She smiled and put both ski poles under her left arm and then stooped into a racer's crouch.

"Sounds good. I've got something," I yelled back, smiling. "My best Italian."

I placed my poles tightly under my right arm and bent in to a compact, fetal position. We were set. Vittorio brought the huge gunship down into the white snowfield, and it was surreal. If I didn't know better, I'd think he cut engines. It was dreamlike, like gliding on air without power. Down, so smoothly we sailed. The heavy Sikorsky turned and listed slightly, gently opening a little sky to us. We were her eggs, and the big yellow bird was softly dropping us in a white, marshmallow nest. Vittorio drove it almost to a stop and the ship lilted. Every flake and grain of snow was suddenly visible in the suspended moment. Our spot came up beneath us.

"*Avanti,*" Franca yelled.

We pressed our ski tips downward. Together we flew and the end of the slick, wooden tracks came fast. Sounds disappeared. We looked at each other, opened our arms like birds and floated, poles in one hand, letting our skis find the pitch of the fall line. Airborne and free-falling, our jumpsuits filled with the air. We smiled again and I yelled.

"*Merda, allora.*"

We skied Gornergrat for most of the morning — not once did I ask about our shoes and socks — and near the noon hour, we crossed over to the runs beneath the Matterhorn. The skiing was complicated, too many lifts and *télécabins*. We made one long climb to Klein Matterhorn — Franca almost fell asleep in my arms on the ride to the top — and then, skied down for an hour into the center of Zermatt.

Lunch was light and sunny at the Monte Rosa Hotel. We sat on the glass-enclosed terrace, exhausted, and spread ourselves and our snowy ski wear on several chairs around our large table. People watched us—the curious eyes again—a bit uneasily, but we cared not and ate and drank and laughed through an hour-and-a-half of luxurious afternoon dining.

Aprés déjeuner, Franca was excited again. She seemed to anticipate great joy from a day's possibilities.

We marched a short distance through the center of town to the Mont Cervin Hotel, where an indoor fitness club, complete with swimming pool, would be our pleasurable indulgence for the remainder of the afternoon. It was obvious Franca had been a regular customer here during her Zermatt Period. Everything was at our disposal, swim trunks, exercise machinery, saunas, steam, mud, and massage tables. Franca and I opted for the deadly-hot sauna, which we shared with two huge-breasted German women. At one point — the point of sauna collapse — the two German women got up and walked through the door of the sauna, holding it open, looking at Franca and me, as if to say "Aren't you coming?" Franca and I glanced at each other, and then followed the two large women, down a narrow hallway, and through another door. Suddenly, we were standing outside, in the back of the hotel, in snow that was about two feet deep.

The two German nymphs whipped their towels off and went frolicking in the snow, naked. At first, Franca and I watched in amusement as their pink, sauna-baked skin gradually turned bright, lobster-red. They were having a hell of a time, and our feet were beginning to freeze standing there.

"It looks like fun." Franca's grin spoke her mind. I flipped my terrycloth away. She let hers fall gracefully to her feet.

" 'Here's lookin' at you, kid.' " I mimicked. She was like a Greek goddess standing there dripping in sauna sweat, a Roman goddess, rather, a Lydian-Etruscan deifying her own beauty. We embraced and dove into the snow with the two Germans. It was nuts. Four naked people, strangers no more, rolled around and rubbed each other with fresh snow.

After a few rounds of *sauna mit schnee* — running from hot to cold like *frei kinder* — we bid farewell to our two naked friends. They laughed and smiled and said nice things to us, in German, that only Franca understood.

Back at the club, our massage tables were side by side, naturally. Franca and I held hands across the space while two Swiss-German sadists beat our bodies into suppleness.

"The two German girls thought we were just married, new..."

"Newlyweds," I said.

"Yes, that's it. Newlyweds." She giggled. "They were adorable, weren't they?"

"Zoftig delights, thoroughly adorable."

"Eddie, why don't you come to Fiesole with me." She said it with a kind of truant glee in her eye. "You would love it, our snowy, little vinyards, the orchards in spring. Eddie, Eddie, pleee-ase, you must. We could go to 'The Palio' in Siena."

She was getting so excited, I thought she'd fall from the massage table.

"Correct me if I'm mistaken, *schiava del'amore*, but isn't 'The Palio' in July?"

"Well, I thought you would stay for awhile," she pouted.

"I'm a crash-and-burn kind of guy, Contessa. I'm good for a weekend – great for a weekend – really. But after that, I seem to have this circulation problem."

"*Ma.* You really are crazy. Such a thing we have together."

"Franca, do you realize we've known each other for less than two full days?" I was contradictory. Of course, I would do such a thing under normal circumstances, previous circumstances. But now there was Céline. Even lying there naked with Franca, that calculation, that time span since I last saw Céline was on my mind, heavily. No thought of myself, my future, could now occur bereft of the thought of her.

"What does it matter? Tell me? Time. Time, Eddie? What does it matter when you feel..."

"Time does matter. It would take years for me to explain how much it matters in my life."

"I'll listen, I'll wait. Tell me anything, *diavolo*, but things must begin, Eddie. And once they do, we must face them as they are. *Madonna!* Forget time."

"What about loving someone, Franca? People invest time in each other."

"Agh. American men. *Che un maschera.* You want to say, 'I love you' after the first kiss, and be together for the rest of your lives. You can't stand the thought of impermenance, chance, living what's here. You don't like it."

"Don't tell me what American men don't like, Franca." I imitated her pout. "We don't like runny eggs, pizza with anchovies, and presumptuous Europeans."

"It just is, my love." She leaned across, very serious, with a very plaintive expression on her face. "For ten minutes, ten days, or ten years. Look at us. We're wonderful together, aren't we? Forget about love. There's only *this* now, whatever we have. It will be there if it's meant to be. This, Eddie, this."

"I know hardly anything about you."

"Come to Fiesole. I won't hide anything from you." Her

look was sultry. "I promise, nothing. You'll see everything. You may be shocked. Now, wouldn't *that* be worth the trip? You can write all you want, and when you stop, I'll be there, Eddie, always."

"Orchards, eh? What kinds of fruits?" I stalled.

"Fruits of love. I'll plant them for you." Spoken like a B-movie super-siren.

"Let me think, Franca. I need to figure some things out. Let me think about spring."

"Whatever you wish. I don't believe in demands. Clarity can be terrifying, sometimes, as terrifying as a bit of doubt. I'm open to you, Eddie. I want you as you are. It's the only true expression of one's love, don't you think?"

She squeezed my hand gently, and her openness drew me in. I was falling into a space that Franca was widening for me. Some women knew how to manage. They did just one simple thing and a man fell into a giant crevasse of understanding and intimacy from which it became impossible to extricate himself. We stared at each other, deeply. *Isn't this what I always wanted?* The two Swiss-German musclemen oiled and kneaded an arousal in our naked bodies that our eyes had already accomplished across the space between the tables.

Vittorio was waiting with the airship at the helipad. Everything had been readied, skis and boots neatly arranged and secured, and of course, our shoes and socks were waiting for us at the health club when our massage finished. Then, a peaceful flight back to Sion, Franca nestled in my arms all the way, and the two of us cradled in Alpenglow and the purple light of dusk.

I drove the BMW back up the hill, into the Val de Bagnes. Franca slept with her head on my thigh. My thoughts were agonizing, wanting Céline so desperately in one moment, reviewing the day with Franca, terrified of hurting her, in the next.

At Sembrancher, at the foot of the climb to Verbier, a

light, wet snow began to fall. The rest of the winding drive
was treacherous, but navigable. The BMW fish-tailed slowly
through La Châble, and spun throughout the "S" turns into
Verbier in first and second gear. Franca never stirred once.
She was off in some orchard dreamland with my warm quad
muscle as her pillow. I touched her forehead and face when I
wasn't shifting, and she grinned, contentedly.

I dropped my skis, literally, at the Eden, leaning them in
the outside rack with the rest of the tourist's skis and drove
the rest of the way up to Chalet Arosa.

We lit a fire and sat curled-up in front of it with glasses
of red Tuscan wine. The strenuousness of the entire day was
seeping into our massaged muscles, and we fell asleep
within minutes to the popping and crackling of the
fruitwood logs, Franca's body next to mine was radiant
warmth to match the fire's glow.

Around nine-thirty, we rummaged for eats. Franca
opened the biggest can of caviar I'd ever seen, and we
scooped ravenously with toasts. We strafed, like fighter jets
and yellow helicopters, with crackers and lemon slices — with
our fingers at times — the black Beluga paste and washed it
down with champagne. The feeding frenzy had begun.

The table looked like a Battle of Gettysburg jigsaw
puzzle. With little squares of toast, cuts and slices of brown
breads and grain crackers all over the place, I quickly turned
the puzzle into a board game. I made the formations and
whistled the battle hymn. She was all ears about Gettysburg,
I had a captive audience in Franca — typical European,
fascinated by our Civil War.

I set the knives and spoons and cutting boards in array,
marking boundaries, lines and battlefields, artillery and
fortifications. The crumbs of poppy-seed rolls and stray
pellets of caviar became the Union and Rebel infantrymen. I
began by showing her the second day troop movements at
Devil's Den and The Wheatfield, The Slaughter-Pen and
Major-General Daniel Sickles line against the doubled forces

of Longstreet, McClaws, and John Bell Hood. Franca was sad. The South had no caviar. The empty can became Big Round Top, the lid, Little Round Top.

Along Cemetery Ridge, I laid down a line of cocaine as thick as my thumb and sounded reveille to the first, white blow.

"Is not fair," she screamed. "The North gets the *bon bons.*" This *petite noblesse* from Tuscany felt sorry for the poor and tattered Rebels.

Franca ferreted through the cabinets for some treat to fortify Lee's men, while I leveled Cemetery Hill to a few white flecks and berms of coca dust. She found two jars of peanut butter, left by the Americans who'd rented Arosa right before the Marchese army moved in. Peanut butter, enough to make any man switch allegiance—I wanted to join the Confederacy immediately. She teased and taunted me with the peanut butter, spreading it with her fingers on top of big squares of Valaisanne bread, on top of Lee and Ewell and Jeb Stuart. The South was smothered in Georgia nuts, and the North was as white as snow. I would have given, gladly, Big Round Top and Little Round Top, surrendered them both—full tins of caviar—for jars of peanut butter without firing a single shot.

The fun escalated, and peanut butter was smeared almost everywhere. So was the cocaine. Empty champagne bottles stood like monuments to the dead and fallen. We were as giddy as two Billy goats, and the kitchen table of Chalet Arosa looked like Manassas and Chicamauga and Appomattox all rolled into one.

And then, during our uncontrollable laughter, somewhere in the middle of wiping a smear of peanut butter from her cheek and Pickett's Charge, she began to cry. Huge tears streamed silently from Franca's dark eyes, down across my fingers, dripping down on bread squares and smears, on North and South along the Emmitsburg line, on Meade and Slocum, and on General Lee, her wet sorrow fell. I clutched

her head in my hands. She cried harder. I licked her salty
tears, and she closed her eyes tightly, pressing her forehead
against my lips.

"Franca, Franca," I whispered, and a deep sadness
burned through to my core. "Franca, you are like a shooting
star, a comet," I told her. "I saw you streak across an open
sky and I took off like a kid, running under you, to catch a
shooting star. That's what I do, Franca. That's what I've
always done. You're right about clarity. But you belong to
some sky, some universe, I know little of."

I held her in my arms for a long time. She shook as she
cried, and trembled like a kitten when she stopped. She dried
her tears on my sweater, and we rocked there gently side to
side, hugging each other tightly as painful thoughts came to
us, memories of the fun we'd shared in the last two days.

"In 1944, my mother, she kiss an American soldier."
Franca wiped her eyes with her hand and brightened as she
began talking. "She told me this so many times, she told me
this story—about when the Americans landed. *Liberazione,
no?*"

"Yeah. I know," I said, pushing her hair from her
forehead.

"She always say to me, 'never kiss an American man,
Franca, because you will never forget.'" The memory possessed
her in that moment, her gaze was far off and remote. Then,
she grabbed a napkin from the kitchen table and blew her
nose in it—a loud honk—a real Contessa honk. So much for
intimate memories. "Never kiss an American, she say, you'll
be sad, Franca."

"So, shall I pinch your ass, instead? The American way
to make you feel better, make you feel at home?" That
brought her back like a cold shower. She looked at me and
exploded with laughter. She grabbed my hair in her fist and
shook my head. Her face lit-up again, the way it was when
we played at the kitchen table with bread soldiers and caviar
infantry. That wonderful face returned, the face I'd seen that

first day on the snow at the races. Beautiful Franca. Radiant Franca. The dark-browed Tuscan face, was fine-featured and mysterious again and flashing with some brilliant glee now.

"*Bestia. Bestia*," she scolded me, grabbing my face between her big hands. She kissed me wildly, laughing and scolding me with each joyous embrace. "*Bestia. Cattivo. Cornuto.*" Names called-out in a shower of affection.

"A guy would rightly need his head examined, letting a dame like you slip through his fingers. But tomorrow is another day, *bella*. And frankly my dear…I've got to face it."

"Don't make it sad, Eddie, please?"

"No, not sad. Nothing connected with the thought of you could ever be sad. You taught me about *this*, this thing we possess now, between us. I can't find the word to describe this something from nothing, but now I've come to understand and accept certain truths. Whatever we've made of it, it's ours alone, Franca."

I brought her into me slowly and kissed her, tenderly. For all the Italian movie stars I'd ever dreamt of kissing, all those luscious, fulsome women who filled those afternoons in the World Art Cinema—the Ginas, Stephanias, Claudias, and Sophias—the dreaming and wishing for just one minute, with Laura Antonelli, one embrace with Sophia, I'd be a Marcello for just one dream. For all those stunning goddesses, Franca filled my embrace and she was all of them in that kiss. She was everything that luck could bring a man, and more.

There was springtime in Tuscany. She'd given me that, like an image from a silver screen. That dream I'd keep. Franca would inhabit me always from those misty Italian hill towns, like an echo of distant *campanile*, the bells in those stone towers, ringing.

Perhaps my days, and nights, of fixing the cat were coming to a close. Something was happening in Verbier this time. I left Franca, determined to find Céline that night.

The cold air snapped at my eyes as I walked briskly back

to town. Down the hill from Chalet Arosa on Route des Creux, I re-played the last two days, touched by this Italian beauty, penetrated by her insights, and warmed in the glow of her constant affection. Why was it like that? Why so easy? Starting from some flirtation, a casual remark—from nothing—and someone was revealed who'd remain in my heart, in my memory, forever.

Ice rain fell around me, making its eerie sound on the crust snow like rushing water, immutable and soothing. I never looked back up the hill. Down I walked, faster toward Jacky's or Marshal's, or the Borsalino, toward some noise that I needed just then to flood the silence Franca had left in me.

Everything suddenly seemed different. I felt older. The faces in Marshal's were new, younger. I was a stranger, invisible and alien among the crowd. The Cup races had ended nearly eight hours before and Verbier was wild. One-o-clock in the morning, and it was like New Year's Eve at twelve-O-one. Standing there in the middle of the disco floor, the lurid lights flashing were making me dizzy. The people around me were unknowns. Where was everybody? Liney? P.A.? Eric? Where was everyone I knew?

I looked in on the Borsalino. "The Gang" had been there, but no itinerary was left me for the nocturnal plan. Outside, the limos crept and slinked through the crowded streets like the chariots of the conquerors during a celebratory bacchanal. The center of town was a drunken bash—a Bourbon Street on Fat Tuesday—typical of the party that followed the final World Cup Races. I couldn't even see the front door of my hotel. "The Gang" must be at Jacky's, and I needed to see Céline, tonight, today, this morning, whatever the hell this was.

chapter Fifteen
RED HORSES

I never made it all the way to Jacky's. "The Gang" — all of them — met me halfway down Rue de Verbier, halfway between the big town-center shindig and Jacky's club. They regarded me as though I were extra-terrestrial. Liney, Eric, Ham and Paloma, Mano and Miguel, Deke Robinson, even Stuart Hartman and Ian Woods stood, a motionless tableau, in the middle of the street.

"Hey, I was wondering where in the hell..."

"Eddie." Eric didn't let me finish. He put a hand on my shoulder. Liney came up close.

"Famous. Famous, you smell...like peanuts," Liney said.

"Yeah, well uh, Verbier Zoo..." I stuttered. "What's wrong with you guys?" I looked at Liney, straight into his eyes.

"Eddie, there's been an accident," Eric said. "We were looking all over for you." Then, Liney grabbed my arm.

"Céline," he said, just as he'd whispered her name that first day at the Eden. My stomach dropped somewhere into my bowels. "She's alive, Eddie, she's at the hos....Famous wait?"

I heard the echo of Liney's call from a distance. I was in motion, had been since Liney said the word "alive." Some hot fluid was speeding through me. Science called it adrenalin, I called it self-knowledge liquefied into battery acid.

Something happens to athletes, some memory in the muscle takes over in moments of extreme anxiety, or determination. It was a calling to peak performance. Some dash I'd made in Ann Arbor for some goddamn goal line, some sprint to momentary glory kicked-in to my muscular memory there on Rue de Verbier. Replace the image, I begged. Call-up some stored frame of the golden past, some message from deep at the center of that sprinting, young halfback to cover the distance full-speed. *Run you bastard.* One Saturday afternoon, a blue-and-gold blurred vision before me and the screaming eyes of some Simian linebacker sent me on my way—to direct daylight. I skipped the light-fantastic scrimmage line, the sky rained confetti, and no one touched me—eighty-four yards over the fresh cut fescue—no one came close. A hundred-and-two-thousand in the stadium became a mountain of sound, and I galloped into the end-zone like a deer. The body, the muscles, remembered. The path tonight was white. The vision was the color of blood.

Ten times eighty-four yards it was, the distance to the Verbier Hospital, to get to Céline. People seemed to disappear from in front of me in the crowded Place Centrale. As I approached, their revelry turned to horror. I must have looked like a serial killer on the loose. I felt like an express train, late in Switzerland. What could be worse?

I hated the appearance, the feel, of emergency areas, the backs of hospitals. The backs of buildings were for garbage. The carriage trade of sickness and death emptied-out here— ambulances, hearses, paddy-wagons, the recycle bags and beds of injury, dying, debility, and infirmity.

And then, inside, there were all those oppressive blue curtains, and wheely things, the chairs and beds, litters and walkers, the white and blue draperies, the bandages and sheets, the sanitary paraphernalia and clutter, stores of medical stationary everywhere, spread over a world of malady and ill. An army patrolled in white and blue, a sickening pale blue that I hated. The air fluttered with a fluorescence that offended the eyes. And then, there were the sobs behind curtains, the unseen hurt, the sounds of sorrow and regret, of mistakes and suffering.

I walked straight through the center of the Emergency Ward. No one stopped me. No one directed me. I was sweating. I felt Céline somewhere in the sprawling room, her prone body called to me through a tremor of our brief history together. Orderlies and nurses and young interns scurried about crisscrossing in front of me as I marched, they disappeared behind those sobbing curtains. And there, near the end, a pale blue curtain hot with light. A blue shroud, just for me, contained some future agony.

Some rude and vengeful god had saved this moment. Some linebacking deity, out to prove my neglect, had prepared a lesson. At the end of my dash, not glory, but anguish.

Some things start out one way, and end up another. Forsake, and you will be forsaken.

Céline's head was wrapped in gauze like a mummy's. It was plain to see from the wrapping why this mortuary art was the province of ancient Egyptians and not the Gauls. The bandages were rough, makeshift, probably done in great commotion at the site of the accident. That beautiful, soft-glowing hair, all hidden now under a crooked hive of bloodied muslin, a few matted strands clung to the tender skin of her neck and bare shoulder. Her face was almost completely hidden, except for her mouth.

I bent over the bedside railing and put my head on her blood-caked arm. I touched her lips lightly with my fingers, and I began to cry. Somewhere deep inside, inaudibly, I cried a cry I'd been saving-up, holding back, for a dozen years or more, and to my surprise, her hand squeezed my arm.

Two people in white lab coats stood back in the shadows of the curtained room. They never said a word. They let me weep, and join the other sobs in the ward. I was grateful for that kindness, that presence, and demonstration of respect. I might have been the guy who hit her. How would they know? They must have sensed my linkage. I really did want to be alone with my guilt, just for that moment. There was something contained in the silence around sorrow, and I had to listen, alone. For the one who caused it, sorrow was resonant with culpability.

Two more people dressed in white entered the curtained compartment, a tall man in a doctor's coat and a slender female. They moved with an urgency and authority. They spoke very fast and very softly to the two people in the shadows. The big guy in the white cloak took a scissors from his pocket as he spoke. The nice young man from the shadows moved toward me.

"*Monsieur, s'il vous plait, attendez-vous a l'extérieur...*"

"No. No. Goddamn it. *Pas, non.* Shit." I was on my feet. The Swiss hospital types were dumbfounded. I'd said something in a loud voice. The four stood paralyzed, looking at me. One simply did not yell in Switzerland, it's just not Swiss. Yodel? Yes. Yelling, loud talking? Not done much. The whole country could pass for a library. Anything louder than cows farting was conspicuous and crass. Oddly enough, on this entire green earth, there was nothing more that made one *want* to yell, than the Swiss. They expected Americans to be loud and dangerous, I hoped.

"Please? Guys, *mecs.*" I calmed, came down two registers. "*Attendez voir, laissez-moi absolument, j'ai besoin a voir.*" My French sounded great, like a pro. I was as nervous as shit, but the courage juice was still dripping somewhere and the French flew off my lips like I was Yves Montand on speed. Odd, too, that at that moment the supremely terrible thought crossed my mind that I could have just said, "*Your mother sucks warthogs in green sweaters?*" The language barrier being what it was, the excitement of the moment, the idioms, the rhythms, the tenses. It was a real pain in the ass. The stunned medical emergency people looked at me compassionately, however, understanding at least the tone of my desperation. "*J'attends ici,*" I said, quietly, firmly. I'd stay and be a good boy.

"*Tout vient à point à qui sait attends,*" the big guy with the scissors said, as he began cutting at the bandages around

Céline's head. I forced an affirmative nod at all four Swiss emergency people. And yet, I was wondering, what if he just said, *my* mother sucked warthogs in green sweaters. You were never sure.

In seconds, the mummy's cap was sliced along her left ear with the doctor's speedy scission and lifted off her face like a piece of eggshell. At that moment, every muscle in my body withered with hurt. The awful fluorescent light overhead washed across the horror, stinging my eyes, shutting-out every other image in existence.

A deep gash ran down and across Céline's forehead, through one eyebrow, trailing-off, nicking the corner of her right eye near the soft temple. So cruel and jagged it looked now, so infinitely damaging and painful a defile, it swallowed all my hope, any hope I had of ever hearing her speak to me again. That was all I set eyes on, that crooked fissure. I was sucked into it. That stunning face was marred, cleavered open across the smoothness of her forehead. I'd kissed there freely so many times, my lips skipping the placid space from temple to temple, the smell of her hair filling my head in almond-scented wishes. Other cuts and bumps—and broken bones—I was unaware of just then. *Comprehend her cloven forehead and bloodied face, and do not look away*—they were all that I could see.

So this was it. This was the gorge I was forced to navigate, a crag that I must peer into this night with solemn clarity. *See what you've done here.* This was what I did. I scarred women. What I'd always done. I cracked open their beauty, their lust, lacerating the soft tissue of intimacy shared, infecting passion and love in a pandemic of my selfish obsessions. A lifelong illness, and perhaps, I'd never heal completely. *Did anyone?*

She lay there motionless, peaceful and breathing. I leaned over again and kissed her lips, softly.

"Céline, I love you," I whispered. The phrase no longer seemed like my native tongue of pretense. I could master this language with some practice. Then, "I'm sorry." The order of things, I had not planned, love, then apology. I was sure she was unconscious. I was wrong. People on the extreme edge often displayed an inner strength that made fools of sobbing mourners. She whispered back.

"Peanuts." Then, "The circus, Eddie. Will you please take me to the circus?"

I was staggered, but so relieved to hear her, and hear my name once again on her lips.

"Céline. I'm going to knock you out first, then I'm going to take you to the circus, you clown." She smiled. Her eyes stayed closed, her lids and long lashes were caked with dried blood, but she smiled. Humor broke remorse into tiny little pieces, then it would blow away on the slightest breath of laughter. Her composure, and droll timing saved me from uncertain depths.

"This is not Dumbo, here. I am a dumbo, yes, but I'm no elephant. You should have seen me run up here." She squeezed my hand. I was half-crying and half-laughing. It was that kind of night. Half of me was lying on that table, inside her, and my heart was half-broken, half-joyous, inside of me. It hurt so much to see her lying there like that.

"The Gang" had finally caught up with me. I could hear them just outside the ugly, blue curtain. The nice young man from the shadows came forward again, and I felt a hand on my back and a voice telling me, in fractured English, that she needed rest. The hand and voice turned me out into the hallway, gently, like re-directing a robot. The sight of Céline on the table in that harsh, white light, the dried blood in her hair glistening—a ghostly vision of things, sights—they would remain for a lifetime.

Out in the hallway, "The Gang" stood as still as Dutch Masters, a perfect picture of unfaltering friendship. I'd never forget this vision either. I had more than I bargained for, more than I deserved, in them.

"Eddie, I told the intern on duty, no drugs," Liney said. "Who knows what she's had, you know?"

"Yeah, thanks. What happened?" I asked. "Where? When?"

"Just up from La Châble, in the 'S's'…the one long straight there, the narrow."

"Well, how? What happened? Was she driving?"

"No, Eddie." Eric was slow and deliberate with his information. "She was found."

"Found? Found what? What the fuck?" Some heat was suddenly building in my head. I felt it pressing.

"She was left in the car, alone, in the middle of the road," Liney continued. "Nobody knows how long. A car full of skiers came along and got help. She was covered in blood and out cold when they found her, luckily."

"Somebody left her there? Who? Jesus-Christ-Almighty. What car, Liney?" I was exploding. The veins in my neck were filling, getting thicker. Everybody was staring at me, stone quiet and frightened looking.

"A red Lamborghini," Eric said.

And there it was again, the heat, the hot sensation, inside. This time, the adrenalin, the scientific flow, became a poison. A venom turned my insides into a heated stream running, filling the dilated muscle, preparing it for some new jettison. Some inner fangs were sunk deeply, locked into my heart and lungs, shooting the terrible, stinging serum through me.

The Emergency Ward, that brightness, became a morgue in my blackened vision now, and I began to walk through it again possessed by some other light.

Horses. I wanted to hear the hill full of horses, the white ones, the roan and paint, the black ones, and the red one. The Lamborghini—a pitchfork through my heart. The Marchese horses, all running beside me, stampeding through a blue morning mist in spring they came, running through Tuscan orchards.

All that was hurtful, was behind me. Céline was alive inside the curtains. She'd live, she would heal, with or without me. Wheelie things flew past me again, in and out of those sobbing stalls. And out of that wailing stable, I ran. I needed to find the master, the equestrian, the rider of the red horse.

I pounded the Route des Creux. Up, I ran. Verluisant, the restaurant at Les Creux was overflowing with celebrants in the street and parking lot. I ran through them, *cheval pur sang*, and they laughed at my braying. The footfalls of a mad jogger had amused. Up the hill, up along the snowy routes I continued. The cold air burned in my chest. The burning air shot from my nostrils in white jets. Across the quarter-mile stretch of Chemin des Luys, steadily up I galloped, to Chalet Arosa, again.

One dim light emanated from the living room of the chalet. Only the black BMW sat in the carport beneath. I walked up the stairs, then across the wide, front balcony and I could see the faint, pulsing glow from the fireplace on the walls and timbers. I knocked. Several seconds passed before Franca opened the door. The look on her face was more than startled, different than surprise. My thoughts clouded. She was in a negligee—pink, tan, I wasn't sure.

"Eddie?" She said, stunned.

"Franca, forgive me...but, something terrible has happened, is your brother..."

As I spoke, my eye detected movement in the living room, from behind Franca, over near the sofa in front of the fireplace, a movement. The movement was slow and graceful, suspended in that moment by me, by my warped comprehension of events during the past forty minutes. It was innocent, really, the movement, innocuous through a single span of maybe only ten seconds, and yet, it was deadly. Some part of me deadened at the sight.

The frail, naked body of Marie Terése, Céline's Paris friend, the *minnet* I'd made playful fun of, moved in that warped space. Little, mute, Marie Terése—so lithe and possessing little, or no, noticeable personality or presence in the every-day social fabric—rose up from the sofa into the firelight and stared straight at me with an unsettling, penetrating glare. That dumb smile on her face crushed me. It devastated the fresh memory of Franca.

The awkwardness of the moment couldn't be rivaled. The air in the world felt suddenly un-breathable and stale. Everything was static, everyone unmoving. Only the fire flickered.

"He's not here, I take it?" I managed only those words.

"Eddie, please, I must explain…" Franca tried, but I had become a wall, impenetrable. I walked across the wide balcony and down the stairs not hearing Franca's pleas, out into a sharp, blue moonlight and away from Chalet Arosa for the second time.

The icy rain had stopped. Wispy, swirling clouds moved fast, like black draft-smoke before the moon's full face. The night was hurrying somewhere. My own shadow on the snow looked withered and pale. Would there be an image in a mirror now? Franca had erased some part of my soul, like a sorceress. She wielded the sharp pitchfork, not Lorenzo. *Nothing inflicts pain quite like the unexpected.* The dark side of beauty visible, and an undercurrent finally disclosed. There were no memories of stunning Franca to follow me back down to Verbier this time, no misty hill towns and no tower bells. Spring in Tuscany would be barren in my memory from this day forward—rows of orchard trees with no fruit, branches of broken sticks with no leaves.

There was a small catholic church—St. Ignace—on Route des Creux, where it met Rue de l'Eglise, just above the town. As I walked down, "The Gang" was waiting for me there by a stone fence beside the church. A police car was parked in the driveway and two *gendarme* appeared to be standing, talking with Liney, Eric, and Deke, there by the wall. As I approached, they turned to me.

"What?" I panicked. "Something with Céline? Tell me."

"No, no, Céline is sleeping, nothing, not Céline, Eddie." Liney spoke slowly, deliberately pulling me in with his look. "There was another car, Eddie...in the accident. They found it after, over the side. There was no chance."

Then, Liney cracked. That pudgy, cherub face turned red and his eyes filled with tears.

"What, goddamn it? What?" I screamed at all of them, searching their faces for some answer.

"P.A.," Eric said. Eric, steady and sober always. Eric the messenger, again.

"Pierre...Alain?" The words came out on my breath. My heart constricted and the tightness followed them up into my throat. I was suffocating. To push the unfairness down again, the hurt, I labored. I toiled and struggled for control but something broke inside, some blocks of stone were toppling, inside. A structure gave-way to strain, relics to truth, and I was coming down. All that heroic enterprise was crumbling, like Roman ruins. I'd fall and no one would hear, like a tree in a distant forest. The ground would punish me and suddenly I wished for it.

My hands were in the pale, blue moonlit snow. The shadow of St. Ignace rose over me, the cross on its spire burned black into the snow just a few feet from my head. I reached for the twisted shadow of that cross, clawing and screaming.

I cried and screamed. I punched at the cross in the snow, scratching and pounding my fists, trying to tear the shadow to pieces. "No god can do this," I shrieked. "Send down a god that walks like a man, so that I can break his friggin' back. I want to kill him. The rams, the chamois, the gods in their eyes would never do this." I said those things. Liney would save the memory of my words and tell me years later.

Deke leaned over me, held me, brought my arms in, folding me together as my energy unwound and closed-down. Propped against his leg, bent like the hunter's kill, he rubbed the back of my neck, whispering something about the two of us water skiing on Lake Michigan one summer.

Not one of these events would have defeated me so, but all together, on this night, were simply too much to bear. Timing crushed even the most stalwart soul, occasionally. Timing alone could inflame bearable heartache into unbearable suffering. Icarian flights to singe the bravest heart, they too burn away and cleanse. Exhaustion finally overtook the pain and anger. *We should be thankful it works that way.* It took that weakened part out of harm's way — the body knowing and instinctively protecting the spirit. What little we knew about defeat, I thought. It has an entirety, of that I was sure. Loss was, at times, final, whole. It could never be undone.

Something new will come and replace our losses, something to fill the emptiness and transform the suffering and anger, and defeat, and in time we will change and become someone else. Loss and renewal. Everything's an exchange. We just have to wait. Everything is an exchange.

chapter Sixteen
THE VISIT

At about four that morning, Liney, Eric, and I drove down in Liney's car to see the spot where the accident had taken place. The news about Pierre Alain was too much for some. Ham and Paloma went back to their chalet. They'd leave for Hamburg at daybreak. Miguel and Manolete, Stuart and Ian went to look-in on Marie LaNoue and then they'd head back to their chalets. Deke had to open the store in a few hours, so he went home to get some rest.

It was cold and still on the stretch of road, peaceful at first sight. No one would ever imagine that a horror was played-out here only hours before. The wall of sound I heard there, the turbulence, was from inside. It hurt the inner ear, that giant funnel of aural agony and racket, the reverberation of cries, screams, and last wishes.

In typical Swiss fashion, the site was as clean as a whistle, no smashed fenders, no broken glass or twisted chrome. Even P.A.'s car had been hoisted-up from the fatal ravine and taken away. A violent swath through the steep forest of broken, bare tree limbs and snow ruinously plowed and ravaged was all that bespoke the frenzied scene of my friend's death. "A routine drive," some police report would read, "coming back from a visit with his mom and sister in Liddes."

The *gendarme* had outlined the action, the probable scheme of things, like a director blocked a play. Strips of orange plastic tape crisscrossed and lined the routes of force, chalk marks indicated places of incidence, confrontation and change, the beats, in the climactic scene.

Pierre Alain's car, it seemed, swerved to avoid a head on collision with the Lamborghini. *Always the gentleman. Why not me instead of you?*

I walked along the tape and it whistled in the breeze, a buzzing sound that annoyed me terribly. Liney and Eric let me walk alone, along the route of Pierre Alain's final moments. The headlights of Liney's car streaked across the slick pavement lighting my path the length of the long stretch out of the "S" turn. They knew I wanted to be with P.A. one more time, to feel his spirit there in the road in the last seconds of his life. We'd been there before together—near the last—this time, my friend went on ahead without me. *A tout, mon vieux.*

We ascended, or sometimes descended, a scale of relativity when catastrophe came close to us. My heart was breaking because I couldn't undo Céline's injury. But Pierre Alain was gone, his wife without him, and little Tarcis robbed of a father at the age of two. I felt like I'd been mugged, and arrested, in Central Park. Victim and criminal, I was Céline's slasher and P.A.'s blood-kin robbed by a brutal murder. A storm raged through my body there in those moments. My mind emptied, a closet overfilled with neglect. Imaginings were not even human during the hours. But in the end, rage took a backseat to the pain and suffering. I simply couldn't overcome the grief.

My room in the Eden felt like one of those parlors in funeral homes. People really did wring their hands. Liney was sitting on the floor, studying the carpet intently. Eric was flat on the bed staring at the ceiling.

It was five-forty.

Paul knew instinctively that something was amiss. He had a sixth sense for middle-of-the-night duress — came with the hotel business, I suppose. Like a true friend, he'd awakened and decided to make "a few things" for the three of us. He'd heard us rumbling in and out in the hours before.

He set a tray of hot coffee and scalding milk on my desk.

With it he'd brought small *baguettes* of fresh bread, butter, honey, confiture, camembert, and on a separate plate, conspicuously, a French cheese called époise.

Why was this piece of cheese worth noting? Céline was on my mind, Pierre Alain, the event, or events of Franca—it had been a night. Why should that cheese be anything remarkable? Well, this was Switzerland. But it was French cheese. That particular cheese, the époise, was the worst smelling cheese, the worst smelling thing I'd ever smelled in my life. It couldn't be overlooked.

"Monsieur Eddie," Paul said, as I stared at the époise. "In my family, for many years this cheese, you know, it will get rid of...things. It chases them away."

"Jesus Christ, Paul. Chases them?" I remanded him. "This friggin' cheese can peel the paint off a Buick Riviera. I can hardly put it near my face."

"When there is a death, we eat this cheese," he persisted. "Like the bitter herbs at Israelian Passover, you know, to remember?"

"This is a French cheese. Is it not, Paul?"

"Yes, monsieur Eddie. I am French, not Swiss. We do this where I come from. It is an act we share to commemorate a change, a passing. I am French. The Swiss? Well, it is difficult to tell when death and life interchange." His disdain for the Swiss was etched in his brow. "You boys should eat the époise, together." After his fatherly command, he walked away, out of the room, clear of the aromatic aura of the stinky cheese.

Of course, Paul was right. The cheese made our eyes tear and every gland in our mouths water. And it marked a point in time. We performed a ritual, together. I'd rather chew on my ski socks, but like my own peculiar set of deities and customs, this was a custom of someone I dearly respected. For all the time I'd known Paul, he had been silently giving-a-damn about me, about my well being. From day to day, I'd never really stopped to realize how he, and others like him in

Verbier, had woven themselves into my life. Odd customs, the inconspicuous presence, there it was unnoticed mostly, until it counted.

Liney, Eric, and I each ate a third of the reeking cheese, more to make it disappear, I think, than to assess Paul's superstition. The balcony doors were opened wide to usher out its odor, and something else left through those French doors, out into the black, cold air. Silently, a spiritual exchange took place. We sat, chewing on chunks of French bread, sipping black coffee and scalding milk. We wiped our teary eyes with our hands, complaining about the rancid event of the cheese, and silently mourned Pierre Alain's passing.

At six-fifteen, there was a knock at the door. The three of us looked suspiciously at each other—what else? Eric opened the door and in walked Patric Verdaguer and Fabian Thibaud. *More odd customs.* The morning was getting stranger by the hour.

Fabian seemed to inhale an authority beyond his own when he was with Verdaguer, the battery never far from the charge. The two men moved in. Patric sat at my desk, directly in front of the Parzival, Thibaud positioned himself beside Patric. Only Patric Verdaguer could look the way he did at six in the morning, as if he were walking into a stockholders meeting. In the brothel of big business, Patric was *the* madame, the pricy top-floor lay. And if he was the expensive carnal bed, Fabian Thibaud was the wet spot.

"*Jour*, Eddie," Patric began in a warm, executive tone. "This whole town knows what has happened. I'm sorry for all of you, more for Marie LaNoue, *oui?* But, he was a special friend."

"Can't be replaced, Patric," I said. At six in the morning philosophy suffered for concrete communication.

"I will come right to the point," Verdaguer said. "Time is important, and we must concern ourselves with the living."

Suddenly, it was just Patric and me. I was on the edge of

the bed. The rest of the room sort of grayed-down the minute he mentioned, "the living." "There is the situation of the girl," he said, very somberly and genuinely concerned.

"Céline," I answered, owing to a name and person who had changed my life.

"She must get to a better hospital, for the injury to her head. She need a good surgeon, maybe even a plastic surgeon. She should be to Paris, Eddie. The scar..."

"Patric," I cut him off. "We've just been through a night. I mean, you're right, of course you're right. None of us has had the presence of mind, a goddamn minute to think this thing through, maybe we wished it, but..."

"You were busy wishing it didn't happen, Eddie." Now he stopped me. "Fools wish to change the past."

"Yeah? Yeah," I nodded, seeing the defeat. "Does anybody wish to change the future, Patric?"

"Bigger fools, Eddie," he said, deftly placed, irrefutably convincing. "People think in miracles when they are under strain. There are no such things."

"But how, Patric?"

"I can have her to Paris within hours," he said straight-out, piercing me with his close-the-deal look. *I can*, to a mover like Patric meant, *I will*. The ones like Verdaguer didn't relate to obstacles. They let others, like Fabian Thibaud, take care of things like hindrance and complication. "We helicopter her to Sion," he continued. "And my jet can be in Paris in a few hours. The American Hospital in Nouilly, perhaps? But then, she must have family there, *oui?*"

"A helicopter in Verbier?" Eric's question suddenly erased any private grayness in the room. "Now? In this shit?" The fuzzy cocoon Verdaguer and I had possessed quickly molted.

"He can land a seven-forty-seven on the golf course if he wants to." Liney wanted a piece of the action, a piece of Patric. "Can't you, Patric?"

There was a bite in Liney's remark. The air had hair. The room was full-color now.

"You care for this girl, Eddie." Verdaguer ignored Liney. "Think on that. Time is precious with injuries like hers. A face like hers, *vraiment*...it is a terrible injury."

"Yes, yes, of course I want her on your plane to Paris."

I was grasping. Someone wanted to talk about the only thing that mattered in my life at that moment. I was in, all ears.

"Eddie?" Liney came through, clearly.

"I want you to do something for me, Eddie." Patric turned an unyielding shoulder to Liney.

"Let's have it, Patric," I insisted. "I want this to happen."

"I knew you would understand," he said, privatizing me fast. He was all business, *this Swiss schmuck.*

"Yeah, Eddie's a very understanding guy," Liney uttered. He was staying in it. Then Liney turned to me, trying to cut out Verdaguer and Thibaud. "Don't jump too fast, Eddie, in with this crowd. We can get Céline down to Geneva. I promise you, we can do it ourselves." I went aside to Verdaguer.

"Excuse my friend, Patric. He's been out of the States for some time, he's not thinking like a good American." In Liney's ear, "You've been out of the States for a long time, Linus."

"Eddie, fuck him. You're not thinking," Liney yelled at me.

"Liney. Goddammit," I screamed. Then, I grabbed him by the shoulders, trying to contain my rage more than to restrain him. "Liney? Please, Liney? It's Céline. I've got to do something. I almost don't give a shit what it is. Her head is split open, Liney. I'm living in there. That goddammn scar stays open for as long as I live, Liney. I've got to do something, just one fucking thing in my life that is decent."

Then I tried to shift the mood in the room. I wanted Liney back with me, on my side. I turned on Patric, quickly.

"I'm not going to assassinate anybody, am I, Patric? No, Patric wouldn't ask me to do that. He needs to make a deal. That's his, uh, his...that's what he knows. Isn't that right, Patric?"

Verdaguer was sitting stone still, expressionless, taking it all in, watching us underlings panic around his proposal. It was all boardroom stuff—pissing distances. This was executive treats, all part of being Patric Verdaguer. His look, his bored satisfaction, was a Swiss erection.

"Just twitch..." Eric in a monotone, moving toward Verdaguer. "...or fart, or something so that we know you're real, Patric. Can you do that?"

"I'm an American," I rushed in, jokingly. "He respects that, don't you Patric? No Free Lunch, right Patric? Hello? Patric, just jump in here anywhere you feel, you know..."

"Eddie have the strength," Patric said, insincerely. "*le,le, fort de...*" he fumbled for some French word. "He have the gut for this sort of thing, Liney."

Suddenly, I got a little worried, about the phrase, "this sort of thing." It was nothing major, a bit of concern was all. The three of us stared at Verdaguer, and waited for the next shoe to fall.

Patric made a half gesture with his head, and Fabian reached into a small knapsack at his feet. He took out a cardboard box, about the size of carton of cigarettes, about as rectangular too. Thibaud held it out and Patric took it.

"I want you to deliver this box, Eddie...in Italy, to some people in Cervinia. If you wish to know more, you must ask me," Patric said, flatly. "Perhaps, it is better to know as little as possible. You must tell me what is to your liking."

"Eddie's a curious kind of..." Liney jumped the gun.

"Liney, Liney, now behave yourself," I said, stopping him. "It's okay. Patric's being a gentleman. It's a courtesy, a business thing, you know?" I turned to Verdaguer, dead-on in the eyes. "I am a curious kind of guy, Patric. Shoot."

He glanced at Liney, satisfied with himself for a small

victory, and then turned to me again, very matter-of-factly.

"In here are twelve electronic devices called klystrons."

"Oh, fuck," Liney whispered, exasperated, as he flopped down on the bed. Verdaguer hesitated and then continued.

"They must go to some men in Cervinia," Patric said.

The guy's the real deal, I thought, some international espionage just to fill-out the résumé.

"A little more, Patric, I need a little more," I egged him on.

"It's a switch," Liney interrupted. "A fucking tube, or some goddamn thing. It's a frequency device, Eddie, for a nuclear reaction. You can't create a critical mass if...Jesus Christ, do you know what you're getting into with this guy?"

"Can't get him away from those Ian Flemming novels," Eric said, dryly, raising a brow to me. "The guy knows, he just knows."

"Patric, tell Liney," I leaned into Verdaguer. "I'm not going to blow up the world, right? Not this part, anyway? Not Switzerland, not Italy?" I went directly at Verdaguer, *mano a mano*. "I'll probably go, Patric, but only if you tell me who...and who." Verdaguer didn't hesitate.

"My client...is American. The people in Cervinia are from Iraq."

"Holy shit," Liney exclaimed, and then he started pacing. He grabbed the box from Verdaguer's hand. Fabian made a sudden move, but Patric raised a hand and halted him. Liney pried at the box, clicking the side-flaps open, carefully, sliding the inside container out at an angle, as if he'd done it before. The neatly arranged dozen switches, lined side by side, sparkled like those plastic-wrapped sets of miniature trains at FAO Schwartz. They didn't look all-that important, or deadly, sitting there in an oblong box. But that was how we'd all get it, I mused. Some loose-cannon fanatic would blow us all to smithereens, the end of the world brought about by toys.

Liney took one of the klystrons out of the box with a forefinger and thumb, turned it over, and read,

"Noritron Systems. Connellsville, P.A."

"The son-of-a-bitch had to be from Pennsylvania," I grumbled, talking to no one in particular.

"What about us, our safety?" Eric asked Verdaguer. Liney wheeled around on Eric.

"What us? What's this '*us*' shit? Are you going nuts, too?"

"If Eddie goes, I'm going," Eric said straight at Liney. "Minutes are flying by, Liney. Céline is lying in that hospital." Then he turned on Verdaguer. "What about us, Patric? Seal the deal. These guys in Cervinia?"

"I will do my best to minimize the risk to you," Patric said. "We can accomplish that, I think."

"Minimize the risk?" I said. "What a guy."

"You think?" Liney snapped.

"The way Eddie is in this town..." Fabian Thibaud spoke up, sarcastically, leaning against the door. "I mean, with his women, *oui*? He must regard some risks as occupational, I should think."

"That's great Thibaud," Liney cracked, moving steadily toward Fabian. "I didn't know you were a goddamn ventriloquist. Can you throw your voice from your asshole again?"

"I didn't even see his lips move," Eric joined in, moving.

"Easy, easy, guys." I put a hand up, halting both of them. "It's nothing, no harm, it's nothing. Fabian's just growing another dick these days."

"Please, please," Verdaguer yelled. "Time is being wasted with this, this...shit."

Then Liney got up in Patric's face, strong.

"I want to know why, Patric? Why? Why a deal all the time? Why can't you just get your helicopters and your planes...you could fly ten surgeons into Verbier and give them all fuckin' lift tickets and limos. Why do you always have to get? Why, Patric? Why always a deal with you?"

Patric never moved a muscle during Liney's tirade. He barely blinked. He looked up at us, a helpless slave to his own ethic.

"Why does a dog lick his balls, Linus?" Verdaguer gazed at each of us with those slow eyes. "We all know the answer, *oui?*"

Fast, heavy footsteps in the hall, then rapid knocking on my door, and we all reacted, perking up.

"Famous, it's Deke." The thin Detroit voice came through the door. Liney pulled the corner of my white duvet over the box of shiny klystrons. Eric and I noticed and looked at each other.

"Ian Flemming, I told you," Eric said.

"Pizza Man. Hey," I yelled. Deke opened the door. The cold air around him came in, too. His eyes darted quickly around the room.

"Sorry, man. I saw the light," Deke said. "Patric, *bonjour.*" He nodded to Verdaguer, a cool respect. Then, to Fabian, "Hello, dog-breath. My, we're up early aren't we? Or is it late?"

"What's up, Deke?" I tried to contain him. He turned to me, quickly.

"Famous, I just...Famous, you know it stinks in here? Jesus Christ."

"Eddie keeps some cheese in his sock drawer." Liney stumbled an excuse away. Deke made an expression on his face to me like, "can I talk?" and his eyes rolled around to everyone in the room.

"Yeah, go ahead," I said.

"Tre just called me from the store, said, when he opened this morning, these three Italian guys were at the door. Said, they bought a load, skis, boots, clothes, snowshoes—all brand new stuff for the big guy."

"What are they doing in Crans?" Eric wondered aloud.

"We open at six, nobody else does," Deke said. "Tre said they were in a hurry, too. Paid cash."

"Bindings. What kind?" Liney asked.

"Marker 440-S. You can step out, and step right into the snowshoes."

I heard the questions and answers in the room, but I was in a daze, seeing in my mind, watching Lorenzo Marchese being fitted for his bindings, watching him snap-in and snap-out. I could hear the snaps in my head, they crushed my temples.

"He's going over," I said. Everybody in the room stopped talking. "He's going over and his two Vowel buddies are going to drive the St. Bernard and meet him in Cervinia." I looked at Patric Verdaguer and froze him, momentarily. Then I went to Deke, fast.

"Deke, as soon as you can, snowshoes for me, Liney, and Eric, fanny-packs, the big ones, hoods and glacier goggles..."

"Two hundred feet of rope. Edelred," Eric jumped right in. "Three harnesses, a dozen karabiners, D-shaped."

"Cramps?" Deke asked Eric.

"Yeah, and some cam straps, a belay plate, and a tubular pick. Short ends, about two dozen." Eric was spit-firing the list.

"Eric, Christ, we're not climbing the friggin' Matterhorn," I said. "Are we?"

Eric cut me right out.

"Don't pay any attention to him, Deke. All that stuff, we need it fast. And a map, a Monte Rosa topo."

"Okay, okay. Give me thirty, forty minutes, I'll have it over here, downstairs by the side door," Deke said.

"Deke, find out from Wunderlin what kind he bought?" Liney interjected, locking-on.

"Right. A tout, chaps." Deke zipped out the door.

Verdaguer was watching all of us with some amusement, perhaps some envy. Friends, pulling something together, working for each other, probably something he'd deeply wished for in his life. But his kind of status rendered him suspicious of others, and very much alone, just like his clients.

"Patric, the helicopter for Céline?" I begged.

"Done, Eddie. The process has already begun," he said.

I looked around the room and realized that Fabian was gone. He'd been dispatched by Patric minutes before and no one even saw him leave the room, we were all so focused on Deke.

"Eddie, it's a small helicopter, it can only fit..."

"No, no, no, don't worry, Patric. Please? Just Céline. We'll get down to Sion." Suddenly, I was beginning to sound like him, delegating. "There's an outfit there, Aereo Pennina – "

"I know it well," Patric smiled. "I put those guys in business. More Italians."

"Patric, we need lift passes," Liney interrupted again. "The armband kind for Zermatt-Cervinia. So that everything looks nice and normal."

"We're not going over that way," Eric stated, flatly, with his Alsatian flippancy. "But, go ahead, get the passes for the trip back." We all stopped talking and looked at him. "No way, man, I'm not going over that way. Not with these cluster-fucks, or whatever the hell you call them."

Liney, Patric and I looked at each other, then glanced simultaneously at the box of klystrons. There was a confusing silence. Then, we all looked back at the self-assured redhead.

"Don't look at me like that, goddamn it. It's too risky," he exclaimed. "What in the hell would we tell the border guards, eh? *Bonjour, mes amis...bonjour*. We're just a couple of wild'n'crazy nuclear physicists on holiday?"

chapter Seventeen
CERVINIA

Seven-thirty. We were downstairs, on the Rue d'Verbier side of the Eden, all gathered around Verdaguer's limo. Fabian Thibaud had turned the back parlor of the big, black stretch into a temporary office, a command center with opened briefcases and papers strewn all over. There was coffee service for everyone from the limo's line of handmade, Swiss pottery. The fresh, strong brew was supplied by Paul. Thibaud and Verdaguer had the office going full-tilt, tending to details for two separate sets of arrangements—our scheme in Cervinia and the transportation clearances for Céline's safe passage from Verbier to Sion and finally, to Paris. One of the cellular phones seemed to grow out of Fabian's ear. Patric was deep in muted negotiations, on another phone, in three different languages.

Deke had brought all the requested climbing and trekking gear over in a little Renault pickup, and he was busy transferring it from the back of the truck and packing it in the trunk of the limo. Liney and Eric went back up the hill to Chez Liney to get their own skis and ski clothing.

"Did you talk to Tre?" I asked Deke as he stuffed the last of the gear in the trunk—a backpack with rope and the crampons.

"Oh, yeah. He bought a pair of Rossignols, 215's."

"Two-fifteen. The bastard's in a hurry," I said, remotely, thinking of Lorenzo speeding across fresh powder.

"Listen, Famous, we usually put a little sticker with our logo on new pairs of skis. Tre doesn't remember if there was one on the Rossignols this morning, it was such a rush-job, but our shop guys are usually pretty good about that sort of thing. We stick it right on the ski tip, sometimes one just underneath the tip if the customer's a real asshole."

"Is it still the Wolverine with the I.M.S. on the bottom?"

"No, it's a new one." Deke unhooked a ballpoint pen from his flannel shirt pocket and then pulled the Monte Rosa topographical map from the side trap of our backpack. He started to draw the circular sticker on the back of the folded map. "Inside the circle...an outline of Michigan, with the I, a big M, and the S, inside. Then, "Verbier" and "Crans" written in the circular border, bottom left and bottom right."

"Blue and gold, of course?" I smiled at him.

"Ain't no other colors, Famous. Shit, you know that."

He laughed, but it was a laugh filled with many difficult memories. We hugged each other there by the trunk of the limo, and I thanked him for the memory of water skiing on the Lake. He was proud that I remembered.

"Hey, now, when you get to the airport," He righted himself. "Check with those guys on a storm coming up in the west. I heard this morning, there's a big one sittin' on Val d'Isere, which means...?"

"It'll close the St. Bernard if it moves," I said.

"Maybe so, Famous. Lorenzo's two pals will have to go all the way around, through Mont Blanc. We might get lucky."

Just then, the evergreen Mercedes pulled up behind the limo and Eric and Liney hopped out fully dressed in jumpsuits. I clamped my skis into Liney's rack as Eric was spreading one of his maps on the hood of the Mercedes. Patric Verdaguer came out of the limo. Liney, Deke, and I gathered around. I could see Paul peeking through the front bar window, through the Cardinal Beer sign, watching the goings-on with grave concern.

"Here's the interface with Italy — " Eric began, pointing to a small gully in a section of the Michelin map called, the Gabelhorn Massif. "The Theodulpass, where we're not going. What we'll do is head east, across the back of the Breithorn, to here—Castor and Pollux. It's a little hairy, and a couple of hours of climbing across ablation and glacial cols, but there's a notch on the southeast wall of Pollux, a deep chute, and then, a narrow, winding slope. Once we reach that, we zip right down into Breuil and Cervinia."

"And no border guards," Liney states.

"No, never. They can't patrol it," Eric said, with surety.

"No need," Liney added. "Only the completely nutty bastards would ski it anyway."

"There's a helipad up on Klein Matterhorn," Deke said. "You guys going to get dropped up there?"

"My choice," Eric continued. "Would be that we just blend-in with the rest of the tourists and skiers."

"Just have our guy drop us in Zermatt?" I asked Eric.

"Yes. We pack tightly and just move with the crowd. Cable to Klein Matterhorn, pick-up some water and eats at Testa Grigia, and then slip quietly east instead of west, like we're going on a little hike. Take a few pictures, a little wine and cheese..."

"A picnic. Everything, *cosi fan tutti*." Liney wiggled.

Just then, Thibaud stuck his head out of the rear door of the makeshift office, the telephone hanging out of his face.

"The helicopter is on its way up to the hospital," he said, and then disappeared again inside the limo.

Céline lying still, bloodied, crossed my inner vision. She was being taken away from me. My chest pained, heavily, just then, longing to be with her, charting the ever-widening distance between her life and mine.

"What's all this climbing gear for, Eric?" Liney asked.

"I was afraid you'd ask that."

"Eddie?" Patric Verdaguer interrupted. "We must start now, yes, to the airport in Sion. Time is rushing away from us. You can see Céline there. I want to make sure everything is in proper working order with the jet."

Is this what made him such a success, his attention to detail? I must admit, I felt relieved by his efficiency. I was learning that in the black-and-white world of Patric Verdaguer, some beneficial ends could be found. We'd made a deal, and suddenly, I had the force of his empire working on my behalf, for Céline. That was his honor system. I'd have to face facts, Patric Verdaguer was it. Switzerland, and quite a bit beyond, was at his fingertips. If it had to be, I was thankful it was someone of his stature. I'd have dealt with Mephistopheles to get Céline into the care of specialists. Patric Verdaguer was something short of a Devil, but how short? And who, or what, was waiting for us in Cervinia?

Our little caravan—the limo and the evergreen Mercedes—snaked through the "S" turns down toward Sion. Down near Sembrancher, Céline's helicopter passed overhead. It sent a rush through my body. Something was happening. She wasn't lying in Verbier Hospital any longer. There was movement.

The sky off to the west was ominous, dark and very moody. If the gods had a storm to serve up, they always checked in with Mont Blanc, the reigning king of mountains in Europe. Storms for southern Europe, particularly, were promoted, or demoted, by the Mont Blanc massif, a rise of earth great enough to often influence weather on the entire continent. I prayed, that this storm might be a blizzard big enough to slow Bruni and Cannegia on their race around the mountain. The snows in mountain passes were like the wonders of the world, one's imagination always fell short of their actual scale. Bury that white Mitsubishi in twenty-foot drifts in the St. Bernard, I wished, just long enough for me to meet with Lorenzo Marchese one more time.

Naturally, Verdaguer's limo commanded complete and unfettered access to the tarmac at Sion airport. We drove directly to Patric's Lear Jet. Some of the seats had been taken out, and they sat, strewn about, on the ground beside the plane.

"Let me out, Liney." I panicked a little, desperate to see

Céline again. "I'll meet you guys over at Aereo Pennina, it's right over there in the next building."

The Pennina helicopters, including the one that ferried Céline down from Verbier, were but a stone's throw from Verdaguer's private jet. I walked fast toward the Lear Jet. It was a hive of activity. A gangplank stair was open in the rear, under the tail, and so was the passenger door on the side. The airport attendants were busy readying the plane, stepping in and out of the rear hatch.

Two hospital types, a man and a woman, were attending to their patient inside. They scurried in and out of the plane, over to the helicopter, then, back into the jet. They were the same two who stood in the shadows at the hospital ward hours before.

My hurried walking suddenly slowed. As I got closer, rounding the wing toward the open side door, I saw a handsome, young man standing by the short stairway that led into the fuselage. He wasn't very tall, slight of build, actually, but trim and athletic looking. He stood military straight, dressed very neatly in a wool, hazel-colored blazer and muted green tie. A full-length Loden was draped over one arm. Gentlemanly, he looked, and very proper. American men used to dress that way. College athletes like the Michigan Wolverines used to dress gentlemanly, before we all became so casual, and sloppy. We dressed in a way that presented manhood at its best—like Claude Decauville.

He smiled pleasantly and put his hand straight out to greet me. Fine French schooling, of course, fine wealthy family. Railroads, Old French money, Chateau life, fine automobiles, servants, manners (definitely), fine wines, haut cuisine, travel, privilege. Handsome boy-man, a brow just like Céline's, same thick lips, too. Strong grip, firm handskake.

"You are Eddie," he said. Nice, forceful presence for a small man. *Another Napoleon?*

"How is she?" I asked, peeking inside.

"She is doing fairly well, I think. My sister is a very courageous woman." I nodded to him and he understood, how much I wanted to see Céline. He nodded me inside.

They'd strapped her litter to one side of the plane, and a row of six seats remained intact on the opposite side. Claude would sit beside her all during the flight. She was still being fed intravenously and that whole hook-up had been secured by a hanging net arrangement suspended from the ceiling. I knelt in the center aisle, beside her. She'd been cleaned considerably, but her color was strange.

Shock somehow changed the hue of human beings. We become a kind of litmus paper that shows the outside world how much horror our frail bodies have just accepted, or rejected. Céline had that odd color now, the color of shock. Her arm was soft casted and wrapped tightly against her body. I could barely see the evidence of some harness strap over her shoulder, the kind of strap that contained a break or a fracture. A clean bandage covering her top like a helmet hid the forehead injury now. Her eyes were closed. I took her hand and kissed it hard, pressing it against my cheek.

"Eddie?" she whispered.

"I'm right here, kiddo." I leaned over her and kissed her again several times on her mouth and chin.

"Cheese, Eddie, you've been eating cheese."

"Céline? Jesus, what are you, like a bloodhound, or something?" She giggled. "When you get better I'm going to take you hunting and you can be the retriever, okay?" She opened her eyes and we saw each other again after four days.

"Eddie, I'm so hungry for cheese now."

"Cheese, eh? Sounds like a healthy Gaul to me."

"And for you, hungry for you. I love you, Eddie. I don't care who you go with, or where. The love, we have this, *mon chéri*, this."

"What? All you girls go to the 'this' school? It's a class or something, this? I'm with you, Céline. I'm inside you. You're right, we have…yeah. And I'm coming to Paris as soon as I can."

"No, Eddie. I won't let you see me until…."

"Céline, I love you. Your scar is mine, too."

"She's beautiful…the Italian." She said it sweetly and it stung me, she riddled my guilt.

"I'm sorry, Céline. It was all a mistake." I was afraid just then to start dredging-up all the missed phone calls, and crossed messages, or my dalliance with Franca and disregard. I needed to find out if I possessed any truthfulness. I'd suddenly painted myself into a corner of new ideals, dreams, and possibilities found with Céline. Would I stay long enough for the paint to dry? Or, simply leave damaging tracks in another life.

"I met Claude." I changed gears. "He's just outside."

"Do you like him, Eddie? He's handsome, isn't he?" She sounded truly proud.

"Yes, he is, very handsome. And all the while, I thought you had all the Decauville good-looks," she laughed and smiled at me again. "Close your eyes now, Céline, and dream of the forest, the soft light and tall trees, our beautiful trees. I'm with you always, in among the pines. I'll never leave you again." I kissed her once more, tenderly, and ducked out the back door, coming face to face with Claude Decauville.

"My sister, she talk about you quite a lot," he said.

"Women do that…talk."

"She say, you played the American *futbol*." Here it comes, the male sports bonding. "Chicago Bears, yes?"

"Chicago Bears, no. I never played professionally."

"You were very big and celebrated in the university, then?" He quizzed. "Céline said you were an All-American."

"I was good in the university, a celebrity to my teammates, only. I was never big," I told him. "Big doesn't mean anything, Claude. I just…I never quit."

I looked at him hard. There was an extended silence in the deliberate pause, and I was looking for some glint, a certain trickle of propane behind the eyes, the pilot light that some athletes have. It burned there, constantly, always ready to ignite a much greater flame and it derived from a hunger, a ravenous hunger to seek an impossible goal. Chasing the rarely attainable—next to love, what else was there?

"I was like a mean dog, Claude, a mean bulldog. You know the kind of dog that sees a bone at the…the *boucherie*? He just won't stop till he gets it. He barks at the butcher, day after day. He growls, he prowls, he snaps at the butcher's heels…" Claude was just staring at me, in a trance, as though I were mad. I'd frozen him like a bug in amber. "I love Céline, I love her, Claude. I feel like a dog again, an older dog, maybe, but I feel the hunger again. I want it. The thing, the prize…the…the…impossible beautiful." I was spouting, scolding him. I had no idea what the hell I was saying. "Call it whatever, Claude. The hungry dog, he will never quit."

Eric and Liney were waving to me from the helipad at Aereo Pennina, all packed and ready to go. I looked at Claude, then in again at Céline. She was asleep. The two hospital assistants were in the seats across the aisle from her, seat belts buckled. I looked at them, puzzled. They smiled at me, together.

Outside, I grabbed Claude Decauville's hand, firmly.

"Take care, Claude," I told him. "I'll see you in Paris."

Then I turned and jogged toward the Aereo Pennina helipad. I couldn't look back at the jet. Its doors were closing, sealing Céline inside, shutting me out and apart from her. I couldn't watch that. Patric Verdaguer was approaching and we met some ten meters from the ship.

"Patric?" I yelled. "The two hospital people?"

"They will accompany her to Paris, all the way," he said. "One is an intern, very nice people." He looked at me in a way that made me feel terribly guilty, like he really would enjoy a single expression of gratitude from me. "Eddie, let me say something very briefly, because we have to go." He began again, very seriously. "I would choose no one else to do this. There are great skiers in Verbier, in Arosa, all over this country, everywhere. A certain quality is necessary, beyond ability, Eddie, some un-definable. There is some tenacity in you, some inner strength. I'm drawn to it and, *vraiment*, I see the way you care for this girl."

"Patric?" I pleaded. "Am I going to end up liking you?" He smiled, slyly. "Tell me. I've got to prepare for this."

"Stranger things have happened in Switzerland," he said. It must have been a Swiss joke — went right over my head—but I smiled anyway. Then, we both walked under the blades of the big gunship. Lo and behold, a yellow and white Sikorsky and the warm greeting came from Vittorio, of course. The way he received Patric, I thought for a second he was going to kiss his hand. He looked and gave me a polite smile, a glimmer of unsettling recognition. Our last meeting was scrawled upon his leonine grin.

"Buon giorno, Vittorio," I said.

"Piacere, molto." He smiled again, broadly.

Fabian Thibaud came up along side of Patric. Liney and Eric jumped out of the ship's hold. There we all stood in the gaping side hatch of the big yellow Sikorsky. Vittorio excused himself and went about prepping the ship for takeoff. Soon we'd all be yelling over that roar. Everyone needed to talk fast.

Fabian handed Patric a piece of paper, Patric glanced at it and began again very calmly, very monotone.

"When you get to Cervinia, my suggestion is to take a room quickly, in either one of two hotels, Grand Cristallo or Hermitage. You can make your arrangements, telephone…"

"Patric, excuse me," I interrupted. "Can you make that four hotels?" Liney and Eric looked at me. Patric smiled with a kind of admiring satisfaction. A show of cunning impressed him, it was obvious. He handed the piece of paper back to Fabian, and Fabian started to write on it, hastily. Patric continued.

"Of course, Eddie, you may have four choices. You will

have no problem at these hotels. If you must, use the code V.N., Verdant Industries, and you will have what you ask for."

"Better be careful, Patric, we could run-up a hell of a tab."

"Whatever you wish, Linus," Patric answered, sweetly. "Now then, you will place a call to a number in Aosta. All you need to say to the other party..." Patric paused for effect and Fabian looked up from the sheet of paper.

"The Wolverine is here," Fabian said. A cool, self-satisfied smile was his only punctuation.

"You really shouldn't have, Fabian," I said. "I mean, that's very touching."

"You give the telephone number, hang up, and wait." Patric took over again. "You will receive a call back from another party in Cervinia or Breuil or Valtournenche. I don't know where they will be exactly, but they will be near. There will be three, and one translator, and he will ask, in English..."

"In Italian, Patric," Fabian interrupted. Verdaguer turned on him quickly. Words were unnecessary. The dressing-down was plainly visible in Patric's glare. "The three took an Italian translator. I told you this, *mon vieux,*" Fabian pleaded.

"But they speak English, no?" Patric demanded.

"Yes, I'm sure, but they wish to be cautious also." Fabian spread his arms, as if to plead *nolo contendere.*

"Patric, don't worry," I split their stalemate. They turned to me. "I can handle the Italian. It's not a problem."

"The person will ask if you have 'The Little Brown Jug'," Fabian continued. "That will be very clear. I don't think you will have any trouble to understand."

"No. No trouble, Fabian," I answered, calmly.

"Now, Eddie, very important," Patric said. "The exchange of the package is your call, completely up to you." We all looked at Patric, waiting. "If you want you can rendezvous in a public place, in the hotel, in a restaurant, that is up to you three and the three Iraqis." Fabian handed Patric the piece of paper again. Patric glanced at it and handed it out to us. Liney took it. "You can make the exchange rather quickly and be back on the lift this afternoon. You realize that, I'm sure."

"Patric." Liney spoke up, his eyes down on the piece of paper. "You wouldn't want to tell us where Marchese is staying, would you?" He looked up at Patric, hard. Everything fell silent.

"I cannot do that, Linus."

"The fuck you can't." Venom spewed from Liney's words. "What? It's not part of the goddamn deal?"

"You know what room, when he checked-in..." Eric jumped in. "When he takes a leak, I'll bet."

"Can I do that, Eddie?" Patric's simple tone again.

He looked straight at me with expectation and certainty loaded into the chambers of his inquisitive frown. There was a long pause, and in it the agonizing sound of Patric's Lear Jet slicing through the still morning air, streaking down the runway, pierced my heart. I pictured Céline lying inside, wrapped in her gauze dressings, bound and held tightly by straps and slings instead of my arms. The nose of the jet tipped slightly up and it slid cleanly into the blue sky, lifting her off of the earth we shared no more. The engine's afterburn branded the moment into my memory. The sound cut into me, and the deep gash it left began to fill fast with loneliness. Céline was gone. A cavern in me echoed the loss. My recklessness had brought about these strange circumstances.

"No. You cannot do that, Patric," I said, flatly. Liney and Eric looked at me, surprised. "It's not about Patric, or Marchese—it's about me. Now, let's get going."

The helicopter's engines sputtered and whirred, and she cranked-up with a tremendous roar. The three of us jumped inside and strapped in. I donned a pair of dark glasses,

stared through a porthole in the side, and never looked at
Patric or Fabian again. The armband passes were tossed into
the compartment. I heard the plastic rattle and saw one
placed in my lap by Liney.

Billet du jour
Zermatt, CH — Cervinia, Italia
valide 08,00 – 16,30

I glanced away again. Vittorio made a few last checks
and adjustments, then ripped into the sky—due
vertical—and we were away and heading for Zermatt in the
next few minutes.

Eric instructed him to land us at *Furi*, a major, on-
mountain crossroads just the other side of the long
Landtunnel that carried skiers up from Zermatt. The
Landtunnel lift was a modern version of an old coal mining
train. From there, we would board the *télécabin* to Trockener
Steg and then to Klein Matterhorn. We'd be at our highest
point reachable by cable car before mid-morning, and
making the fast schuss down into Breuil and Cervinia by
noon or shortly after, if everything went as planned.

After a few knowledgeable estimations, Eric made some
executive decisions about our equipment. He decided to
leave the snowshoes. We'd travel the glacial stretches of flat
or upgrade with only the faster crampons. Speed was a
priority up there, an advantage, not a liability. Among
climbers, speed actually became a safety factor when
crossing snowbridge and crevasse zones. We'd buy bottles of
water at Furi before boarding our first *télécabin*, and eliminate
the lunch stop at *Testa Grigia*. Blending-in will have been
achieved, said Eric, by the time we reached *Klein*. We'd then
bolt for the vast expanse of glacier behind the Breithorn.

I'd have the cigarette carton of twelve klystrons, "The
Little Brown Jug," in my backpack along with the water
bottles. The rest of the gear was split between Liney and Eric.
Eric had also figured, that such a division of the cargo made

us all approximately the same weight. He'd always be the
lead on our rope team, but in terms of his fast computation,
we could now assume that if a surface or snowbridge held
him, then it would in all probability hold Liney and then
me—each crossing was not a new test, or re-calculation.

Judging from the crowd on the cable car, we were
probably part of the second wave of skiers to go up that
morning. It was brilliantly sunny when we disembarked at
Klein, but off to the west an intricate sky still held the
promise of dramatic change. We were safe as far as weather
was concerned. Italy beyond was bright and blue and almost
cloudless. "The Sunny Side of Winter," the ads in the New
York Times always read. We'd find out in the next few
minutes just how sunny, and hot, the sunny side could get.
We'd all feel like three, over-easy.

We pushed hard away from Klein Matterhorn, east
toward the great wall of the Breithorn, trying to get as much
out of the slope as possible on our skis. Eric wanted to get
clear of any other skiers, out of sight and over onto the
backside where we would re-group. We finally came to a
stop on a flat expanse. The three of us were already warm
and in need of water.

"Alright," Eric began. "This, here, this ablation zone is a
boring, pain-in-the-ass to cross. So, what we'll do instead is
climb." He turned and pointed up at the massive wall of the
Breithorn. "Up along there. That's the ridge of the
bergschrund, right there where the glacier pulls away from
the headwall of the mountain."

"Can you believe this guy?" Liney whispered to me.

"We walk the spine of that moat, see, then ski down
across an accumulation, or another ablation zone on the far
side. It'll be climbing, but we'll spend a little and get a lot
afterward, skiing instead of walking."

"You ever get the feeling he's not telling us everything?"
I said to Liney.

"Yeah, yeah." Liney went along. "These climbing types

explain stuff like it's just a walk in the park—we'll walk along the berger-sound and the framerstam." Eric laughed at us. He emptied the gear from the backpacks and sorted everything out under the hail of our ribbing.

He carefully placed things in the snow in three distinct piles, in the three positions he wanted us to assume in the rope team. The hoods, masks, harnesses, karabiners, piles of straps, and crampons, accumulated under Eric's intense and systematic procedure. He methodically unlaced all two-hundred feet of rope like a rodeo cowboy and began to mountaineer coil its entire length, checking it every foot of the way. The simple truth about climbing redoubled itself with Eric's concentration and competence. In the mountains, people would give anything to have someone just like Eric along. He was our security. His knowledge and leadership would carry us all through. Minutes from now we'd defer to his every judgment, his decisions, every step of our journey up here. That was as it should be. Someone must lead with total authority, and others must follow with total compliance.

Liney and I watched him work to set up our rope team, looping the rope through our karabiners, making knots and hitches, tying-off short lengths in *prusiks* and *Bachmanns*, *Kleimheists* and *Kleimheists* with karabiners. He formed clutches and more loops to hold skis and poles, working feverishly, thinking and making mental pictures of the dangers, then whipping together some hitch, some piece of rope, to combat the perils.

Finally, we were strung together with Eric in the lead, me in the center, and Liney, third. I watched him tie-off a series of loops on his own harness through the tiny belay plate. He did it so fast I marveled at how complex a simple thing like a piece of rope could be in the hands of a master.

"What the hell are you doing?" I asked.

"This is our little transmission and brake," he said. "When one of you Bo-Bo's fall into a crevasse, as fast as I can react, I can slow the fall, then brake it. If both of you go down, I can get out of the rope and go home," Liney and I laughed.

"What if Eric, The Red, our fearless leader, goes down in a crevasse?" Liney asked.

"Well, I brake myself to a stop with the extra coil, then...I hope and pray that my friends hold me in their highest esteem."

"Where did you learn all this shit? And how come I don't know it?" I asked him.

"P.A.," Eric answered, somberly.

"What do you mean? P.A. took me everywhere. How come I don't know this stuff?"

"What you and P.A. did together Eddie is called hiking," he said with his ever-handy Alsatian smugness. "What P.A. and I did is called climbing. There's a big difference." Liney and I looked at each other.

"Well, gag me with a belay plate," Liney quipped.

"P.A. You big lummox," I yelled up into the sky.

"Yeah, you'd better be watching out for us today," Liney shouted. "And I hope they have that French cheese where you are, and you get some stuck in your nose."

Eric just looked at us and shook his head.

"Alright, you two, here's the program." Eric commanded our attention. "We'll each be about fifty-five feet apart. Keep the slack out as much as you can. The extra is over my shoulder and Liney's. Somebody punches-in, sit down and dig your cramp spikes in. I'll tell you about anchors and tie-offs when we hit our first snowbridge. We don't gather together unless I determine a safe zone. I'm going to go fast, so keep up." He started to walk away, toward the lead position as he talked. "We cross that little compression zone, up over the tension zone...doesn't appear to be a problem... then, up on that spiny ridge, should look pretty spectacular down in that *bergschrund*."

"There he goes, talking funny again," I said. Liney started singing.

"The berg-shrund connected to da tension-zone, da tension zone connected to da safe-zone, da safe zone connected to da 'cummulation-zone...'"

"...And here's the word of the lord," I recited. *Amen.*

The line tugged at my waist and I left Liney standing, singing. Once our fifty-five foot distances were achieved, we'd keep a very brisk pace going. Three dots along a line, like three notes on an endless, white sheet of music, we trudged the breathtaking and desolate glacier.

The sun beat down, and we all started ventilating our suits soon into the climb. The wall of the Breithorn sent shears of wind down upon us, stinging the left sides of our faces. We walked with our left shoulders dipped into the cutting wind. Castor and Pollux rose steadily on the horizon, two ice cream cone tops, vanilla-white in the Italian sun.

As Eric had promised, the walk along the top edge of the *bergschrund* was spectacular. The wind and elements had carved towers and cones and smoothened boulders of ice in formations and clustered groups that were truly magnificent to behold. The depth of the crevasse was frightening and the towering pieces of stone and wind ice were reminiscent of the Grand Canyon, winterized.

Everything was going as planned. We came across only one small snowbridge. It was solid and very safe, but Eric took a few minutes to show us how a three-man rope team anchored and belayed across any tentative span. Thereafter we called him, "Teach."

We'd traversed a few arduous miles when Eric called us forward onto a white, bulging *arête* that looked to be the highest point of the entire ridge along the *bergschrund*. The snow and ice cliff protruded, out over a steep, sloping transverse of windswept "dry" ablation that looked like smooth animal skin scratched and gashed by giant claws. The ablation field was cracked and opened a thousand times or more in crescentic crevasses, gentle little half-moon arcs, some looked to be slivers no wider than a fist, and some were one and two feet wide. Each crevasse seemed to swallow the sifting, blowing, granular snow like holes draining water from a colander.

"Pretty sight, isn't it?" Eric smiled.

"Pretty scary, yeah," Liney replied.

"Piece of cake," Eric said. He'd already begun to coil the rope and get his skis down off his back. He just gazed out over that deadly looking expanse as if it were an amusement park. There was a joyous glint in his eye. "P.A. and I did something that looked like this one time. It's not that bad. Normally, we'd stay roped together, but I think it's going to be too fast. The skis are better. We ski *over* the crevasses…skis perpendicular, always. Just glide over the cracks, edge and brake in between. It'll be a lot of chatter. The fillings in your teeth may come loose, but just let the skis glide, over the crevasses, and don't worry about speed. That's why I don't want to go roped."

"Isn't that the mountain right there?" I wondered aloud.

"Yeah, that's Pollux, and Castor behind," Eric said.

"Will this get us to the base of Pollux?" Liney asked.

"Not quite," Eric replied. "I don't want to get below a descent line for Pollux, so we have to turn east again somewhere down in the middle of this crevasse field. Now, that gets a little hairy."

"No more gliding over the slits, eh?" I ventured.

"Right. We rope-up again and glide parallel, in between the crevasses. It's called *en echelon*. We fan out a bit and let the rope span the crevasses, and we just skate the chatter."

"Just like changing lanes on the freeway," Liney mused.

"More like the Cross Bronx Expressway, with a thousand friggin' potholes," I said.

With a hop off of the cornice and two turns in the accumulation powder directly beneath it, we then turned our skis straight down the mountain and onto the glacial ice pack. The crevasses looked like some giant razor blade had touched the straining, stretching ice shelf popping it open like taut skin under a surgeon's scalpel. The chatter started almost immediately, and it was worse than any of us anticipated.

Our skis bounced and vibrated across the rippled ice. My knees were pumping up and down involuntarily, firing like pistons in a fast-idling engine. The cuts and crevasses were more numerous than they had appeared from the high *arête*. We rumbled down like three skate-boarders speed-surfing a concrete ramp, only someone had forgotten to smooth-finish the cement. The noise was deafening. Edging sent sprays of ice crystals racing across the surface, the sound was like thousands of heavy dice rolling across a marble floor. After a hundred yards or so, as they shattered, the tinkling shards of falling ice became like a rushing, white-water flume.

Liney and I watched Eric and mimicked his every move. We were almost even with him when he suddenly waved a ski pole in the air. He dug his edges in like ice skate blades and nearly disappeared in a huge spray of ice. He did two complete three-sixties and came to a stop straddling a small crevasse. Liney and I scraped and slid in a shower of ice spray. Then, we fell on our asses and skidded for another twenty or thirty meters.

I hooked a pole on the lip of a two-foot crevasse and screeched to a stop. The falling ice crystals caught up with me and in seconds it looked as though I was covered in broken glass. Liney's final rest came a few yards below me in a crevasse just big enough to fit his butt. His skis and arms were high in the air, and his better half was stuck in the tight deep-freeze.

It took us ten minutes to finally reach Eric, edging back up across the rippled ice, and the Redhead laughed all the while we struggled to gain parity. Liney complained about his rear-end hurting, and Eric made sure he whipped it with the rope at every opportunity. Eric then began threading us together again for the last push across the easternmost edge of Breithorn's glacial side and down into the notch at the base of Pollux.

"Now Castor and Pollux are right there, Eddie," Eric said. "...almost feel like touching them, don't you?"

Two milky smooth and sensuously rounded domes thrust heavenward like city cathedrals, as though nature hired Renaissance architects to perfect their stately vaults. There were no jagged sides — unusual in these Alps. Wind and snows had turned and polished these two giants to show their Italian host some of nature's equally Baroque inspiration.

Some vapor went up from my heart at that moment. Some unsettling breath of spirit left me—P.A., Céline, my children, I couldn't explain what it was. Those two white peaks, so still and majestic there took a raging storm within, and brought about a calm. Everyone and everything seemed so far away and Castor and Pollux sat waiting for me, offering me peace. *Never ask, the gods never intercede. Weather the storm alone. Take care of the mess in your soul, and never ask of these gods.*

I crouched down and put my head between my knees, breathing deeply, taking my eyes off of the silent twins.

"You all right, Famous?" Liney asked.

"Yeah, yeah. I was just thinking...nothing," I mumbled.

" '...*passion, and the death of a dear friend, make a man look sad,*' " Eric said, as he continued fixing our ropes, threading the karabiners on my harness. I looked up at him.

"That's the Duke," I said.

"I played Theseus, once," he said.

"What the hell are you two talking about?" Liney asked.

"*A Midsummer-Night's Dream,*" Eric said. "I was in a school production, in America." He pulled the rope through, tethering us together again. " '...*and passion ends the play.*' " He whispered the line to himself.

We were ready to fan out abreast of each other, and Eric began to glide away from us slowly, uppermost on the fall line, opposite a crevasse, putting the deep gash between us and him. "Liney would have been good in 'Midsummer,' " he yelled down.

I looked at Castor and Pollux once more, then smiled at Eric. I rose and began to slide now, second down on the fall line, as the slack between Eric and me came up, spanning the crevasse.

"He would have been a good Puck," I teased. Liney watched us both with a suspicious leer, as the rope from me to him dragged across the ice. "Or, maybe one of the Fairies, Mustardseed or Moth?"

"Nah," Eric hollered down along the rope. "Bottom, I think, definitely a Bottom." Eric and I smiled in the bright sun. Liney touched his rear-end and winced. Then, the slack between Liney and me came up and we were all under sail, drifting on the wind along a gentle, icy downgrade — three across, dodging the cracks—Liney at the bottom, *en echelon*.

We did this for the distance of about five or six football fields, I guess, and stopped as the accumulation snow began to top our skis. Only a white, swerving river separated us now from the entrance to the "notch" Eric had told us about. The top cone of Pollux loomed directly over us. Castor was all but hidden behind his brother. This white river was a two-hundred-foot-wide col — a col that moved and had all of the properties of a small glacier. It snaked down from the ice shelf on Monte Rosa, around the east shoulder of the fourteen-thousand-foot Liskamm, and skirted the west wall of Pollux.

"We've made it this far," Eric said, looking out over the frozen stream. "I'm going to be extra cautious."

"Whatever you say, Teach," Liney wisecracked.

"What's another twenty minutes," Eric said. "I'm looking at the margins, and there just might be something under there."

Liney and I both looked down, puzzled at the white blankness, then looked back at each other.

"What the hell's he talking about?" Liney ruminated.

"You two dig-in here and belay me," Eric instructed. "Let me have as much rope as I need, and all of the slack. Just keep the twenty at Liney's end. Let it slide through your hands. If I punch-in, I don't want to go far. See you chums."

With that, he pushed on his poles, onto the white stream and started across very slowly. Liney and I sat down and crossed our skis, sinking the rowels into the powder. The rope crept slowly through my karabiners, then my hands, letting Eric out.

"You okay?" Liney asked. "I mean, back there."

"Yes. I'm okay. These mountains get to me, that's all." I was comfortable again with Liney beside me. "I can't think it through sometimes, know what I mean? I lose my way, or something. I want to be like them. Why can't we be like them?"

"Like them?"

"Yeah, like those two mountains, still and natural, knowing without thinking…a knowledge that would give us a kind of peace, Liney. We think too much, we do, we cock-everything-up."

Liney sighed and rested his arms on his knees.

"Everything important in this goddamn universe is beyond thinking anyway, Famous, beyond our intelligence." Liney just stared out, watching Eric gingerly cross the col. "I'm telling you, it's beyond intelligence…but it's not beyond feeling."

"Linus? *Mon vieux*. I hope we survive this little trek. That thought deserves another hearing. I'm glad I'm up here with you and Eric. Whatever happens we're in it together." I put my arm around his shoulder and pulled him into me.

Just then, the rope snapped taut with a violent pull. It yanked my harness and the twenty-foot coil over Liney's shoulder. We both reacted, grabbing the straight rope and leaning back, hard. We looked up in a panic only to see the Redhead standing about a hundred-and-fifty feet away, on the opposite side of the silky col, pulling on the rope with a huge smile on his face. He gave out a banshee yell of triumph, and waved his arms wildly for us to come across. Liney and I looked at each other, then back at Eric, who'd started doing some gyrating dance-move atop his skis.

"I'm going to bury that little Redhead's face in the snow," I said. Liney just shook his head.

"Beyond intelligence, what'd I tell you, Famous? Beyond intelligence."

Eric's notch, in the west face of Pollux turned out to be a narrow, steep avenue that widened quickly in the descent. Shaped like a halfpipe, it snaked like a bobsled run, or a luge track. Fantastically fast and untouched by skiers, we skied the hard tension zones along the banked turns, keeping out of the softer, slower accumulation in the center of the track. It was roller derby and three-man bob at hair-raising speeds. We cut and ran, passed and let loose with an abandon, and for most of it we were parallel to the snow, like three spiders running along the white walls of Pollux's back alleys. In minutes, we emerged from her broad flanks onto the wide top of Plateau Rosa.

From the plateau, the Cime Bianchi trails led us down among the Italian skiers, down beneath the chairlifts and *télécabins*. The modern hotels and apartments of Breuil and Cervinia appeared to rise up from the deep, white snow mounds. The Valpelline, the Valtournanche and sunny Italy — the Val d'Aosta — lay beyond. We landed at the base of the main lifts looking like arctic explorers covered in a white frozen mist.

Breuil and Cervinia were two stations — two communes — about as far apart as Grand Central and the Library on Fifth Avenue. The ski slopes melded smoothly into the narrow streets and walkways of both villages, connecting them as one in a maze of white, hard-packed trails for strollers and skiers alike. We snapped out of our bindings opposite the veranda-style café of the Breuil Hotel. Liney checked to see if the Breuil was one of the hotels on Patric Verdaguer's list. It was.

We locked our skis and poles in one of several long racks directly in front of the café. The three of us made a thorough inspection of those racks, and five more at the front entrance, hoping to find the tall Rossignols belonging to Lorenzo Marchese. We found six pairs of Rossi's, but nothing longer than one-ninety-five, and none had Deke's Iron Mountain sticker.

We were in need of something hot to drink, and so decided to sit in the sun-drenched café of the Breuil and plan a strategy over a quick *caffé e ciocolatte*.

"Three more," Liney said, studying the piece of paper and correlating the names of the hotels to a plan of the two villages. "The other three are all in Cervinia. That's good. I'll take the Chalet Valdotain. Eric, you take the Grand Cristallo, and, Eddie'll take the Hermitage." He pointed them out to us on the colorful plan.

"We meet back here?" I asked.

"No," Eric said. "Waste too much time. We snowball. See the way the streets go around? If you come up with nothing, you move to the next hotel and help. Whoever finds Lorenzo, sticks."

"What about asking at the front desks?" Liney said.

"I'd like to hold off on that if we can," I broke in. "Let's try to find him without asking first. Front-desk people never keep quiet for some reason. This is a small town. I know we can do it. He's here. I know he's here." Liney and Eric looked at me, hard, but didn't question. "It's one-thirty now. We won't go past three on Lorenzo. At three we've got to start making the big phone calls or we're going to be in deep shit. A deal is a deal."

"Okay, we'd better get moving," Liney ordered. "Skis and poles stay here in the locks." He folded the paper and map. "Eric and I can cruise the cafes and restaurants in these joints, too. He doesn't know us. He won't jump." Liney looked at me. "You've got to do something about that handsome puss of yours, Famous."

"It's a Harrison Ford-thing he's got going, I think," Eric teased as we walked out of the restaurant. "The chin scars, the moody eyes...the pained-oversexed-intellectual look."

"Yeah, yeah. I can see that," Liney fueled him.

"A kind of, James Caan-DiNiro-ey attitude thing, too, you know?" Eric kept at it. "The women like that."

"Hey, Redhead?" I came back at him, brightly. "How'd you like a belay plate up your ass?"

"*Ouuu la,la*, Famous. *Oooouuu la,la*." He wiggled on ahead.

An hour later, Liney and I had turned-up nothing, so we converged on Eric at the Grand Cristallo. Cristallo was the high end of accommodations in Cervinia, befitting the Marchese more than any of the other three hotels. It was modern but the decor was classically sumptuous and the amenities plentiful. There were three full restaurants, of varied fair, situated off of the main lobby—two had café-bars and one looked more like a breakfast room. Eric met us in the spacious main lobby.

"We hit it," he said, quietly. "I found the Rossignols leaning against the wall in front with a thousand other pairs of skis. Deke's sticker, *voila!* Under the tip."

"Did you check for his room?" I pressed him.

"Not yet."

"The house phones," Liney said, enthusiastically.

"Easy, easy—" Eric quieted us down. "He's in there having lunch."

"Where?" I rose slightly with my question.

"There, the Crystal Room. I've been watching."

"Oh, how nice," My heart was pounding. "Why don't I just go in and sit down, and choke him before dessert comes."

"Eddie, Eddie, easy, he's not going anywhere, take it easy." Eric had his hands over my shoulders. "What do we do? Start pounding on this guy? Here? How do we explain that? Don't forget that little box of cookie cutters you're carrying." He puts me back on my heels again, thinking. "You and Liney go get the room, and stay out of sight. I'm going to hang here. I'll get his room number, don't worry, just leave it to me. I'll get it off the check when he signs it. Now, go, go ,go, both of you."

I fought the impulse to run in to that restaurant. Most of life was a series of stifled impulses. *We think too goddamn much. I'm sure of it.* But, Eric was right. Lorenzo Marchese was here. We had him. The horseman and I were in the same barn.

Liney and I got the room — a studio — on the fifth floor. It had a simple daybed sort of thing, a loveseat, coffee table, some lamps and end tables, and a small balcony with sliding glass doors. There was a mini-refrigerator, stocked. The bathroom was tiny with one of those tubs-for-dwarfs. We were in Italy, but the room was typically Alpine — designed by Swiss midgets.

The view was spectacular. The backside of the Matterhorn was less imposing, gently curved like an old man bending on his climb toward Switzerland. All of the hillside slopes and lifts serving Cervinia and Breuil filled the complete panorama.

"If Patric's paying for this, how come we didn't get a big room?" I asked, pacing around.

"Eddie, chill-out, for Christ's sake," Liney said. "What? We're going to be here all of an hour, hour-and-a-half?"

We laid our stuff out on the day-bed thing, the klystrons were still tucked in my backpack. We both opened our jumpsuits all the way to our waists, then we raided the little wet-bar refrigerator for cold drinks. I slid the glass balcony doors open and a cool afternoon breeze billowed the draperies and freshened the room. Eric came in only a few minutes after we'd settled in.

"He talked to the waiter forever," Eric said. "Jesus, Italians can talk." Eric started throwing his stuff off.

"So, what have we got?" I asked.

"He's in two-sixteen," Eric said.

"We're five-two-four, we're on the same side."

I rushed through the open glass doors and looked down along the rows of balconies. They fell away like a grand staircase, in a descending line, down into a snowbank so deep it came up even with the second floor. One of those balconies, on the second level, was Lorenzo Marchese's.

The snowbank came straight down from the slopes. I could ski down that slope, across the back hump of a drift, right onto his balcony like a painted bird, and fly through his glass doors. The balconies were all empty now, no one was sunning today. I left my daydream on our little terrace and went back inside.

Liney had laid out the paper with the phone numbers on the coffee table in front of the loveseat and pulled the telephone onto the table. He sat behind the phone and picked up the receiver. Eric and I jumped. He tapped a key, and listened.

"Just like I thought," he said. "Italian phones, they go direct, to an outside operator."

"Is that good or bad?" I asked.

"Perfect," Eric answered. "When they call back, they don't get the front desk or a room number."

"They come directly into this phone," Liney continued. "It's great. Every room is wired like a separate house."

"They'd have to trace the call to find out where we are. Imagine that," I teased. "From the same people who put tomato paste in a tube." Eric hit me with the coil of rope.

"Come on, let's get this thing rolling," Liney insisted. "It's after three."

I sat down behind the phone, on the loveseat next to Liney, Eric stood over us and they watched me dial the number in Aosta. It rang three times. I let Liney listen, his ear was up against the receiver with mine. A non-descript voice answered a simple,

"*Pronto?*"

"*Buon giorno, signore,*" I said. Then, I said only, "the Wolverine is here." Silence. I reeled off the telephone number that was on the phone. The voice asked only that I repeat the number. I did and hung up. "So, now we wait," I said, and we three stared at the silent phone.

"It sounded like a bakery or a restaurant," Liney said, excitedly. "The background noise…maybe a pizza parlor or something."

"Oh, shit. Ian Flemming is at it again," Eric said.

Just then, the door burst open and the room suddenly filled with six more people. Liney and I jumped up. Eric skirted around the table. The three of us now stood, a bit shaken, with the backs of our knees pressed against the little sofa.

"Don't any of you move. Please?" How polite. The British accent was soft and mannerly, but loaded with sincerity. He was stern looking, a sharper, harder-featured Cary Grant. The two behind him wore tams and long coats, they went to the sliding doors and stood sentry. The other three, in military browns and greens against olive-tanned skin, were definitely a cultural league-and-a-half apart from Great Britain.

Two dark, stunning women in muted brown parkas guarded the door and a short bald man was just to Liney's left—lots of khaki and brown, and black shining boots.

"Getting a little crowded in here," Liney said.

"Told you we should have gotten a double," I mumbled.

"You didn't tell me you were having people over," He said.

I was getting very nervous. The Brit had a presence, I could feel it, but a nice, non-threatening presence. The little bald guy was homicidal, for sure. I didn't see any iron, but these six didn't need anything else to make an impression. So I thought.

"The two Go-Go girls..." Eric whispered in my ear, lips twisted talking out of the side of his mouth. "They're packing Uzis underneath the parkas."

"Parka packing. Hmmm," I said, side-mouthing. "Now, that could be some rough sex, semi-automatic, rapid fire, rough sex."

"Shut up you two, goddamn it!" Liney said, with gritted teeth.

"Gentlemen, please? I'm Major-General John Tiffen, British Intelligence." Cary was direct, forceful, very firm and secure. The black beret was cool. Nice touch. "This is Commander Ari Urist." He nodded to the deadly, short one. "Israeli Counter-Espionage in charge of Middle East activity in central Europe." Perfect name, big title, but he still looked homicidal. Urist didn't move or make a sound, but his eyeballs screamed.

"Hershel Bernardi," I blurted out. "A young Hershel Bernardi. Don't you think? I'll bet you get that a lot, Commander. Boy, was he a great actor."

"Eddie?" Liney scolded.

"Listen, I love Israel. Honestly. I'm from New York. I love the Jews. I've seen all your wars on T.V."

"Eddie, shut the fuck up."

"No shit. They're like mini-series, you don't know about mini-series?" My mouth was just going, uncontrollably. The nerves, the guns, I had a lot I wanted to say before I died. "Really, Commander, I love Jewish people. There's a deli in my building."

"Eddie. Damn it," Liney again, forcefully.

"Can I call my kids before you kill us?"

"Eddie, Jesus-friggin-Christ."

"Yes. Linus?"

"Shut. Up. Now. Please?"

"Okay, okay, I'll just...General Tiffen, by the way, I'd just like to thank you for not yelling 'freeze' when you came, I hate that, you know, when you came in...thanks."

"You're here in Cervinia," Tiffen began, officiously, dismissing my chit-chat. "And should you pass on what you're carrying, the consequences of your actions could be very grave, very grave. Under the Geneva Convention..."

"Major, Major?" Liney interrupted. "Spare us. Just tell us what you know, and if you're going to waste us."

"We're not going to harm you," Tiffen assured. "You'll be dealt with accordingly. Possession alone of those twelve switches is a serious breach of international agreements."

Just then, my cranial light bulb went on with unusual brightness, and the courage juice kicked in again.

"Wait, wait, hold on a second," I spoke up with some reserve of energy, or was it a ton of shit-scared gall? "Major Tiffen, you're a very intelligent man. I can see that. But, your timing...well, it's just a wee bit off, you see. Leaves a lot to be desired. You seem to have caught us in the middle."

"Sorry, Yank. I don't quite follow," He said, nicely.

"I mean, you can have *them*...and the twelve gadgets, of course. Or...you just get us. And who the hell wants us?"

There was total silence in the room. Even Liney and Eric were stunned, giving me crooked glances. Ari Urist perked up like a bloodhound in a duck blind. He and Tiffen shot looks back and forth like Western Union telegrams.

The phone rang.

Six people suddenly got debilitating gas pains, simultaneously—exactly what it looked like. They all froze with uncomfortable frowns and shocked expressions.

"Now, I wonder who that could be?" I jested, politely.

Second ring.

"Maybe it's Ed McMahon from the Publisher's Clearing House." I went eye-to-eye with Cary Grant. "Think fast, Major Tiffen. Three Iraqis. They're right here. One more ring, you can have three Iraqis, or a handsome ex-jock, a debonair ex-pat, and a redheaded Alsatian." Third ring. "Excuse the rags, we don't always look like this. I'll throw in the Italian interpreter for nothing." Tiffen held his breath.

Fourth ring.

I lifted the receiver and cut the ring in half. The room went even deader. The six were rigid like statues, with gas.

"*Pronto?*" I answered, brightly. The voice, a different voice, bid me good day.

"*Grazie. 'giorno, anche, si,*" I returned, then listened. The voice asked if I was the Wolverine, and I responded. "*Si, signore…ecco?*" I was smiling broadly at Ari Urist and Major John Tiffen.

Then, the voice asked, in Italian, "*Quello che, un piccolo brocca marrone?* eh?…the Little Brown Jug." The last phrase was unmistakable even in thick-accented, broken-English.

"*Momento, per favore—*" I held him, and clamped my hand tightly over the mouthpiece. "Come on, Tiffen, here it is. I bring them in, or I tell them to scram…your move." The veins in Major-General John Tiffen's neck suddenly thickened. I knew I had him.

"Eddie, are you nuts?" Liney jumped in, whispering fast, his face beet-red with pressure. "What are we covering Tric's ass for? Give them the god-damn stuff…"

"No," I whispered at maximum volume. "You guys don't play enough poker over here, too much of that faggy roulette. Come on, Major Tiffen?"

"Bloody Yanks," Tiffen whispered, at maximum volume. "What the bloody god-damn hell…"

"I'll tell you what the bloody, Maj, fast Maj, they're on the line. I want two of yours, Maj, an escort to the lifts, the last lift over is at four-thirty. Come on, Tiffen, let's make a deal. Door Number One."

"You bloody bastards. All right, all right, goddamn it." Tiffen was fuming, blasting under his breath.

"My, my," I tried to soothe Tiffen. "You chaps are still pissed about that Tea Party thing, aren't you?"

Thwap! I popped my hand up from the receiver. Everyone went still and stonelike again.

"*Mi dispiaci, signore,*" I went sweetly on the Italian again. "*eh – no, no, no nienti problemi...il toeletta. Si. No, no, gas, gasso e stomaco signore, solamente,*" I continued on. Everyone listened, hanging on my every word as I gave the caller the name of the hotel, and then the room. "*Si, signore,* you come to the room, *il camera, camera,* yeah, *si.*" I looked at Liney and Eric. "*Numero,* two-sixteen...*due cento sedici, al secondo piano,* two, one, six – *due, uno, sei.*" Liney and Eric smiled. I was feeling pretty good, full of myself, then the voice on the other end stunned me.

"Your Italian is very good, Eddie." Sarcastic and low, remotely familiar. The voice was deep, slightly accented, European, nebulous. I glanced at Tiffen and Urist. Suddenly, I was on a tightrope. The fun was over.

"*Grazie, signore,*" I smiled.

"You're a man who likes to touch beautiful things," the voice went on. "Women, antiques." Malouel. Henri Malouel.

The picture of him exploded into my head. Liney and Eric were losing their smiles. They wanted me off the phone, urgently. "How poetic," Henri Malouel continued. "That an American brings these beautiful things to us. Look how far you've come, Eddie...Michigan to the center of the world." The phone clicked dead, abruptly. I placed the receiver on the cradle and stood quickly to face Tiffen. Inside, my heart was racing at full throttle.

"Major Tiffen, I apologize for all of the bullshit theatrics." I was trying to be sincere with Tiffen, with an image of that bastard Malouel still in my head. "Believe me, we're relieved. We respect you, all of you, honest. I'm glad you're getting the Iraqis, and I'm thrilled that those tinker toys over there are in your hands. But, we can't help the way we are — a deal is a deal — if you know what I mean? Now, I hate to be a traitor and run, but we really must be going."

Liney and Eric and I moved quickly. We started dressing again, zipping-up, snapping on our fanny packs and ski gear. It was three-fifty-five.

"We can't figure you Yanks," Tiffen spoke up. "You go cocking around in the Middle East with these bloody chaps."

"Major Tiffen, I can't figure it either," I told him. "I thought I knew a little about my fellow Americans, too. I guess I don't know shit."

"If it's any consolation to you, mate," Tiffen said. "We think it's the ones coming in, not the ones going out."

"Yeah, well, not a hell of a lot of difference to me. Turn them upside down — Democrats, Republicans — they're all the same. Now, look..." I drew Tiffen to the glass sliding doors near the balcony. "You and Hesh can stand on that snowbank there and watch the action in two-sixteen. I think you'll know when to move in, right Major?" I looked him in the eye again. "Tiffen, I mean it, I'm sorry. We're really three good blokes. We're not into this stuff, honest. Ian Flemming novels are about as close as we want to get."

Tiffen leaned into me, knitting his brow sternly, and said.

"Tell me something, Yank. What bloody tea party were you referring to?" He winked and we shook hands, very firmly.

Liney and Eric were at the door and fully suited for the trip back over. The two stunning Israeli females were on either side of them. I headed for the door but stopped and saluted the Israeli females — Sabraesque, dark and so tempting, skin as smooth as Sunday morning cream cheese on a toasted, sesame bagel. Holy Moses, they were beautiful women. I turned to the nearest.

"Hello, beautiful. Is that a pistol in your parka or are you just happy...?"

"Commander Urist?" Liney cut me off. "Would it be possible for the young ladies...?" He started to say.

"No," Urist replied, emphatically, in a booming voice.

"Hey, he talks," Eric said with dramatic surprise. "Little Hershel, he actually speaks."

chapter Eighteen
BLUE WHALES

On the lift ride back over, Liney and I argued almost all the way about Patric Verdaguer's role in the events of that afternoon. Eric closed his eyes and sang Mick Jagger songs. He couldn't be bothered with either of us.

I thought Verdaguer set the whole thing up in Cervinia—Tiffen, Urist, the Sting, the works—to save-face with his American client, and to make sure the little nuclear switches did not fall into the hands of the Iraqis. Patric Verdaguer could have it both ways. Liney was adamant. He thought Tric was dirty, head to toe, and deeply involved in dirty business.

Patric was one of those restless souls dogged by a certain pattern of behavior, a persona he had to maintain. *Sounded like somebody else I knew.* He found small measures of acceptance through a few good deeds, and thereby something honorable within.

I never mentioned Henri Malouel to either Liney or Eric. Some part of me wished that Tiffen and Urist would snatch him in Cervinia, and some other part of me knew they wouldn't. He was too sharp, too cunning. The Iraqis would take the fall, and somehow, Malouel would slither-off into the invisible cities of international terrorism once again, plying his trade.

It was something of an art with Henri Malouel, like collecting antiques and fine furniture, he knew every edge and knurl, every hidden contour of prized workmanship in terrorist activity. We'd meet again someday, I was certain, in Verbier. The meeting would be interesting.

Lorenzo Marchese slipped through the cracks that day, too, the cracks in my armor. I deserved it, I guess. It was the reason bulls were fooled by the red cape nine times out of ten. I had to console myself that any measure of justice, even the meager one he'd receive in room 216 with the Iraqis, was the best I could exact under the circumstances. I told myself that Marchese was a timely messenger sent to warn me about neglect and obsessions and carelessness with those I professed to love. He ran. And I ran after him to punish, when it was me I needed to punish all the while. My recklessness and improvidence was courting tragedy almost every night of the week. Marchese served a purpose. He was a trade-off, another exchange.

He'd remember that I was but a few steps behind him. The thought would haunt him. A humble settling of scores, but I was content to live with the thought of him out on his daily ride, in full command of his steed across the Tuscan hills through his orchard trees, and occasionally seeing my face come out of the morning mist.

Verbier, when we returned, had already changed. The World Cup Races were finished, Winter Festival ended. She wore the face of the typical Valais resort once again, it was back to business as usual.

There was always more sadness in return than in departure. Something changed while we were away, something irretrievable was gone forever in a kind of betrayal of sensibilities. We counted on a certain permanence in Verbier, our gang of friends in our little resort. Nothing would change unless we changed it, we believed. The familiarity and comfort we sought in each other we also found in the same places, and in the same rituals. We shared a wish for constancy. Then, we turned away for one brief moment, looked the other way in some idle distraction—a kind of betrayal in itself, I guess—and some part of it vanished. Or, was it some part of us?

Tonight, the town was relatively empty and unusually quiet. I slipped in and out of the Borsalino and the Sacconaix, alone. Liney and Eric were back in Chez Linéy, sleeping. The Italian rock music from Marshal's seemed oddly out of place tonight, tinney when it filled the deserted streets. In the cold night air, I stepped briskly through the dark *ruelles*. Snow flurries were light and intermittent, giving the streets a soft patina. The infrequent flakes gently settled on the wet pavement and then vanished. Ideas, answers melted just as fast before me and the absence of Pierre Alain haunted the very places I walked.

My mind, my heart were in a Paris hospital. I wanted Céline in my arms and I wanted to find a new constancy with her. Back in my room, I tried to write about Cervinia, about Liney and Eric, the hurt of Franca, and about Céline, but I could not. The letdown was so great, I felt even more depressed than before. I fidgeted and paced about the room. I tossed in the bed, and finally I embarked on the most difficult journey, sleep.

I slept the sleep of sea creatures, drifting at the mercy of prodding currents, asleep with the mind's eyes wide open — restless, thinking, navigating, never reaching the still and silent depths of the much-desired slumber. I'd never been a sound sleeper, but now, the night was filled with agony and much too much thinking. I labored at sleep and the memories came like blue whales. In dance-like cycles, they surfaced, they breached and bared their shiny backs to the light. Then, they returned to the darkness. The whales cried and squealed, they murmured and rolled softly. They called me through the liquid. I was immersed in the shallows of memory, tossed and spun in the eddies of blue whales.

Certain moments in the depths were intense. A screen of illusion flickered and jumped, chattering, scratching like an old projector — the dream gods threading up the nightmares again.

Horrific thoughts of events gone wrong — cars, planes, helicopters, horses, bare branches, falling dreams—were intercut with warm visions of Céline. Why this mixture?

Pushed over the edge of eroticism in one moment, then spun-round in violent schemes the next. Why couldn't I rocket to Paris, right now? What was keeping me here?

Up again, I paced out on the small balcony in the frigid air. The snow had stopped. Beneath a cloudless black sky and half moon, I watched the hill in a blanket of mist. The hill that sparkled every evening with the chalet lights was hidden now under a dense fog. And rising above, breaching the thick clouds, there they were, the mountains, silent and resting like blue whales in the moonlight. Sonorous, deep and thundering, they spoke in tones. The mountains moved, and moved me within. When I trembled it was the voice, the resonance of mountains that unsettled me, and I was compelled to listen.

What I'd gone there for, what held me there, they conveyed, ardently, that night. They had my undivided attention. The mountains told me, I was not done.

chapter Nineteen
THE DONNA

The balcony doors were wide open. I stood three stories high again over Place Centrale and watched dawn light spread like a white glove across the broad blue flanks of the vast snowcap. The sunlight fanned over the humpbacked mountains above Verbier and tried to seep into the deep cols and ravines, but they remained cool and dark like the folds in an old whale's skin.

The hill looked like Swiss suburbia. A Levittown of chalets wedged between chalets, on top of chalets, stacked like Legos, their glass-faceted prows jutting outward into the bright sun over plank decks that seemed to overlap. There was hardly a path of white to see linking anything together—collateral damage of the great skiing boom of the eighties and nineties.

I marched back into the room and crossed to the desk for a refill of Paul's strong Eden brew. Goddamn Parzival still watched me every step of the way. The Stirner diaries sat unopened in my attaché on the desk, next to a ceramic beer stein full of flowers. Nothing had changed. And everything had changed. Paul manages, but no longer owned the Eden. He sold-out to a Swiss resorts conglomerate—an offer he couldn't refuse. They were buying-up the whole damn Valais.

Two days. Two days and nights locked in this friggin' room like a monk. My rental skis were finally ready at a shop in the alley that used to be Iron Mountain Sports. Deke sold Iron Mountain in the mid-nineties. He and Tre had the first snowboards in Europe, I think. They made millions selling and renting, then moved to Tignes with the Gen-X and Gen-Y crowd. His e-mail was a warm welcome back to Verbier,

"Break your neck falling off a barstool, Famous, just call me, man. I'll send two rescue Bunnies."

Liney and Eric were down in New Zealand, sailing. They entered some racing series with a new ketch Liney'd bought last year. He sent an e-mail to the Eden wishing me *"bon ski, le Eddie."* And Liney sent flowers.

I strolled back out onto the balcony. The top of Mont Gelé was in full sun now, blazing white hot. A scalding sip of Joe charred my lip and I remembered Madame Desnoyer's words to me as I left the Balzac. "You don't seem to age all of these years, monsieur, you seem to grow more sad."

So, what's it going to be, Famous? Old or sad? What was I doing there? Why Verbier? The Eden again. The truth was like a train hurtling through the night. One stop or express, it was a liar's ride, Stirner and I had made the swift passage. I was seeking some Verbier truth, a mountain truth, the undeniable kind of veracity that burned in my memory, and scarred the hell out of my past. Like the candor of Madame Desnoyers' words, thunderous in my dreams, mammoth in their portent—this must be my stop.

That scarfaced mountain stood waiting. The white couloirs scratched in Gelé's headwall cascaded down inside of ashen narrows of glistening wet stone. Wind-whipped snows streamed from her eastern flank like paint spray on a cobalt blue wall of sky. A tremor rattled the coffee cup slightly against the saucer in my hand. "Gelé, damn you," I whispered. *You have some part of me. Once, you claimed my soul. Now, you want my life.*

The bright red lift ticket dangled from the long chrome chain around my neck, twisting and turning in the breeze. Quatre Vallée—the four-valley area above Verbier from Veysonnaz to La Fouly, a full day's worth of varied skiing interconnected by lifts and cable cars, honoring a single day-ticket—I was on my way up.

Verbier had become *the* spot for the hardcore double-black-diamond whackos. Family skiing had to be found elsewhere. The annoyingly prominent cliché of the day, "extreme" got generous play around the ski world. Verbier somehow avoided such Pop Culture labels. Verbier never needed classification. It had always been a Telluride Of The Mind, a place to weed-out and separate the casual and intermediate skiers from the borderline obsessive expert. We were all like that once, obsessive, and out to prove something to a mountain, or some god. *Ski d'sauvage* whackos, they all came here.

I was not alone. The morning crowds were sizable. There were even some lines at the ticket windows. Expert or dreamer, when the lifts began cranking in the Valais dawn, skiers materialized out of thin air.

Then, in the *télécabin* to the top of Greppon Blanc, a glance, a woman's glance, took me by surprise. The power in that first second of acknowledgement lured and unsettled me, and I was completely unprepared for my own response. I felt a sudden weakness come over me, a faltering, then a crushing sadness in my chest, pressing down. Some weight in her stare pained me.

Was this the recoil for the past few days—young Elissa peering through this woman's eyes, punishing me? Or, was it Céline Decauville haunting me after all these years?

When our eyes met and held for a moment, I felt the woman in the *télécabin* was taking something from me, depleting me. Knowledge in that intent look attended some unrequited need. Somehow, the woman had fixed herself onto it. I wanted to convey with my eyes, but I was frightened, and then I lost our line of sight in the crowded cable car. I panicked and searched, trying to re-establish our eye contact, but I'd lost her.

We were nearing the top station and in the usual discharge of skiers from the car, that great rush of bodies, it would be impossible to see her again. Encounters of this kind that suddenly disappeared, men can sometimes think on them for days. I was chilled and discontented. A woman's unnerving glance, a face as mysterious as an alien being, all the more puzzling for its beauty and sudden power over me, had broken through. The still, clear gaze, the silent soft look of the doe—glassine, irresistible, and hypnotic—her perfect wet eyes, brown, translucent and alluring beckoned me to something, but why? I wanted to see that face again. There was some comprehension of her much more than beauty or desire or innocence that I'd missed. *Lovelessness nurtures such wishfulness.*

Perhaps I was losing control, reading too much into it. But I did feel unweighted. One more glimpse was all I wanted. The face, her eyes said, "follow."

Out on the snow, across the broad expanse of Greppon Blanc, I searched frantically, trying to spot a white furry headband, white fur, encircling scrolls of shining auburn hair. The crowd moved in waves now, groups of skiers dashed or cruised to the trail markers. I was crunching through the hard-pack at the mouth of piste Nundaz, shoving my way at times, skis in one hand, poles in the other, scanning the huge crowd.

Suddenly, I spotted a woman in a white ski suit, her brown hair flowing through a white fur bandanna. Her body was shapely and young, muscular and energetic. Without thought, I approached, walking fast, then jogging, dragging my skis and poles at my side. She was on her skis and beginning to push off. My mind was a jumble, words were hopelessly unavailable, my heart pounded with excitement, or apprehension—I couldn't tell which. What would I say? Then, one last foray, one last gasp, and I charged at the woman.

"*Ehh...donna? Madame? Eh, mademoiselle? signorina?*"

The sounds startled me, the choice. The words frightened the woman who now glared at me, and we two stood still and paralyzed, facing each other for a long awkward moment.

"*Pardon, madame.* Sorry," I mumbled to her, backing away like a bashful dog. "*Excusez-moi, madame.*"

Mistake and pain. Not the magical face I so wanted to see, not the mesmerizing beauty from the cable car. The woman in white said nothing. She sailed-off, her haughty haunches and nose high in the air like a Kentucky mare, onto the fresh snow of the Siviez traverse, leaving me stunned.

The moment's hope and expectation had been replaced with despondency. The long sought-after burst of feeling had finally come, borne I thought, on an angelic vision. But I'd just paid a price for the brief commotion.

I felt cold and empty, ready to walk back and leave the mountain—vanish somewhere for the day. Down in the village, I'd walk my narrow streets and bemoan my foolishness, flirting with a young beauty on the ski lift. *How original.* Brief exaltation and thrill were rushing away from me, fast.

Then as I turned back toward the cable car station, the sudden shock of her presence jolted me once more. There she was smiling at me now, fully recognizing our secret game of glances—the brown-eyed sibyl—just as before, drinking me in with her eyes. There was no time to contemplate. She was beginning to ski away, smiling at me ever so sweetly. There was only time to act, to do, to move toward her, toward the uncertainty, toward some omen.

I watched her glide over the snow, side to side softly, gently touching the powder with her poles, beating a sensual rhythm. She descended rapidly into the billowing, white terrain.

I snapped into my bindings and flew into the pursuit—jumpsuit open, goggles hanging about my neck, gloves dangling from my clips, trailing in the wind. I spiked and slashed at the ground with my poles, skating across the snow, running over moguls, beginning a desperate chase after my precious lady—"The Donna"— the white-tailed doe who now drew me into a forest abyss.

I was, at worst, two minutes behind her, a distance I'd easily close once I knew where she was going. The trails away from the Greppon were limited to three and only one, piste Cleuson, would take her directly away from the area. The other two led halfway down the east face of the Greppon and the Combyre into the bowls of Thyon 2000. From there, short chair rides then returned skiers to Greppon Blanc. If she were aware of my pursuit, which I was now certain she was, she'd avoid those short runs and head for piste Cleuson, a longer, narrower trail full of switches and tricky wooded sections that ran near the Lac de Cleuson, and then, down to the large crossroads station at Super-Nendaz. Piste Cleuson was a labyrinth of hopscotching terrain. The big verticals were sometimes treacherous and icy, and the lake-effect drifts near the reservoir were deceptively deep. Two steep double black-diamond narrows always made things extremely interesting. And it was fast, everywhere. Somehow, I sensed she knew that.

The crowds, the restaurants, and the hub of activity at Super-Nendaz afforded her the best opportunity to evade capture. *Capture? Christ, what am I thinking?* At Super-Nendaz she could hide and watch me, monitor my frantic little search. She'd have a good laugh, I was sure, at this crazy American racing after her.

What if she was just having a good time with me? A handsome young woman, idle, bored, alone, looking for a cat-and-mouse partner for the day? Some European women loved to engage in little *affairs du jour*—wistful little afternoon pursuits, teasing fantasies played-out in the span of a few hours. It was all part of the titillating legend and lore of the European *femme fatale*—such playfulness and movie-screen intrigue — flirtation of the most obsequious kind.

The task of shortening the time between us and catching "The Donna" was, in fact, next to impossible. At times, the distance between us broadened. She knew where I was, at all times, and seemed empowered with a control of the chase, intensifying the possibility of a catch when the probability of my giving-up became greatest. Of course, I obliged in kind by picking up the pace right on cue.

Near the base lodge at Tortin, she passed right over me on the *télésiège*, fully ten chairs or more ahead of me, sitting alone, the seat beside her empty. She smiled down at me. It was a teasing invitation to occupy that empty seat. I laughed. So close was she at this point, her face appeared even more radiant and soft than the first glance revealed. Rapturous beauty — taking in all flattery of bright sun and blue sky, the white light of snow, and blushed like a mountain pasque — she glowed now like an icon.

A sense of overwhelming desire suddenly welled-up in me. Any second-thoughts I had dissipated. My resolve to catch her returned with stiffened ardor.

We skied the short runs above Lac Des Vaux — Argentiére, piste Dariane, and Le Marge — as though we were tethered together by an invisible line. She was able to feel when I pressed the advance and compensated with an ease of acceleration and faultless skiing, always maintaining our separation. She was an exquisite skier, rhythmic and efficient. Her speed, technique, and sheer strength were transformed into a kind of recital and ballet—performance art of the highest order.

It became apparent that she also knew these runs, and the mountain, very well. With such knowledge over difficult terrain, the game would advance on her terms, and by her design. I felt certain, however, that I had a stake in the outcome.

We went on skiing the entire morning that way. Shortly after the noon hour, I stopped for some lunch at Les Ruinettes, the huge restaurant complex situated directly above Verbier. Ruinettes was the largest on-mountain food and services station in the four valley area. It was a sea of red-cheeked, boot-clopping skiers, the famished and frosted who began their day, as I had, on the first morning runs. Into

that mix, throngs of half-dayers now poured off of the lifts
from Verbier below. This was, logically, where either half of
the avid skier's day connected. Ruinettes was a terminus and
the most trafficked crossroads in the valleys, a ski metropolis
complete with clothing stores, pro shops and souvenir
kiosks, snack-bars, cafeterias, even a posh *après-ski* restaurant
and bar — it was a mall.

Also from Les Ruinettes, the largest *téléphérique*—a
hundred-passenger sky vessel—transported skiers to the top
of Mont-Fort. At more than three-thousand three-hundred
meters, Mont-Fort reigned mightily as the skiing pinnacle in
the Val de Bagnes. The 25-minute ride to the top was well
worth the special fare for skiers and non-skiers alike.

I took lunch standing at a snack bar on the main
thoroughfare at Ruinettes overlooking the vast indoor Alpine
concourse. The mid-day crowd moved in unbroken currents,
a 42nd Street and Fifth Avenue without the business suits. As
I stood and watched the great colorful tide of skiers, I
suddenly decided upon a new strategy with "The Donna."
What had I to lose? If she had her sights on me, I'd play
oblivious and disinterested. Not too disinterested, but casual.

I slowly made my way to the south end of the complex
and sat alone, face to the sun, at a table on the sprawling
outdoor deck for the remainder of the lunch break. The
"mall" was at my back and the north faces of the magnificent
Grand and Petit Combin were before me, thirteen-thousand-
foot giants that seemed to scrape the southern sky clear.

As I sat, I imagined myself scored in the crosshairs of a
sniper's scope. I felt she was watching me waiting for my
move, that somehow the tenuous string between us had
fallen slack and I had only to tug at it gently to change the
balance of our engagement. She belonged to me now, as
much as I to her. I could feel her eyes on me. I fought the
temptation to seek hers.

The chase was in transition. Maybe the prey needed the
predator's cunning and gamesmanship as well. I was risking

all. She might walk away. Then, I'd be on the one-thirty *téléphérique* to Mont-Fort without "The Donna."

Stone faced, I parked on the concrete waiting platform of the Mont-Fort cable car station. I had not seen "The Donna" at all for more than an hour. I was pressed in, waiting among the damp bodies and the hundreds of skis and poles, a subway rider's karma. It was like waiting for the D-Train at Columbus Circle during rush hour.

We all watched solemnly, prayerfully almost, heads craned heavenward as the great chrome and glass cable car descended into the hangar—the Ark sent for the chosen beasts. The great bay windows of the Mont-Fort *téléphérique* slid in front of us, reflecting the hundred-odd sunglassed-and-goggled skiers, a stand of bug-eyed gnomes peered like insects, readying to light-upon the silvery vessel. The creaking boxcar-of-the-sky moaned and belched as it settled into its steel and rubber mooring.

This marvel of Swiss engineering opened its gaping doors and a mob of the most ill mannered, cackling, rude, pushing and shoving, aggressive-but-colorfully-dressed people wedged their way into the soggy cabin. Like a giant centipede, we trundled *en masse*. I remember moving, but I don't remember my feet actually putting pressure on the ground.

The doors closed rapidly with an accompanying ceremony of bells, buzzers, and beeps. A voice, speaking too rapidly at ear-splitting volume, garbled by electronic amplification, barked-out unintelligible instructions through an overhead speaker. The sensory assault was complete. It was the D-Train. I'd found Switzerland's D-Train.

With a great heave and sway, the bulging *téléphérique* cranked-out over the Brunet Crevasse. The first big bounce of the fifty-ton cable car was a real tummy-dropper and the collective sigh of the "insects" served only to fill the car with savory luncheon aromas.

The towns of Sarreyer, Lourtier, and Bruson down on the valley floor looked like dabs of dark acrylic paint on a white piece of paper, getting ever smaller as we climbed faster toward the huge wheel junction at La Chaux.

If for nothing else—save chocolate—this tiny country astonished the world with the overwhelming scale and ambition of its Alpine cable car system. It was impossible to appreciate its magnitude solely as a technological feat, one had to feel its effects. Of the few impressions that truly last a lifetime, this occupied a special place at the heart of awe.

At La Chaux, the gigantic wheels and gears and steel cables of this Swiss Erector Set swung our dangling compartment, with clockwork-perfection, out over the wide *passe* at Fionnay — the Lac de Mauvoisin barely visible in the distance — and, in a flash, the Bruson Valley disappeared completely, and with it all reminders of inhabited civilization.

We began the long, steady three-thousand-foot grind to the top of Mont-Fort. A thousand feet beneath, an arctic terrain, a white, lunar sea, foreboding and breathtaking in its starkness. We'd entered upon an empire of the snows, and a reverent hush fell upon the passengers at once. The silence was a wonderful gift—unquestioned, shared by all, as though we'd just entered a cathedral of nature's unified denomination. No matter how many times one made a journey over the Alps in a cable car, this vision, its impact, returned fresh and new and deeply moving.

I was at the window, childlike and trembling at the sight before me. At once, significance and insignificance, my own, synthesized. A greater greatness, an immensity, revealed itself, opening me, inhabiting a limitless volume within, an immense, mysterious volume. Man was too much in awe of himself to see the truly awesome, I thought. Wonder had its own wisdom.

I was all sweat and emotion, glad and frightened in the same impulse. There were sights such as these, when the proportion of things came full and vividly real, and we were suddenly permitted that rare sight of a world that could begin anew.

I felt an expansion, a fission of immeasurable energy, the whole of experience multiplying, dividing, and diminishing in the same fraction of a second, my life imploding, being sucked back down into a black hole of self-worth. Never had I known such solace, such transformation. Never had I felt so alone.

I turned my head back into the crowded room of the rumbling cable car, removed my sunglasses, and there she was. We looked at each other calmly, steadily for a long, long moment. The sensation again reaffirmed the power and tenderness she possessed in that look. It would be different now. Whether my actions had forced an adjustment was not clear. It didn't matter. Something had changed. It was the same stunning face, but the look had changed. We acknowledged an obedience and commitment to something undefinable, yet present in our stares.

No one between us stirred, our line of sight was unbroken. We stayed, locked-on to each other's visage, submissive, unabashed, knowing, sealing the contract of our need. We stayed, watching just this way for the rest of the journey to Mont-Fort. A reassuring calm settled between us on the long ride. Only the sound of the wind whistling about the cabin accompanied the stillness and peace we shared.

At Mont-Fort, the *téléphérique* opened its wide doors once more and the usual push and shove exodus was replaced with a much more civil disembark. The traveled masses had been somewhat humbled by nature's impressive display of the Alpine landscape, or by the Swiss physics of wheels and pulleys. The common experience had made a congregation of disparate peoples—small kindnesses and courtesies proliferated.

Without ever taking my eyes from her, I walked beside "The Donna," away from the *téléphérique* station to a sunny rondure in the snow. We walked silently, not more than six feet apart, then stopped and methodically began to get into our skis—adjusting bindings, goggles, gloves, and zipping zippers everywhere. Like two altar assistants preparing for high mass, we spoke not a word. I watched her hand as it went into a glove, smooth and olive-skinned, strong and sensuous. Mediterranean, I gauged, a Phoenician exerting a power over me all day, and I, like the wine-drunk sailor, given to obsessive love. I wanted to touch her, just place my hand over hers, but I did not. We didn't speak. It wasn't an urgent consideration. We seemed to understand the communication of our glances. The silent looks spoke to our most pressing needs. The sound of our presence there beside each other was sustenance enough.

For these past few hours, I could only be thankful. If she disappeared in the next few minutes and never returned, I'd be grateful that she saw me at all, chose me, and truly stirred me, if only for one brief moment. I did so want to touch her, but I sensed it was not "The Donna's" way. She was like St. Vincent Millay's precious doe,...*monstrous and beautiful to human eyes, hard to believe.*

She looked over at me, without smiling this time, and I knew it was time for us to go. We turned out together, gliding gently over shallow moguls and onto the wide expanse of Mont-Fort. Side by side we skied, easily rocking with the softly undulating mountaintop terrain. The new skis were the shape of butter knives and we spread the snow like marshmallow before us. "The Donna" was skiing with me, mindful of our closeness, as if wanting to be together now in perfect rhythm. Breezing along on the rounded slopes of this top section, we swirled through wide turns in tandem—our parity had finally been achieved. Had I found acceptance in those clear eyes? Would she ever let me know?

From the top of Mont-Fort, the mountain spread open like the Ohio River. Some twelve hundred meters downriver, the Ohio became a Monongahela and an Allegheny flowing-off to the east and west, the Gentianes Col and the Tortin Glacier, respectively. The towering skyscrapers of a rugged granite city, a Pittsburgh of jagged outcroppings and jutting peaks, was situated squarely in the milky confluence, its majestic centerpiece the icy monolith that soared above Verbier, Mont Gelé.

After the first few hundred meters, the broad front of Mont-Fort dropped unassumingly onto a steep head wall. It was a tremendous release, not intimidating, just a wide, long runway that novice and expert alike could simply cut-loose on—it was a drag strip eleven-thousand feet in the sky, a place to feel an over-the-limit abandon, that derring-do of the downhill racer.

Every rollercoaster in every amusement park in the world had the most terrifying downhill immediately following a long, chain-dragging, gear-clinking climb to its highest point. Before hang-gliding and skydiving, it was the closest a kid could come to flying. The summers of my youth brought dreams and longing for the annual family outing to Coney Island, where the great Cyclone loomed over our awestruck nerve. That first tenuous assault each summer scaled a mountain of diffidence. Once the Cyclone's first run was breached, the sheer happiness and excitement we derived from subsequent rides was enough to sustain us for the year's long privation. The heart-racing exhilaration of unforgettable summertime rides, rollercoaster sensations, were re-lived and enjoyed again and again in each flight of an all-out downhill—and the child was never far from the man.

A Christie, an unweighting hop, and "The Donna" and I flew together into the fast downhill schuss, crouched down, knees bent, poles under our arms, the wind rushed through our suits as though we were airfield wind socks. Fast and wild we skied, whizzing like new playmates laughing freely we shot straight down the long boulevard run of the great Mont-Fort, side-by-side. Then, as we came nearer the wide confluence, she turned west toward the Tortin Glacier, and then sharply down at full-speed, in toward the "Pittsburgh" of jagged rocks. Without ever breaking pace she slipped underneath the orange rope that marked the trail. I followed, staying in her tracks. We poled off-piste and her expert ability was immediately apparent once again. She spun through turns and pumped arms and legs vigorously, riding an invisible bronco, knees flexing, easily navigating the narrow and cavernous passes in the Monts de Sion, the snowy serpentine foothills that formed the backside of Mont Gelé. Our carefree downhill suddenly turned into serious, hair-raising, skiing.

I mimicked her moves, staying glued to her tracks. Again I marveled at how assured she was in this maze of mountain cones. She knew just where to brake hard, where to roll and run, when to control and gently edge so as not to break the crusty cover in the shaded sections. I was skiing beyond my own means—given an accelerated lesson in-tow of a master skier.

We skied tight trails, skimming along the sides of dizzying cliffs. Her surety instilled a confidence in me, or a recklessness, I couldn't tell which. I skied these places, without thinking really, right behind her, trusting that some ability and some faith would pull me through.

We soared upward through mist and alternating sunlight, drawing ever closer to the summit of Gelé. Through and around rocky passages we skied and sidestepped against sheer inverted walls of *schist* and *gabbro*, slowing, edging and sliding, picking our way. Carefully, we pushed across narrow snow bridges, windswept ravines, and thread-like ridges barely the width of two skis. She'd look back at me from time to time and her eyes always encouraged, *Do as I do.* There was fervent hope in her look and I obeyed, the longing in my heart and the tender entreaty in her smile.

The granite boulders of Gelé fashioned the walls of what seemed like small, white chambers of ice *séracs* and glistening rock. Up and around and down I followed her, playing a hide-and-seek game in the uppermost marble towers of an Alpen castle. We chased in and out of the "rooms" created by the weathered rock and drift snows, through a constant interplay of light and shadow and mist. I'd lost all track of time and place.

Then, like the playful doe of the deep woods, she disappeared, her bubbling laughter echoed among the rocks. Her clever escape begged me search after her. I followed the sweet sound of her giddy laughter, sidestepping cautiously, then edging hard to slide across a tiny col. The cap of Mont Gelé seemed very near now, beyond it, the great round ball of the sun was yellow-diffused by fast moving clouds. Around another crystalline boulder I inched, and then stopped suddenly, clinging to the cold stone cliff face with one arm.

At first, I only saw her, perched above on a snowy ledge, smiling, nodding to me, radiant in the sky and sun—her arms outstretched to her ski poles. The sudden relief brought a smile to my face, and she signaled a happy reply.

Between us lay an eggshell bowl of white, icy crust, a near-perfect dish forty feet across. Down in the smooth bottom, a crack split the bowl in two, a deep crevasse about four feet wide emanating no light severed the small basin horizontally. "The Donna" stood high on the opposite rim.

How did she get across?

The sides of the bowl dropped severely into the flatter, dish-like bottom. There were no tracks, not the slightest scratch of a ski's edge over the glassy surface. There was no place to stop or even side step, the crevasse would swallow anyone who miscalculated.

Skiing it was a trick to be performed in one daring move, a push downward to the middle, a weightless glide over the crack, and a feathery lilt upward, like a bird landing on a thin branch. I had to catch the lip of the bowl on the opposite side, with both skis, directly in front of where she was positioned.

My mind raced, my eyes pleaded with her. I was getting cold standing there. The slab of frigid wall beside me sent the history of its coldness through my shivering body. She was a silhouette now against the afternoon clouds. Raising her arms slightly from her poles, she beckoned me once more, turning her palms open. Her smile radiated.

Quickly, I jammed a ski pole into my binding release and snapped out of one ski, then another. Picking up my skis in one hand, I stepped gingerly down into the glazed side of the bowl, digging the edge of my boot into the ice. I'd walk across, crawl if necessary, to reach the ridge on the other side.

I made each step slowly, down and across, wondering all the time if the shell would hold, listening for telltale sounds of cracking ice beneath my boots. I came to the crevasse. I looked up at her, then planted my skis and poles on the far side of the break. She stood motionless watching me, smiling down all the while. I leaned over the gaping crack and looked down, but saw no bottom therein. The dark void reported back only the bellowing sound of an unspeakable infinity, of a vast underworld sunken in millenniums of ice and time. *What now?* The last beautiful woman pursued leads me to a dark, empty hole in the world.

With a racer's push-off of both my arms and an even lift at the hips, I jumped to the other side of the split, landing between my poles and skis with a light thud. I should have enjoyed the success of the crossing, but the hollow sound of a crack that followed right after my light thud sent me scrambling on all-fours, digging-in, climbing and clinging like a panicked cat up the other side of the icy bowl. Would the crack follow? How much time before the collapse? I struggled. I reached the lip and threw my skis and poles up on top ahead of me, pressing them into the solid snow above the edge. Hoisting up, I managed to get half my body up onto the ledge before swinging my legs up. I rolled over onto my back and sighed with relief, deeply.

I was expecting to see her standing there, leaning over me, breathing down a heavenly mist—the wonderful warm breath of "The Donna"—her stunning face blushed and close to mine. But only sky covered the expanse high above me and the clouds belonged to the heavens. I rolled over again and pushed up to my knees. The space there was empty. She'd gone. I jumped to my feet to see if there might be another cliff, or another snow ledge she'd skied onto, but I saw nothing. "The Donna" was gone.

The white sound of high snows, devoid, resonant yet vacant, returned, bringing with it a desolation I had not felt since the moment before that dazzling face, the angelic gaze, pulled me up and filled me with desire. A certain darkness contained me now. Another crack, another void was swallowing me, a bellowing crevasse, final in its defeat.

My idolatry had left me in a blind alley. How could she leave me there without even a word? Without some gesture? Or message? I didn't hurry after her. Somehow, I sensed the pursuit was over. There'd be no more game, no more glances, no more discovery with the angel in white. Had she sensed, wrongly, that my need had turned to lust somewhere during our innocent play? Is she all women, and I all men—abandoned, unfaithful, and hungry in a garden frozen? Or, was this my penance for coveting the messenger?

She'd gone. And there before me, I saw where she had led me. Now, I understood why the chase was over, why our game had ended. There at my feet was the place. The couloir. A gorge so steep and blinding white, so pure in horror and dizzyingly perpendicular, it swallowed my loneliness and despair whole. It sucked my eyes down like a whirlpool. A vertical tunnel stretched endlessly below from where I stood, it pulled and sifted the granular snow down like sand in an hourglass, distorting the vision, making an eerie sound like rushing waters. The couloir flowed like a great, white river from the peak of Mont Gelé, cascading down between funneling rock and icy chasms—a seamless frozen waterfall. A granite dome of Alpine mountain pressed against the slate-gray afternoon sky above me, and a white stream of terror led below from my feet. I stood alone between a heaven and a hell. "Every man has to find a place among mountains that makes him feel alone with his gods and demons," P.A. said.

The couloir beckoned me down. *The descent beckons.*

I was delivered there by her. My fear now was a deafening scream. It rang across the barren mountainside, bouncing down into the cavernous canyons. It was the rim of the world, a nothingness, an unsuspected outland, alien and deadly. And yet the couloir contained me, contained my spirit, almost instantly. The fearsome shaft was so enticing, so helplessly mesmerizing, that portents of destruction and liberation swept over me like a burning wind. Wonderful sensations raced across my skin.

Standing there above the savage crease, a crooked alley never intended for skiing, was to behold evidence of an unparalleled violence and fathomless beauty in one sight. The brutal seam of some glacier's icy surgery was torn here, never to fully heal, an endless wind and torrent had frayed this stone. Volcanic fire had tempered and compressed this crag with elemental ferocity. Born of these forces, how could it be anything but an unforgiving and hostile place for a man?

Was this Mont Gelé's famous Hidden Couloir, *couloir caché?* The talk of it in the small towns by the great Valais skiers always sounded like half Swiss yarn, half myth—The Funnel, or the Narrow of Death, *étroit du mort,* or *hélice bleu,* the blue helix. The names and the stories said it all. Was I staring down the throat of a spiraling deadly legend? This fairy-tale suddenly seemed very real. My heart railed against my chest. I was overcome. *Get me the hell off this mountain.*

But the fear was relentless in its seduction. It played

with me, locked itself in, between reason and estimation—despising reason and infatuating estimation. There was no compound, no complexity, no shade to the fear I felt there. It was pure. It coursed through solid flesh and fluid, through mind and spirit. I was inextricably drawn to it. I had never known such purity until that moment. In sudden starbursts, uncontrollable impulses collided with deep psychological predispositions. The death here was certain. Or was it? As certain as a will to live.

Easy come, easy go.

Relish the moment. I'd never known solitude like this before, and I may never again. I'd never thought about God, any god, as a viable intervention, until then either.

Minutes passed, and I was still terrified. I thought of leaving, alive. I thought of turning around and walking back, through the ice bowl, over the crevasse, back down the mountain. The couloir did not need me, there'd be no shame or embarrassment. *It's my life. Not outstanding, but the only one I've got—a course of descent since puberty.*

A chalky screen flickered in my brain. I retrieved the amber message across the mental monitor. Fact, more than 250 skiers from, [A]Austria, [CH]Switzerland, [F]France, and [I]Italia lost their lives in the mountains, annually. Some were the brightest people in Europe. My legs understood the message. They wanted no part in this stupidity. They shook. My legs wanted to abandon the enterprise. Never count on the legs for support. The instinctive system preempted learned foolishness. My legs were already in the chairlift, or in the *après ski* café resting comfortably. They shook uncontrollably, they tried to convince me that I might be in over my head. *It slopes gently to the left at the start. Hesitate, you're done. Get over-confidant, and you'll end up in Liechtenstein.*

Death Row, I had the view from on high and I felt every bit the condemned man, my appointment imminent, the prescribed time of execution, there and then. It was right in front of me—a tangible truth. *Life is like a ladder in a chicken coop, Famous, short and shitty.*

The narrow top had to be done aggressively, rapidly, attacking the turn—death to the dim-footed. The legs need to rise, like ship's pistons, moving, pounding, side-to-side, up and down for fifty, sixty, seventy meters, without stopping. It was a kind of dementia, a madness of physical and mental extremes—madness and desertion with undecipherable warnings.

A bird appeared, floating on drafts of air. The bird struggled to fly higher, but couldn't—limitation revealed benignly by nature. What did that mean for me? Cities, towns, villages, railways, and roads, all lying three thousand meters below. An entire civilization thought to settle the valley floor, to live among cows. Why was I standing there holding two thin, funny-colored boards? Two planks and two sticks, and straps, buckles, clamps and pins to lock me in. Even the clouds had sunken into the valleys. I was skiing into the tops of clouds. *Stay left on the blinding front wall.*

The couloir remained. I looked down into the fearful corridor and sunlight bounced up from the snow, burning in my eyes. Sharp rock outcroppings and ledges cast cold, blue shadows across the beginning chute. It would be just like first sex—an unknown escapade, a freefall—and just as terrifying. *Turn away. Call on some gods. See what happens. Step into the bindings.*

Snap.

Commit, Eddie.

Snap.

The crack of the bindings was deafening. It echoed down the mountain calling a new awareness to my insanity. Did they hear it, the ones having lunch in the restaurant below? The fur-clad fanatics, the *blasé Milanese*, the bored Nords, the *al fresci tedesci*? They must have. They were looking up here now. Tanned jowls slackened, momentarily. Chewing stopped—the *croûte de fromage, the asiette, the raclette, the pommes frites,* the crumbs of the *pain Valaisanne* scattered across the sunny terrace beneath their feet. My nerves took flight, my mouth dried. I struggled for breath. My skis turned out over the edge of the world and the *beau monde, the bella gente,* sipped their *fendant* and stared up through their blue Vuarnets.

Gentle snows swirled about my red skis. Tiny white whirlpools curled and shimmered, touched my skis, then danced down the couloir. I did this once upon a time. I could do such things with P.A., with Liney and Eric. I could do this shit alone. I was young, *young-er.* My knees were shot now, every joint hurt. I didn't get up in the morning, I got out, onto the floor crawling, then I got up. My Salad Days were gone, only the dressing remained.

I am with you, mountain. I tried one last plea. I loved the power mountains had over me. I fit within their cool protective niches, slid softly along their green mosses and ice, their ramparts. I hid and I played among the rocks and bent in the wind like the Arolla pine. *Let me live, mountain.* I was stalling. Survive my own fate, create it anew, or die.

Still, the couloir waited. My sound began to diminish. I strained to hear other noises, other sounds like "The Donna's" giggle, Newell's cries, Céline's whisper, "I love you, Eddie." I heard none. The sound I heard was the avalanche of my fear beginning. Blood pounded in my head. Temples pulsated. My ears rang, a whirring noise, whizzing like a sailfish strike on the line. The banging blood coursed through my ankles and wrists, and tears streamed from my eyes, freely. My hands grasped the poles, the black straps lashed me to the commitment. I bent over the skis and stared once more down the couloir. The pounding stopped. The sound was gone. All the sound was gone. A white acoustic deadened the aural world.

My poles go in.
           I lift.
                    The earth
                              falls away.

I saw my son, kicking in the crib, then my father lying in his bier. The sum of everything flew through an aperture in my time and I was in the sky searching for open arms.

Suddenly, the earth returned, slamming against the bottom of my feet, my knees flew up past my chin. The blue couloir pulled me down into the vertical track. A vortex, a Cyclone eye, sucked the muscle down from my bones. A centrifuge was separating my blood to my bottom, an uncoupling force—times ten—tried to quarter me, wresting my limbs. It was frantic. I wasn't ready. Everything was too soon and I was in the middle of a race. Where the hell was the start? *Move or fall, idiot.* The choice index flipped through memory. Where were the legs? Goddamn it, where the hell was the mountain? Earth and sky all tossed together. *Ease-off some.* Give a little, I'd get a little. It was all an exchange. Slow it down. Slow the time down. Oh, god, oh, god, rearrange the seconds. Calibration was a universe you could control. I knew about the elasticity, the divergence, the flow—master it and re-create it. Creation called to the creator. Imagination had nothing to do with memory. The steady march of moments could be re-ordered, re-paced, wound-down, the altered state re-used. Oh, Jesus, Jesus, my body burned. I really was going to die. The expense, the depletion was too much. My ankles were exploding with pain—my thighs shined, they beamed and stretched. They were tearing open like skinned carrion. *Take me down, god, please show me some sign, finish me.* If I'd just let go. If I'd just sit down and let the mountain have me—I wasn't afraid to die. Dying was easier. *Living's the bitch.*

There. A rock. The rock juts, it would slice me. Over there. A narrow, a chicane to the left. Too narrow. God-damn-it.

Turn, ski it. Turn or die. I hacked and chopped at the snow. The jutting rock tore at my shoulder, ripping my jumpsuit. Ski it, dammit. Attack. *Pianta su.* Plant the pole. O, Mother of God, tell me where to plant the pole, come on, tell me, when to unweight, how much to turn, run, edge, push, sit back. Tell me, please? Caress me, *Gelé. Down, steeper down.* The couloir beckoned me down, it wrenched me into a hellride.

Over there, the spot, I saw it sparkle. The mountain spoke. I listened. Ride me, feel me, feel my beauty, my contours, slide me—come down with me, with me, she said.

The left hand. *Plant the pole, Eddie.* Plant the goddamn pole, stick it in the springtime side of Gelé. There, the fields of cotton grass and swaying hare-bell. I raced through the blazing Alpenrose, skimmed the blue campion moss over the rocky moraine, and I'd struck the sleeping grasses. They awakened and grasped my pole. *Hold me, Gelé?* I was floating, turning in space, winging lighter in the air on the gentle waves of the tall grasses. Cold April rivulets were fast at my feet. Ride. Ride the rushing waters like a leaf spinning down a mountain rillet. My feet flew and bounced on the white waters.

I'd make it now, I'd make it. I had found the rhythm of the couloir. *I have you now, Gelé.* We danced a dance in triple time, embracing—a fandangoed ecstasy, a swirling and breathless fantasia—all light and ice bursting up from my flashing skis. Burst and flash. I jumped into the mountain's arms. Softly, we undulated together, Mont Gelé and I, we waltzed the great waltz. The ballroom was suddenly ours alone. We tossed each other around and around. *I am with you now, Gelé, we are together.*

The couloir widened. To the left again—a slope, a drop, a release. The sun shone brightly. Over there, a bonus, a gift, a cradle. The mountain cradled me. My legs were beyond pain, beyond habituated suffering, a white heat radiated beneath my ski suit condensing and wetting the innermost layers. Time lapsed. It was my own now. The frenzy had become a descent.

Wider still the couloir opened. I followed the shadows and streaks, the broad schuss was just ahead. I would make it. The turns were wider. I had it under control now. Springing softly, I kneaded the fresh snow with my poles. Sailing the horizontal line, I floated-up easily on the turn and began the line across again. The new drifts sprayed high up alongside the red skis, the powder lapped against the sides of my legs. I carved and cut the white waves. A sailor on the snow had found his way.

The beating was like the intimate pulse of lovers, the rhythmic union of movement and purpose—an elemental harmony. The wind and the sounds returned. Down. Into the life again, down. *Steeper down.* The laughter of children filtered in, people talking, the scraping edges on the snow, laughter and the movement of life, I heard again.

And my sound returned. My movement returned, rekindled in possibility. The sounds of a joyous deliverance reverberated through me. I felt reborn in my exhaustion, delirious with fatigue, and laughing. An exchange had been made. My eyes teared, my hair flew wildly in the wind, and the warm clouds of my laughter trailed back behind me, back up into the couloir.

Verbier was below, already in the blue mist of evening, waiting at the end of a thirty-minute ski through kindly wooded trails. Up here, everything had become pink-hued in the Alpenglow of dusk. I stopped, just briefly, to feel the cold freshness of my own sweat, to feel the vastness that had just come into me, to feel the completion.

I looked back at the couloir, at how nature had gouged a long, deep gash in the face of Gelé, how she had commanded the memory of creation in the stone tablet of the mountain. My ride, my accomplishment, had branded me with self-evident scars, endless and indelible gorges, my couloirs, that beckoned my descent forevermore.